The Quiet Spaces Between the *Whirlwinds*

Paladin Chronicles Book I

ERIC OLSON - WHITE SHIRT

Kravitz & Sons
INNOVATORS IN PUBLISHING MARKETING AND ADVERTISING

Kravitz and Sons LLC
204 E Arlington Blvd. Suite B
Greenville, NC 27858

Published by Kravitz and Sons LLC.
ISBN: 979-8-89639-524-9 (sc)
ISBN: 979-8-89639-525-6 (e)

Library of Congress Control Number: 2025920543

Because of the dynamic nature of the Internet, any web addresses or links contained in this book may have changed since publication and may no longer be valid. The views expressed in this work are solely those of the author and do not necessarily reflect the views of the publisher, and the publisher hereby disclaims any responsibility for them.

DEDICATION

For my Sons,

My love is as constant as the North Star. It has never wavered. Let my life be a testament to that. May you come to know the truth, and may you come through it. I'm sorry for what happened. It was no plan of mine. You are _innocent_. I love you always. I hope against hope that this meager lamp and rough map may yet guide you home, through the dark and cold steep waves. I will be here with you always.

Love, Dad.

For Anghiel,

My bounty is as boundless as the sea, thanks to you. I love you with my whole heart too.

For the Crew and Deckhands, all of you, past, present and future, you dear, beloved handsome bunch of Gallows Fruit… it has been my honor to have served with you. You know who you are, the real samurai, my family, my brethren. There are too many to name. Don't ever, ever compromise. Spit at Death, sound the Charge, and we will laugh our farewells as we all ride out, together, one more time. The Code. I bid you now, always and forever… Not good luck… Good *Hunting.*

Let us be who we are, that we may meet our destiny. There is no justice here. It's just us.

The Way of the Samurai is Death. This is to say that one should live as though already dead. Then, whatever presents itself in way of challenge or obstacle, there is only action, without thought of life, or preserving oneself. Therefore, though death be certain, a samurai will act rightly, no matter what, without hesitation, or thought. And achieve his goal.

Hagakure: Hidden Among Leaves
Japan, circa 1611

Acknowledgement

The author wishes to thank the gallant nameless many who toiled into the wee hours to see the ship all the way to shore.

A full list would double the size of the book.

See yourselves here; hear your voice in mine forever.

Thank you.

TABLE OF CONTENTS

$\mathcal{A}$BOUT THE AUTHOR

Eric Olson, aka White Shirt Pierce, is an enigmatic individual possessing a wealth of experience that he has very effectively put into words in his debut novel, *The Quiet Spaces Between the Whirlwind.*

With a career spanning almost three decades as a counselor of children and families in crisis, Eric has dedicated his life to making a positive impact on the lives of others. He has also worked as a CPR and first-aid instructor for 20 years, and a driver's ed instructor for 10 years. Instructing professionals on how to safely manage aggressive and violent behavior, and teaching remedial driving courses in Maine to people under the age of 25 who've received speeding tickets were among some of his other career endeavors.

When he is not busy with work, he can be found river canoeing, fishing, and hiking in the wilderness.

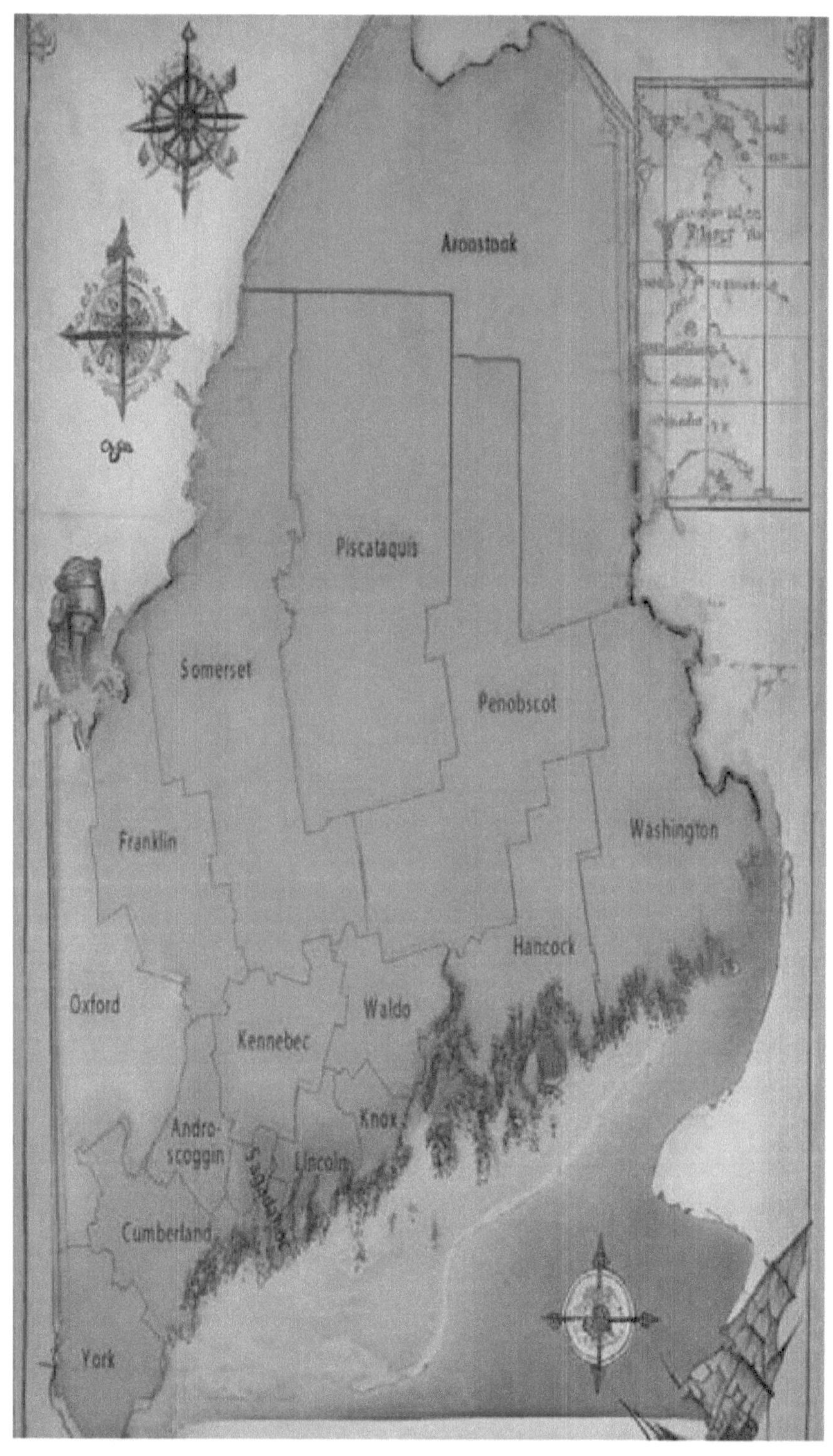

Aroostook
Piscataquis
Somerset
Penobscot
Franklin
Washington
Hancock
Oxford
Waldo
Kennebec
Knox
Andro-
scoggin
Lincoln
Cumberland
York

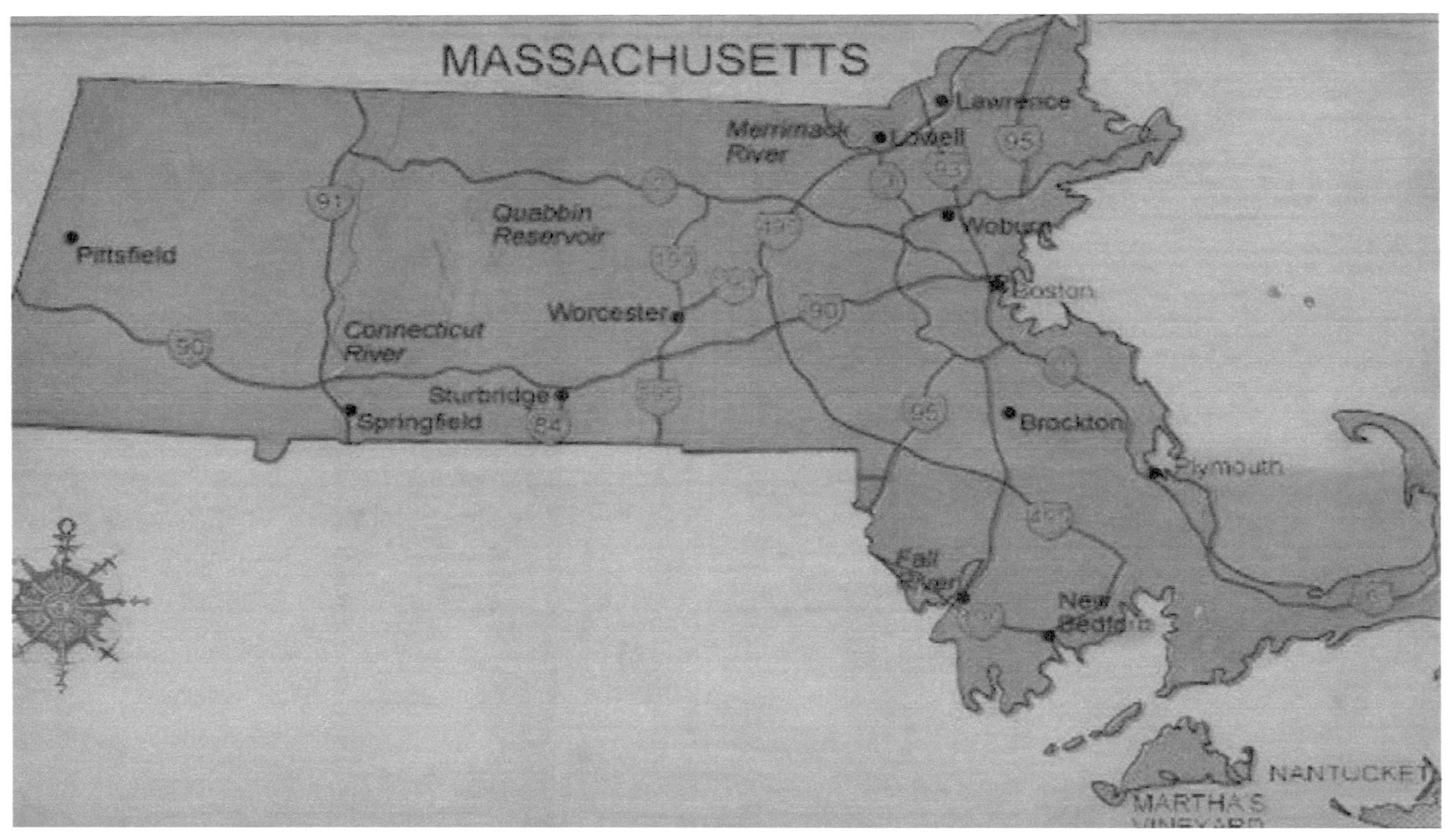
MASSACHUSETTS
Pittsfield
Lawrence
Merrimack River
Lowell
Woburn
Boston
Quabbin Reservoir
Connecticut River
Worcester
Sturbridge
Springfield
Brockton
Plymouth
Fall River
New Bedford
NANTUCKET
MARTHA'S VINEYARD

PROLOGUE

(1)

South Twin Lake, Maine.

Spring, 200-

Brethren of the North.

Every year they come, as the spring up here yields slowly to the summer. Ten years and more now. Not quite a lifetime, but a good bit of one. They look forward to it, planning menu and bar for months through the long night of Maine winter.

The winter wind can blow so cold. We hear them, for four days, they laugh and tell each other the same stories. They drink and sit around a huge white man fire. Too much wood. Never last through the night, when the night gets dark and the skies are clear and the stars look down and know but can do nothing but bear witness, stoically and silent, for the ages. These tenderfeet would never have survived up here in the olden times. Except that one.

There are usually five of them, and a dog. The dog and the one, they do not come every year. She never leaves his side. When they are not here, the others are not so loud. They laugh, and cook, and drink, and… relax, but he and that dog bring more. Pirate flags. Fireworks. Canoes. He scares the shit out of everyone every year, screaming and running into the water without warning, and he always (always) catches them by surprise. It's a running joke now, a tradition, and the other one is whenever that pair doesn't come, they reflect on that absence at some point in the first afternoon, and miss them.

The early spring dawn is rent with the call of a horn. Only when they are here, the pirate and his kooky little dog. Every spring they gather, and mark the years with rituals and antics.

Not a horn. A shell. A large brightly painted Conch shell.

He slipped onto the water one night some years ago and shelled them around the campfire with bottle rockets. Sent the lot of them scattering. They laughed after that for some time, otherwise in silence, at their big bright fire, the chuckles circling around the silences like waves returning softly, every few breaths, gently diminishing as they ran out with the tide.

He works with children, they tell me. He always jokes with them about how he loves his work, and accepts that it is a friar's choice. He works more than one job, and is generally a Teacher and a Healer in his vocations, when they are not here. They are all fathers, this crew. They speak of graduations and drivers' licenses, so they aren't young men. When he is here, they all laugh like college kids, frat boys, for four straight days. They smoke prodigious amounts of marijuana through a tomahawk. It's his, of course. They laugh, and smoke.

And he listens to the loons and knows them. Birds of prey, too. This one walks on Earth and is acquainted. Once, Eagle flew over their cabin on the first day and shed a feather right into his hands. He gave it away to a mighty medicine woman, for her own journey, they say. They walked together, went to war together, laughed and cried together as the cancer crept its way in, all the way down. He almost beat her there, they say, shortly after being here. That was five years ago, now, when he almost just quietly slipped away. Just after being here with the crew.

So, they say…

When one of the regulars found a loon whistle in the cabin, he was on the water with that dog, watching the sun set. He heard the whistle and turned back toward shore. They beached and I heard him explain to them that the Loon whistle must not be blown. It disturbs the real Loons. It frightens them. The dog barked, as if to reinforce it. The energy of the moment became calm as the lake did. This one knows things from long ago. He speaks with the trees and the Stones. He is… tapped in. I have watched him grow in power through the years. Always, here with them, he speaks of finding lost children. He is a Healer, a Medicine Man. A real one.

They listen to him. He's the one with a compass, a first aid kit, and a knife, that serves as a cocktail ice-chopper. The only one who looks like he has what he needs and knows how to use it, and when.

He always cooks on the fire, never inside. In fact, when he comes, there is a perfect little tent site nestled next to the cabin, but it could be surrounded only by that glorious forest up in God's country, Maine. The tent doesn't look out of place. The cabin does. They got rained off the West Branch in 2006. The Pirate and one who does not come anymore wanted to hold out, but they ended up in a strip club called La Casa Mia in Marlborough, Maine, down the road from Millinocket and you can use the Gazetteer to find it, just like you would Castle Rock, or Derry, or Crabapple Cove, or North Kennebunk. But… La Casa is very real, and the building still stood the last time they were in those latitudes.

Last year, he wasn't here. They were quiet, landlocked. Just men, this weekend, with jobs they were off from, and sunsets to watch, but without the pair that brings that vibrancy. Horseshoes, alcohol, and the same old tales, leatherbound stories that never get old, but are more relished with a side dish of spectacle of pirate-y acts and the energy he brings them, and they know it.

For many years they have spoken of hallucinogens. They all have dabbled, when they were young. They remember Pink Floyd and Grateful Dead and dorm rooms and campuses. Bright lights, big cities. They laugh at it, and joke that it would be fun to introduce that element to this trip. For seven years this discussion happened, like clockwork, right between the story about Gary Farmer from their hometown punching his wife in the face at the Annual Drunken Barn Dance, and the time in college when the Pirate and one of the brothers, Mikey P, were roommates that summer long ago, and the pirate watched him drill some girl that followed them home from the bar. Mikey Poulin and the Boothbay whore. It's a time-honored classic. They talk and share stories of tripping on Acid, but they never have here.

They never did bring the medicine up here, in that First Age. The Sacred Medicine. It was not truly needed.

Until the First Age ended, just before Easter, in 2017.

(2)

South Twin Lake, Maine (*Turkey-Neck*).

May, 2017.

Before the Sun Sets on the First Day…

This year, the pirate returned alone.

He arrived here on a wave of bright and searing pain.

Without the canoes, I would have thought it was someone else, but it must be him. They are happy to see him, and yet sad for him. They know how much he loved her. He does not run into the lake.

And then something new happens. They all went inside and got quiet for a while when he got here. He came down to the shore alone, without his canoe. He put his hands in the water. He washed his face, and wept in silence for a time, and the laughter began from inside the cabin. Before they started to spill out of the cabin, through the opening Doorway, he came out alone. There is an air of solemnity. The ancient Doorway is opened with modern medicine. His brothers have no idea the gravity of it. But they sense it now. They have some time to get up to tempo.

He brought down the canoe… only one this year. Two of the others were sitting on the sandy beach between the rocks, and the afternoon sun came from behind the trees and bathed them all in warm liquid gold. Pauly from Connecticut and one of the Boothbay boys were seated quietly. The pirate is standing on the point of rocks that juts out under the birch tree. One of them, as they began to trip, breathed in the lake and mountain and said one word, just a whisper…

"Healing…" This is not said for him, rather they are suddenly aware of the rising energy, and the true reason why, this year, after so many years saying we should, this is the year that acid finally made it to the Great North Woods, and became the center of this retreat.

At long last and from great need, the medicine of hallucinogens has made its way into this Circle, and nothing will ever be the same again.

The other one made a sound of acceptance, and acknowledgement of all of that in one "Mm." Healing. They were both watching him now. They feel it too, though no one here walks in the other places this one does. For them the Doorway is Pink Floyd and dorm rooms, far in the past, a thing of nostalgia. A treat for them, here away from their wives for a few days. He doesn't have a wife, not really. Not in any sense of reasonable definition. For him, it has become a tool. Now, he will use it to quench the Fire in him. In the heat of the anguish emanating from him, they hear the notes come through the other symphony of sun and water and sky now gaining crescendo… They have also lost. They realize, maybe, they all need some healing.

… The pirate's chest was heaving deeply, and his tears washed him in silence. His brothers become aware, and he turned from them without a word, grabbed a Red Stripe and that horn, sorry, shell, and shoved off onto the lake. Straight for the island. A straight line, gliding over the whitecaps like one of those little bugs, the skates, that sit atop the surface and flit about without effort. That's how he handles that vessel, without effort. With precision. His antics may be foolish, but this one… he isn't just playing dress up. He's a mariner, one with real skill, and experience, and it shows. To be a fool here is no joke. Death is in the water, in the form of cold. He demonstrates for them, just in fun, but always teaching. Teaching how to survive. He makes play real. Fun, and serious, and knowing. With laughter. It's how he talks of working with hurt children. How to Heal. Teach, and Love. He plays and laughs at Death but respects the reality of its existence. And its real-world power. Today in his agony he tests it, standing, rolling on that cold deep lake in his tiny clamshell

of a canoe, that little green sliver on all that quicksilver water. He will flirt with Death more and more in the years to come, daring it, but today, he still thinks his Life exists as it had been. It is rather, the herald of change to come, though that is still two years away… He has found kindred Pirate spirits in all of them, and they have watched as the gag flags became more a philosophy and a Code, when he realized the weight that symbology carries in the hearts and minds of children of all ages. He has become a pirate, and so have they all. Indeed, they kind of always were, too. Together they have evolved into a special group that is now sealed together forever. And now, today… today it all comes down to this. They have spent a lifetime getting here. They have spoken of the Doorway for years. This is the first time, and the setting is one of anguish juxtaposed with this beautiful place they come back to year after year for fun. After today, nothing will ever be the same again. His heart is bleeding on the sand next to them and they cannot unsee it. They are uncomfortable with the Power he has summoned today. There is no denying that this is no joke, and we are not kids anymore. This is real, and it will have its own way.

I can't see the other side of the island from my spot here among the stones. I have been here thirty thousand years, like the island. Same as the Lake. Same as the Mountain behind me, Mighty KTAADN. We are one here, in this place where time passes slow. I am Pk'tAA'dn, the Piece of the Big Rock. The Eye of the Earth, and Scribe.

I heard the shell blow, as the sun set. Once, again. Something else, faint on the wind. A bell, or something. It was a long time before I saw him come around from the lee of the island again, back onto open water. But before I saw him, I heard a howl of pain and loss that I felt deep down in my roots in the ground. It split the lake from skin to cold rocky depth. It sounded like the anguish of a Titan. Nothing like that has been heard over these healing waters for three hundred years, when the people of the forest and the lake up here waged war on one another and there was blood and grief. So much grief. Raw and hot. Suffocating grief. I haven't heard a human being cry out like that for three centuries; what in the name of Cosmic All-One who made us all, the rocks, the trees, and the creatures of the air that this man appears to speak with in the manner of the Old Ones... what has happened to this man's soul to bring that sound out of him? For one human heartbeat everything, absolutely everything, was silent.

Later, they watch thunderstorms across the water and great flashes and symphonies of light. They are more impressive in their silence because it shows how faraway they are, yet visually spectacular. The Doorway seats are good ones, for natural phenomena.

Since she has been gone, he, and they all, are... diminished.

Maybe it was not fair of him to bring them to this place and turn it into something else. It is done. The pirate was not okay when he arrived here this spring. When he left, some of the bleeding was stopped. Thanks to the magic. They helped him pick his heart up off the beach. He washed it in the lake and the last of the tears, for now. He put it back into his chest. His face is grim, yet he is smiling. This is a Warrior. He will survive. There are other things ahead, in Destiny, for all of them. He hopes they can forgive him, someday.

They cannot share his pain, only help him bear the weight. And he loves them back, and so did that sweet, silly dog. She will be missed, and part of her remains here, with us—the watching *stones.*

Love Heals. Even the Stones know Stones can Love. Everything in Creation can and deserves to know Love.

Love is infinite.

The pirates returned to South Twin Lake again in 2018 and 2019. As of 2020, when the entire trip was cancelled for everyone for the first time ever, there had yet to be another dog. There was speculation, leading up to it, from the others. They were disappointed to see him arrive alone both subsequent years. Silver changed hands.

Both times he has made straight for the island alone, full colors flying. The old flag. The original flag. The Wynne flag, that has at least countless river trips, night marsh bugouts, and twenty years on it. It is the one in some of the best photos ever taken in this group. Strange sounds come from the lee of the island. He returns. With her gone, he returns here, and he is still diminished. But he never fails to observe this ritual…

… before sunset on the first day.

(3)

Time and tide for no one stay.

(What has gone before…)

I took LSD for the first time my first year in college. Mick Mack was there, and Kenny. It was Sean who spearheaded the whole thing, of course, he was our leader. No magic mushroom bunny slope ride, straight to the high test, Sean said. He said he didn't have time to remediate what I should have done in high school. I learned so much from him. It was 1988. The before: I was what I was. It is hard, now, to look back at what I was at 17. A young man, yes. I was recently moved away from home and going wild in college, of course. It was definitely the right thing for me, the freedom. I did not have much of it growing up, and I was low on the social food chain in a small-town high school.

From the first moment, the effects of LSD can best be described as this: immediately, my perspectives were blown wide open. It was basically… "Oh… *okay, then…*" I felt happiness and fun, without filter. I felt what pure love is. I had a loving family growing up, this was… *universal.* It was a dimension of existence I had never seen before, and now I look at people going through their lives angry all the time and 35 years later, I think, "<u>That</u> motherfucker needs to eat some acid." Or mushrooms. Those are good too. I learned that at the Blue House a couple years after this. I did not trip a lot in my life, get me. I didn't follow the Dead, and unlike Hairdoo Bob, I never got a taste for psychedelics on a regular basis. In fact, it almost slipped away into the past, relegated to the things of youth, which should be gracefully surrendered. What would have happened then… well, without the sacred medicine there would be no tale, and no hope of survival.

That was the after, and that morning in 1988 I awoke as they say, with a new outlook, but… you know, people say a lot of things. Sometimes they say one thing and do the very opposite right in front of you. As of now, this fine morning (that's 2 p.m. on college hours) when I resurrected myself after that wild first trip, I truly had a different outlook on life and this cannot be overstated. It really changed everything in an instant. I had attained… *mellowness.* It was a Healing thing, but I was barely 18 years old then. What did I know of Magic?

All I knew of magic at 17 was play magic (hocus-pocus you're a frog!). Then, there is fantasy, like *The Hobbit*, one of my all-time faves, of course, and good movies with wishes and miracles. Then, there is real magic, and it is about good times and good memories, like Christmas and graduations and the intensity of feelings that accompany. I would learn, after that night long ago, much more about the workings of the mind, and dynamics between people and families. I would, in time, become a legitimate, if uncredentialed expert.

And, that wishes can come true with a little help and luck, and that miracles happen all the time.

LSD, however, after long years of exploration, in my experience, will do more in the right hands in twelve hours than ten years of traditional therapy and medication. Is that magic? It sure feels like it, and packs results to back it up. What is magic, anyway?

***

After Uncle Jimmy died, Barbara moved out to Colorado to be with her relatives now that my cousins were grown up. It was the very early nineties. The town was one I never would have been able to name, except in 1995, as I began my professional life trying to help kids find the way out of the dark. A couple kids from the local high school in Aunt Barbara's new home really put their town and school on the map.

It was Columbine, Colorado.

For years and years, I taught two things, how to be funny, even for the hopelessly cringy dad jokes, and how to stand back a bully. Also, hopefully, how not to, you know… do that. Matty Mango and I used to joke that if we ever wrote a book together it should be titled How Not to Raise a Kid That Gets Guns and Murders a Bunch of People in School.

Teach someone to fish…

***

I have been in training my whole life. Everything I ever experienced in life was training. My parents took me to amazing places, and I learned about the world. I read for hours and hours in the car when I was a kid, and my memory is forensic. My parents sent me to a long list of camps, and I enjoyed that. I was not a kid who called home and wanted to go home. One summer when I was about 15, I did a three-day basketball clinic (which is funny, because I suck comically hard at basketball to this day) a week aboard a sailboat in Rhode Island, and a week at a Boy Scout camp, practically back-to-back. It put me, as I would explain to my father one day, in different milieus, and because of that I was able to reconstruct things internally and externally later, with more than one experiential reference point.

***

So, one of the first things to teach young people is that their experience now is so limited, that the world is full of beautiful people, and some of those people are their *people. I learned this, at that Old Blue Lambda Delta House, and I think it helped me survive.*

***

Me and school were never a good fit, and school was the source of much trauma to both me and my family. My mother was a schoolteacher to the bone, always the teacher, and having a neurodivergent kid (ADHD) was NOT something she had factored into dealing with. This, of course, affected me and our family. More training. Having to deal with not being able to have a "normal" baby fucked her way up. I get this now deeply, and of course, I never knew her before this skewed her. My father and I discussed this, and many other things, when I returned to West Allenton after one life was over. College was completely different. It was my mind-wipe. I heard people say, "The military would be good for you." To me, and to others. I did not serve. I did pledge the Lambda Delta house in the fall of 1988 and got reprogrammed. If you know, you know, and that's some of what I'm trying to bring to everybody, here, now.

The Treeherder pledged **three** times. Maine Maritime plebe year, Navy, Lambda Delta. No wonder he plodded through our hazing rituals numb.

My mother hounded me, *hounded* me relentlessly throughout high school that I was going to college. I made it there. I found education there, and they paid for it, and oh God am I blessed. The education I got was the one I needed, if not the one they technically paid for.

I was lucky. I was able to find my people, my vocation, out here in the wilderness. I went looking, and I found. I worked with a thousand parents who are hobbled by anxiety and fear. I found dozens of schoolteachers and staffers with mean streaks and petty tyrant syndrome. I recognized them when I saw them. I was no longer a child, but one who was protecting children, and my sword, figuratively speaking, found use. Healing became the work of my life. I am a healer, and a teacher. I am a man, no more or less. And I found my own battlefield. The years went by.

'92, Boothbay, the summer before my last year in college, I went down the Saco River for the first time. I came home from Boothbay because I missed the summer house life, and I stumbled onto a group of brothers headed to Fryeburg. They snatched me up. I had not seen them all summer. I had not canoed since I was a kid at Rocky Pond some five years ago now. This was an eternity then, and I was a man now, my experience of college, and especially the Old Blue House, almost behind me forever.

I discovered that on that little pond, so big to me once, I had learned something. The Saco is packed in the summer with people partying hard. I fell in love with the scene and for eight years. While I got married, had kids, I contemplated how to get back to the water, how to return to what I once had known and loved, and had maybe almost come dangerously close to forgetting, or losing. I left it all behind to come to Maine so long ago. We ate mushrooms that day. Besides laughing our asses off for six hours I felt an awakening of something that had been missing while I was getting my education. My mother rolls her eyes at that. The education I got was far more important and useful, and Mom came to accept that, although she never did fully understand. Dad did, though, before this yarn would end.

Before I left the Blue House, I acquired awards. Four different classes of new brothers over the time I was there recognized me as the best of the best teachers, and fearsome in the face of ignorance ("IGNANT" in the parlance). I accept that. Mom, like many parents now and then, saw things in terms of accolades and certificates. Trophies. There's nothing wrong with trophies and ribbons, as long as everyone remembers what they're there for, and how they work, and what they really mean. What their true significance and value is, in other words.

After losing a longtime job I encountered a kid I had worked with in my community. He ran up and greeted me, and told me how much he loved it when I used to work with him, and all the fun stuff I had taught him. I can't put that on a wall, or a resume. I can't eat it, or use it to fix my car. But I still treasure these things that I have, that matter. They matter where few other things do. Money, car, what kind of cigarettes you smoke or house you live in, or what you did for a living… oh… but there are places where none of that matters at all, and it is just you, and what you are, and what you believe, and what you can or cannot do. And what you must or must not do. In those places, who you are and what you have done, nay even to what you think in your heart are what you want to have with you, when the reckoning comes. If those things be riches, then I bathe in the wealth of Midas.

There is a t-shirt, or a poster, or a coffee mug, or a meme. You've seen it, I hope, or we're all fucked. It says, "A hundred years from now, it will not matter what kind of car I drove, blah, blah, blah, but the world will be a better place because I was important in the life of a child."

***

So, I came to understand. I am a Pirate…

And a Medicine Man…

And a Samurai…

PART 1
SACRED SPIRAL

The Last Night of My Old Life

Circles open and close.

This story begins and ends in the same place, in the same manner, and among the same main company. It is Midsummer's Eve, 2019.

My old life began when I left my home at 17 and moved to Southern Maine to go to college. I met the woman I would marry there, and we bought a house, and had a family, and lived our lives. I found my own calling in life as a teacher, and healer, and the perfect job for me did not really exist, but I found a way to make it up as I went along.

Working with children and families was how I spent my professional working adult life, and it became my purpose, my cause, that which I took satisfaction in. Along the way I met many people, friend, foe, and the in-betweens… teachers, all, in their way.

I also had a great dog for a time; I should probably mention her now…

I had to jump from one job to another every few years or so. That became the norm. I would have loved to find a place I could just stick with, but something always went sour. One time everything was great, then all the good bosses quit, and the good staff weren't far behind. At another, again, people moved around, and it changed everything for the worse. I learned not to hang around too long, or get too attached, but I managed to pick up a good friend or two in every place along the way, friendships that outlasted the jobs. I walked a path of solitary seeking, to heal. A ronin, of sorts. At least I fancied myself so. How I found my way to that was a mystery to me once, but now…

Now, after all this, it kind of makes sense. The silver lining in this was that I met a *whole* lot of people I would not have, otherwise. Colleagues, and people we served. In those eyes, it made sense. My path took me to the people who needed me most; it was how I came to see it. So, chaotic though it could be, and risky, the plus side outweighed, especially looking back at all those faces.

In the end, the last place I worked in Maine was that *something* I had been seeking, and thank God, I found it before the journey I was about to undertake.

And my kids grew up into men, and the marriage was a dark lonely hole. So, when my boys got old enough, I knew it was time to go. Two more years went by. Ella was gone. Pete bought a piece of land on a river in the woods, and that became our place. I escaped there a few times over the first couple years since he bought it.

Tonight started like that, like any other night just buggin' out to Pootown with the Treeherder, but I should have known it was going to be different, going in.

I <u>should</u> have known so many things.

In Need of Medicine

June 29th, 2019.
Midsummer's Eve, Pirate Stronghold.
Pootown, Maine.
8:51 PM EDT.
81 degrees F.
Clear and still. Visibility unlimited.

This is a special place. I love it here. I wish she had lived to see it, but then, our time was already done, and this place represents what will come, what may yet be, or be again. The dog, of course. Not the wife. Jesus.

Since October of 2017 we have been here, in this little patch of woods. The bank is due south, the road due north, and the river runs east out to the Saco, and from there down to Saco Bay, Camp Ellis, on the mouth of the river. We know that river, the Treeherder and I, as did she. This one, coming in low from the west below Cornish Station, was new to us, and the memories we share of here have been accumulated over the last two years or so. As far as knowing the flow of the waters for roughly a hundred miles around, that comes from Pete and I (and Ella, until…) spending fifteen years becoming expert wilderness canoeists, river trippers and Pirates. I canoe the sea routinely, at night on the estuary near my home. I have seen things. Ella and I used to ride the tide out to the furthest sandbar and watch the fireworks over the pier at Old

Orchard Beach, sometimes just us, sometimes with pirates who made it out here with us. God, how I miss her and that. I don't go out as much these days and, when I do, I do things I would not have done with her. Dangerous things. I have come here many times to sit with the Treeherder to get council, mayhap to give it, to remember. To… *take stock*. To work through life's challenges, friends putting their brains together in this safe place.

The Treeherder put a road in here early, but before he did the first fire ring was on the hill right next to the road, the one that we would fortify in other times and places in this world, like when if the zombies came. This place itself was developing into something special. Energy pumps through the forest along the river, raw and unspoiled. This is an unremarkable location; it was not strategic when wars between red man and white were fought here centuries ago. Few, in fact, have ever really paid it mind, since the time of Ice eons ago. It has just… been here, waiting. At first, it was just us on the side of the road, the river to our backs deep through thick woods, a fire, and council of matters of import. And of Honor.

A good friend is that: a highwater mark to navigate by; a lighthouse in the dark. We have been that through the years, and not just we two—all of us, we happy few who have somehow found one another from time to time in the Dark…

My medicine is my weapon, professionally. As a young man I was given some sacred knowledge by the Crocodile, and I had lived by it, and been guided by it. Years later, it was Gundy who explained to me that not only was it very real, but it held great shamanic power. Uh, okay…

So, I learned, and believed. I used this energy to work with kids and families, and I came to believe that while magic isn't Harry Potter, it IS very real. Understanding it, that it is energy in a scientific sense, allowed us to walk a Path of true healers, medicine guides.

I have studied martial history and militaria my whole life, and I had cultivated the notion of modern samurai values in working with children. This was a solitary quest. Gundy put the capital on Quest. Quests, Chivalry, Bushido… all real, alive and waiting to be cultivated and nurtured, and so we did, over years. By the time I arrived at the Poo this evening and took my medicine, I was cognizant and respectful of the Old Ways and Magicks, a Practitioner in my own right. I had to keep that energy clean (I'm a family therapist, in-home; a field agent; a specialist; I had real concerns, this night, about my future and… staying healthy and sharp amid the potential acrimony of a divorce).

I've heard stories of every abuse and neglect and torture one person can inflict on another family member. Many of them have come from the Treeherder himself. He was married to an abusive demon, and she dragged him in every imaginable way, including with his kids, which is just despicable. It was his experience that had me terrified of leaving my marriage, and something that told me waiting till they were grown was the right thing. I heard so many stories about the horrors of divorce, it was one of the reasons I waited to leave her. I knew I wouldn't be able to be the father I wanted to be if I put my needs first, because she would use every edge and angle, even the kids, to hurt me. I needed to get free of her, and preserve my relationship with my kids, and my career. The kids were men now, launching themselves well, and I wanted to move onto the next stage without being anchored to this marriage that was not. I had come here tonight knowing I was at a crossroads, and knowing I was done.

Divorce is catastrophic to children's lives. That's not a judgement, because they need to happen when they need to happen. But the reality of it, the ugly unseen parts, the effects of it, are NOT fully realized. I have breathed people's air for twenty-five years. I waited and tried to survive. I was very much in the positive as a family man, and when the four of us were together in my old life the home we lived our lives in was always full of laughter. Literally, I realized one day some years ago, that whenever we were all home together, we were always laughing.

Child abuse seemed like a good dragon to slay, so it wasn't hard to stumble into mental health and discover an awesome way to make a living, if one can roll with the big dogs.

I think I always wanted to find minds like that. I wanted to fight. I have been a warrior, in my fashion. I have contemplated long in the dark and lonely hours of the night what the nature of evil is and where it lives. And how to kill it. And from what places one gets things like courage and honor. Where is meaning found in life? Can it be created?

So, if you can, consider that it may be possible in this world now, this time and place, this society, for one to rediscover, recreate, and live by a code that would be more recognizable centuries ago; there may be something here for you. If you can believe the power of some of the things I will speak of, maybe, just maybe, all of this is worth it. I hope so. Every day, with every part of me, I hope so.

Air, Water, Fire, Earth & Spirit

The preparations were complete. The fire was lit. I had moved from Prima Nocturne to High Hill, where Pete had put an old rusty camper he holed up in and found his shelter. He had taken his own shelter over the years, mostly in the form of working a lot, and picking up cans along the road, and wandering the woods of his land where his boys grew up, but not with them, because she always kept her sharp eyes on them, and what they were doing, and how close they were to him.

The fire caught, and leapt awake, casting pale gold around us in aura, high into the trees. To my eyes only, they extended their warmth further, up to the high treetops, still against the sweeping curve of sky silent and deepening dark, peppered with early stars. The audience was arriving. I began to hear the forest. Ah, sweet spirit world, come and show me what I must do, through the Doorway. Into the Sacred Spiral. This was Act 1, opening number, full swing. Be. Be Still…

I have never sought the Doorway here before. That was something I discovered in college, but for many years I had not thought of it, because I thought it was fun to take drugs and hoot it up, partying with your brothers and jamming music, just living and eating life as we did, drinking life, I guess would be more accurate, at the Old Blue Lambda Delta House.

Last fall I slept rough on a tarp, here on the ground, curled up next to the fire. I had taught myself to live without the love of a mate. When I rediscovered psychedelics a few years back, on the Saco of course, it was very much more, and I held this medicine in reverence, and took true counsel from the voices I heard when it was in me, when the Doorway is open. Psychedelic drugs heal. In the right hands and manner, and with the right reverence, they do. I will say it now. I would not be alive to write this tale if that were not true.

Here, the seasons express their wonder raw and primitive. They start to zip by one after the other, faster. It is getting harder to find space and time to connect with the things that bring me sustenance, like water, and night sky in summertime. The dog is gone. Fuck it.

Whatever comes, it was time to take some agency over my life. One thing I trusted, is that we both had the boys close to heart, that we both wanted what was best for them. I was counting on that to make this separation work. I was terrified about moving out of my house.

How many people come to crossroads like this without years of exploration and experience for reference and perspective? I had waited. Until mine were grown. For them, and for my parents, too. I just spent twenty-five years learning about people and life, and mental health; my own and others. I have tried to be well in all aspects of my life, so that I may be a better… instrument. It is how I encouraged others to think, and practice—Way of the Samurai. It's the only reason I'm alive to tell the tale, that I spent my whole life preparing for what was now manifesting, here, in the forest, as the boundaries that separate worlds continued to fade, and things began to walk among us, unleashed from that other place. They spread out into the night air like the ills of Pandora's box, but the energy here was neither good nor evil, it was neutral and illuminating.

I was protective of my power once I came to understand

that it was real. I had worked hard for it and bore the wounds and scars of its earning inside and out of me. It took me long to manifest and understand it, and I had many Guides to be sure. But it was Gundy who told me that the time for fuckin' around was over, because when you wield power like yours, she told me, you cannot hide any more than a candle can hide in a dark forest from the things among the trees.

It started here, tonight, in this place, and through the open Doorway, the one to the spirit world, where I have walked and learned secrets of the universe. Where I have walked, both at the beginning and end of this journey.

The Juice was now running *HARD*. All senses heightened. I began to think in universal terms. One must be able to introspect without cloud on the eye. The air gave faint hints of bamboo chiming, the sounds of its essence and energy. The stars began to look like jewels. Another effect on the other side of the Doorway is hearing the voices of all living things around you and seeing things with less distortion of the physical world. Stars, for example, gain visual clarity because the effects of atmospheric distortion and lensing are negated by the drug, which shows things in their more elemental state, unfettered by physical factors like light and gravity. It shows things more as they truly *are*. Learning to interpret that is a course of study, though not recognized as legitimate science or treatment. Not yet anyway.

From **DESIDERATA:**

So, be ye at peace with God *whatever you conceive*
God to be…

And amid all your labors and aspirations in the noisy confusion of life keep peace with your soul.

The Treeherder fed up the fire, watching me stand there in wonder and breathe with the Earth and Night, joining with the forest, and the river through the trees. It was a dark night without moon, yet the sky was alive with wisps of Milky Way and meteors. The silence and the sounds were deafening in their contrast. Pete knew the show was really starting. I heard myself laughing.

The Wind Across the River/Acid Theater

So, the Doorway had just been kicked open, again, again at great need. Now, we were settled into the night on High Hill, my little temporary fire on Prima Nocturne glowing and fading out across the frog pond, back toward the road. No road, now. Void. Emptiness. Pause. Breathe. Be. Be still. Be still and know.

The forest continued in pulsing sentient awareness. I could sense the tens of thousands of living things around me. There were plenty of critters out there, little ones with fur, not just bugs. Birds. Reptiles. As if reading my thoughts, far off I heard a large noise from the river. It could have been anything, but I sensed a large fish catching a snack. Some things, there is no way to ever know. The rolls of faint magenta and violet passed softly away from me, sliding over the hood of my vehicle, reflective, and out into the darkness of the trees. With the medicine, the drugs, the magic dust, I really don't care how you look at it… with the LSD in my system starting to take hold, I was relishing the chorus. LSD is medicine. Illegal. Dangerous. Powerful. It is time to make decisions and commit. Time to leap into the sky.

The road I am on now leads to Death. I am losing myself. I need cleansing. It began to come as the night fell, and the fire crackled and hissed and lit the trees behind the Treeherder, watching me now with familiar amusement and clinical curiosity. He's a nurse, a navy medic, combat vet. Eagle Scout, as are his two sons. He has never done drugs, but he and I have been brothers since before he went to war in 1991, back at Old Lambda Delta, and he sure as fuck has seen plenty of drugs done, mainly by me, but not only. My sons are grown. I can't believe it, that ten years went by so fast.

The forest and the river were speaking with the stars. We sat in on the conversation for a bit. Blues and golds throbbed through the green. Inexplicable, that the green is perceptible. It was 22:45 EDT.

Blue Fire

The Fire began to glow deep indigo around the edges of its dancing pink and metallic orange flames. The air was light and comfortable. The sounds of the night were crisp and clean. I heard insects conversing, and small furry things whispering to each other, telling each other that the night is long and dark, but this little patch of leaves is warm and safe, and in the morning, there may be some food to fill our bellies. Sleep well, honey. I'm here. I'll protect you if I can. Love. It is known to everything, not just human beings. We are just the species that makes it complicated. The species that weaponizes Love, uses it to hurt.

I began to laugh at the wonder that is Creation. That is how acid works. It opens the mind and drops all barriers between you and the world and cosmos, between you and time, and inside your own mind, it shreds the barriers you build for yourself, to avoid looking at the dark and dirty places in your soul. Acid shreds that curtain. That's what a bad trip is. It brings all repressed memories to the surface. And once you learn to handle that, and face it, you are ready for what it really can do. It can offer you audience with the universe.

The first time I was 18, with Mick Mack and the old crew. The second time, me and Mick and some people we didn't hang out with that much all got some together, but we took off on our own, roaming around the woods near campus before settling into his dorm room for some serious communion. The second time was when I realized that the human mind contains the Godhead, but the Godhead is a real living entity. We don't make it up, we sprang from it, as did all things.

***

The conflict between science and religion is not real. Throughout history it has been used to dupe some people into oppressing other people. In Fact, of course, science and religion are but two studies of the same thing, but one of those disciplines refuses to recognize the legitimacy of the other, because it thinks in terms of exclusion, superiority and power. – Acid Wisdom. It abounds.

***

Ella was the sweet quick brown love of my life. Her loss had devastated me, and had he been capable then of feeling, it would have Pete as well. We were a pirate trio, we had put many miles under our keels together, us, and others, over the years. We had become expert canoeists. There had been many adventures and hilarity. Ah, the addition of a fine dog to anything, and she was the very best. Pete said her name, that he missed her. The air of the night was hot, thick, and still.

With the invocation of her spirit, the night changed and a wind began to rise.

Out of the silence, the wind rose. Slow at first, but slow and wide. It continued to rise as we stood, and I felt the hot tears begin to stream. It has been two years, and when I think of her now, she mostly makes me smile, but there are still tears, too.

The wind rose and blew the flames around, tipped with platinum and shooting silver flashes off it only I could see. It rose to a roar. The trees began to sway, pulsing, breathing, awake and here with us now, through the sacred Doorway. The stars shook above the rising wind, between the two worlds. Everything vibrated with energy, the energy of love.

On the front face of that wave of only air, as it crashed through the trees and rolled over the last few yards of forest straight into us, and shook our little hilltop like an earthquake, my chest exploded outward in a blast of bright white light, and her face came rolling out of that wind, smiling, huge, looking down at me. Her love, her spirit, had arrived at the party.

"Can you feel her, Pete?" I shouted from my promontory, atop a large rock, the Starwatching rock. My face was hot and wet with free-flowing tears, but I was smiling, and laughing, and crying, all at once. "Can you feel her here?" I didn't hear him answer. I could not over the freight train thunder of the wind now. But I saw his eyes grow wide as he watched the power begin to flow through me. She was there with us, of that there is no question. Pete was also smiling. In awe, but smiling. I was too, the unfiltered smile of having set aside the world for a time, to gain perspective from another angle. An unpolluted smile, which was about how I was feeling. Still dirty, but a filter was softly humming now. The medicine… it was working.

The wind and our tears died down. The fire dwindled. It was 11 PM. Had it really only been two hours? It already felt like days. Like I had learned years ago, standing waist deep in the current of the Holy Saco raising my hands and heart to the glory of the universe, laughing and loving life and being alive, I let the wonder and unity with all things flow through me. Breathe, and walk. And know.

Be Still, and Know that I Am.

We were in the current; inside and within the Sacred Spiral now, gaining speed.

Mr. Treeherder's Wild Ride

Pete needed beer and he chose this moment to inform me that he needed to go get some. I was laying on the ground in giggling mania and awash in tears of joy and wonder at the same time at the amazing heavens above me, so to him this seemed like the right moment to ask me to function enough to co-pilot him. He isn't always good with timing, but then again, the store closed at midnight and I sure as fuck was not going to become any more serviceable in at least ten hours.

I had the undesirable choice of staying here alone, which I was not prepared to do, or ride with Pete to the store we always pour ourselves into at some point when we are out here. They're probably expecting us. It is Friday night come to think of it. I wasn't afraid, but I didn't know who all was coming through that Doorway next, and I didn't want to meet a fucking wendigo or a Level Three Orc fighter by myself out here. The truth is, I felt safer on Acid there than not, because I could see, hear and smell better, in either world. Also, I was on a spirit walk. Warded, right?

Not on Acid, there's no way, NO WAY, I was going to stay there by myself. We have both heard large things moving around in the forest at night, between us and the river, and I sure as fuck did not think sitting there alone tripping balls with one of Pete's firearms was a good idea either. I had lit myself up to be seen with the right eyes and there are many things that walk between the worlds. So, I poured my laughing, crying, drooling ass into Pete's disgusting rolling dumpster of a car, a Toyota Yaris filled to the brim with trash and miscellaneous pack rat shit, coins, cans, fast food waste, a shovel, a backpack, a Model 94 lever action carbine, axes; it's a Hoarder-car. It looks like someone lives in it. He kind of does.

The ride was unpleasant. Pete has only had two beers, or I would have taken my chances alone here, wendigo or no, and he followed the speed limit into Cornish along the hilly wooded road that felt to me like the amusement park rides where you ride a cart through a haunted house and shit jumps at you from every corner. I closed my eyes until we arrived at the store. It is a point of fact that Pete is a terrible driver, except not an angry aggressive one. Just… not good. He doesn't drive technically well. He drives… poorly. He doesn't speed, not like a speeder, he just doesn't pay attention to his speed, the speed limit, or what a reasonable speed is, so he may roll into a 25 mph drop at 50 and not realize it. On the other end, he may do 25 after it turns to 50 for a mile or two, until people start beeping and passing on hills.

Pete got his beer. I tried to hide among the trash in his car. We went back, a complete reverse playback of the wild hallucinating ride out. It felt to me like we were driving in reverse. I held fast, my jaw tight and sore. Pete was amused that I kept reaching for a brake pedal on my side. I taught Driver's Ed for ten years; I'm used to one being there. We tripped our way back to the safety of the stronghold. The night was still there, and I relaxed, and smoked, and took breaths, and through the clear mind's eye of LSD, I knew that my decision, and my Path, was right, and set, and begun, now, irreversibly. It is a good thing I came here, tonight, the last night of my old life. It set me on the path. That was the end of Act 2, Mr. Treeherder's wild fucking ride. It was 12:56 A.M.

In the rising light of the fresh loaded refueled fire, Pete cracked open an ice-cold beer, well won. He likes weird beer. This was Fin Du Monde, from Quebec. I find its taste about like its name. I think he only drinks it because it's from Quebec. Not known for discerning tastes, my old friend. It's an old rib between us, and I love to give him shit. This, however, was big. He casually asked me if one of my sons was gay.

How close have you ever been to a lightning strike? The Treeherder and I once saw a bolt come down at fifty yards that was six feet wide, and when that happens, just like right now, with that question, as soon as the last word came out of his mouth, the night went instantaneously silent, and still, and deep velvet black for just… one… heartbeat.

Face-Melting Acid Show/A Voice with which to Scream

Act Three kicked off with a blast of love that lit me up and made me shine like one of the stars looking down. I thought of both, the might-be-gay one and the other. My fine sons. Everything I ever did that mattered was right there. Everything was bright. The pale blues and purples running through the trees in waves returned on the next pulse of the heartbeat of this night and morphed into the warm pink and orange of an evening sunset like the one that had capped this fine day, on my way out here to open the Doorway, now wide open with the love of a father for his sons blasting through like a supernova, fierce, hot.

The sounds of the forest and the river came rising back in slow crescendo. I could hear two hundred yards to the southeast, there were water birds roused at the power that had just shot through here, and the shift of energy to pure bright love and life. My own shamanic powers were manifesting now, three or more hours into this journey, and I began to feel like I had climbed atop the wave of the Spiral. This is all normal and gets easier with experience. I felt so much love for them both then, my sons, and I never got to tell them one more time. I could have, but after tonight things were never the same again. I still do. Love them. I never did not for a moment, even when I lost my fucking mind, later. The night was clean after the big wind had come through and sounds of other life were everywhere.

A large old fish slid by along the rocky bottom of the river. I felt his spirit greet mine in recognition. I was in commune with Nature. *Phew.* Liftoff was rough, but then again, this journey tonight marked the beginning of my full manifestation, so there wasn't really experience, much of this was new. Drugs, that's one thing. If this were just about drugs, I wouldn't be writing it. This isn't about drugs. It's about how without this medicine I write of here, I would not be alive to tell this tale, and I hope others will find their own way. What happened to me after tonight is hard to believe, but I was prepared, and I survived. Well… I don't know if *prepared* is correct, but anyway, back to the Spirit world, and my yarn.

I did not need to answer what I would think if T.C. or Keelin was gay, or trans, or anything. If they could find love and happiness, I will have also. That simple. The love I felt for both my sons at that moment made the question so irrelevant I dropped to the gravelly ground and rolled around howling in laughter at the absurdity of it. Next to the love I felt for them, bright, hot and pure, there was nothing in all the cosmos more… elemental.

We sat in silence for a time after that, he in his thoughts, I in mine, and in the company of the souls of the forest, the living physical animals, the trees, the Spirits of the Old Ones, watching and awake now to witness my journey through their world. An interloper, perhaps, but one who had come at great need. It is good to know the appropriate courtesies and rituals. Now, my eyes were not on the misery of being married and alone, but what there may be in the promise of the future now. There was nothing then, ever, in my life that felt so pure, and clean, and beautiful, as the love I felt for my sons right then. There was only that, and nothing else, for that moment.

When I would return to the Stronghold two years from now, it was that love that was still there, that had never wavered, and that which carried the voice of my heart into the universe when this Circle closed.

Act Three saw a new arrival, one I had not expected. This next guest was a most welcome addition to my little company that was gathering, preparing to jump off the cliff I was going to jump off of tomorrow, when I returned to the Prime World from the one I was in now.

This guest was Musician-me. There was a musician in here all along, and he found his voice out here tonight, around 2 AM, listening to the college station out of Portland as they whanged out some ripping honkytonk southern rock, that the harmonica set I had with me, the one I carried for years before this, that my mother and dad gave me for Christmas a few years back. I actually picked one up and played with the music, and I was born again. Somewhere in the vast data archive we now generate, there is a record of what happened, this birthing. There is something called Spinitron, and on this date one can search, and around 5 AM, the DJ says that they are "supposed to be doing Perky's Auditory Canal, but

Jerry is out in the woods, on the river, by a fire, and playing along to the radio, so he is kind of running the playlist." For people who tuned in to hear the David Bowie thing they were going to do, my apologies. I hope you enjoyed the Little Feat and NRBQ. I sure did.

There are Truths here that will be real and manifest in the real world. Pieces. Clues. Breadcrumbs.

The birth throes of the muse inside me were red-faced and squalling, and went on almost until first light, as Pete tried to sleep in his trailer he bought secondhand, and dragged out here to High Hill, next to the Star Watching Rock, as I played and played and screamed in my new voice. I thought I was screaming in relief, in escape and joy. I was not. I was learning how to scream in pain. I once screamed in pain to the limit of what a human heart, a human voice, was able to express in this world, with mere tissue and muscle and air to work with, frail flesh. I needed something more. My own voice was not going to be sufficient. If I ever tried to cry out to the Heavens the way I did that day in the shattered spring of 2017, when I split that lake right in twain underneath my green canoe, looking at those old muddy footprints from her last ever boat ride, I would tear myself apart. I was going to need something else. I did not know, then, so many things.

And so, under the guidance of The Allman Brothers, and Stevie Ray, and Little Walter, and Howlin Wolf, I learned from them as I called WMPG over and over between licks with the band and asked them kindly to keep it coming. Coming in the full darkest depths of the summer night, as I played, and played, and played. The house was full, and the place was rocking. Act 3 was at its peak, the light show playing among the tree all the way to the river. The show that night was hot, hot, hot. The music echoed out through the trees and I felt like I was sitting in a jampacked honkytonk bar, thick with smoke and sweat, and full of that real live true rock-and-roll energy. What happened here tonight… I had no idea at all I was a real musician. I played trumpet in high school, but, like… I was awash in tears and gratitude at this new voice I had found.

I realized I could see a little further, that the dark no longer encapsulated us the way it had through the night.

I had been playing music for about three hours. I was soaked in sweat. Baptisms. I knew I was not done. I drank some water, breathing deeply. The clarity is tempered by the physiological effects of the drug. It takes some experience to remain cognizant. It helps not to be overweight, diabetic, and a heavy pot smoker, too. Spirit Walking is physically grueling, there is always something, a hill, a river, an all-out sprint away from slithery hungry things that tend to lurk in the shadowy places… always, one way or the other.

There is something to be said for four hours in the fetal position with awesome music on, but this was a different thing. I had been *in* it.

Dawn was approaching.

Be Still…

And Know…

That I Am…

The air was thick like a warm sponge and there was dew rolling down the inside of my windows. I watched the moisture evaporate in the cool of the deepest last gasp of the night and the breeze swept through my car and all around me through the forest. It was time to move. Curtain on the rock-and-roll. For now.

First Light

As a child when I first ventured into the forest for the night, Skylab fell. We didn't see it, I just remember it happened, finally, that day, somewhere far from the little spot in Allenton, on Sewell Pond, Camp Harrington. That would make me seven years old at the time, I guess. It was the first gray light of dawn, and I heard one of the older kids say, "Guys, its six o'clock, let me know if Skylab falls," and we started to wake in our sleeping bags, children still, but older, having spent our first night away from home, among friends, at Camp in the woods. This was day camp. The overnight was the end of the session. The stars had faded one by one the night before, slipping into the dark of sleep, like we had slipped away one by one as the sky went from obsidian to slate, then slowly granite, along the golden riverbank of dawn, atop the diamond sun, and finally into the blazing sapphire sky of full day. But the stars do not sleep, they wait in the bright of day, invisible to us. But always there. Children sleep.

Time passes. In years to come, I would try to catch this moment when the night slips away into the dawning of a new day. For years, working third shift, I would slip out for that moment, sometimes to smoke a cigarette, against regs. To catch the wakening of my surroundings, the little creatures waking in a hug, to try to survive to cuddle again into safe slumber. Like humans do.

Of course, now, unlike then, I was the Adult, the one in charge, of the innocents upstairs asleep, starting to stir themselves like little cute furry things, but ones who did not have another to cuddle with, and whisper to, to protect and be protected by. Not these little ones. They were wounded. They needed the kind of love that dispels a nightmare with a cup of hot cocoa and a picture of a dog, or a tale of a pirate. A real one. A fierce one. The one who is watching over you now. Good night, little one. You can sleep for a little while yet. I am no saint, but that doesn't mean I can't be a good example to you of what a man should be. Or a father, or big brother. Of what Love is. We can do that in safety. I am between you and all danger, on my life. On my honor, and my life, God grant it so.

There are many paths to service. To self-worth, self-esteem, self-respect. This is one, and I found it, in spaces where quiet lies and time slows down, and you sit with yourself under the watching knowing stars. To know who you are starts with what you have done. The Path begins when you realize this, and what you do next sets your course. Free Will. Law, Chaos. Good, Evil. The spaces in between, in transition, on the keen steely edge of change. The edge so sharp you cannot find it, like the places between sleep and waking, or Heaven, Earth and Hell. Everywhere there is an edge, spaces in between things where Knowledge lies and Peril. That is a valid pairing. More? Okay… Dreams, Nightmares, Pleasure and Pain, Love and Hate, Healing and Hurting. Oh, and of course, Sanity. Sanity and Madness.

Go ahead, everyone, take it from there… we don't really have a plan.

I knew this, this early summer dawn, unchanged since my childhood, unchanged since the last Ice Age. Life is crazy and unpredictable. Everything I had ever worked towards was in play. I was so scared. The only thing I was hanging onto at this point was self-preservation in my professional life. This "Samurai" thing… it started because the values of Bushido are Compassion, Respect, Humility, Courage, Honor, and Service. I read this and I had a moment of power. These are the exact values that people who work with children should follow. I began a long contemplation, about these ancient values and how they hold up now. And what they mean, now. Here.

I began to think it was possible to be a samurai. I mean, we were already Pirates, right?

My whole life has been training for the next challenge. That is consistent, at least. My God, I had no idea how many circles were going to close. And Open, too, of course.

As the dawn lost the cool of night the faint rose began to glow through the tree line on the horizon across the river. It was Morning. Bugs were buzzing, and I felt alive and healthy. Exhausted, maybe, but also energized.

Me & Myself

The deep blue-black night had given up its jewels one by one and slid up from its depths to slate gray. Shadows shot about the Forest as the night retreated behind trees and into the little hollows of the forest. Pete snored through the walls of his camper, at peace now that my antics had died down. Act 3 closed as the day opened one pale blue eye. Musician-me retired, resting up. It had been a strenuous birthing. We were both husked out. I paused to smoke. I could feel Ella beside me, bemused. She bid a soft sad farewell for now.

The moment between sleep and waking is tough to try to catch, like the one between night and day. The residues of dreams hold truths. As day woke, the first thing she saw was me, and I was there too, another unexpected (Was he? Had I not come here looking for the man I saw here now?), Essence-me. The soul under the face I see reflected in glass, or water, or windows into strangers' houses as I walk by on my own road, passing you in your sleep, just on the other side of the glass, me on my path, you upon your own.

Essence-me has been away. I have held on to the ideas of my career and tried to make them practice and even maybe legacy. Essence-me chose to weigh in now. Behind me is twenty-five years of walking and seeking, that to be a Healer. I have met many powerful souls, alive and dead, and some have gone from one to the other and remain with me here, or out there, watching, on the wings of the Hawks that greet me now since Candace the Grey died, and came back as Candace the White, the Hawk.

Ella, of course, never went all the way away, and her voice I hear as much as I did when she was alive, and could rouse me with a thought, seconds before she had to make any sounds. Telepathy. Love, some parts of it, I have learned, never die.

Essence-me knows me. So do I. I must be able to trust myself, my path, my character, my integrity, my destiny. I must be able to love myself. I have forgotten. Essence-me and I held commune, getting to know each other again, reminding us of who we were, and what we have already done. Wondering if that was firm enough to give buoyancy over depth, when fatigue sets in, and always, the cold. I smoked, and laughed, and remembered.

Be. Be Still. Be Still and Know. Be Still and Know That I am. I am. I am…

I am.

Essence-me, long a picture on the wall, came home and reminded me. I do Trust and love myself, warts and all. Some warts may need removal; I never said I didn't have any. And this morning, this glorious morning as the curtain came up on the last chemically inspired number in the concert of the cosmos that the night before had been, I made my way through the hungry tiny bugs to the river, trying to take care not to taint the energy of the moment with killing, not the smallest of God's creatures. That is the Way of the Samurai as well. Aversion to killing. I am speaking of the modern Samurai. The Ancient Ones loved killing, especially themselves.

Those are good markers to guide if what you seek matters to you. Sometimes you must redefine what matters to you. The dawn air was fresh and clean, and still held the cool of the night before.

Essence-me walked with me, down to the edge of the river, and when I first saw the water, he had slipped away. Back into the place he should be, close to my heart, so I can find my way.

For a long time, I think, I have only thought about Essence-me, who I hope he is, what others see in him, how he uses himself. It was good to bump into him. Musician-me stirred a harmonica melody. Not one I was coat tailing by ear and luck; one coming out of myself. My new voice, even just to sing a little of my own new song to myself.

Candace Gray was her real name. The first time I saw her, she was standing in the stairwell of the old brick building at Sweet Shores. She was a medicine woman. She was a clinical social worker. She was a field rat, like me.

Far to the North are the Sun-Dancers. She was one. They call her Gundy. I can see her now in full indigenous regalia standing there next to that spooky grandfather clock in the stairwell. But of course, she was not. I just remember her so.

Candace and I became more than partners, more than friends. We *served* together. My boys loved her, especially T.C. T.C.'s first car was my father's Mercury Grand Marquis and when Candace died, she came to T.C. and he and her did donuts in it in his dreams, roaring with laughter. I remember his face when he told Keelin, Marla and I… he didn't want it to be real, but he knew it was.

Candace also came to me. I was asleep and had what they commonly call a waking dream. It is a little more than that, I know now, but here she was. I regret to say, I have never been able to recall the conversation, because I suddenly blurted out, "Wait… how are you here?" and in the blink of an eye, she was gone, and I was sitting up, awake. And holding the sweetgrass bundle she had once given me. The one that was on my hat brim when I went to sleep the night before. My body felt like I had just jumped in a cold morning lake, but it was good. Frightening? Oh, hell ya, boy. Tighten up ya pucka, frightening, but also… welcome.

Death can be bridged. After Candace was gone, I mainly saw her as a hawk, and without fail, said hawk, or occasional eagle, would do something un-hawklike, just to let me know. I am not making any of this shit up. I swear, it's all true, and it's going to get fucking weird and deep. You should try living it. It's been quite terrifying, in fact.

Candace died from melanoma in early summer of 2012. She worked up until the days before she died. She had the illness two years before it claimed her. I understand that for melanoma, that's a long time.

She was the mighty medicine woman I had known, the one I gave the eagle feather to, the feather that had fallen right out of the sky in front of me at South Twin, right before I had almost died, and right before she really did.

If what I tell you moving forward is not real, then everything I have come to believe in this world is not real. It also means I am just an insane drug addict, and I can't live with that. There is really magic, real power in this world, and it is accessible.

When Candace died, without telling me, she passed her power to me. For a while, I did not realize what had happened. I ended up reaching out to her sister in the Circle. She told me what had happened. I was initially too astounded to even appreciate the magnitude of it. That was five years before this night. I also understand that some people are not happy about what she did, but I hope they understand what I will do with this power, and that I will be its most humble custodian. That's as good as it gets. I did not ask for it. But now I need it for what I must do. I'm not giving it back while I draw breath, even if I knew how.

Pieces

On the banks of the Ossipee river. Pirate Stronghold, Pootown, Maine. Sunrise.

78 degrees F.

I carried the feelings of the moment and the night with me through the last bit of these sacred woods. The spiral was slowing. It had given me vast doses of what I had needed. Clarity, Reflection, Accountability, Responsibility, Duty, Humility, Satisfaction, Awakening, and Oxygen. I was exhausted. This wasn't a Grateful Dead concert in my twenties. I'm 49. But I was somewhat hard and strong under my doughiness. Exhausted, but awake and alert. And as ready as I was going to get.

Always, blessed Grass. Marijuana… it helps us be sane in a world that is not, and isn't even trying anymore, just gaslighting us about what is right and normal. About what has occurred. I evened out the jitters with some good smoke among my pieces.

Everyone has their Pieces I had learned. Nowadays they call it EDC gear. Its Pieces. Pieces are the things you carry in your pocket. It's a joke from when I was a kid; my cousins started it. I had developed the concept. Pieces are your gear. Pocketknife, matches. A quarter. Bits of string. I had to carry Pieces for membership in Old Lambda Delta, a big and early part of what made up Essence-me. We didn't call them that. But all the pledges I hazed afterwards did. It became Lore. Lore is Legacy. Legacy is immortality. Legacy marks the course to Destiny. We spent a lot of years on rivers figuring out what the Pieces were that you really needed, and

I approached life kind of the same way. I got into hot water more damn times carrying a little pocketknife, but it was used many times in emergencies over the years and I was glad to have it every time.

I broke through the woods into the clearing by the river's edge. Two beavers swam together on the far shore leaving slim white trailing wake like little furry happy boats. Happy, until they saw me. I greeted them in the Old Way, and they went about their business. I was not an interloper. I had business here this day, but not with them. They moved on downriver.

The top rim of the sun came above the bank with clouds to the south and off to the east, toward the Sea.

And I stopped and looked again. I know, and remind you, yes, there were drugs on the road to this vision. But it was why I had come, and what I had been seeking, along with everything else I told you about.

The City in the Sky

It wasn't clouds, not at the top. It was a city. A shining city, not of this world, but sitting there, atop a nestled bed of celestial cloud. And improbably, among the spires at the furthest earthly south, I was able to see the last stars of that world faded out one by silent, distant one.

Stars much, much older and more distant than the ancient stars I knew and loved, and their light I had of late drank deeply of, within the Spiral. Much more holy. In my earthly orientation, at the northern end, I could see tall shimmering gates of gold and opal-like white. Like almost pearl. If I were to go in a straight line and stand there now, those gates were between me and the rest of the city. Shut.

It was a city, in the sky, across the river, atop the sunrise. Made of jewels and precious metals. I knew as soon as the image resolved in my eyes what I was seeing. I could see them glimmering and flashing with the sun coming up over the pine trees on the south bank of the river running east to the Saco, to the sea.

All the acts of the night came slowing down, the winds had died down, the night had scattered like smoke with the flipping on of the Sun. The first sun of new things. And it all came home.

Be

Be still

Be still and <u>know</u>…

<u>Be Still, and Know that I Am…</u>

<u>BE STILL AND KNOW…</u>

<u>THAT I AM….</u>

<u>…GOD…</u>

BE STILL AND KNOW THAT I AM<u>…</u>

Be Still… *And know…*

…Be still…

…Be…

***

The forest around me was silent. The river was still, and I stood there for eternity, in one moment. My old life ran away with the river's inexorable flow, and my new life began.

***

The quiet was like thunder. Just soft river sounds of this little snapshot of the here and now, in contrast to… what? The limitlessness and awe of all that has ever been, is, or will ever be? Yeah. Exactly.

The last guest had arrived, but this was as close as we were going to get to Paradise today.

Don't make me say it. No matter if it was only in my self-induced psychosis, in my mind, or not, what I describe can surely be only one place, and one way or another, I was looking high across the river and saw what I saw.

In all of God's Creation, what else could that be, that I saw as clearly as I saw the tree under my hand and felt how tight my fingers were gripping the bark? I have glimpsed the Gates of Heaven before. That was in 2012. I knew this was not some invitation, or anything like that. I hope to walk through those gates someday, but I will not walk through them without certain things. And, I was very much interested in staying here on Earth for another forty years or so. For unfinished business. Like the things I just alluded to, and hopefully meeting someone special, preferably with long auburn hair and nice legs. That she would wrap around my face. Come to think of it, not being a sadistic abuser was going to be in the interview moving forward. I laughed myself silly at that and the creatures and spirits of the forest and river around me were watching. Another fucked up human, but not howling drunk. Something else… They were not troubled by my one-man comedy show.

I would eventually turn my back on this vision and

make my way back through the woods to this world, to the morning, to end Pete's brief slumber. My journey had been long, but I could not put the blankets on this day, just yet. There was work to do. I left the riverside a man, upright and clean. I had not swum in the river this morning, though a baptism did not feel inappropriate. I was conserving my fuel. I didn't know how much I was going to expend my last reserves. Before I turned away, I wanted to reflect, to remember this moment and my perspective. Thank God. Thank God I did that.

Time enough for baptisms. Tonight's, of Love and Starlight, was complete. There are many others. Darkness. Sunrise. War. Fire. Blood. Shit. Pain. Flesh. Sweat. All first things baptize you. The night and forest had just done so me. It isn't a one-time one religion ritual. It is an expression, of being washed clean, and made anew, and ready. Baptisms are lifelong and take many forms, for all God's children.

The Code (War)

I reflected as the drugs began to wear off, having shown me what I needed. I took inventory.

I am a career professional. There are few who have done what I do longer. Simple Fact. It was my dream, someday, to encapsulate the ideas and practices we learned along the way. Some of these best practices were met with severe resistance from our management and superiors. There are many people in this club, these lone renegades that we were. We did not all work together, at least not all at once, but many of us had worked together at different times, in different places and often in different roles. Gundy was one of these Warriors. Rene 2 K. Jill B and the Quimbus. Jack the Deacon. Whatever we all are, we are Practitioners, and that holds to no one company or team. We are unique. We have all spent the last twenty years just trying to survive so we can do the work. For some of us it's a real crusade, or jihad. I like that one, *jihad*. It's so spoiled now, to use the right way. With politics. There is so much old knowledge and secrets just out there, all you have to do is look. But you have to learn how with clean eyes and pure heart.

It's hard to map this out now, looking back, but basically, it started with pirate flags and canoe trips, camping and fun. But… something happened. The Pirate shtick crept into my professional character, the guy with the telescope, the briefcase with all the rocks and crystals, that. It bled into that. Maybe some kid saw a picture with a pirate flag, and that was all the spark it needed. I always seize on the things children are interested in. They *loved* all things pirate, and sometimes, the grownups, the colleagues, the managers (such as they were, with rare exception) and the parents… they ate it up too. Magic begins with curiosity and is birthed in knowledge, especially fresh and new knowledge.

What is the brightest Star in the night sky? Hint: Not Polaris.

And then, something *else* happened. That was when I put it together that the same thing applied to the Bushido Code. If people ate up the pirate thing, I thought, wait till they get a load of samurai. It was an easy leap, strangely, but the culture was fostered and nurtured and never really seemed to take hold, not in a way that satisfied me. Individuals bought into it, but I wanted the whole crew to get down with it, and that never happened. Until I made it to Pathways.

The Code had evolved to be (loosely):

No Addiction.

No Abuse.

No Sexual Misconduct.

Broad reach. Covers almost everything. If you boil things down enough, to their essence. Their Essence.

Essence, again.

You must keep your Essence clean. It is not a new concept. Old, actually. Ancient, really. So Ancient.

I saw many people try to balance careers and try to juggle these things at times. It's always a trainwreck.

It comes down to this, moving forward. As I stood on the banks of the Ossipee River that morning a lifetime ago, I believed then, and still do, that I had successfully captured much of the essence of what it means to truly be a knight, of sorts, in the modern world. The old values hold. And when working in a service industry, they are sacrosanct. But they are also corrupted and diluted by time and modernity. I spent many years in contemplation.

I also spent many years under what in another time and place, would be vows of Poverty and Chastity. More on that later, I guess. Back to heaven… these were the things that I studied on as I beheld the wonder I was seeing.

Actually, it was time to move out. I turned my eyes away from that vision and moved away from the riverbank, back toward the campsite and reality in the growing heat and buzzing bugs heralding this morning. I gathered my Pieces.

Act 5 wound down. The pace of preparation was picking

up. I could hear orders being barked in the Ship of my mind. Making ready. Ready to set sail.

By me, though. I was in command.

I thought.

I know who and what I am. I can look myself in the eye in the mirror. I made my way back enjoying the Zen of the insectile music of the Forest in the growing heat of the day. It was getting warm. The sun was shining bright and hot, and there were birds laughing. I went forward into the future.

The Red Sun

It was time to call T.C. and say hi, and I loved him. I missed him this morning. He was so busy, so motivated. He came and went, always up to something. This was our way, to stay connected. He was always stopping to show me videos of everything. How we used to laugh and love.

Before I did, fresh and raw, there was some business. As I saw it, a matter of honor and respect. This was my new life, and I had just taken agency over it. The way I was feeling was simple. Last night I had given up for good on the marriage. It was time to bury the dead before they start to stink up the place. And hopefully, not hurt anyone, their plans, their stability. I foresaw a smooth transition out, and it really depended on Marla.

The sea and space… are voids. Voids are not empty. There are things out there in the dark and cold and vast. The vast and deadly.

This was not the first utterance of divorce. Far from it. But this was the first tangible step. This was it. No more talk. Playtime was definitely over for good. I was pulling the plug. With this message, I struck the flint, and the tinder caught quickly. It was so very dry. I did not smell the explosive fumes in the wind, the rising wind.

I have never for a moment regretted marrying her, even now with secrets revealed I could not have even taken in then for their magnitude and depth of their roots. Never, for one second, did I ever regret marrying her and wishing it away, because with such a wish, I would surely have been damned. To have the sons I have I would go through the Hell of being married to her all over again. Maybe I am damned any way, and all truly lost, but I would do nothing to change the sons I had or the relationship we had, except I wish I had protected them, but I had no idea.

I sent this message this morning, because this is what I truly believed at this moment, even though I knew I had to leave her.

"Thank you for being a mother to my sons, you are the very best. And I am sorry for everything else."

But now… the earth has traveled many millions of miles since that morning, and at this moment as I type, is on the other side of the sun from where it was that day.

It was time to call T.C. and see what was up. I missed them both in that moment, and I never came back from that. I miss them still.

He is not amused by some of my antics. I have been a poor role model in many ways. When he was young, I was a tobacco smoker. Since he has been old enough to comprehend (And what age do you think your children start to comprehend? I tell you; it is far earlier than you know. That's how they learn.), I have been a blatant pot smoker all my adult life. I use it. I utilize it. I embrace it. It helps me to regulate. To go with little sleep, little food. It helps me keep pace with coworkers half my age. The ones who learn, and grow, and the ones who see something slow, something that holds back the herd. Hey, let's run on down there and smash one of them cows. Old bull says, I have a better idea. Walk down. And smash every one of them silly. I am no saint, never claimed to be, but I tried to be a good dad, and a good role model. This morning, I felt we had a good relationship. This next part was going to be tough, but I had waited two years while Keelin went to college. I cherished those times. I was going to miss being around them all the time. I wasn't sure how we were going to do it. I would follow their lead. Whatever else, I believed this morning, as a family we worked together.

In our family we were quite unfiltered. I believed in letting children see the world, see the blood on the streets, and not try to tell them it's just fucking ice cream. So much of my work was this, simply exploring the truths right in front of our eyes, and it worked. Be Still and Know.

There is nothing in the tale to come that they ever need forgiveness from me. I had in front of me horrors that rivaled the worst nightmares of my small childhood, waking up in the dark of night that only a child knows, the dark that presses in. When you wake up from a nightmare as a kid (and horror movies did it to me, but I loved them and I swore they wouldn't every time), there's a delay of a few seconds while you come fully awake, and you're still as scared as when you were dreaming. It sucks. That feeling, that despair and fear, was about to become the landscape of my universe. I have no idea today what I believed that day was not what I thought it was. Not knowing what their recollections of our lives together are is why I reside in Hell now, but that's getting way, way out ahead.

They are innocent. I live every day for them as I always have, from now until the ending of the world. Sorry. *ALL. All Worlds.*

When I called T.C. to say I loved him and I'd see him soon, he gave me something unexpected and out of place. This was not the first time he had caught me off guard.

I tried to set an example for my kids around what it means to be a real man. Not a toxic, abusive bully, like so many men I had worked with, young and older. There are other ways to be. We see so much of it. You want a close look at people's pathology, pay attention to what kind of driver they are. Some people are angry, beeping their horns and telling everyone to hurry the fuck up, moron. Some people do dangerous shit sneakily. Who is the real evil? Anger is pain, hurting others intentionally is evil. I taught Driver Education for ten years. As a mental health guy, it was eye opening. People think it's okay to beep and abuse a student driver. It is not. I used to tell my students, with their parents in the car, that if we encountered that, I would become "psychotically belligerent". "It's the only way to deal with a road-raging bully," I told them all with a straight face. And I meant it.

When T.C. and I got into it, it seemed wrong. Wrong like

out of place. Like he was speaking in another voice, someone else's voice.

It was in the open, I thought. I wasn't seeing that it was also alive and well in the dark corners, when I was not at home, out working and trying to make enough money to survive. Being fed, and nurtured. And made ready, to be awoken fully and revealed.

I saw the first glimpse today, the first real glimpse, that I can mark as the first clear red flag that something was wrong. The essence of the conversations we had in our home had circled around how, in theory, we could split up, and not mess up the boys' lives. I was trying to keep this discreet. Marla was not easy to have a conversation with anyway, but now… it was like to speak to her invited accusations of being some kind of asshole.

I called to check in with my son as the Doorway started to close. Just to tell him how much I loved him, how proud I was of he and Keelin, how much hope I had for the future, and that everything was going to be okay. I never got the chance to tell him how much I loved him that morning. It's been more than three years now. The pain that I have learned to live with had not yet arrived, there was only foreboding. It is hard to pinpoint the beginning or end of things, sometimes, but I mark this moment as the moment when I realized something was fucked up, and that things were not even close to being in control from my end.

T.C. started by yelling at me, telling me not to fuck him. Not to fuck his life, his plans. How? I asked. We were all going to work together to keep things as stable as possible, for both he and Keelin. The effect was jarring. I was confused.

I put the conversation away when it ended. I had said I love you, but I don't think he was hearing my voice at this point. I am struggling, in 2022, to recall my state of blindness after all I now know. Something was not right. I mean, a lot of things had been very wrong for a long time, but they were hidden from me and went back much further than I would have thought. I have often wondered without the use of drugs how I ever would have even been able to comprehend any of it. That's what all this is, I hope. A map. A map to survival, or healing, or something.

This was the moment that I first knew something was wrong.

What is the brightest star in the sky?

Athena.

Sometimes, we make coffee. I do, he doesn't drink it, and I for the life of me cannot figure out how my friend, a Navy man for Christ's sake, and a nurse lives the life he does without it. I sure couldn't live mine without it, and sometimes I wash up and freshen up out there, as we are learning how to do that beyond camping, into homesteading, but not today. It was time to move. I shelved my bewilderment at the conversation I had just had with my older son and assessed how much tripping I was still doing. I did not realize. I was now inside the Doorway, **and it had closed behind me**. Everything seemed to look the same, of course, perspective change from within, thanks to the acid, now, slowly trickling away as the Spiral wound its way all the way down. Of course, it never does, and we are all within the Sacred Spiral, sometimes flying, sometimes looping and laughing, sometimes, falling, down and down, as the walls of reality move faster and faster, to be imperceivable, on the flying screaming musical laughing ride in such strange and wonderful company at times, at other times all alone, all the way to the end.

So, Athena and I have known each other twenty years. We met at Old Crisis, at Sweet Shores, a residential facility, and crucible that forges together that which is broken, or perhaps, also into tools. Instruments.

Athena is Greek and beautiful. She is smart. I liked working with her briefly at Sweet Shores. She was gone six months after I arrived. I stayed there, leaping from lily pad to lily pad, for about twelve years. Keelin was born my second year there.

Athena was married to the guy who hired me, one Vinny Pataglia, a one-time airborne ranger and veteran, avid golfer and all around badass. We all worshipped him back in those wild west days. He, too, was gone from Sweet Shores shortly after hiring me, but long enough so we all had some good times together, and in the first days, I picked up some other brothers and sisters too, like Matty Mango and Cristobel. Athena had some long awesome Greek name that sounded enough like Baklava, that I called her Athena Baklivakis, and she giggled when I did, so I guess it isn't racist. She and Vinny departed Sweet Shores, and it was about twelve years later, I shipwrecked right into the lap of her and Candace the Gray, who also bore the dirt of Sweet Shores on her, although she and I had never worked together, only met. Candace. The White, now. The Hawk. They became close friends at that next place, old Sweet Shores alumni, refugees, whatever. The place that was named after the holy Saco River, what an omen, I thought then. We were three, then four, before that melted away too. Met some really great people there. These were the good years. The kids were young, the work was hot, the steel was sharp, you know? Candace and me, we went to battle, every day. Athena, too. We all quit, eventually. These were the places I had trod, and buried my dead, before I came to the Poo this night.

About a year before the last night of my old life, I had approached Athena about something. Something risky. I guess I was starting to think outside the box. By then I was four years without any human touch. I made my peace with the code around sexual misconduct by telling Marla that I saw no evidence of marriage here, and unless I did, I would consider that here was none. My kids hugged me a lot then, and I had a great dog I might have mentioned.

There were compensations. But that only goes so far. Vinny Pataglia had had a long, ugly, and spectacular meltdown that involved meth, divorce, and outrageous behavior. He almost beat Athena to death; that was their last act under the same roof. This guy used to belt golf balls off the hill at Sweet Shores in the afternoons, horrifying the overlords in their ivory tower over Brown cottage. Family Focus, it was then, back in the first new days of that place. I was one of the first people to join there as it started to get so big not everyone knew each other. Cristobel had been there five years. He remembers little Sweet Shores, before it tried to take a bite out of every dime it could find and became a gargantuan monstrosity with neither honor nor code.

Only the trench troops keep the Light alive when a workplace is sick. Only the young, who will work 70 hours a week because they love those kids, and not think to question why they must. Why there aren't more people there, as many as we need, we were never given a good answer. It's because it doesn't pay shit for what you're really supposed to do. I have known many heroes. Vinny Pataglia was one for a time. He was a great leader, a real warrior. Before he went fucking insane. Too bad. It hurts when heroes fall. People get hurt, too. Innocents. Collateral damage, they say in war. The Way of the Samurai, the military attitude toward our own selves as practitioners; it was born here, out of a sense of honor and accountability to one another. Vinny was 82nd Airborne. We emulated certain things.

But he was in the wind now, down the river. And Athena was no longer married, or with anyone.

I caught Athena on the phone, as we rode with the rising sun at our backs into New Hamster, and after I had sternly admonished the Treeherder, just Old Pete now, to shut the fuck up while I was on the phone with a girl.

Athena and I had got along at Sweet Shores, but not really joined. When she circled back into my life over a decade later, I needed friends like her like the one I found in Candace the Gray, exactly when they resurfaced, together on the Saco River. Like I said, I took it as a sign. Of course. Of course, it was.

The thing I approached Athena about last year, was maybe, you know, getting together. And she had agreed to go for it.

I'm going to make this quick. It didn't happen. As soon as she put her hands on my chest, after taking off my t shirt slow, I short-circuited. I felt it. That fuse, it just blew.

I went back home to the roof I would share with my family for about another year, the last year of my old life. The experience, though unsuccessful, had been a huge positive. Athena had just hit me with the paddles. We fooled around, we just couldn't smash. It was still fucking awesome. So, yeah, there was a ramp up to this point. I knew I was not staying married for a long time before I left.

I called Athena that morning with the idea of maybe having another go, since, you know, I was about to set fire to my life. I told her that things were about to be official on that score. Was there any chance? She said that there was. Holy Fuck. McDonald's has never been more delicious than it was that morning. The ride back to the Poo I couldn't stop smiling. I could not wait to set myself free. I could not wait to return to Scarborough, where I still lived, but I knew now not for long. I could see the first siding, the first harbor, on my way down the river I was sailing now.

I have to laugh now. How did I not know that I was headed all the way to the open Sea and across? And the Tempests… just one after another.

I have been no place worse, more bleak, more windswept, bare and scoured, more barren and lifeless, no more terrifying than the marriage I was in. I would face ten times the horrors I have seen before I ever let myself be led down that little hallway again, where there were people waiting. Waiting to watch me die, properly, and decently, and justly. I've already said in the universe's logic, I can't wish I never married her, and I do not. Never once. I'd do it all again for my sons, the ones we had together, no matter what manner of monster their mother turned out to be.

The LSD in my system had faded away, leaving the feeling it always does. Regenerated, clear-minded, with a whole heart. I was back on this side of the Doorway, I thought.

And so, with the last night of my old life now receding into the outgoing tides of time and memory, I saddled up, and mustered out, back home, home for yet a little bit.

Home to Scarborough.

***

Scarborough, Maine.

June 30th, 2019.

On the first day of the life ahead, no longer trapped in a loveless, sexless marriage that showed no prospect of change, one I was finally able to leave, on this morning, smartphones were still not a part of my world.

Later I would marvel, as I began to appreciate the dimension they bring to the work I have done, teaching curiosity, modeling wonder, inspiring imagination. I had a chance to use it, my trusty cylon, before I was done.

I remember coming home feeling great, for the most part, like, great before a surgery that is supposed to go well. I found Marla in the small front yard of our home for 24 years, filling a hummingbird feeder. I tried to greet her with a hug that would have been sad, but not cold. Trying to add heat was automatic by then and I did it, even knowing I had no more fuel. After almost 25 years of blowing, trying to coax the fire to life, the weekend had passed. It was raining. It was cold. So cold. It was time to leave this part of the river. To pull camp.

She pulled away from me, the last hug I was ever going to give her, when still I believed she was a human being, that she had at least been married once in more than name, that she had ever had any love. I knew there was none now, although she said otherwise. Actions, she always liked to remind me, are louder than words.

Two years earlier, I don't know how, but I had caught her off guard. And she surprised both of us in different ways. She said something I did not know, the kind of thing you can only suspect until you hear it straight from the horse's mouth. It surprised her, not because she did not know, but because for some reason she said it out loud. She had revealed some horrible secret unintentionally. She looked surprised at herself. Even that, that little slip, might have been intentional. Meant to leave a mark, but so swift it was like it had never passed.

I was leaving for work one day in the afternoon. I had spoken to her, rolling out to battle, hoping to leave it for later, to circle back having prepped, without trying to blindside or sideswipe, to talk about who we really were to one another, because I have many best friends, and a best friend she was not. It was almost like, and I say it now clearly, almost like she hated me.

And she raised her eyes to look in mine and said as crisp and clear as the fall wind outside that day, "I do. I do hate you."

For two years after, when I tried to have a conversation about that, the truth of it, I could not. She acted like she never said it long enough to pull off acting like that wasn't what she said at all. That's gaslighting. Everyone knows what that is now. But, as crazy as it sounds, to me, too, it isn't apparent to you when you're in it. It happened right in front of me, right to me, and I didn't get it. Not then, I did not. For two years and more since Keelin turned 18, I would look at her, and ask her, not yelling, but in the same way I would approach the most difficult no-fly zone on the streets on the job. "Marla, this marriage is both sexless and loveless. What are your thoughts on that?" And I would get silence, or accused loudly and shrilly of creating drama.

Beyond this point on this road, there was no returning and no improvement coming. So, I went to the Pirate Stronghold, walked among the stars and communed with the universal life force, and came home and pulled the fucking trigger on leaving her. I did not know many things at this point, but had I not done so when I did, I have glimpsed the other paths, and all are far more terrible.

Trim Sails. Tighten sheets. Tie down that stay. Sharp, sharp, and steady. We still have shallow and familiar waters under us, but they are turning dicey. Treacherously dicey.

Captain's log.

July 2019.

There is a storm coming, and the water is turning dark.

Steady, lads!

Pathways, Part 1

I had a great job that summer and I had landed there two years earlier, just as Ella and I sang our last song together. I was pretty happy about the job situation. Other than the thing, Mrs. Lincoln, did you enjoy the play?

***

When Ella died, I laid down and found myself for a moment unable to breathe. I felt suffocated. I rose and quickly walked out down to the marsh. To the bridge. She and I had been familiar here, a little secret that mainly came through when no other people were to be seen, when normal people slumbered. Only the skilled and brave venture onto the marsh at night. It is a holy place. That night, as I stood there alone, 3 weeks before I would open the healing Doorway in South Twin the sounds of life returning with the spring to the marsh, the myriad birds and insects and their myriad noises went utterly and instantly silent as soon as my feet touched that bridge.

In reverence, you see. That, and solemn respect.

***

For ten years I wandered. If Sweet Shores had been my Iliad, my time there longer than the actual Trojan War by two years, then after Sweet Shores had been the Odyssey. And I was no Odysseus, riding home from war with the taste of victory. No, in my Iliad, I had received my own Trojan horse, not gifted one for the big win. I left my Troy in defeat, and bitter. Let me explain. I spent around 12 years in a place that was many places in one, many group homes, many programs. It was easy to move around. So, it wasn't really one job, it was an amalgamation of jobs, and I cultivated the persona of a staffer who could go anywhere and handle any situation. When I left Sweet Shores (fired, I'm not sugarcoating shit), I began a ten-year journey, the last ten years I was in Maine, of seeking people like me, passionate about children and families, and prone to difficulty because of their annoying tendency to do what people need to heal, and not always follow stupid rules that are contrary to working relationships. Example? Sure. In our work, talking with people, like by phone on the fly sometimes, allowing them some level of access to you, is part of the job. Every single agency I worked for pushed back on that, sometimes (Saco River) just for the sake of doing so, being in control. This aspect of working for other people sucks ass, but you're also in the field and not in an office all day. Big plus. Most controllers are lazy and rely on fear for compliance without doing diligence. I used to shoot blowgun darts with kids. Best tool for it, and I died on *that* hill more than once. It wasn't exactly an approved activity ("I'm sorry, did… did you say *blowgun?*"). It drew reactions. Kids *loved* it. No one ever got hurt. If any of you pontificating know-it-all fucks are reading this now, suck my ass.

I dedicated myself to modeling the modern Way of the Samurai and applying it to the work. You know who really dug it? The kids and families I worked with.

Pathways. I knew it was the last stop. Don't ask me how. When I first started there, I came out of the office after a late spring sun shower in the late afternoon, still in pain over the loss of my sweet pooch, I saw a double rainbow across the sky. I knew then although the idea of leaving my marriage was more of a wish than a plan, and the idea of leaving Maine was nowhere in the picture, that Pathways was the end of the line for me in many ways.

One afternoon, I was leaving the office and I was sad, as usual, about my dog. At this point, I had not had sex in five years. Well, except Athena, kind of.

Over the roof of the Pathways building was a double rainbow. I saw it, and I knew that this was some kind of end of the line, and I needed to make sure we did it right. I knew this was the last, but I could not have known.

Pathways was different. Team meetings were vibrant and dynamic. They had certain key things worked into them, things that were… sacrosanct. Things that were lacking other places I had been, wearing out my shoes. One element was we split up into different groups. You might be sitting with six other people, and all of you do different jobs for the company. Whatever the topic was, everyone had a voice. To that end, and this really impressed me, the two services were deliberately mingled together, and talk of the different streets we saw, the tools we used, was nurtured in spirit, executed in practice, and facilitated in the culture. This was something unseen behind me, where mental health services are compartmentalized and people don't even know how to guide you to what you need, because they may not know what else is out there.

The entire culture was not only different, here there was pieces that simply did not exist elsewhere I had been. I always tried to draw people's attention with the pirate flags, all that fun bullshit, although, yes, fun is memory and memory is sacred, but bullshit nonetheless, at least for the tale here and now. I drew attention with Pirate weirdness. Then I struck with the Way of the Samurai. Me on my solitary path since pulling my marriage, then my career out of the ashes, defining to myself what I was, what I was made of, and how to use it. I like lore. Lore is powerful. The right lore, over time, as small imaginative minds grow up into, well, grown up ones; it is good to preserve imagination. For the future.

***

The original name of Old Lambda Delta, way back in 1899 in Illinois… was The Knights of Classic Lore. I always dug that, what with growing up down the road from the largest collection of arms and armor in the Western Hemisphere.

***

So, after everyone knew the new staffer was a pirate, after the pictures, bringing Ella to offices, the tales of the river, being written then, shared fresh, like warm bread, fresh out of the oven, after my intro, I would start talking samurai shit. Explain, I would, that pirating was fun, but what we were in fact were samurai. Enter Bushido 101, how it fits our work.

When I had time off, I tried to take to the river, and the forest, and the sea. And the marsh, of course. The Scarborough Marsh, especially at night.

When I found souls with enough hunger, I dragged everyone I could out in the canoe every single chance I got. Even my dad made it out onto the marsh way back when the kids were still young. He actually came out in a canoe with me during the First Age. We even caught a striper, right off Seavey's Landing.

We had some good times in those years with Ella and all the rest. Now she was gone, but I had found a place to hang my hat, my sword, and I was going to hang it way out. Draw it, even. Unlike the crews I sailed with up to now, save the one or two I had gleaned at each stop along the way, all of them absolutely ate this shit up. I had found a true home, for now, anyway. There was no one after, no one better. This I knew, prophetically it turned out. I dropped all anchors and got to know some awesome people closely.

Thank God. Thank God.

The first, the person who hired me, was Brittany. I was beginning to recognize I was in a state of Not-Give-A-Fuck. Dangerous. But here, they rallied to it. After more than twenty years following a path in faith, a quest in courage, and acts of kindness and justice, I found Home. They validated all of it. Almost all of it. More to come on that much, much later. My faith was restored. I had always wanted to write the book about the art and science of family rehabilitation. While we were writing it, in our work, our experience, our refinements and our struggle, it turns out someone actually DID write it. Put that in the hold for now. For now, what I found here was not only enough, it was more than I ever had hoped to find, and far less than the great truth I found on the other side of the desert I was about to cross by quitting Pathways, after two amazing years and more friends than I had ever snagged out of one place.

In my time there, people had come and passed through, but this place had the power to really stick people together. I don't remember Adam's last name, because I did not know him well, and he has passed over the horizon in this tale, but I asked him about getting an apartment, when it became my reality, and he had been a wanderer, out in the world alone, and he made me less afraid. Like many here, this was the first way station from the Hell of addiction back to Life and recovery. They made excellent soldiers with the intellectually disabled kids.

My dear friends, so many, so new and fresh when things were falling apart. Mackenzie. Derick. Lono. Daija Pear. Kary. Rob. Jenn A… Nancy. Kevin the Canadian. Aiden and the missus. Haley Mercury. Jess. Angela. Blackjack. Ryan. Kyle. Brando. A gorgeous redhead twenty-five years my junior who was the spitting image of Botticelli's Venus. And one guy who loved baseball. This list is criminally incomplete.

Man overboard! I'll circle back to my shipmates.

The Spark

Shortly after returning from the river that morning, I jumped back into my old life for some few days, maybe a week… I don't know. I was still in the house, it was still July, and the spark happened.

I was trying to be honorable because that is my way. In all things. In that way I have come to this point in life, happy, successful, depending on your measure. I felt rich in most ways except with her. She made me feel poor in many ways. No, in every way.

So, after I snapped (*I hate your fucking guts and I wish you were dead*) at Marla, in the following days, I know they three talked. Then, me and the boys took a car ride. I never said anything like that before. Never. I let myself give way after years of her just being fucking difficult about everything, and more and more displeased, and disappointed, and hurt, etc. She had never been able to say anything of substance, and simply refused to engage. So, I quit. I almost quit once ten years ago. She said it was all going to be okay, and it was, for about six months. And now it had just gotten worse than ever, over the last two years. Maybe I just realized it when Ella died.

I asked three things of them, not knowing what mind they were in that day, what they thought was driving the car, what their father was. I spoke to them as their dad. They thought they were in the presence of a demon. They were not, not with me, not ever. But they were and had been for a long time at this juncture, and I still didn't get it.

So, it was easy for them to promise me the three things, based on their understanding. That's why they are innocent, but for a long time after this day, I felt betrayed by them, and it did not make sense to me. Looking back, now that I know what they thought that day, I am so very proud of them. They acted like soldiers. Thank God they are not soldiers.

At this point, all I had on the horizon was divorce. I was going to stay in Maine, stay at Pathways, like all jobs, until I did not, and move on. In Maine. Close to them. Away from her. Or I was dead. I already had one close call by misadventure, and that still did not make sense to me, but I almost died in May, 2012, from an accidental opioid overdose. I still don't really know how that happened, because I was not an addict of the Poppy death flower as that scourge ravaged Southern Maine for ten years. I had seen many people just… be no more. It was almost me, and I don't really know where to fit that into everything else. But it's there.

The three promises were:

Please, don't let your mother fuck with or taunt me. She does and now she really will. Please don't let her force me to take all my stuff in that house, my trinkets, books, photos, memories, my Pieces, of a lifetime. Please don't let her fuck with me, play control games. And please do not let her promulgate lies about me. She is threatening my reputation, to cause trouble, to drag me through court, to make me pay, and pay, and pay. When I said it for real, that I was going to move and divorce, she first reacted in her way, shrilly telling me I was going to do all the work and she would not! Foot stomp! Hmph! That was her base face, the one under the mask. Her own true Essence-me. A spoiled brat, who was either going to have her way, some sour grapey version she could tell herself she won, or make everyone pay for denying her. It sums up her conduct throughout the marriage. What do I know?

They assured me. Keelin said the words, "<u>We will not allow that to happen</u>." They lied to me that day to get me gone as quick as quiet. They would have promised anything. Because they were afraid. Afraid of me. That is why it is not their fault. I know that now, but it took me a while to get there. I'm sorry, boys. I am sorry I let myself think you guys fucked me. You did, but if what you believed were true, you guys did exactly the right thing, and I'm proud of you. Please God, if you can hear me, let them know. Loud and clear.

Be Still and know, please…

It's the sense of disorientation, of frantic running, like in a dream when you can't get up the basement stairs fast enough. In dreams you mercifully wake. In life the feeling just sticks with you.

I didn't know what she was up to, boys. Neither do you.

The Last Family Meeting

By the time we sat down to talk it out together, Marla had already gone to a lawyer. So much for me having to do all the work, which is what she had said when I finally said that I was done, for real and for good. She had the papers in her hand, ready to push them at me. Otherwise, she sat almost in silence, as the boys told me their plan *they* had come up with.

I could sign my half of the house over to them, and so could she, and I could walk away from the marriage. They get the house; she would live there. They were going to support her, their choice, and I advised them against it, but it was theirs to make. I had told Marla that I would not allow her to be a parasite on them and their future. She took my words. I admit, they were dangerously close to what she was able to turn them into. She twisted all my words for them, these were just the last. The deal was done. I was moving out.

It wasn't a hook she was about to sink into me, that's what I had been allowed to fear. It was a needle. A lethal injection. Not for me, exactly. For my sons' love for me, for the man I was to them, the real me. She executed me and enjoyed every second of it. She was right against the glass, her thumb on the plunger. Smiling that smile that never touches her dark glittering brown eyes. Always, one or the other. Eyes or mouth. Never both. When her eyes smiled, her mouth was pursed tight against what may slip out… reveal. When her mouth smiled, her eyes were cold and black. Like a doll. Or a shark. Or a corpse.

When the Circle closed on this, when I really knew, when I really saw, when I really heard my own voice *BE* heard, my own heart stopped for just one beat. And everything that is, everything that ever was or will be, for that one arrested heartbeat, everything in all of God's Creation, stopped too. Like it had on the bridge on the marsh. Like it had when Pete asked me about T.C. being gay in Pootown. For just… one… heartbeat. Everything, *everything*, stopped. That was later. Read on.

101 Degrees

The conflagration that had been smoldering for years finally ignited. It was 101 degrees at noon on the Sunday before I moved out. I had about three hours till my work shift. It was now or never. T.C. was sleeping. I fetched the pick and spade the Treeherder had placed under my canoe the night before. It was all the help I was getting on this one.

The idea I had here was universally unpopular. I had made my intentions clear, and the boys were not supportive. It had come up as we had navigated things up to this point but there was no way. No way I was going to leave her behind, and it had been left like that. T.C. was sleeping. I couldn't do it at night, and besides, I shouldn't have to. I was taking her with me to the stronghold. In broad daylight. Not in the dark. To the forest and river that would always be a home to me, the only one I had now that I wasn't afraid of ever being lost. Marla saw me going across the backyard, and I saw her scooting down the hall to wake up T.C. and point him right at me. By the time the pick sank into the grave I had always said was temporary, T.C. was awake and I could hear him yelling in his drama-voice, the one now, looking back, I never heard without first hearing Marla's. Or its echo… its foul aftertaste. The signs, the breadcrumbs. They were always there. It's funny what you don't see when you can't imagine looking for it.

That scorching day I tackled a physical task the like of which I had not attempted in many years and no idea if I was even capable of. I believed it fully possible I would have a heart attack. I was kind of hoping for one. I was being tested now. Crucibles. I've tried to learn to recognize when in them. No way to know, down and down, through the spiral. My son called me an abuser that day but did not say why he was saying that. He told me he hoped I would just die. He postured me and threatened me and tried to get me to fight. Marla was watching the whole time, hoping. Hoping I would snap. T.C. crossed a line, because he took everything out of the car I used, the one he bought but we paid for, so he could build his credit. The car was technically his, but I used it, and when he tried to tell me I no longer had a car to use, I called the cops on my own son. Because what he had just done was domestic violence. The fact that he legally owned the car I drove, that had been another of Marla's plots to make T.C. think he had to take care of her because I wasn't able to. Later, I realized these things with the Pieces in front of me. For me at this moment everything had the real sensation of spinning and spinning and feeling unbalanced.

T.C. lied to the cop and said he didn't want me using his car to transport a dead dog. But he knows, and I know, that he didn't say that at first. He told me I couldn't use it at all.

He was over the line, blinded by hate now, unmasked, red-faced, and incoherent. The things he said did not make sense to me that day. It was orders of magnitude above what I had expected. I could see her behind the glass of the doorway she once told me she hated me in, then gaslit me around. She was smiling again, this time, no face. Only in those eyes; those were black and shiny with glee. I understand so much now as I recall these events. I need to stress that at the time I was struggling to remain conscious and failing. In this time and place, I was only trying to breathe and dodge fire. The feeling stayed.

I tried to take Ella with me, and everyone told me I was crazy but I didn't care. I was going to put her out at the stronghold in the path of the sunrise. It would have been right about where I had seen the city in the sky on the morning after Midsummer's Night. I wanted to put her there with a treasure of silver buried with her, a shrine, a real pirate treasure, for a real pirate dog. A legend, which indeed she was. A treasure in a secret shrine in a pirate stronghold on a river in Maine. Fuck everyone. Lono, alone, told me how beautiful that was.

I dug the hole through all that screaming bullshit. She was just too heavy. Too heavy. The Code demands, I tell it true… that while the Treeherder, my friend of thirty years, the first pirate after me, had refused to help me in this beyond sharing his tools… Lono did offer. Lono, who I had only known for a short time, offered to come help me, but I couldn't. It was so, so hot that day. It was also Lono that had joined me in canoes after Ella died. I dragged him out to the marsh and he brought his dog, Mr. Nimbus. Nimb is a big, goofy pit bull and it was the first time a dog was in the canoe with me since…

Out there that day, shortly after I had first met Lono on the job, been part of his training, I told Lono that we were becoming friends at a point in my life that I did not really know what was next. That day, for the first (but not the only time among my last best work family) time, I got solid validation that the situation I was in in the marriage was untenable, and that it wasn't that hard to believe or uncommon. This was huge because Marla always blamed any conflict or problem on me no matter what. I just did not know, all I had was my own perspective and experience. Validation, that day gave me much for days ahead, and Lono turned out to be a long-term player.

Keelin had come home to this scene: TC screaming at me, cops. Marla had zipped by me in the driveway right after the cop left. I don't know exactly what she said to him. I would not have guessed it then. I know the gist of it in 2022. Keelin and his girlfriend, Marla, and T.C. all scrambled off and left me there with my hole(s).

So hot. I had to get to the street, to a family's house, and try to be of service to them. I knew I was… emotionally compromised, but as I have said, I stayed on flight status and did not crash through any of this, even as hot as it was getting. This is the Way, in action. I lived like this for many years, one foot in front of the other. The momentum kept me in motion.

***

I know you don't agree, sons. I'm sorry that hurt you. But I hope you come to understand that there was no way I was going to leave her behind. She belongs in the Holy Poo, and there is a place for her there, waiting. There is another treasure there, in the spot that waits for her and me. Or rather, the map to the rest of the treasure lies there now… for you.

It was so very hot that day.

I'm sorry.

***

One Week.

That was the last Sunday before I moved out. In the next week I functioned in the spaces that were not occupied by my job. Years of practices and habits were jarred by changes in physical locations and the changes happening now. In the homes with the Folkie, I shut it off and did the work like I always had. It was the only thing that did not feel like it was in flames. The week went by scorching hot and blinding fast, and I could not wait to get to the place I had somehow found. The only drawback was it wasn't all mine. There was a roommate, and that was a twist. She was female. She was also, it was immediately apparent, completely out of her fucking mind. Two, then. Two twists.

The Cid

The Cid lived next to me when we first moved to Scarborough. He was 15. I treated him like what he was, a kid, a young man, a friend, and neighbor. Before he was 18, we didn't share cigarettes, for example, and all the rules implied by that. I was a professional, all the time, at work or no. You cannot do the work we do and be another creature in your own home. You cannot be in the light of healing and the dark of abuse. Or addiction, or sexual misconduct, it turns out. So, I was a safe grownup for him until he turned 18. By then, shortly after, he had left that home. The Cid had been in tough places his whole life. He is one of the strongest people I know. His character has always been impeccable. He sometimes hates himself. I love him. He returned to my circle in December of 2001. I saw him on the road behind me in the morning. My smile split my face as I rolled my window down and waved at him at 35mph on Payne Road, the air chilling my hand.

We slowed at the light and he stuck that big ginger bear face out his car window, aged now, and tempered… the face of a man, no longer the boy I had once known.

"Are you ready for the end, old friend?" He called and I saw us laughing together, my face in the mirror, his behind his windshield, as if across the time that had separated us, together again, as we always had, laughing as the world rocked and rolled and shook. Of course, he was referring to 9/11, still freshly burned into our eyes; that morning the world had changed for all of us in an instant forever. I did not need clarification; it's how it is with real friends no matter how much time has gone by.

I called The Cid when I needed a new home. He helped, as he always had, and sometimes the only help around. He has a habit of showing up and leaving me with a flower in the winter to bring a little peace. He has been there with weed many times when no one else has in the days when it could be scarce.

The Cid did not help me find an apartment. I found

that through Adam at Pathways, one of those friends that just comes and goes. He did, however, hook me up with aforementioned roommate.

I mean, it isn't really exaggerating that I would have been content to find a homeless person who just needed a shower, a shave, and a cheerleader. I was desperate and the boys were cold to me, but I chalked it up to them being in shock about the divorce, something not unexpected. As he has in many ways over the years, when nothing else materialized, The Cid found something a little better. At least she had a job. Regardless of how it shook out a few weeks later, he had done me a solid. I was free. The apartment came from someone I worked with and liked—Aiden and his missus—but I did NOT like the idea of mixing friendship and business. In all this transition, for the first time in all my years as a family man, I began to avoid going home for the last month I was there. I began to carry weed and smoke it, not before work, but I did not go home right away anymore, to see my boys. My boys were men now, and I was leaving. And I needed weed. Lots and lots of weed. As he always had in thin times, The Cid kept me in the green. A friend with weed is a friend indeed, and The Cid… he is that, and much more.

Maggie was chaotic, and right away I knew I was going to be setting boundaries, and setting them hard. She complained constantly about not having money and drove a vehicle that was absolutely one late-night-and-bored-cop away from me hearing her whine about not making rent, always trying to get me to offer help. I gave her rides to work with Athena on the phone and her trying to write me notes with unimportant questions on them, while I tried to close the deal with Athena, again. I had to mute my phone and whisper to her, please… get the FUCK OUT OF MY CAR! That did the trick. She fucking terrified me. It was still better than being with Marla. But something was wrong with my sons and people trying to help were filling my head with shit based on their own experience with divorce, mainly. Static. Debris to dodge. Well-meant, all of it. Not all debris. Food, water, and oxygen also freely flung at me from loving, supportive friends, way down there on the Earth. It was cooling rain, washing dust, while I went up and down the exterior stairs to the basement to do laundry. Okay. I could do this. Breathe.

Mulligan's

Cristobel, always there in the dark, showed up and took me to Mulligan's for dinner. I relaxed for the first time since Pootown at the beginning of a summer now on the downward slide. Not good sleeping weather, yet, but soon. The heat of July had passed by as nothing—the blink of an eye—and nothing compared to the other fire in me.

On the way home, I saw something in the street, and someone. He picked it up as I braked for him to cross the road. He came over to hand it to me. It was a dollar bill.

"Here you go", he said. "Karma dollar."

"It's all yours, you earned it." I laughed with him, and Cristobel joined us, two friends and a stranger offering a gift.

"I don't keep found money," he said. I know Code when I hear it, mine or no, and the voice of one who follows his own. I took the dollar and wished him peace as I looked into his eyes and we were friends, for a moment, as I was counting mine. Chris laughed, and we went back to my new little home with him reassuring me that I was not going to have to worry about meeting a nice girl. I was a nice guy, and not hideous. I still have the karma dollar. It has traveled beyond this world with me. I had need of it, after all. Thank you, stranger. Just as Cristobel went down my stairs bidding me goodnight, it began to rain.

Athena came to have lunch, and to discuss our new status shortly after. We could simply date, now, and why not? I was in. Maggie joined me on the deck as I was smoking and smiling about this new prospect. After Athena went back to work, Maggie expressed that she was uncomfortable with the idea of me and Athena having lunch, and sex, in the afternoons. I expressed that Maggie could fuck herself, that I hadn't been with anyone but myself for most of my marriage, and now, I was going to, for riz, fuck someone else. Do not get in my way. The electric tense feeling I had lived with so long came roiling back. I hadn't really realized that was why I had been feeling so good. Stress had been my normal, for, well, for a lifetime.

And that's when Maggie showed me her inner psycho. After getting away from Marla—so good at showing her face so quickly no one else ever picked up on it—after getting free, onto this little piece of flotsam after jumping ship on a hope and a prayer, the little piece of flotsam burst into flames. I had just gotten away from this, this anger and hate and meanness. That was a slow roast, twenty years (and of course, I was only into the second course, and didn't know that). This was a grease fire.

Fuck. That soured quickly. The situation did not improve

when I sought out Aiden down in the tiki lounge, the great outside rec area that this place came with, and proceeded to share with him, guy to guy, that my roommate was going to try to cockblock me and I might need some kind of backup. Because Maggie heard me, freely speculating on how I could solve my Maggie problem with a car door at 35. Just spitballin'. I knew better, as funny as it would have been to make jokes about how easy it would be to just bury something out to the Poo. Not a treasure this time, but a problem. My God, if I had even breathed it… My senses were kicking in on automatic, protecting me now.

Through all this, the move, the next week, up to now, I had kept pace with my job, and my laundry, etc. I did not miss a single shift, and it was good, gritty work, right? But something did not feel right no matter what I did, no matter that things seemed to be pretty good. I sold my wedding ring for 90 bucks at a pawn shop in the Biddo. As Code-honoring as it would have been to pay that same 90 bucks for a date with a nice girl, i.e., working girl, but that's not my style, and I think I'll try my hand… sorry, I've had quite enough of my hand… ahh, I'll try my *chops(?)* at finding me a woman who wants me to do the dance, like a regular guy. I was psyched. Not soon enough, to shed that collar and collar that had truly been, and nothing else. The days were hot for about a week. I was disoriented and in shock. I did not really know how bad. I should have, because I felt normal, but numb.

Mary Pierce called me from out of the blue from Old Orchard Beach on Saturday morning. She and her brother wanted to know what I was doing. She's married to my cousin, Jon. They have three sons. Mary grew up with 8 brothers, with her right in the middle. They were an Irish Catholic family, and my clan and theirs had coexisted for generations. My mom and Mary's mom had been friends growing up. Small town. I often forgot I am from one too.

Of course. Of course, I would love to go see them at the beach. I was in my new life, had held on to the old like my job, and come out the other side. I thought my transition was done, out of my house, in my apartment, ready to recharge. I never even thought for a moment how much I was about to shift perspectives. My family from the old country had just shown up and reminded me I was still one of them.

Seavey's Landing

Mary, Barts, and Me and my Pieces (Genna).

My cousin Genna has always been more of a big sister because I don't have any siblings but a lot of cousins. Genna and Jon on one side, and Nicky and Kevin on the other, were the closest things I had to siblings, but we had all gone ahead and lived our lives. So many of the Pieces, my Pieces, left behind, but it was the way of things, right? Everything had changed for me and I was psyched to realize I had time for reconnecting these relationships, just like this. Genna had been floating in my orbit once in a while via phone calls, updates, and news on occasion. This for me eased the transitions coming, the shock of being through the Looking Glass. But it turns out, the Looking Glass, it was only the first one. And the easiest.

I raced down to the beach and caught Mary and one of her brothers, Barts. We went the six minutes to Seavey's Landing, smoked a J or two, and talked the talk people talk, when once they were part of everyday together. Not Barts, he was a little kid when I was a teen, but now… we are all older. Lifetimes behind us. So, we mainly talked about what our last common denominator really was, except weddings, funerals, and the one Christmas Marla and I, still newlyweds and childless, had returned to Massachusetts for the last time. Nana and Papa had come every Christmas after that and made it awesome, for twenty-five years.

Until 2018.

We talked, of course, of Rocky Pond.

We laughed that day, and I started to think about the things I had left behind when I moved to Maine for college thirty-two years ago, how I had had a life here, how that life now was over. I thought about the lives they had lived, and the one my parents had, my mother so excited, calling, planning, discussing food, trying to get an idea what presents to buy people. It was her greatest joy, to give Christmas presents, Birthdays too, but Christmas… she was always happiest, and we had had a whole lifetime of great ones; the years go rolling by. Now, my mother had been in a state of decline, as was Mary's father-in-law, my Uncle Ritchie. This is the Pierce Curse. Die young, or this. Many had gone to kidney failure or cancer. No mishaps, like accidents, or suicides. Jimmy went in for a gall bladder procedure and died right there in the operating room. My mother and Ritchie were the first and oldest of their generation to live to this point. My family in Maine and I, we knew Nana was declining, that the Christmases had come to an end, because in 2018, we had gone down on Christmas eve, and for the first time in twenty-five years, there was someone actually in this house, on Christmas morning.

Not us. We all returned to Maine. It was sad. It was our last Christmas together too.

Seavey's Landing is the number one spot, ground zero for me. I took my sons there when they were little, and as they grew up. Many children I worked with had come there, some even on the water in the canoe. Mostly fishing. Sometimes cooking food for people, parents, too, if I could get them here. Depended on the kid. It's also the main spot I would take people who wanted to canoe. It was probably the one place Ella and I had spent the most time and been the most often. It was 6 minutes from my house, and mainly pig free, at least when I had lived in Scarborough. Today was gray and breezy, but warm, and the sun danced in Heaven behind clouds that spread out every so often and bathed everything in sunbeams. I love when you can see the shadow of clouds go across the water and the sand and the dreamily swaying grasses of the estuary.

Mary started to reminisce about when we were all kids together. She asked me if I remembered that they used to tease me and say if I wanted to hang out with them, I had to make sure I had all my Pieces. It was all in fun, but the Pieces…

I told Mary that I have never stopped being mindful of my Pieces. I showed her my gear, unaltered from my everyday usual, whether I was working or not. Swiss Army knives, bits of string. I told her that Pieces made up a pretty big part of me, and I always taught kids about them. "And Mary," I said, "I still think of them and call them… my Pieces, Mary. I never saw it as teasing, more like teaching. Or training.

That's no shit."

We all laughed that day in the blazing Maine summer sun. I felt pretty good. When I drove back to my apartment, I drive back to my apartment. *My* apartment. Yeah, okay. I could do this. I could live, work, and love in Maine. And my boys will come around. They're pissed about Ella.

I had a good time at Seavey's Landing that day with Mary and Barts. I took a pic of me and Mary and sent it to Genna. She sent me a message that made my heart soar. Not a whole lot about my life really needed to change. I still had my job, I still had my friends, I still had my sons, even though they were pissed about Ella… right?

Genna replied with a text to my pic. "Single life seems to agree with you because you look great!"

Awesome.

More company was coming.

My Apartment

My apartment/Biddoton 2:21 AM EST.

One week, again.

Hot peppery raindrops… (make stars on glass).

I was scrolling Bumble. Maggie was at work so I had some measure of peace. It just did not feel quite right. I couldn't pin it down. I was listening to the sounds of the streets. Streets I had walked for many years, and returned up and down Route One, out of this… this environment, so close to my work. Too close. Way, way too close. It was hot and humid, and the air buzzed with the sound of bugs, traffic, and the voices of the hood. I breathed. I breathed free air.

The second woman to pop up on my Bumble feed in Biddoton was someone I graduated high school with. *That* was weird. West Allenton… so long ago, so far away.

My parents. They had been isolated for a while since last year. They hadn't come up as they always had, all through the kids growing up. They were always around. Close, even when down here. They gave me, and my family, absolutely everything.

My relationship with my mother was complicated. It had ugly moments attached when I was young, and I failed to appreciate the great things they did for me as a kid, the formative experiences and adventures made available to me, the vacations. But I did love my mom, and I knew she did me. I had worked at it. The truth is, it had guided me in my vocation as well.

Be still, and know…

I thought, now. Of my life, looking around at where I was. I had signed a lease. With a friend and coworker. It hit me. I had been worried about the situation with my parents, but what could I do? I was here. If they needed me, I could go to them, but what? Genna had done just that at this point, a couple times, returned to Mass for a couple weeks at a time to help her mother with Ritchie, and she was about to return there for good.

But I could do something now, besides wait for a phone call I dreaded.

"There are no beginnings, or endings along the Wheel of Time. Ages come and go, and one Age fades into memory, then myth, then silence, until it comes again. Nothing begins or ends. All things are new beginnings, and all things end. This was… a beginning."

----------Robert Jordan

I'm sure seeing Mary and Barts at the beach earlier was the catalyst, but I felt my mother at my left shoulder. I now know, without doubt, she came to me for real. Her spirit, trapped inside her dementia brain now, was free, and clear, long enough to find me in my little apartment and tell me, it was time to get home. She was going to be dead. I could do something. What was to become of my dad? I could intervene in a way I never really thought. It was an unbelievable chance. To give them back, something now at the end of the tale, and perhaps to see beyond? Whether or not Dad would even function without Mom to take care of was one of many unknowns. Be Still. To know that we know what we know…

It was a crossroads. The journey about to begin was going to be longer, more arduous, and unimaginably more of everything, both terrible and wonderfully beautiful than the one I, up to this second, thought I was on. The road forked, as I leap from land and sea here… that is how it was and is. Neither land, nor sea or sky… all of it, together, at once indistinguishable. Inside the Sacred Spiral. Inside the rising whirlwind. I wasn't through the storm at all. I was just about to get onto big water. Big, rough water.

As I always do, when no one else is awake, I called my friend halfway around the world, in Hawaii. Of course, I called the Crocodile. The streetlights shone in all distorted by the rain like stars.

The Crocodile and I have been friends since college, and he was my best man. Since moving to Hawaii twenty years ago, it's been phone calls once in a while, when the moon reminds one of us of the crazy shit we used to do at the Blue House, and we check in. He was awake, I was sure. He had been half a nomad his whole life. He told me to pull anchor without hesitation. I was decided already. I just needed to hear it from him. We laughed for a time about the old stories, like the time he fell off a three-story roof and landed on his feet next to a crowd of brothers, and just walked away without a word leaving us in awed silence. He did shit like that a *lot* back in the day. Some crazy drunk redneck fuck from the house next door came out one night with a shotgun and started talking shit between the houses. I realize now how easily someone could have gotten killed, because people were calling him a pussy and telling him to go the fuck to bed. And that fucker started to raise that weapon towards our house. You read this nowadays and it seems commonplace. Trust me, they all would have gotten famous.

But the Crocodile, unbeknownst to *any* of them, was on top of it already. Next to that stupid Pumpkin was a small bush, a weed really, between the two frat houses. It was about the size of two stacked milk crates. As soon as that drunken asshole's hands started to move, they all saw the bush suddenly spit a Crocodile out of it, and in his hands was his Colt Python .357 Magnum. He just appeared next to the guy with the shotgun and poked his little Snaky right in his ear without making a sound. Correction: he did whisper something to Tim, who went ghost white as he heard that hammer come back, but none of the Blue House boys even felt curious about what it was because the Crocodile scared the shit out of all of us anyway on a daily basis without guns. They didn't even want to know what had just surgically removed Punky's drunk-balls with what looked like five clipped words. We were used to that shit from him, but not like this, with like, guns and shit, but their reaction was basically Crocodile was the *Deus ex machina* here, and that didn't surprise anyone at all. That's funny, looking back. The other Punkies talked Timmy back inside to change his underwear, and the situation broke up quietly. Crocodile was there, and then he wasn't, and when we went back inside, he was already in there, pouring a pitcher of beer for himself off the keg on the fireplace, and smiling. He kept the revolver in his belt the rest of the night, completely against all rules and for two days he was in the Chapter room, armed, watching over all of us. I sat with him through many nights, praying for a chance to whoop some ass side by side with the Crocodile, but that was later. The gun story preceded me by a semester but I heard it many times.

It was about three-forty in the morning, Eastern Time. It was a little more than a month since I had moved out of the house, and just a little more than that since my old life, I thought, the biggest piece of it, changed. I had other… Pieces. Friends. This great place to live, all the little places I had come to know, that had long years of history, me finding out who I was, and then making myself into what I was now.

Now, it was all going on the fire. I was leaving. Leaving it all behind. The last of the Pieces of my old life, the one that ended on the drive out to Pootown a few weeks ago. One that I had traveled ten years to find, crossed an ocean of time.

My Job-family.

Pathways, Part 2

This part was going to be tough, and I faced it now as I walked outside with my bamboo sword and began to take myself through the forms. Robert Jordan pointed the way for me, long ago. It took a long time to find this crew, and we had already had some good times and good work under our belts. I loved them all, and I had just spent weeks on Fridays at a Leadership Seminar put on by the company, invitation only and many of us had become close.

Matty Mango and I walked many roads together over the years. Peers, boss/staffer, Friend, and Business partner even. He called me once, afraid for the safety of his mother on a date with a man he did not know. He called me, and I asked who was driving. That had kind of defined our friendship ever since. Cristobel and I also walked more than one road and became family, as they, like me, nurtured and protected and planned for our own families, but together, like ships in sight, within one horizon, though to each the horizon they perceive, unique to each of us, but navigable. Especially with friends who might know part of the way or have a couple extra limes, when you run out, to fight the scurvy. The scurvies of the world.

I am a wealthy man. I never have had any money, but I have vast reservoirs of friends and brethren. Love. We have lived and some of us have died. Some of us now are a little bit of both, as I had been for so long. They are all warriors out there, those who watch over the ones who need protection, old, young, weak, sick. All of you. Anyone who serves. Serves any quest of Love.

This is who we are.

I used to say that long ago. Teams. Crews. Shipmates. You facilitate enthusiasm through culture. You share philosophy, encourage others to explore and define their own. Every last man-jack of us can. Boys, girls, others… all of us. Philosophy… Indeed, I had done it. I would do it again, far away in both time and space. The Pathways crew… They were they very finest of them all. Would that all the troopers I shared the road with along the way could be on the same team. There were crossovers, other *ronin,* like me. I stretched my arms and shoulders out and checked my distances around the deck with the shinai.

I talk about these great people but there was always a plethora of control freaks, demagogues and idiots, too, that kept on turning up, like bad pennies fouling the wishing well, not belonging in this false but beautiful koi pond environment that is residential care. More, in fact, than I care to mention. Only to remember. Friends, they come and go. Enemies, they add up. Poolside Ruth, suck my ass. You committed fraud every summer, sitting there by your pool, and never shutting the fuck up about it. I was on the streets. I didn't see you. You were AWOL. Nice tan. Mine is darkest on the arm that hangs out the window of my car, like most of us here. You were in the Army during Vietnam. So was my Uncle Ritchie. You were in San Diego, I think you once bragged, as you were calling yourself a Vietnam veteran. Ritchie served at Da Nang, Vietnam. He said he didn't see you there, before the dementia took him away too.

I am very proud of my friends. They give me strength and guidance, even when they are not around. Hear me now, I am just as proud of my enemies. So are they.

Fast. Accurate. Fast. Accurate. I blew sweat off above my eye. I felt good. Strike. Strike. Block.

My own journey had carried me from place to place, points on the map, sometimes twenty miles, sometimes three or four, but most of the time, on Sunday nights, I wrapped up the week before as the new one began to stir. Late night Sunday paperwork, after my family was asleep. As the kids got older and the locations varied the lineup did too, like a good TV show that doesn't get stale, just richer and funnier for the changes. So, my workplaces changed, but my work really didn't, except for my year-long trip to the other side of the river for Matty Mango. But I found my way back, across the river, back to working with children, in their homes, with their families. The biggest change had been when I no longer had Ella to ride with me late night, wherever it was.

Until now, of course, with everything changing. But I reflected now behind me.

***

The meeting that morning at MAS devolved into staff shouting over each other. I had never seen anything like this, and I had been around long enough in this game that I knew what it meant. I met Meg Scott here, and we became good friends at Pathways, later. I met Dr. G here, and we became friends too, and Meg and Gina and I all worked together later at other companies. This is how it is. This place was ridiculous. The guy who hired me was one of the stars, but he had gone. I had not been involved in the shitshow this morning, but when my phone rang twelve hours later to get my side, my new boss was three glasses of wine into forming conclusions and she was not interested in my side, even though I had not been party to the bullshit in team meeting this morning. Before Terry called me, Matty Mango had called me, and he said words that reminded me who my friends really are and why.

He said, "I need you to come to my company. No one else. You."

At first, I wasn't down. Matty Mango wasn't sure his boss would meet my pay number I had thrown out. He was going to call her. He told me one of his residents had lit herself on fire because staff wouldn't give her an ice coffee at ten p.m., and he was beyond enough. Fire. She lit herself on fire. He was spooked, and desperate, and he knew who to call. That was when my boss, Terry, called me. About five minutes in, I decided I was not interested in trying to rehabilitate this place that had shit like this going on. I did something I don't often get to do. I calmly told her I had concluded that I could not, nay, would not, *serve under a leader like her, and I stuffed my notice right back at her. Polite and professional-like, but firm and clear. Like in a SafetyCare prompt. I worked out my two weeks and said goodbye to the active client families, but there were only a couple anyway, and the work with them had gone well. I was grateful for that, because leaving work undone sucks and is sometimes unavoidable. Matty Mango called back. I was still in my driveway in Scarborough. I accepted, and went off to work with completely different people, adults with Intellectual Disabilities ("retarded" no more), this time. For neither the first nor the last time, I marveled at what I may have done different once, if I knew what I was learning now.*

When my… when I finally made my way back across the river to mental health, kids, and families, I found Pathways.

***

All those years, talking about how Samurai values and the values of a healing practitioner were the same, and like bushido, if one looks it up, does not always present identically. I spun and reversed the bamboo shinai. Some say seven values, some say nine. They vary. Most things, they vary in some fashion. A man. Steel. But the ranges, and the possibilities… And some things do not. What is required. What is and is not possible. These were the things I had contemplated, when I was a monk. For monk I truly had been, a warrior monk, so I thought of myself, because it was the only way I survived being with someone who was dead in every practical way, except when she woke up like on the fucking *Walking Dead* and tried to eat my brain, figuratively speaking, but it was pretty much like that. I found compensations, as I am certain all monks always have. It could be risky to share these philosophies. I did anyway. I was past caring about many things by now, but it could be risky. I went down on one knee and lunged up and forward. I eyed a single leaf in reach and smacked it off its little branch into the yard. Pieces of it fluttered down in the porch light.

Until my seeking took me to Pathways. They loved it, from the first, and I dared, once more unto the breach, to hope, to run at this football one last time. Pathways ate it up, and I served it. We rose high together in those last days of the setting sun of my time as a samurai in Maine. I made a few, there.

Humility. I still lack it.

I did not make any samurai at Pathways. I found some. Raw, perhaps, and motley, but real as steel. And they recognized me. It seems, as I had been looking for them, not knowing if they were out there on the wine-dark stormy water, they had been waiting for me. Maybe, I hope, I showed some of them what they in fact were, all along. Naming. Powerful. I explained to them what they really were. Does it make a warrior fight better if you knight them? It does.

I always wanted a seat at the big table, even if the big table was small in stage or scope. I believed we could leave a quiet mark on the watching stones, for someone, someday to find… But, the table… it needed to be round. There were things in those days, and now, that are above, beyond… indeed, anathema to the idea of compromise. I got it all here. Finally. One day as the spring was getting hot, I came out of the office, missing the freshly departed Ella, I saw a huge double rainbow that went right over our parking lot, framing my last office home.

It's funny, looking back on the Swan Song of the Samurai, as spring again gave way to summer, that infernally hot summer, two things.

One was, there was validation, and real strength to be found here. I was not always sure there even was a quest, and if there was, I was worthy. There was, and they believed I was, so I tried to be, and felt like I may yet be. I have played such a spectacular fool.

The other thing… I did not own an actual sword. Just a blade. I had not in this world, beyond Philosophy, ever needed one. But I did have bamboo practice ones. So, I practiced, for years. I practiced, tonight, on the cusp of the wave.

Philosophy leads to Practice.

The blade I owned had been washed in holy water Uncle David gave me years ago, when he went to where John the Baptist baptized Jesus. David always, always gave cool shit.

Near the end of my time with those merry gallows fruit, I was invited to participate in a leadership training series, and it was awesome, because it magnified all that long-awaited validation I was talking about, and it made a tight pack of friends much tighter, and we picked up a few that might have been passed by as the Spiral whirled its course. So many names, so many friends, so much love and laughter. And shared tears, but in a good way. Together. Back-to-back, and swords out. Let them come!

And now, in one week, I sent the emails, I made the calls, I did the visits. I wrote the notes in the office late at night with music echoing these halls I had come to love. Wagner. Twilight of the Gods.

I went to the meeting. Ah, my last team meeting. Sendoff, part 1. I gave a hell of a speech. Tears, laughs, hugs, and well wishes. If you were there those days, read on. Read on, and I'll tell you what was over the horizon. But first, we must honor the code. All the way.

The bamboo sword was whistling as I went low and high across this great deck. It really was perfect for this. I was sweating, but hungry for what was coming. It started to thunder over the Biddo.

Blackjack Swayze & the Rest of Goodbye

Jack had joined our team after some of those other names had left. It was truly a revolving door there, but it was also a dynamic time for everyone. The other service too had a company of heroes, and almost every one of them had seen a Hell I did not know (chemical dependence and recovery), and they were gallant, hardworking, and trying to make their lives less of a mess. Like I was now. There was a prevailing theme to the last couple years of my old life, and the last act was great, weird extra shit going on with my boys or no, things were okay.

But this guy… he sized up the energy immediately, and just jumped right in. I loved him on the spot. I felt like the replacements were arriving, the next generation, as the sun went down on me. And they were damn good too, Jack, Ryan, and Brando. They all had master's degrees, attitudes, and were lean and hungry. They particularly loved all talk of pirates, samurai, and jedi knights, especially Ryan, movie and Star Wars nerd at heart that he is, but a true scholar. They encouraged and uplifted me, the Old Wolf, and I relished my place with them, mutual respect and balance. Just fucking professional camaraderie and *esprit de corps*. Thank God these guys all knew it, had picked it up, or sought and found. We had a blast, too, and kicked some real ass on the streets. I had already crossed an ocean of time to find them, and I told them so, and they understood.

At Pathways, unlike the rest, they really make it a point of introducing you to the team at a meeting. It's awesome and awful, of course. A rite of passage, a thing in short supply in today's world. Some say such things are not necessary. I disagree, having benefitted greatly from such practices, even to make up a few of my own along the way.

Jack, upon being introduced to all of us, with a smile that says I will eat that for the right laugh or the right money, casually deadpanned that his parole officer said it would be a good job to work with people. You know, to get used to it. My absolute favorite… silence and hesitant laughter, like I always knew I could count on from Jessie Lee and Angela. I heard it now from myself too. This cat was one cool customer. We all, like I said, immediately thought he was the shit. And he could ball, too. We worked some hard streets those last days, and it was Jack who called me and tried to say he was hoping to get a beer, since I was leaving and all. Just us. With a straight face, he said it. I was most happy to accept, knowing it was going to be everyone, and more hugs, inspirational calls-to-arms and the future, and tears, and laughter. Always together.

So, he came to pick me up in a car beyond its last legs, and I said I would drive. I'm diabetic, I told him. If I drank enough to be funny or interesting, I'd probably stroke out.

What a cool place that is, the 88 on 302 in Windham. Everyone was there too. I felt bad about that. All my talk about wanting to stay there for a long time, and their love they showed me, and all of us. That little shining city, the clean empire… small, but pure all alone in the wilderness up North. They did it right, in my book, and that's the stamp, if it's worth a damn. Thank them all too, they truly made me understand something that I had not looked at enough over all my contemplations.

Gratitude. An attitude of gratitude.

At Pathways, they said, life is short. Work someplace awesome. I did, and it was. And is. Short. Far too short. But for a little while in the summer of 2019, in Brunswick, there was a vision of what the future may have been, what may yet be.

Because this quest, this life's work and legacy did not end here. This was only the first age, as there had been a first age of Piracy. It was over now, for good or ill, and I did not know really what that meant or what was next for me professionally. There would be another Age, it turns out, and that is really what this is all about, this journey that started on acid way back out at the Poo, on Midsummer's Night.

Blackjack and I were not the last to leave. I mean, it <u>was</u> my party, but the Pathways brethren were still there as we rolled out into the night. They had forgotten the party, had said goodbye, and now were simply out with friends and coworkers of an evening, laughing about the crazy awesome work we do that doesn't pay shit but we love it so. I was quite at peace, to leave them quietly and for us to remember our parting so, unable in days to come as time and memory stretch out, to remember exactly when I slipped away. It's how we try to leave the families we work with. They had given me so much attention, I wanted to ride out gracefully at last before I wore out my welcome. On the ride home, Swayze and I took a long, long winding road, through ins and outs of the neighborhoods and towns I had worked, he was and would continue to, and what I had to share as I passed what counts as a torch, the last and most bit of honor I could give, to one most worthy, here with me now, making sure I wasn't alone before I left.

We went to the bridge on the Eastern over the marsh, and I told him how when Ella died, I had come down here screaming inside, and the whole marsh had gone silent as soon as I stepped onto the bridge where we now stood, smoking a J and laughing under the same salty, briny moon.

I dropped him off where he found me and, not wanting to go into my apartment, I decided to take me a little tour, since I was leaving and there were places here that I would see one last time with the eyes of a Mainer.

Starting with returning to where he and I had just been. Not the Bridge. The landing. Seavey's Landing, again, one more time.

I had a long moment. How long do you sit and remember her? All the years? All the love? I watched the stars and the water and the grass and remembered all the many people and things attached to this place for me, and her. Going away from her was fucking with me. Was that it?

From Seavey's Landing I went down to the fishing dock at Pine Point and watched the water and the stars some more. Lovers and freaks floated about as they do perpetually in places where you can find a little privacy and beauty, me a little of each. Lover and freak. The salt was in the air, and I took it in, knowing it was for the last real time as my home.

And I had to finish up over at Pine Point beach, because I wanted to look out into the sea, not our little estuary with its secret hideaways and islands… I wanted to look ahead, and big. So, I did. I stood there for a long time on the sand looking east. Nightwalking beachcombers went by me like in a movie, someone standing still, people zipping by too fast to see.

Before I turned away the last time, my eyes looked down at the sand, and right next to me, the whole time, someone with some other unknown connection to the name, had written it in the sand, right next to where I had been standing. Just the name. Her name.

ELLA.

No… fucking… way. How? Come on. I don't even question anymore. But that's now, while I recollect. Things were still weird. No drugs, just… otherworldly.

I began to really accept that there were forces at work here quite beyond my control. I had taken agency of my life, yes, but… things had just gotten way bigger, and way more serious, and in no way or fashion were they even a little under my control. If I didn't know about drugs, I would have really felt like I was going way off the deep end. With drugs, you know what the deep end looks like, at least. It's a marker. Something white to mark the water level from afar.

I was chomping to get home to my father and mother, to my family. My cousin Nicky lost his wife some years ago, with two small boys. He still has them, still small. I am going to be in the mix, around my family, my cousins, who knows who may yet surface? After 32 years, I was going back to Massachusetts.

My father had taken my call after some sleep. It was the day after I called the Crocodile. I told him I was coming home to help. I realize now he was kind of in a fog, but I just took it as a surprise at the abruptness of the decision. He needed my help, that was clear. I had called Nicky to see if I could borrow a thousand dollars in case I needed to. He said I sure could, but I never needed it. I made it home to them all, maybe just at the exact right time.

There had been two bits of business to close with the mandatory *accoutrements* of Honor. Departing this crew properly had been the first. We had honored the Code. Now, to finish it.

Cassiopeia (The Code: Love, Law & Mojo)

She had been kind of like my lawyer all those years on Death Row in a sexless, loveless (*solitude; chastity*) marriage. Cassiopeia and I had worked together for almost a year twenty years ago. Things got hot, but nothing ever happened except a hug goodbye. A long, long hug, that almost became a kiss. I had never forgotten. At the time I had two small kids, and no reason to cheat on a marriage. There were no ideas in my head that anything was wrong, and if I went outside my marriage sexually, I would be in the wrong. I would also pollute my medicine, as I was starting then to understand it. I could text her, and call her, and we had a real friendship. I joked that if we ever ended up single at the same time all bets were off, but she knew she could trust me, and she never doused me when I expressed that I really appreciated that I knew because of my friendship with her, that when the time came to escape the marriage, I was going to be okay. She was very gentle and loving as a friend, and she also gave me a window into another reality, one I knew was real even if it wasn't mine and was being told my eyes were lying. Even now, I can hear Marla's shrill accusatory voice saying this was an emotional affair. Cassiopeia kept something alive for me for twenty years. She knows how important she is to me and has made me understand that it has been a bit of a two way, because she always knows, even if she doubts it, that she is beautiful, and she truly is. And, like all truly beautiful women, she does not think she is, so she is kind also, further magnifying her external beauty like a soft light under a Bonsai tree. She had never asked a single thing in return. Until now.

She called and asked me to help teach her daughter to drive before her road test. I did. I did my job and now truly single I breathed her in and gave her a little bit of everything I could to help her be safe, and just breathed her in, reviving in the warm, warm sun after an unbelievably long, bleak winter. I was being reborn. That last dose of her, in person after years of just a voice on the phone, or a text while the clanging of the bars in my mind got louder and the walls thicker… my sweet attorney, my… advocate, it was exactly what I needed. Thank You. I hope you like your name here. And your… avatar, how you fit, what you did, how it gets explained to the world, from the other side of the looking glass, the gift you gave to me, mayhap to the world. One Oasis. One Angel, early along the way doesn't do it justice. You were there, from the true beginning. And every step of it, for twenty years. The sacred vessel that had kept Essence-me alive. Cassiopeia. I have always loved you, honey, and I always will.

***

A kid with ADHD or Autism has a lot of people in their world, and people sometimes talk out their asses. It isn't supernatural, it's all about knowing. Being still, and knowing how to listen with a child's ears, and hear a child's voice. There are many tools and practices on the Path I sought. I have ADHD. I had to make my own Path, because the ones already extant were not mine, and I had always seen much conventional anything as a thing to be interpreted fresh. Like how a child does. Somehow, this one person had never stopped hearing the voice of the child inside, and it had spoken in the voice of a man to many, many others, with the desire to speak as a Man should in this world. Walk tall. Protect the Innocent. Speak up for what's right. All I have now, all I had then, I would give, save that… I had no regrets about the walk behind me, which is not to say there were many foibles and my feet in my mouth, and hilarity often ensued, at my expense, because it's hard to be taken seriously in the conventional world when you can seem like a child and struggle with grown up things. Survivors compensate. I had learned much, and much was about my own self, my greatest teachers the very people I once deigned myself somehow on a footing above, to hand down my service. The first step on the Path… humility. I still struggle with it. I knew myself, and I knew who was around me now, friends who are family, on their own pathways, many met in the field, in the trenches, and bonded that battlefield bond. They were all here with me that awful summer when I cut everything loose to get free of a loveless marriage, by phone and text, laughter and memories, but also the promise of a bright new future.

But Mary and Barts and my mom had passed through this version of my new life, the first version. The larval version. And I had made the decision hot on the heels of starting to not spread my wings, but hope that there were wing buds there, mayhap someday to burst out. Out of its chrysalis.

If my career-a-kiri isn't assured by now, what with tales of drugs and Peter Pan-like pirate fantasies, I will finish that part, before we get out of sight of shore. I had learned how to do this and got better and better at it.

There is a place out there, and you want to watch for it. It is the line to one side of you, or ahead, where you can see, really see, the demarcation between different waters. A water-boundary. As the calm brackish water of the Saco River began to be dwarfed , simply absorbed into the vast and timeless bitter brine of the chill Atlantic, the last hands on me, the ones who had thrown me that last line and ran alongside me on the bank of the river as long and as far as they could follow, all the way to the sea and beyond, I could hear them calling to me, telling me they loved me, that I had been an angel, of sorts, to their family, wishing me Godspeed. That was always and could only be the Murphy's.

The Murphy's

I have known them since the middle of the first ocean, the 25-year journey as an in-home therapist. They met Ella when I first took her home. My skills grew in the time I knew them, both working with them and others. The Murphy's are one of a handful that crossed over another kind of river, the one in our hearts that, as professionals, we are supposed to keep everyone off. Stay on the other side. If I have to give account for my time here to my Maker someday, these people here with me now would be my star witnesses. Indeed, I could not prevent them from doing so. Some people earn their place despite rules. Some rules are for the restraint of fools and the guidance of the wise. As far as being real friends with these people, there were a couple factors. One, they thought of me as one. Two, respect with real people is earned. They knew both Candace the Gray and Mikhail, both gone now, my partners. So, we had shared loss, and seen and shared tales of terror, and their kids were now grown up. I helped, a little. Them, and hopefully others, too.

There was no reason to not allow these people to share their friendship with me freely given and asking for nothing in return. They earned it. So, they came to my little pirate apartment, and I stopped peeling the photos off the wall I thought would be in place for at least a year. I went and sat with them in the Tiki Bar at Aiden's place, and said not goodbye, but rather hello to a new time. They gave me a great gift as I began to pull up the anchor. From it I drew a larger measure of strength and power I would need. It was a near thing, in the end. Inches, between me and that fire. Right to the buzzer, but that was two years away, when the first journey would yet end back on the river. They were there the whole time with phone calls and such. Like all my people were, starting now. They also kept Maggie out of my hair the last night I was there. I knew she had some drama up her putrid skirts, and I was not going to be able to handle that, and for once, just now, tonight, I wanted to stop running and catch my breath. Maggie popped her head out on the upper deck, took one look at Tammy Murphy and the crew, who went silent as soon as she appeared, and promptly vanished out of sight for the night. I had a moment of horror slap me in the face like déjà vu, but I realized that her departure, thwarted, outfoxed, and bitter, looked familiar. I was free of *that* exactly that, and besides this three-week-long little false start and misstep, an encore of terrifying cuntery, like escaping a shark and noticing something else out there, lurking, waiting for you to get tired and complacent… I was FREE. And I just burst out laughing. Phil looked up at me, in my eyes, saying

I was okay and joined me not knowing why. For that alone I am grateful to them. They scared her right back into her nasty little lair. If only it had been that easy with Marla. I laughed out loud and popped a round of beers and lit up a J with my adopted family. We laughed into the depths of the night. Dickie-Kai, baby, Dickie-Kai. That's Gypsy talk. When you know, you know.

But now, the goodbyes were said to living friends, ghosts, and sacred places—everyone but my boys. And what I was about to do was drop everything and go help my parents. They gave me everything as a kid to continue my journey as an adult, they filled our family life with awesome spoiling machines of grandparents (really, she had a shirt) and at this point, I had no real idea of everything they had given me and my family. No idea at all. If I could give back, to ease this change and transition, I would at any cost. My father was not going to be sitting in the house, alone, while I tried to put Pieces together here. No. I had the power to make the choice. With all the uncertainty, I felt pretty fantastic. Except for T.C. and Keelin, and already I was realizing how much I used to talk about them, all the time, because they, we, had been close, I thought. When I thought to refer to them, or mention them, or think about them now, there was a crushing wave of all these new feelings. I had set down the mantle of being in a miserable, loveless marriage, but I had just traded one set of bad feelings for another. I was slipping around, trying to find my footing.

Something was very wrong, and it stank. On the shores of the Saco River, on Pike Street in Biddoton, I was making big changes that affected what I still thought of as my family. And yet, I have been exiled in a way that was not in the plan.

Not my plan, I thought not any of our plan. Its six miles to the sea on the Saco from here. The last dam is in my sight. I know the others going upstream. Sand Pond Road. Skelton. Hiram. Swan's Falls. I know them well. The river isn't going anywhere. My parents were, and Dad had some time left, to enjoy his grandsons, to help his sister in a parallel Hell to his, to do right by Mom. All he ever wanted to do, ever in life, was make her happy, make her feel safe. I was going to be there to help him, as they always had for me and my family.

The Murphy's left, and I finished putting everything I currently owned on the car, save all my shit in Scarborough that I was confident I could retrieve, at some point. My boys had promised me as much, even though something was clearly not right. The canoe went on. The doors shut. I walked through one more time, and said goodbye to my little lifeboat, well begun, too soon done. I had not been with a woman here. Soon, God willing, please. It was 6:20 in the morning.

The sun was up low. The tide going fair. I could see it and smell it down over Pike St. Fuck sleep, I'll sleep when I'm dead. I said goodbye to the heart of the community I had worked in for twenty-five years. I pulled the last line, began floating free and clear, under my own power. I left Maine for the last time, running out into the Sea, on the shifting, glittering, undefinable crest of the outrunning morning tide.

"The warrior maintains his daily ablutions and his cleanliness of mind, body and spirit always. It is not necessary to choose between life and death, there is only how to attain one's aim."

------Hagakure: Hidden Among the Leaves

PART 2
THE SHIRE

Baptism

Rocky Pond, Allenton, MA.

8:45 AM EDT.

91 degrees and clear with no wind.

I rolled down 95 south at 75 miles an hour, not caring much about John Q. Law. Two hours at a time, all the trips up this road, all the trips down, me as a kid with mom and dad… Maine was Shangri-La, Vacationland. They had come up a lot throughout the years. Taken the boys down to the rolling hills of central Mass back up again, cars laden with presents, twenty-five Christmases—more; I had been in Maine longer than that.

While I was in college, through the fall, through the winter observing and falling in love with the changing seasons in Maine, I noted how different it was when you stayed after summer, when the boards are across the windows of the stores and snack shacks all along Old Orchard Beach Road. Staying, living, watching, learning. Growing? Teaching, working, fathering, friending, husbanding… pirating…

My parents were always very supportive. They gave generously to me and my family. More than I ever knew. And as I was thinking about what I could give them back in thanks, they had given more, and would give it all to me, all along, every day. I had not come south on this road enough, but there had been two trips down to Rocky Pond with my sons to spend time and catch up with John and Mary and their three great kids. The littlest one was almost 18. Jesus. Truly a lifetime, for all of us. I had left them in Mass and went and had mine. Mom and Dad were happy, satisfied. They had dreamed of moving to Maine someday, but that had never materialized for reasons ultimately unclear. Probably because by the time they were ready to pull their own anchor, the tide had not stayed; their grandkids were no longer little and the Pierce curse had begun to grip both my mother and Uncle Ritchie, John's father. It was evident, but in early stages that last trip to Rocky Pond, in my old life, when even Nonnie had still been here, and for the only two times, those two summers only a couple years apart, but bookends of sorts, was when Nonnie and all her greatgrandchildren had been in the same place.

And now as I rolled south, the sun swinging behind me as I leaned west, away from the sea, the cascade of all the memories and all the years, muted in the world of here and now as I had made ready to set sail, came crashing down with all the force of a great wave that stayed with me and intensified the closer I got. I saw snippets of time over and over… laughter… so much of it. I felt empty in one profound way, yet good, at least, that I should feel good, the closer I got to home. Home. Home, again.

The Shire is how I think of the area I remember as a kid.

It is pretty much all connected, and encompasses Allenton, West Allenton, North Village, and parts of Shrewsberry. Places I knew as a kid, before I left, when Rocky Pond was the biggest water I knew. The Woo is not the Shire. I remember it, of course, where we went to roam, smoke, listen to music, watch movies, and, as we got older, to kiss. To get into, or narrowly avoid, trouble. Everyone had a Monday morning tale of horror at Woo center: fights, cops… I never really saw anything like that. It's a small American inland city. Industrial. Past prime. Crackling with the 21st century. Not home, not The Shire.

I will never even want to dream about how I wouldn't have made it through all the little things we had to do without my trusty GPS cylon phone. And the Tinder/Plenty of Fish action was not what I had heard. I had no hordes of thirty-year-olds asking me, "Heyyyyy!"

No time, really. What I needed… well, I just wanted to meet a girl and have a drink and a laugh. Wild rampant sex repressed for years and on life support, optional but free with or without purchase.

I did not need GPS to find my way to Rocky Pond. This is one place I never left. I had even connected this place to my other world, when me and my pledge class bugged out for the weekend in that crazy fall of 1988. I changed in so many ways forever then. I brought them here. The trips back here a few years ago, within the bookends of the memories of childhood, both mine and now my boys, Jon and Mary, their sons, all of us now had that one common memory pool and memory, the power of it occurred to me now, as it washed over and over me in waves as I crossed the invisible imaginary boundary, across time, back in time, into the Shire. I was here, home at last. I made it.

I was still, for a moment, and knew that I was. I was still. I was.

I rolled into the old familiar parking spot, the one right out at the front, not the little secret pockets every step up the road that held capsules, all, only needing to stroll into my sight to release their history for me to be seen and enjoyed. The memory cascade that would occupy my attention wherever I went now had begun on the ride down and intensified on every stop over the next thirty hours, and never slowed down again.

I took the canoe of that SUV with yesterday's eyes that had last awoken from sleep in Maine some thirty-eight hours ago and put my paddle into the water. Instantly, the focus went from blasting fuzzy color to conveying all the range of emotions I was trying to reset to gain some clarity.

I was home, really home, in Mass, and I wasn't going back to the house I shared with my family ever again. Not that family. I had no idea if what I was shooting for as a plan was even viable, no backup plan, and no money, really. A few hundred dollars. I was done. I needed a bath, and some sleep. I was beyond coffee and adrenaline. I was beyond all EENs unless we got into some amphetamEEN. The record was starting to skip, and that is dangerous. Like, when driving. I rounded the bend that blocks the real body of the pond from the road. To really see this place, you have to put a little work into it. I came around swinging my prow towards the North as I cleared the massive vegetation bog that occupies a big chunk of it, like a divider in a big Japanese garden. It isn't in its natural place. It was moved there. But as a kid we knew the Bog well.

George the Rock peeked around a patch of bush in the water anchored down, down where large things move. Everything in this little oasis is larger than you would think. Fish, bugs, plants, birds, reptiles, and amphibians, too. There are big things here, especially at night. George is out of scale. This bush is the size of two basketballs, George is the size of a bus-and-a-half, made of playdoh, mushed together, and dumped out of the Ice as it receded and released this land to its most recent incarnation about fifty thousand years ago. I thought about this, this one, and all other places I know, mostly including waters, the footprints of the Great Ice.

It took twenty thousand years for the ice to recede to reveal KTAADN, and SouTwin Lake. I can drive that in six hours. All I have to do is sleep a bit and fill my car with gas. I wish I could make this feeling about my boys go away and call them; tell them I made it here. Nothing had been the same since the morning I had driven out of the Poo.

It would be some time yet before I saw KTAADN again, and I was still inside the Doorway I had entered back in June that had closed behind me and tricked me into thinking I had emerged back into the old world. The old world was in my wake, and no matter what, there was much to do, before I could ever go home to my sons again. Of course, at this point, I still thought, they were freshly pissed about all the ugliness that had just been puked out in front of them. I had no idea… no idea at all, and I was focused on duties of the moment.

For a quest there should be proper trappings and rituals. I

had to look at it this way. I had dropped absolutely everything in my life, and rushed home on fire to lend aid. I was trying to be okay with the two years that I had remained with Marla instead of doing this sooner, but that had been the sunset of our family. I knew this now, and I had to let it go down. I had taken on Service, not because I had to, but as Lono, of course, had understood, because I had a chance too. A quest was the only way I was going to be able to look at it and give it what it deserved. I was, on the morning of that first day, profoundly grateful. The sun was bright and hot and thirty plus hours of nonstop running gave way to quiet pause. I could breathe, and I realized, I had not been. Not regularly, for a very long time.

And I beached my little clamshell of a canoe and climbed up onto my old friend to see the sun catching up with me now that I had stopped, really stopped running. Then, with no-mind, the void, as achieved as I could get, trying to distinguish and balance that with fending off numbness, to know the difference, I launched myself into nothingness, perfect Zen, for the .35 seconds it took for my face to break the surface of that water and baptize me clean and washed for what was coming.

After a while drying in the sun, sitting on my canoe, remembering two different Ages, the first, me, a child, this, the biggest water I knew, and me, now, and all the miles under the keel of that old canoe. Three Ages. Those two now gone, and the one that had just officially started about sixteen minutes ago when I hit the sacred water.

***

The waves of feelings, emotions, the exhaustion, the stress…

100

the whole sideways shitshow my supposed new life was going to be—apartment, slut parade—it had come and gone so quickly it was like it had never been. But it had. I had set off on my own. Part of me wished I had put this all together two years ago when Keelin turned 18, but sitting here now I knew that things had unfolded as they should. There were things I did not know at this time, this morning as I watched the sun come over the trees behind where Old Camp had been. That was then. The floods of memories were assaulting me on all sides, and it wasn't all bad. There were laughs and good times remembered as I looked across this little pool, still astounded at how big it once was to me now that I have been so far out on water you cannot see shore all the way around you, if you can see land at all.

Contemplating this now I felt right. Grateful that I made it here, grateful I could do what a good son should do now. The life I had just left we always, I thought, functioned as a team to survive. Now, I had to guide my dad. And also, Noragee and her crew, Jon and Genna, et al. And then there was Nicky and his boys. His brother is in California, but me being here near Nicky will hopefully afford an inroad there. I bring experience and knowledge back to this circle. This family. I am the lost returned. I'm not special, don't get it twisted. My grandmother and her sisters lived within a quarter mile of each other. My mom and her cousin were all neighbors. My generation did not grow up so near each other. It is the way of things.

But now, I have returned. And so had Genna. Jan and Mary got run out of here unfairly, unjustly. I have no idea at all how any of them deal with trauma and mental health, and my own is now not only clearly altered (it was the boys, you see. I think I would have been okay, except for that. It was new to me and small in my mind, but... I would learn many things), it was under assault when I left. That's the thing, here… my sons were treating me like I was some kind of fucking dangerous animal. It just didn't make sense, and I could tell I was fucked up about it. It was vast, and gray, and in the way of what I had before me.

***

Behind me, in the woods to the North, is a rock twice the size of George, and tucked back into a little nook is another rock. It's big, but not as big as George or The Indian Rock. It's about two-thirds the size of George, and it just sits there, like the other glacial erratics that litter the water, and the woods all around this little scooped-out pool. On this rock, set in its little frame of trees, the last on the edges of the picture frame of this place, are three names and a year, done with a brush, and never touched, added to, or marred even by the intervening years. They are still there now, and even people well familiar with Rocky Pond may not even know they are there, may never have noticed this rock marked by three teenage girls so long ago. The paint was yellow, or beige, originally. It says, "Sherry, Judy, Bev. 1960." I know Judy is Judy Abrahamson, but there is no surname here. I don't know who Bev was, here with Judy and Sherry, when they were 16 years old.

Sherry is my mom. She painted that a long time ago with her friends. Now, her son sits in this place, and sees. And remembers. My mom has had a good life. I am a product of it. So are her grandsons. Breathe.

All this washed over me in the morning sun. It was powerful. I don't know what it's like for any other person. For that matter, neither does anyone else, but… we have our own experiences and knowledge. And choices. I was here. I was going to be a factor, a force. I needed to show my sons I was not going to flame out, to crash. This could go either way. They could see it as me just pulling the plug and running home to mom and dad at 52. Maybe everyone would see it that way. I was grateful, again, not only for the chance I had now to give something back to my parents, but that I had a fund of knowledge that was going to be helpful.

I felt the old familiar water resisting my walking through it knee deep. Sunfish flicked about around me. I saw some larger fish. There are big fish in this little pond, and monsters too. There are snapping turtles here bigger than a basketball hoop, and snakes as long as your leg. The last time I came to see Jon and Mary, Mary told a great story about how something broke Jon's line night fishing, and it had a lighted float, so he chased the light around for two nights in his canoe before retrieving it from the depths, still lit, and still hooked into the three-foot eel that had made off with it. Jon is a pretty rugged guy; hunter, fisherman, trapper. But neither one of us would have tried tangling with that Leviathan, fuck *that*.

He cut the line below the float light, and we had ourselves a story. That's Rocky Pond. It's a little glacial scoop of a thing, but tales to equal Moby Dick play out on its scale, and the idea of Jon as a crazed Ahab chasing his quarry round Perdition's flames is not only epically hilarious, it also isn't a stretch, it's how he really is. Give Jon a White Whale and he *will* chase it. Me too. It must be a Pierce thing, adopted or no. No, I have no idea how they will be dealing with the same hard shit I'm here to deal with now. But I *do* know a little something about mental health and trauma. I definitely have work to do, and a chance to put things right. I hope. I was.

This sucks without a dog. I miss her so much. It's been two years, and now everything is just… burning. I shoved it off. It was time to go to work, and I itched to just go get some beer, lock down my Superglue SUV out front, and fish and drink and sleep until nightfall. Then, starlight and moonrise over Rocky Pond. It's changed, but it has not. Not on the long timeline. I was really here. Overwhelmed just became my state. It never went away after this morning, I just learned to live there. I think people know what I mean. Whatever else I could say right now breathing in the last of that good muck and fish fragrance of home, old familiar home after a whole other lifetime, I was glad I was here and now, with what I had behind me. I was Samurai, and now I had to really live it. Okay. Tallyho. In that defiant pirate-y spirit, I hung wang off the side of my little vessel, and pissed a salute at The Mayor's cottage, which sits on the spot our two camps had occupied when I was a kid, up until the Mayor told Jon and Mary that if they could come up with a ridiculous amount of money, they could stay. Jon worked on Gram and Gramp's old camp for fifteen years. It had become so much more refined and beautiful. They came up with the money, and the Mayor told them he never thought they would, and it was better than telling them to just go fuck themselves. But go fuck themselves. They were still pissed, to say the least, and I was aware it was a sore topic. Fuck the Mayor. I wonder what he will think when he sees the Skull and Bones over George the Rock and hears my harmonica and my voice for the first time in twelve years. Maybe there were some hidden treats in being back here, not just tough stuff. I was hopeful, and anxious to see Genna and NoraGee and Ritchie.

Loading a canoe on an SUV sucks ass. I grew dry enough

to smell like clothes washed in the pond, still a little damp, dry enough for camp. The smell of the place lingers, and I'd love to say pine or sunshine, but the living smell of a pond is organic and silty, uniquely flavored to its origin, every one like grapes from the right branch of the special tree on that one hillside that make this unique nectar-hooch. That. That kind of stuff filled my childhood from the people around me, Ritchie, David, my mother and all the old uncles and Aunties and grandparents. It was time to go see Ritchie and Nora. The morning was hot and I felt alive and vibrant. The release of escaping the marriage, and the relief I felt at the opportunity that had presented, the one where I got to alter the future I expected to be profound, was quite something. I had not yet lost my boys, which is to say they were not talking to me, and it was still new enough that I expected some of it, and knew I had caused some trouble about Ella, but there was no way…

But it was still fresh, and I was feeling good about my own situation, bad about Dad and mom's but still…

They live right up the road, and Genna and Jon were here virtually whenever they wanted as kids, a short bike ride away. I always envied that. They were truly part of the place all the time, me, only sometime, a fair-weather guest with a solid pedigree to be there. The kind of pedigree that doesn't go away. Blood. Real blood, not genetics. For me, it was summers living there, and the face of the pond in its other dresses I did not really know when I was young. Flesh, separate and apart, apart from, a part of… I came here in the off season rarely, until I got my driver's license and for my last two years of high school it had been one of my favorite haunts. I hadn't done the deed for the first time here, but almost, and I had done the deed for the second time here, with the same girl who I was with the first time. The second time we were at Rocky Pond in my 77 Cordoba. The first time we were at her parents' house, inside an antique vehicle her father owned, an old dairy truck he drove around as a gag. I knew woman for the first time on a summer day, in dusty sunbeams, and it was awesome. Her parent's house is like four miles from here, in Dawn Village, not really a town, just a special little sublet of Allenton. Dawn Village is Shire ground zero. I went to Sunday School across the street from Dani's street about fourteen years before she let me into her own Sunday School, for the first time in her daddy's toy truck. Dani. My first. No bad memories or hurt between us, either. Just brief, hot, and forever seared in its own place, the place no other can have. The First. (And second, as a bonus, woot, woot, here in my Cordoba long ago.) First, Warren Street.

Ritchie is my mother's cousin, and he also has the cognitive decline, having lived to see his own children grow, Jon a family man and all around awesome regular guy, and Genna, the artist, the gypsy, his wanderer, who had come home now to help her parents, as I had, and this put us all together again for the first time in many years. I was excited about this, and I couldn't understand why I wasn't happy. I told myself I was, but I was not. Logic said I was, and something was not logical.

Ritchie's response to my arrival was logical and expected. It was identical to the one I got a few years ago when I saw my grandmother's sister for the last time. Stella is Ritchie's mother. The other camp at Rocky had been hers. Seeing someone you have not seen all the time, and for a time, can jar someone with dementia back a little, for a moment they return to a time further back, when you were there, when they were still more here. It's kind of like TiVo, as I understand these things. Kind of? Ritchie knew me, and reacted with joy to see me, hallo lost nephew, from whence come ye, briny bloody burned and torn? It was good, good indeed to be here now. It primed me up for West Allenton.

We laughed at old tales of people and things for a time as I watched the sunlight and the trees and million little pieces of dust and bug, the little universe floating through their own ocean all white to me, but I knew under scrutiny and the right lenses could reveal shade and colors unimagined, exotic shapes like aliens or snowflakes. Like real life Horton hears a Who, when they almost boil the whole town of miniature beings alive? Yeah, Gram read me that when I was little. It terrified me, but this was real, and it was cool. Whatever else was going on, I was safe. I was around and among my people. They took me in like I had never been gone. In some ways, I realized, I never had been. Genna asked me about my Pieces. I told her how, funny she should mention it, but Mary asked me the same thing the day I sent you that picture, and it gets better. Fuck, Genna… it is good to see you. I explained Pieces philosophy and discipline as a professional, which of late I was. We laughed like we did in the old lost times, not forgotten.

About two weeks later I rolled through Rocky Pond and found Genna there with one of her friends. She and I stood at the water's edge for a while, two ships on like course sending signal and comfort in the dark. We watched a group of civvers doing their thing, and suddenly I realized that among the weeds underwater, hiding and pulled back in half-cock, was a snake, hunting. There is a dozen or so snake species in Massachusetts. This one is both rare, and venomous. It was a Copperhead. He noticed us hovering over his well-set ambush, and quietly slipped out and down through the water and thick forest of pondweeds, away, looking back directly at us, annoyed.

It was getting hotter as I rolled the last 3 miles from Allenton to West Allenton. I was almost unconscious now, and I knew, I had to land, at least for a little while. It was time to go home.

West Allenton

I pulled into the driveway of the house I lived in for ten years, from the age of seven to seventeen. I did not like it there when I was young. The town. Cruel faces hide in safe spaces. This I knew as a kid, but not the way some do. Some people know there are monsters among us, true demons. As a young man, I did not understand, for example, that some people around me had real demons, real danger. Drug addiction. Domestic violence. Sexual abuse. Emotional Abuse. Violence. All of it, violence. Now, when I meet anyone, I first think of the scars that they try to hide, or the hurts inside. Like many things, I was a little ahead of the curve of the world in my understanding of such things before words like "trigger warning" became something we did not need explained, and a period of "you've got to be kidding me" before we could really appreciate the value of empathy, walking in the moccasins of another.

***

When Ella died in 2017, I went to SouTwin howling inside, unable to breathe. I was on autopilot for about a month, and I opened the Doorway up there, with them, and when I rolled south after that weekend, I was on my way to OK, no matter how long or how far, even if never all the way OK ever again, I was… swinging back. We talked about tripping up there every year, because I had, in other places. South Twin was their one trip into the wilderness each year. It was my kickoff to Pirate season. They had other pursuits that I didn't do back then— sports events, trips to Disney. Some people have several things they do every year: Go to the beach; Fireworks at the park every Fourth of July; Down Home days around the town common every Labor Day. I didn't live life like that. It isn't a judgement, it's just the way it was in a lot of ways. Rocky Pond, I was part of life there, but there were people who didn't live there who had more connected experiences, for example, with John and Genna.

High School, year-round partying at the pond. I was adopted too, and that always gave me an alternate perspective. I once took solace knowing I wasn't made up of the same DNA as my mom. That I wasn't locked in to it. I was ever, and I embraced this, when I read the words in a book, and thought, yeah, that's me… a flesh separate and apart. *Also, once, at Sweet Shores, I had worked as a residential worker, but the ones who go to school all day with the kids, not the evening troopers. The 3-11 shift is where the fun is, consistently, and not at the expense of living like a human being. That's the night shift, of course the real fun of the fun but a higher level of discipline… the 3-11, that's where the meat is. The 7-3 crew, they get the kids up, and out, and to school, sit with them in school all day, and do the whole romper room school thing (which has loads of awesomeness, don't get me wrong) and then return the kids at 3:30 and unleash them on the fresh meat coming out of the staff office with their coffee and information already a whole day old, and thus pretty much moot. Also, the first shift is its own brand of horror, starting with waking at 5 A.M. So, over the years, 3-11 was where I mainly hung my hat, except for OT weekends when I pulled doubles in cottages all over the place. I could have worked a hundred hours a week, then, for years straight. Thank God I was jealously protective of my time with my family.*

So, the 7-3, yeah, we were like that too, and the flip side… A part of, yet apart from, both teams. *The school, and the cottage. This problem isn't just at my little corner of this vast and timeless Dickensian Forest that is Out of Home residential care. I think anyone reading this, years later, will recognize the same problems. Overworked staff running on Love, Balls, and EENs (CaffEEN, NicotEEN). The next shift has no idea what has happened today. The collective experience of the staff is six years between four staff, and 34 years between ten kids. They are outgunned, most of the time, staffers. I had many years of experience, in a way, right off, as I had my 3 years of inpatient night shift, and I threw that curve, and evened the game, and my teammates and I got on well. There are always a few idiots, and the kids shred them, but they learn, or they go, like the idiot who ripped his shirt off, or a kid did, and he was running around in a panic. Dan, his name was. He was a guy who could quote Shakespeare or Carl Sagan in the same paragraph. He had come after me by some years, but people occasionally made comparisons, and it pissed me off, privately. That yoyo was not me, he just knew a bunch of trivia about a lot of stuff, like me, and shared with the kids. Okay. Well, even a stopped clock is right twice a day. It takes a certain way to be successful with these young people and if you don't get it, you don't fucking get it. Most do not, and the ones that do not, stand out. You know who they are. Prison screws have no fucking business working in* residential after they work in prisons, ever.

I had been there and done all of that. Over and over again. Rather than let the turkeys jade me, I appreciated that there are a lot of eagles, too. You need to find silver linings. It is a good thing, if you can lift people up. Raise their game. Covet honor. Made many friends. Some even became family, and it was always and ever that, the Code, the bond of the battlefield, honor. That is the criteria for this club.

My path, 25 years before I sailed out of Maine… I had learned a lot about myself, about my own family and upbringing. I had unpacked and processed a lot of feelings over the years about my mom and how it used to be, how it had been all the years since. As I rolled up the driveway, marveling at all the trees and lush green that had been windswept and bare when I was a kid, when these houses were first built, I knew that I did love my mom. It had taken work, but I did. I knew they always loved me, and they certainly, if any, like, debt was owed, had paid back many, many times as grandparents, and just by being great. It was a love I had taken for granted and invested in my own family and the concept of future, and my own grandkids someday, and now when I tried to look to that I couldn't see anything, and it made me appreciate the love that had always flowed freely from here in a heavy way.

In 2017, before the dementia really took her away save the little moments of brightness that never went away all the way, especially when she saw me and Dad, I called my mom, from SouTwin, in the arms of one set of brothers, way into the open Doorway, like three hours in, after my canoe trip/funeral. I called her, and I told her how much I loved her, and how great all the Christmases had been as a kid, and all the ones ever since, *even the year they were really sick, and we didn't go to Gram's and David's on Christmas morning for big breakfast. I opened my gifts, and my parents went back to bed, sicker than dogs. But that didn't suck, as a kid. It had been different, and special, and I always remembered it so. It was the only time I watched some of the classic movies, the black and white ones about bells and angel wings. I also ate so much leftover Christmas food and unmonitored candy and cookies and fudge it remains a high tide personal best of gluttony to this day.*

I called her, and I got her. I spoke to her and told her I loved her, and the last Christmas they came up was 2017, 7 months later. As I rolled up to my old parent's home now, I was at peace with my relationship with my mom. There was one point, one thing between us, undisclosed, unresolved, and I had put it away a long time ago. It was an ugly business, I remember, but what I knew about it then, was not Truth. It wasn't the Truth of that matter at all. But I made my peace with the small unsaid, un-unpacked thing... but I hadn't forgotten, and somewhere in this house before me, this time capsule like many others I have known and made, were secrets and truths yet to be discovered that I could not imagine.

Mom & Dad

It had been nine months since the four of us—Marla, me, T.C., and Keelin—rode down together to Nan and Papa's house to have a Christmas with them because they were no longer going to be coming to Maine. They were no longer going to be coming over the river and through the woods, bringing Grandmother's house and all its Christmas joys up to Maine where their son and his family were. It was the story their friends knew well, my mother's circle, how they went to Maine every year, and how my mother got excited for months. There is so much fun and joy remembered in those times. It was the spirit of that that I carried out into the field, the streets, whatever. People's homes. In my work, I thought of Christmas memories as something to be protected and defended, for everyone. It is the Whole Year philosophy. You think, operate, and plan in terms of the immediate, the 24-hour picture, the week, the month, the year. We spent time in July tamping down toxicity and preparing for the emotional stress the holidays bring. I trained a mom how to fend off verbal microaggression from family members verbally by teaching her how to find the Void of the Sword. We used bamboo practice swords. For this woman to see herself as a blade wielder was empowering to her, and from that she smacked people up at holidays when they commented on her parenting, her life choices. You know, holidays.

I wished everyone had Christmases like the ones I knew my whole life, and I am always a little sad at the holidays, and I think of the lost, the alone, the poor, and the hungry. But for families that are trying to spend time together, it helps to teach people what loving someone looks like, 24-hours-a-day, seven-days-a-week, etc. It's a sacred thing, and the modern battlefield of how we wish each other happy holidays, the idea Christmas is under assault... that hurts too. If Christmas isn't yours, here's my happiness. Jesus? Sure. What? Di what? Diwali? Cool. Hannukah? Awesome? Let's just take December and make it a holiday free for all. I want to eat Hindu food while lighting a menorah and singing fucking Jingle Bell Rock. Not Jingle Bells, not Silent Night. That's for the other parts of Christmas, or The Holidays. The kid part, the family part. This is just the America Part. You celebrate the Winter Solstice with your lesbian coven? Cool. I'll see you between Christmas and New Year's. Wiccans like Irish whiskey? Awesome. What about eggnog? Okay, Wiccans but not vegans, got it. (*Weed? Cool, I got some stankly-dankly!*) Okay… this is going to be a blast. It's the Holidays. Fucking smile, we only get so many with our own people and with each other. This… this is called fruitcake. It's a genuine Christmas old timey trad… hold on, no don't eat it… tradition. Don't eat it? Fruitcake is *terrible*. No, really. No one knows why it even exists, except it goes back to like Good King Wenceslaus or some shit? Who cares? No, we don't *eat* fruitcake, we just have it at Christmas as a conversation starter, to laugh about. My dad loves fruitcake, and he's the only person I know who does.

"What's your name, honey? Raven.?" I was roleplaying this out for Dad in one of those spaces we were waiting somewhere, I don't remember. I filled spaces where he would have been alone and scared and bored with the spectacle of tale, and sometimes, acts. He realized I had slipped into characters and was running with this and he watched me.

"Come on over here, Raven. This… is Jameson whiskey, and *this* is *mistletoe*." I winked at Dad as he grinned broadly seeing the punchline coming. And, every once in a while, like he did right now, he took over and finished it, and that was just superb.

"Yeah…" he reached and made it… "Come on over, I'll, uh… show you how it works."

These were the moments it was hard to remember how terrible so many things were, because no matter how you slice it, they would never have been, and now, they have been. I am blessed. We both were, in these early days, I hope. Dad was without a doubt relieved I had shown up. I was too.

In the few moments that Dad and I had to talk, we spoke of the state of Mom. She was worse than I had feared. She had declined significantly in the eight months since I had hugged her on Christmas Eve. And I explained again that we could not stay, we had to get back to Maine. We had a little dog still at home. I left her standing there smiling and waving and laughing, like they had left my own house all the years before. The world started to flip upside down then, I guess, in hindsight. It was the last Christmas we all were together, or you might say my first one back in West Allenton.

Dad and I checked in and I hugged Mom several times. I was happy to see her, but I was very sad immediately, that the little dream I was holding on to, that we may be able to be here for a while together and wrap things up, was definitively gone for good.

I had just gotten home, and I had been able to stop moving. Dad and I were trying to make small talk and keeping an eye on Mom. Mom was engaging us but was confused, and my presence here was unusual and that was not lost on her. She had greeted me much as Ritchie had. Dad looked tired now as I recall, but there is a lot of perspective between that day and this one, and I was aware, it was expected, I was in Ops mode, shit needed doing. Assessment, first. Sorry, first, sleep. I spent a few minutes with Dad and Mom and took the temperature of the situation. First thing was, Nana had slipped since Christmas. For a few of the last years we thought of her as happily confused, and she was, and we speculated, T.C. and I, both experienced professionals, about what the next layer of this would be. The thinking was that they were doing what they were doing, what they would have talked about as she slipped away. My father was following his last orders. None of this was unexpected. What was, was that the "something has happened" call never came. I did. I came home, to help, whatever the original plan had been. There was no more plan. No plan survives contact with the enemy. We needed a new plan.

The enemy was this degenerative disease. Dad was still, I realized to my horror, trying to collaborate with Mom, to have her make the decisions like she usually did. He loved to make her happy, and she couldn't tell him how anymore, and it was going hard with him, this I could see, right away. I took what I believe is the last picture of my mom and me, with my phone. It's a terrible picture, it's very rough, but it's beautiful, and it captures the purity of the moment, even with all the swirling whirlwinds of the Spiral whipping faster and higher, carrying me away. This picture looks like I am trying to talk my mom into the other room, where people are waiting, and she doesn't know, but she is suspicious, the sweet kind of suspicious when someone you love is setting you up for a gag, not a mean gag, a funny gag. In this pic, Mom looks suspicious but bemused, and I look like I'm up to something, and I love her a whole lot. I love it. I'm so glad I caught it. I remembered another time. Thanksgiving. And Kevin was here from California with two of his three girls. Nicky was there with Nathan and Cody, my Mom and Dad, Uncle Dave, Jackie, Wendy… everyone. Now there's no putting that assemblage together again in this world. Mom had this ridiculous gag hat that looked like a table set for Thanksgiving, and we were going to gag Kevin into putting it on. He saw right through it, and it was fun. Kevin can put on a hat that looks like a table set with a Turkey dinner and pull it off. My Mom loved to create these venues, pre-script conversations. As a gag, or, for keeps. Indeed, it was how she and my dad first got together.

Nicky & the Boys

I managed to sleep for a few hours, but by the time Mom woke me up the third time, agitated now, not bemused, demanding to know what the hell I was doing here, I knew I needed another plan. Staying here was not going to work, and it also appeared that I wasn't going to be able to be here without factoring in Mom's state. Dad had her in a status quo for some time, it appeared now, and my presence was disruptive. I had to think like a pro, and advocate for both of them. It seemed a good way to repair the rift with my sons. They loved their grandparents, and this was an unexpected silver lining to the divorce. It should be a positive thing, and I hoped they would be talking with Papa soon and frequently. I made my way over to my cousin Donny's house, but that wasn't going to be an option. He had a room, but it was filled with junk, and I was not up to that, so homeless now, for the moment, I called Nicky. I hadn't needed to borrow money, but maybe he had some room. It wouldn't be a bad thing being close to Nathan and Cody, or Nicky.

Nicky is seven years younger than me, putting he and his older brother both below me in kid rules, but we got along as kids, and they were my closest cousins, my mother's brother's kids, as Genna and Jon were my father's sister's kids, and my mother and Ritchie were cousins like me and all these guys. My father and his sister both married Pierces. In Maine, especially rural Maine, for reasons I did not understand, my first few years there, people raised an eyebrow at that, but it isn't weird, two siblings married two cousins. If Aunt Nora and my father weren't siblings, Genna and Jon would still be cousins, and they still would have been at Rocky Pond. Either way, Genna and Jon and I must have been destined to grow up together in the summertime, close. We still were. Me and Nicky too, because after not really having regular contact with him for years, besides the usual (weddings, funerals, you get the theme), he called me out of the blue, again in the summertime, while I still lived in Scarborough. This was summer, 2018, about a month before the last night of my old life.

In Scarborough, near Old Orchard Beach, that was. This is ground zero for the annual ritual of a vacation for many, and I had done the same with my parents as a kid so many times they all ran together like all the Christmases had. It was the same, really. I experienced Old Orchard as a kid, and it was just that, the yearly trip to Shangri-La, the long car ride and the two weeks of surreal bliss and lifetime memories. As a young man had come here in college with my fraternity brothers, with girls, with groups of other friends, all those little bands of a lifetime, sometimes just together for that one night, then to part to the four winds, each with their piece of it, and their tale to spread it out to the world. Later still, when the kids were young, we brought them to the wonderful fried dough and fireworks, and still later, or recently as we measure these things, I had come to the beach whenever I needed a dose. It was great to live next to a beach (next to: within a few miles). That's why Nicky had called me, when I lived there. His bad shit was still too fresh.

Nicky and Wendy had two boys, Nathan and Cody. My Uncle's grandsons, but he had hardly known Cody, because David died when Cody was, like, one, and Nathan was four. I met them, not really the first time, but early for small children, and I knew I was just one of those faces with no context other than someone who is known, one of us, like my memory of my mother's uncle Pinky, one single snapshot of living memory when I was very small on some holiday or gathering, this one at the house we had in Allenton. That was long, long ago, and yet these days I drove by the spot of that memory about twice a week. I had not seen Nicky, Nathan or Cody since David's funeral. I didn't see them again until the next one, but it wasn't the Pierce lottery this time.

Oh, God, no. No, No, No.

It was Wendy.

It was my father that called. That should have told me then that things were worse with Mom than I thought.

Nicky had grown up around Uncle David and his many toys and gadgets, old engines, motorcycles, fire trucks, tractors… David loved all things awesome. He remained a profound influence on me in my work with children. He made everything interesting, explained what wasn't known. I had sipped Coor's beer for the first time, maybe one of the first times, when it was something you COULD NOT GET in New England. Don't do the math. I was five, and he was sharing it with my grandfather on the plane to Hawaii, but he never ever left anyone out of the fun. It was his Playboys in which I saw a woman for the first time. I was probably six. David was that uncle, and I had Ritchie too. When Nathan was born David lost his mind in the good way and it was awesome, too, and his love shone so hot I heard it trickle up through my mother, through Marla, in snippets of overheard phone conversations. When David died it was awful, and it was unexpected, but David had diabetes and a love for life and its pleasures, especially food. I say especially, as far as I knew, but my soon-to-be new bestie, Aunt Jackie, shared that he loved ALL the pleasures of life. Not today, she didn't share that, thank Jesus. That would have been weird. Even, against, you know, the three-month acid trip that had followed me out of the forest back in Maine and was still going on. He had married and left two other women before he got with her, so I guess the third time was the charm for him. His loss for Nathan's sake was felt more by the rest of us, knowing not what he had lost, but that he could never know. All that was left was that firefighter motorcycle, Nathan's now, gathering dust and cobwebs in Jackie's basement.

Nicky had that love of things that go vroom and surpassed most normal people in genius with them from a young age, quietly watching David tinker away at this or that, growing up, one day at a time in one of those quiet safe spaces that hold treasures that never die. If Nicky couldn't fix it, he wouldn't even call you. He would just make whatever he needed to. New bracket, new spring, new whatever. David always specialized in the things that were not ordinary, so did my mother and my grandfather. I guess it's a family trait.

Nicky and Nathan had went haring off of a Sunday morning to the Straw Hollow Antique Engine show, long a staple in Dawn Village at that sweet spot in the Swan Song of every summer. They left Mommy and baby happy and barefoot and her humming and arranging their penguins. Nicky and Wendy loved penguins. They were so happy, so in love. So lovably quirky and silly.

When Nicky and Nathan got home, they found Cody locked in the bathroom, but the first thing they saw as they walked back into a home that was no longer, that existed but for those last few moments only in memory, swept away by the storm, like the cherry blossoms, was Mommy, his dear Wendy, on the floor. She was all the way gone already. Cody was crying.

I never asked. I imagine Cody's crying soon was drowned out that day, and that sound never really stooped for any of the three boys left behind, Wendy's boys. It wasn't suicide, or drug overdose, or one of those things that make people who have no stake okay with the death, that it makes sense that all these lives got shattered. When they ask how someone died, which people never need to, but always do anyway. It's because we are afraid of it. We must stare. The bereaved, they get sick of telling, especially when it is something tragic and sensible. But Wendy took medication and it had side effects. You know on the TV, we get blasted with ads to take drugs for everything from Triple A (that's Abnormal Ass Aroma) to drugs for hating yourself because other people have hurt you… and they always say, some people experience sudden death in cases with this or that medication, but these are rare. Yeah, she had a rare side effect, and experienced sudden death. She had enough time for one final act, even knowing she was going right through that doorway. Just like a samurai can. If you get close enough to strike a samurai a mortal blow, he can and will still kill you. He has one act left in him, all that lifetime of training… to delay death just long enough for one final act. A single extra heartbeat. A lifetime. Wendy pulled it off. She protected her little cub. Way of Samurai, to be sure, is also the way of the mother. That is how I remember her now, perhaps more essential because I did not know her well, and all I can feel is her presence on you guys, her love, Nicky, Nathan, Cody. Mama was a grizzly bear. I hope you're old enough when you read this, but there are good deaths and bad. Hers came too soon, but it was still a good death. Do you understand that?

That was the year before Nicky called me in Scarborough. He was with someone new, and they were up at the beach with her family like they came every year, and Nicky wasn't ready to stay with all of them, her whole family. I got that. He had been severed by death from his wife's siblings and such, and though he still kept up with them, he wasn't ready to adopt a replacement crew. I got this, so he left his Nathan down at the beach with the new kid in the mix, the new girl's kid, who was the same age, and asked me if he and Cody could come stay in my driveway, like they camp out and tailgate at engine and motorcycle shows. It was unexpected, but of course he could. Of course, he could, what a great surprise.

Cody was fussy that night because he was legitimately tired, and he wasn't whiny, or cranky, or a little bitch like some kid's parents feed into. Also, his mommy had been gone just long enough at that point for him to start understanding what not coming back means. That we have a new summer vacation now, with new people. He was just done, and he was still cute as fuck, the poor little guy with no mommy now, and Nicky got him settled into their snug little truck bed well capped and locked, and in sight in my little driveway, safe and sound. They go to engine shows, and antique car shows and stuff. This is not new, in some ways, but of course, some things have changed forever. Nicky's visit tonight is random, and unexpected, and joyous for me although I am sad for him. I am reminded I have a big family, and I've been in Maine for decades becoming a healer and being a father. Also, I watch and listen for certain things. Is he really OK? It turns out, he is. He had to white-knuckle his way back, but he did. For his kids. A father will endure any pain, cross any barrier.

Nicky and I had a couple drinks, that night and I smoked my earthflowers. T.C. came out and hung out for a few. T.C. is so sincere and loving, and he was warm to Nicky, like we saw Nicky all the time. I was grateful, although it wasn't needed. It was exactly how I felt. We caught up a little and, in the morning, they quietly rolled out such formalities as goodbyes truly unnecessary. I did not feel disrespected, quite the opposite, I felt like he had honored me and my home greatly, to view it as a safe place, the kind of place you could just call and ask to crash. I was totally charged that he knew that though we had absolutely no such precedent. It said something, to me, so when I woke and they were gone, I felt warm and happy in the afterglow of the ramifications of that, and when I might see them again. Especially Nathan, because Nathan was a little older at his mother's funeral than he had been at David's and for the first time, even though I had no plan whatsoever on my charted horizon to make any kind of helpful or healing hay out of it, at Wendy's funeral, using an amethyst crystal I used for years to join with kids, I had been able to make a genuine connection to Nathan. I loved those two little cousins of mine, and between them and the prospect of being around Jon and Mary's massive clan was warming my heart…

My heart was broken, that's what this feeling was, and shock and confusion. My family, seeing the next generation I had not expected to see from close up, was water. Cool, clean Rocky Pond Water. Baptisms come in all different forms.

I called Nicky as I roused myself that Sunday afternoon and he sent me his address. Mom pretty much chased me out of the house. I thanked God, again, for legal weed, which I now made completely illegal by smoking the piss out of some, before driving, and for the cylon I plugged Nicky's address into it and did with the blue teeth and the talkie car and the Cosby voice just took over in my head as I smoked and laughed, cried and screamed inside, and thought how lucky I was that some of this shit was the way it was. There is a lot to be grateful for, though we approach the Horn. Too bad about Cosby. It's sad when heroes fall. When I was a kid, I loved all his old shit. My mom introduced me to it via the Chicken Heart, and I was hooked, and I know most of that stuff well enough to spit a taste from memory even now. More the Noah, and my parents always lost their shit over Little Tiny Hairs, and the one about the go carts and Old Weird Harold, and my eight-year-olds interpretation and recital of all of it. We did laugh, a lot, we three, through the years. Things I want to write now, but no one alive would know, just me, and mom, and dad, lost on some back road in Nova Scotia, laughing, me and Dad also secretly and not in conspiracy, each our own, hoping that Mom didn't stop finding it funny. She usually didn't but if she got pissed it wasn't funny, because dad hated when she was unhappy so it stressed him out, and I would duck down and try to be quiet, but be annoying, and NOT HELP. You never want to be the one who RUINS A TRIP, and I was the only kid, so…

It was hot. I was on 290 through Wootown, and the nonstop memory cascade extravaganza gave way to something old, yet new again, and fucking terrifying. This was Massachusetts, the benchmark of kamikaze driving and this was as hot as it got this side of Boston. Or Mumbai. Or Hell.

Well, at least I'm not afraid of being bored. I looked at the cars next to me, close enough to touch, and realized I was laughing. Or screaming. I'm not really sure now, either. Both, I guess.

Aunt Jackie

Jackie was at Nicky's when I rolled in. Twenty years we plied the woods and waters in Maine, being pirates, but also campers and trippers. It takes some measure of skill, and now I marveled as I set up my little grill and cooler and *accoutrements* and began to cook the first meal I had had in a couple days. I used camping gear and skill as a tool in my work for years, and now, homeless for the moment, I thought about how much harder life is for a lot of people every day all over the world. The gear and skills develop interest, and I wanted to make a quick connection with the kids because besides their mother's funeral I hardly knew them. It all hinged on the amethyst crystal I showed Nathan that day, at the funeral, as we were headed back to Maine. Nathan and Cody watched me fascinated so it was working as I cooked the chicken I had hauled from the other life, the other world. I had been in Mass for all of eight hours. Maybe I couldn't replace David, but I could bring my memories and experiences with him into my new life in their orbit, so they may know him, a little.

Jackie and I did not really know each other that well. She was with David for twenty years so she isn't a stranger but she was his third wife. I don't know. We had been to their wedding just a few years ago, me and Marla and the kids, at the little chapel at Bug Light on Casco Bay. My sons had a close bond of their own with David, and I would have given anything to have his voice there with me then and in the days to come. T.C. had flown to California with him to see Kevin and his clan not long ago.

I cooked my chicken and was about to ask Nicky what my options were, when he flanked me, having put it together without being told or asked.

"How is Sherry?" he asked me.

She was not good. He did not seem to know. My dad had been on his own, but what could anyone do? I was in the house with him and I was already having to figure out what he needed. This would not change, he was uncannily preemptive at anticipating my needs, but incapable of asking for help for himself. And NoraGee appeared to be in the same boat. It doesn't matter if people are close by. It's like being in a prizefight with no rounds and no timeout.

Nicky threw it right out with Jackie sitting right on the stone wall in his driveway watching her grandkids. "Jackie says you can stay with her."

Had not occurred to me. My grandparents' old house, David's house. A place where I had years of memories, my earliest and best memories… the luck of it was unbelievable. I would love to stay there, holy cinnamon toast fuck.

"Doesn't your son live with you?" I asked her. I was still feeling this out. Like I said, she doesn't know me directly one-on-one that well.

"He's got nothin' to say. You're family." That was as definitive as it gets. She had already told him, apparently. I was caught up in their love and protection.

It was time to commence my new relationship with Jackie, the one where she really knows me, all of me. That escalated quickly. Time to roll the dice, full disclosure. Dickie-Kai, Baby.

"I smoke a LOT of pot," I told her.

"Just don't smoke it in the house."

I… would not. Not in *that* house, no way. I had been smoking pot under new rules for about three months since I first untethered, and sitting in my car at Wal-Mart, or just about anywhere, was something I was way too comfortable with already. I was in a state of *Hagakure,* true lack of Give-Fuck. But smoking weed in Grandma's house, I couldn't have done it if she did, anyway. She lit her cigarettes in the house and walked out on the porch and I could feel the disapproval from the white mist that was my Grandmother's spirit, near me a lot in the coming days. All the ghosts came around when I went back to Grandma's house. I even had a couple I brought with me. Getting crowded in here. Even my grandfather had never smoked in the house at all, at least not in my lifetime. My grandmother's ghost disapproved, but she knew she was long dead, and the world had moved on.

Okay. I had a home, for now, and it *was* home. Home never stops being home. I guess it could be. To some Cuiviénen there is indeed no returning, so says J.R.R., writer of Tomes.

Tomes

Tomes… are not just books. Tomes… are things that contain knowledge. Secrets. Ways to be strong. Knowledge truly is power, and the first repository of Tomes in my life as a child was the one I was about to crash at for an indeterminate amount of time.

Yes, there had been books in my grandmother's house… unbelievable books. What made this place special was also that this great repository of knowledge and experience of my life was sitting in between two others, all part of a greater whole, but each with its own piece of my heart, and claim on specific areas of life experience (Horton Hears a Who!). You see, by 2019 the two houses on either side were inhabited by strangers, but what had been my mother's childhood home (my grandma's house, the one over the river and through the woods, my Uncle David's house and its own incarnation of awesomeness, now the home of his widow, sad and hurting on her own, alone), had been flanked on either side by family too. She was mightily being a grandmother to those two little boys so dear to the heart that had stopped beating in her arms, right down the hall outside the room I would be sleeping. When I was a kid and stayed in that room, the house on one side was where David lived with his family, and on the other side was where my grandmother's youngest brother lived with his son, the youngest of my mother's generation, and close enough to be a young adult when I was a wee one, my cousin Scott.

I was surrounded by a huge chunk of my earliest memories, and a large percentage, really, of all of them. I read old books here about the origin of superstitious beliefs, tales of hauntings and ghosts, science books, history books, encyclopedias by the hour. I watched Star Trek as a small kid when my parents came for dinner and to hang with Gram and Gramp, cartoons in the afternoons, and my grandfather taught me many, many things that had held up and been built upon. I held a three-foot-long snakeskin once on the spot where David died years later. There were ancient microscopes, instruments, and an old balance scale made of agate. To a child, it was a limitless house of wonders, both in objects, and the words I heard there exchanged, my grandmother had several brothers, and all of them had gone to fight WW2, the big one. I heard war stories when I was a child and old men think little boys don't pay attention. When I played in the dirt, I listened and I heard men who had been in the hell of war talk and share about that Hell, unmindful that the horrors they were sharing as only those can among like souls were being… attended. David's house had its own treasures, and he had been a firefighter, and as I have mentioned, had a love for the taboo, that which you COULD NOT JUST GET, the unusual, the unique, even the forbidden. David was always my best and loudest advocate for those things which are not mom-approved. *Through him I saw my first Playboy, firearm, and tasted wine, one that was HARD TO GET HERE on a Christmas morning when I was ten. My mom, I would always look at her in moments like this, and if David was involved, she seemed to know it was one battle she would not win. She deferred to her younger brother in these matters, to my great salvation. I saw a nude adult woman in a photograph for the first time in David's house, and later as a teenager, and Scott was a young man living next to Gramp alone, I would take refuge there, and smoke and drink beer, and timidly ask my cousin if he would sell some pot to me. I can still remember him laughing, handing me two raw handfuls of swaggy homegrown wrapped in the Wootown Evening Gazette. Uncle Peter's house was a time capsule Tome in its own right, because as a small child, Scott's teenage room was a snapshot to a time that had passed by since he was a middle schooler, but virtually unchanged. The 1960's. Scott had this poster in his room that scared the fuck out of me when I was a kid, and now I'm going to buy it. I first read the words when I was four, but before I could read, the picture depicted an ogre of a caveman carrying a club though an orange and blue 1960's velvet acid poster and gave me bad dreams a couple times. Then I read the words and I liked the caveman. I tried to live by them ever since, such was my understanding of their ramifications as I grew, but they too speak a Code, and it can be a handy one, when things get... dicey.*

The poster said, in big blocky, rocky blue, orange color vibrating blast:

"Yea, though I walk through the Valley of the Shadow of Death, I shall fear no Evil. Because I am the meanest son of a bitch in the valley."

***

I snapped back from that recollection like I had been snatched by a mantis and hauled rudely backward. I crossed a hundred feet, and 46 years of time and memory, in one second or so, from the room where that poster once hung, in the house next to Jackie's, Uncle Peter's old place, to the front seat of the car next to the Bonsai Garden. I shook, again, like a dog.

I loved that poster. It works better with "meanest motherfucker". Meanest <u>motherfucker</u> in the valley. That's how I say it, when I do, when I need to reach down and grab a hold. Another Tome was the Dungeons and Dragons Player's Handbook. I never played the game, but I loved spectating it when I could and I read all of those books with true scholarship. Pete the Treeherder had found an old Player's Handbook, identical to the one I had had as a kid, at Pick-a-Pound a couple years back. I love recovering old books, old tomes, once had and lost in the rough waters of life's voyage and all its shipwrecks and losses. I was starting to think about the belongings I would not see again, at least for some time.

The Last Autumn

2016.

Ella was 12. We had had some crazy good times. Earlier this summer, knowing she was getting on in years, I had contemplated the Doorway. As I have mentioned, psychedelic drugs had affected me profoundly and positively. Twice, freshman year in college. Twice, in the Old Blue Lambda Delta house. Twice more at (one each) Grateful Dead and Jerry Garcia shows, the latter, Old Orchard Beach, Sept 9th, 1989. Keelin's future birthday. I had eaten mushrooms about three times in the interim years from 1992 to now, 2016. There had been many years without the Doorway. Most of my experience with it was dorm rooms and Dead shows, with a side of frat house and river trip. Until now.

In the summer of 2016, Ella and I went to the marsh with two hits of acid, blessed Pieces grass, and a bottle of Jack Daniel's Sour Mash Tennessee whiskey. I was Type-2 diabetic and would not know until the fall. That night, we saw two different thunderstorms frame the horizon, and a meteor shower in between them, with the Milky Way blazing in the background.

The Marsh, as always, was alive with life and sounds and this was the first real time I opened the Doorway, consumed LSD, as an experienced professional healer, teacher, samurai, and father with an almost grown family. This was the same water Lono and I had come to with Mr. Nimbus after Ella was gone. It remains in our memory together as our greatest, bestest, most funnest night we ever had together. That night our souls were truly joined together forever, and Ella and Candace the White have both since taught me… Death is a Doorway too.

Come to think of it, Candace died five years before Ella, and Ella and I had been out here a few times in remembrance. It had been the last time I drank wine for what would be quite a very long time and many miles indeed.

The morning found us among great flocks of birds feeding on great schools of fish, and in the middle of this a small white fluffy duck with a jet-black bill flew through this cacophony, oddly out of place with the dive-bombing terns and sweeping gulls. There were even Great Blue Heron at this dawn breakfast, and Ella and I just watched together in awe, and laughed, and laughed. We traveled into the marsh interior that day, two salty pirates in a canoe, encountering yuppie paddlers from the bird center who were far too horrified by our appearance and demeanor to even try to mask it. I heard kayakers whisper, "Don't make eye contact", and Ella and I just rolled in the canoe. No one took me up on a draft of the John D., but it was 7 am, so…

The second most funnest night Ella and I had ever was the last time we were at Turkey Neck together in 2015. I had taken her off on a solo fishing excursion, and it had worked out that the Boothbay boys had just drank and drank all day and watched TV, so when Ella and I rolled in after dark on the last day, I was still in Rock-and-Roll mode, and they had moved on to we-have-to-drive-home-tomorrow mode. Ella and I listened to music on my truck radio until dawn and I drank Jack Daniels under the spring moon at South Twin Lake.

That last autumn, Pete had the idea of taking a long, lazy exploratory trip up through Rangely so we did, with Ella, and we made it all the way to the top of the long Richardson lakes, where we three had shared so many miles under the keel and would never return to together again.

As we reached to the apex of our journey that day, on the shores of Anklebreak, where I had last been a month before she had come into my life, where we stood now, about to turn back towards southern Maine, this… this was the farthest point we ever made it to together. Like Moses and Joshua seeing the Land of Milk and Honey for the first time, we looked ahead over that little pond that day into the future that we would not make it to together. Our time, our love and experience were behind us now.

Ella drank from Anklebreak Pond, and we turned back toward the car, and the first light sharp snow of winter began to fly around in the swiftly risen wind. Winter was almost here, in Northern Maine, and would come south to us all soon enough.

Later, as we made our way south, Pete and I stopped and scouted out a lot of land. I found a rock there that was gray and round on the back, but when turned over, it revealed a red heart. I gave it to Marla when we got back. Later, shortly later, when I told Marla I was going to really leave her, she cried and asked me, how could you give me that? That was special, and I thought it meant we were going to try? I felt sad about that that day, and I had not taken the Heart Rock. There are three others. There's a gray one with a fossil clam in it from Blueberry Ledges

Trail near KTAADN. There's a smooth brown one that looks like impossible polished mud from Gould Island in the holy Saco. And there is the Laughing Dog.

Pete and I, and Ella, showed up early and went to put in for the Old Stretch, the Swan's Falls to Brownfield run. We had good liquor, and we were old salts at this now. It was simple to us now, we had done it so much, and we own this river.

Usually, you throw it in, and get underway, and commence to drink. As I did this, Pete overturned his canoe getting in, and Ella and I were laughing so fucking hard at him thrashing around, I had to just go over to the far side and ground and wait. We were hysterical. I looked down and saw a nice hunk of stone with some nice large fluorite in it, but nothing special. We got underway, and I tossed it in my aft scuppers and we drank our asses off and owned the river like the pirate kings we are.

The next morning, we woke up on the island, in the pond that lies secretly off the river. We had the island, and apparently the whole lake to ourselves for now. Pete was gone, fishing, I figured. I went to the canoe to get about the day, and that's when I saw the rock from yesterday. When I turned it over for the first time, there was a beautiful perfect crystal pocket in it. It remains the most geologically interesting specimen I ever found, so far. There are three rocks associated with the First Age of the Pirates, with Ella. The fourth is the Rangely Red Heart rock, but Marla spoke of it like she did, and I had left it in Scarborough.

***

I had some flowing emotions as I landed at Jackie's and the whirlwinds started to quiet down a little, and I was able to stop moving long enough to get a bearing, a fix. No use trying to plot a course yet, and something was missing, and foul. The growing feelings I was having about my boys were starting to fuck with me, and I tried to fight it, but I started to feel betrayed by them, and it didn't make sense. I did not realize, but I was in a state of shock and confusion.

I landed next to the Old Japanese Maple tree, the first sanctuary tree. For the moment and foreseeable future, I was home. Not just landed, but home.

Ghosts, Bonsai, Sun Tzu & Max

My grandmother was there with me in those weeks, and so were David and Gramp. All three died here, and whenever I went into the basement, the most charged and focused portal in the house, out of the corner of my eye I would frequently catch a faint white mist, and a feeling of warmth, safety, and confidence. Be Still. Ride the spiral. Ride the Whirlwind. I did.

I was just learning how to use a smartphone. I had had one now for about six weeks and I was astounded at the difference it made, especially since I was driving around unfamiliar territory. The amount of hassle I was avoiding was profound and I could not stop recalling times when I was young without a talking car map and I would get lost looking for shit. Once left an hour early for a job when I was first driving and I got lost on the way there.

One of the things that just kind of happened was I somehow started getting a daily Sun Tzu quote on my phone. Every morning, there he was. It became a little piece of flotsam to hang on to, since shipwrecked and adrift was how I felt. I was trying to focus on what to do, but the blood from what had happened with T.C. and Keelin was still everywhere, and I was in shock.

There was a lot to make happen. David and my grandfather both manifested as senses of presence, both admonishing me, in a good way. Not with voices I could hear, words, but rather a knowing they were there, and an ability to perceive. They were helping me transition to the now and look ahead. I began to break things down. David had a bonsai garden throughout his front yard. He had been years tending and growing it. T.C. had helped. He loves Bonsai. I wanted to connect with them and share these moments. I should be in a positive place of peaceful healing, having escaped Marla unscathed, I still thought. Next to the stone walkway that is not used now, there is an old Japanese Maple tree. My grandfather planted it when I was a toddler, I recall it. It drew every Japanese beetle in the area for years. Later, I understood Earth and Nature, and invasive species, but the little bronze beetle was the first for me, and the hate my grandparents had for them, my father too, was visceral and personal. The Bonsai Garden is lit at night, and I sat out there and smoked weed and played harmonica, screaming in pain in this Godsend of a new voice. I called Geary Sloane one night from the Bonsai Garden and we spoke about my mother's state, and my father's. Geary without hesitation validated for me that it was okay to facilitate my mother's transition out of the house, away from my father, before one or both got somehow to level three of fucked. Yeah, you were spot on Geary, and I already knew it, but it was a lot easier that someone helped me spell it out to myself. It was good I was here, I was away from Marla, and everything was as it should be, except something had happened with my sons.

As I settled into a safe place, as I got used to the memory cascade that went on all the time, the new discovery of old places, and new, starting to assemble new Pieces, I started to think about the two most important Pieces of my life, that were suddenly and inexplicably absent.

Jackie and I went from almost strangers, really, to close friends. She spoke of David all the time, his memory, and we spoke with excitement about how I could be here while Nathan and Cody grew up. Not David but the Pirate King ain't nothing? We both, I think, were trying to find something in the now to make up for what was lost. I should have felt great, and I definitely did not. I was also mindfully trying to be focused on priorities, like helping dad make funeral arrangements, procure a cemetery plot, and purchase a headstone, one for mom, someday probably not far off, relatively speaking, and someday, hopefully far off, for him. These are three separate things, a funeral, a plot, and a monument. Dad also needed to get a lawyer. I did *not*, and Dad never once mentioned it, that they in fact had a lawyer for many years. The fact that this never occurred to him, in years to come, would tell me what I first started to suspect now. I was worried that Dad was in shock, a little, and not fully operant, but he gave no indication of it, not really. Maybe I just couldn't see it. Maybe I will never know. I did, however, find Nicky the Gun, and I will come back to him. First, Max.

Max. I met Max at Wendy's funeral, for a handshake. When I had connected with Nathan for the first real time, too, that was. My parents were both there, and people who had not seen Sherry in some time, even the ones who had seen her at David's funeral, were visibly shocked. All four of my family were there and me and the boys worked together working the room and keeping an eye on Nana and Papa. Yeah, when Wendy died, things were normal in my family, as far as I knew. We were a good team, and on the ride back to Maine that day we did, I remember now, discuss the Nana situation, because her decline was obvious, and had kicked up a bit. We were all still together in Maine then, and I never thought I would be moving back to Mass as I had now, except maybe to help out temporarily. Now, about Marla, there was no shock, no sadness, there was no love to be lost and had not been for a long time, far longer on her end, and in secret, than in mine. I shed no tear when I buried that marriage. Like Ella, it had to be put down, because it was in pain. Unlike Ella, who I miss every day, I did not grieve the marriage, not once. I was nothing but relieved. Then I looked down, once I got to my first safe harbor, and saw that I was covered in blood, my own, and it wouldn't stop. In fact, it was starting to run.

Later, it was later, when it started to spurt. I was wounded. I did First Aid in Maine and ran. Now, I peeled off the field dressings and looked metaphorically, and gasped, metaphorically, in appalled dawning horror. Not metaphorically.

It was the boys that had me fucked up, severely fucked up. I was attendant to my responsibilities, and I knew I was compromised, and I didn't know if I was headed for some kind of crash. Max had been at Wendy's funeral, and all I knew about him was 1) he had had a tough life. My parents both had a soft spot for him, and he and my Uncle David had gotten along OK, but were not particularly close. No one, I would soon learn, was close to Max. 2) Max had had a run with the drugs, but was clean now, suboxone aside, and had been living with Jackie and working a job, and was stable. And in profound pain. I felt it from him immediately, as soon as I walked in that first day, disguised as anger, not at me, just there. In fact, Max and I got along from the start, my own aversion to any drama or conflict notwithstanding and the practical point that I had to live here, and didn't want to test Jackie like that after her merciful intervention. This guy was an angry driver, a loud, opinionated son of a... sorry, a loud, opinionated <u>motherfucker</u>, and had a really short smoldering fuse. It was pain, and because I could see that, not only did I like his Orange-Clown-President-loving ass immediately, but I also didn't much give a fuck about politics at this point, or really much else, except the wind and the storm and the confusing happenings swirling all around me all the time. And the blood. What was all this blood? Thank God for the self-induced insanity of LSD. Perspective. Also, practice. Practice maintaining. Maintaining, like for example, a straight face when the blue lights come on behind you and you know its jedi mind trick time or who really is that one phone call to? Max's part in my story, it turned out to be bigger than I thought it was going to be, at first. He was intelligent, and between coffee on the back porch with Jackie unpacking all the Pieces of my old life she did not know, we found time to watch the HBO Chernobyl docudrama. What a terrifying event. Perspective was coming from different directions; I was in an eye of one of the storms. There was some measure of quiet and peace. Uh, perspective... I was in a place that oozed warm memory and laughter and love from every pore of its old wood trims. There was a fucking bonsai garden I could walk in and try to think like, to try to be samurai. If ever there was a time for toughness and discipline, loyalty and duty, I was in it, in it to my eyes and felt fit, felt like my whole life was training for what was coming next. The situation with T.C. and Keelin, it stank. Something stank. But it was a place of much healing, early on, and I needed to replenish my reserves. I did not have time for it, but I was bleeding.

As I spoke with Jackie those weeks, between my errands out of that sanctuary and bacta-tank, for the first time, with some perspective, I started to postulate what might have happened. Another mistake. I should have thought about what was happening.

The first night I was there, as I ran out of things to keep me in motion, on three hours sleep in the last fifty hours or so, it was Max who told me that it was time for me to hit the rack, and hit the rack I did, but not before a quick triple scroll through the Big Three. Bumble, Tinder, Plenty o' Fish. Nothing. I awoke in the full sun feeling like I had actually slept, like *really* slept. In the very same bed, in fact, that I had stayed in when I was four, and had been here with my grandparents on New Year's Eve and had stayed up to watch the BALL DROP! I felt like King Midas and King Kong that New Year's Day, 1974. I felt kind of like that now, and before I sat up to carpe the diem, I reflected on the journey that four-year-old had had, what had transpired in the world, since the last time I woke up feeling so rested, oddly, in this same bed and room and house, so many long worlds and miles ago. Circles. Closing, opening, all over, all the time. I could feel the vortices of energy and power, and in it, on that wind, was something fell, and between harmonica screaming and smoking in the driveway, walking, washing and cuddling Lucifer the West Highland White terrier that Jackie pampers to the point that the dog is visibly embarrassed, all the coffee talks, trips over to West Allenton to do whatever the order of the day was over there, I started to look around me, and ahead. Jackie and Lucifer the West Highland White terrier kept me busy, mostly spoiling him.

Lucifer helped, a lot. He's a stone-cold killer at heart, a well-pedigreed ratter, and he was loving the Man. I was the Man in his dog mind. I can connect with dogs, and since we shared a house and he loved me right away, and I missed my sweet old girl, it was kind of like it was with Max. It would have been weirder if we hadn't become buddies. I knew how to talk to him, and he sensed my state internal, and he did his job well. I miss my girl. Ella. Not the ex, fuck. No, I have to say… that's the one thing that feels pretty good. The new despair was clouding the relief at the absence of the old. I sat in my car and smoked and missed Ella and screamed through my harmonicas to the universe. See me, motherfucker. I am still standing.

Max was exactly like a hundred young men I had known, but this one had not met me when he was young, and I felt sad about what could have been. You can't help wondering sometimes, had things been different, had I never left but somehow found my way to work with youth. You just never know what may have been different, better, or worse.

She babies Lucifer and puts bows in his hair. I encouraged him to chase shit on walks. Jackie can't run around and chase him, and I did, all of that as the Autumn came on. In the last few days of summer, I was outside with Lucifer, and he was running through the tall grass snuffling and snarfling happier than a pig in shit, and he stopped suddenly to look at me, and like the developing theme here, I saw something that was both a little horrifying, and devilishly hilarious. Because this little hunter was smiling from ear to ear, and completely unaware that smack dab on top of his head was a dark black field spider, a "Wolfie" the size of a Franklin half dollar. Neither one seemed to care, and before I could reach for my phone, Lucifer darted into some thick grass tufts and the spider was gone. Later, around Halloween, I took one of those plastic spiders and staged the shot, because those toy plastic ones you put in fake cobwebs are the same size, so it was accurate. It's the same principle I used years ago at Sweet Shores to demonstrate blowgun skill. I wouldn't kill a real spider for this, I'm no hunter, let alone trophy hunter, but that doesn't mean I can't have the skill of a hunter. So, one trip down the Saco, with witnesses, I picked a relative target, an inanimate one, like a leaf, and sent a dart straight into it from my canoe at forty feet. Later, I took a toy spider and put it in a jar with a dart through it and explained in my best pseudo–Aussie Crocodile Dundee voice, "I took 'em from me canoe, I did." And that was how I used to explain to Sweet Shore kids about a no-kill path, why I would not kill a spider, or a butterfly, to put into a glass case, or to show off some notion of prowess by taking life without need, other than pride. Blowgun: the best of the best tool for working with kids. No contest. Magic. Has all the elements, especially the forbidden fruit, not-mom-approved appeal. I got fired from at least one job for using it, and argued with virtually everyone else why it was awesome, but I stand by it. So do the kids who got to play with it, and learn that they could do something well, and there may yet be things like a blowgun, that they did not know existed yesterday, and actually have some talent or skill with. That's a good thing to teach kids, especially hurting ones (or ones that hurt). Teach Curiosity, Inspire Wonder. My alternate way of looking at things was blessedly challenged while I lived with Jackie and Max. I have had a near death experience, and recently viewed Heaven in the sky across the river. My own perspectives and expressions were jarring to the unfamiliar. Fortunately, they ate it up. Some guy came to work on Jackie's house and his kid was with him. I dragged out my work stuff, the rocks, the harmonicas, the coins and games and other trinkets that were manifestations of David and my mothers and grandfather influences on me. I could feel their legacy, as I watched Jackie watch me with awe as I blew this cool little shy kid's mind and dragged him out of his shell so fast he was laughing when he realized, too hard to be scared, or shocked.

Hey… I am a fucking ***professional***.

***

Right now, at this moment in Jackie's house I felt that wave come over me. This may have been the first time I noticed this consciously, but when I heard this kid laugh, I felt my feet land on stone. I was… grounded in this. What was done was done. I was trying to stand on a tripod that had two legs kicked out. The only thing I had right now was this, the power of who I am. Whatever else they say about me when I leave this world, let them say children loved me, and I them. It was all I had to hold onto that felt life flotation, where the challenging stuff felt like it was a drag. Its energy balance, of course, and I knew it, but when you're really in the Spiral, it can be really hard to see. I took a moment to enjoy the simple timelessness of making this kid laugh in this house, as I had, and my own sons, and all the other things that had happened here. It felt good to be sitting here, and causing laughter to soak into these old walls. I was clinging onto everything I could that would float. Being good with kids, that is something no one will ever take away. The kid's dad finished his hammering and gathered in the kid. He looked at him, and saw him smiling, and saw the spark of curiosity and wonder in his eyes. He looked at me and smiled and nodded. A high compliment, in today's world, to know you can show people immediately that you are safe, a shelter. An Ally. I wanted to preserve these things I had, these skills and abilities so it was good to know I still had it. I didn't have much, but I had that. I practiced with my bamboo sword in the Bonsai Garden.

***

Speaking of skills and abilities, I was in the lifeboat of my cylon in all things. I wrote my resume on it. I looked for jobs on it. I looked for the lawyer for Dad, places to buy this or that… everything. I showed Dad all the things I was doing with it as I learned. I went over to Jon and Mary's and Mary walked me through uploading my resume. I wrote cover letters and sent them out. I went back to Jackie's at night and screamed through my harmonica in my car. I missed my dog. I missed my kids, and I wondered how long it would take to normalize things. My father's journey with Mom was front and center, and the idea that the boys were withholding and how it affected Papa started to piss me off. I fought it. I broke a harmonica in the fog and the breeze was picking up. I tried to breathe. It was becoming normal that I could not, but laughing along with these strangers that were my own eased the transition.

And, I was feeling untethered from the big show, the work. The kid at Jackie's that day was more cool water, and

Jackie's bemused smile and pride, I think, for my mom's sake, put the water in a tall frosty glass for me. I had been so distracted; I didn't realize how parched I was. My spiritual piss would have been dark gold swanky syrup. That means you need to drink. Drink deep, as ye can.

***

… and fill your canteens, lads. Some of you are going to be in Hell by nightfall, and you will have need of water.

-------------------- *Col. J.L. McDonough*

Shiloh, Tennessee (The "Place of Peace")

6 April, 1862

***

We talked at length about those two little ones in my life now, or rather, I was now in theirs. Jackie is their de facto Grandmother, and this house made that even more real. They do not know what they have lost, but I feel wrong somehow, and the idea of being here with them during these years felt right but I did not understand why.

It was time to think about a job, so I had been exploring mental health jobs and what I was looking at, for options, money, the future. With my boys not in the picture. I could not see them. I looked for them, and they were not there. There was so much blood in my eyes. As the initial tempest that had raged from Midsummer's Night died away and I saw some sunshine, the waters calmed a bit, and I tried to navigate. To get a fix, gauge the stars. My eyes…

My eyes were stinging. I wiped them with the back of each hand and shook myself like a dog.

Breathe.

Jon & Mary

Jon and Mary have three grown boys and two of them still live with them, along with a girlfriend. I last remember Little John, their youngest running around the old camp at Rocky Pond the same way we used to. Chris, their oldest, was getting married in October, and they were building their new house while living in the one Mary and her family had grown up in, a short drive through the heart of the Shire, on Cross Street in Allenton, five minutes from Jackie's. My first stage of transition that I had Pieces moving and under some modicum of control, what little I could, was in view, as a stage, a place, a *staging area*. Mary was indispensable in those first days, helping me get resumes together on her computer nights between getting food for mom and dad and coming back to the Bonsai Garden with Jackie, Max, and Lucifer. They absorbed me into their bustle of all of them together without even a ripple. Home again. Jon was elated to see me, and that I was home. He gave no indication of this at all, except to act utterly convincingly as if I had never left. It was like I never had left, we just picked right up like it always had been. Thank God I can't drink anymore since I'm diabetic now, just trying to keep up with any of them would have leveled me. Barts was younger than me, and we didn't hang out as kids, but I commented to him and Jon that without my tutelage at Rocky Pond growing up around handling one's drink, mostly with Chipper and Jon, I probably never would have gotten noticed enough to join Old Lambda Delta, because the first friends I made in that house freshman year were older brothers who marveled at the little freshman that could drink all night with the older Lambdas and still find his way home. It was unheard of (okay, I did not find my way home every night).

Some of these guys were serious alcoholics when we were in college, but I never had any problem with that and I was almost always the last man standing. Okay, there were times I was down and out early, to be sure, but I had earned those and their tales, too. No big deal, it was just growing up at Rocky Pond with my cousins, the Pierces and the West brothers, Chipper, and Wonderboy. Talk about life training. Barts laughed. After growing up on the Pond, I had graduated to Animal House. It just was. No room here, really for all the tales of Old Lambda Delta, but they creep in. Lambda Delta guys are everywhere. You probably know one. And if you put a bunch of us together, it somehow makes sense. I explained to Barts on Jon and Mary's porch in Allenton that knowing his older brothers and Jon had kind of prepared me for college.

"Yeah," Barts said in his huge baritone. He looks like Mr. Clean let himself get a little fat.

"I've met a lot of people that Chipper has, uh… mentored."

We all roared with laughter the way they did all the time, the way they had without interruption all the way back to those muddy damp sunburnt days at Rocky Pond, and my voice joined theirs like an instrument that has long been silent, now part of the orchestra again, again, at long last.

Mary was there whenever I blew in to answer questions I had about whatever, and ask me about Allan and Sherry, reminding me that all those years I was up in Maine with my life, my parents had their life down here, and had been at some of the graduations and barbecues I had not. She pointed me toward the three death tasks I mentioned, and the idea of needing a lawyer. I called a lot of different people from their deck in Allenton for jobs and those other arrangements, and I also had ongoing calls and messages back and forth from the people I had left behind, notably the old Pathways crew, and my friends up there. The beacons were all still lit. I was absent, not gone. Not departed. Exiled.

Nicky the Gun, like many lawyers I have met, was impeccably professional yet also personal. Unlike many I have known since, he remained that way after my father wrote him a check. He doesn't do much, in this tale, not really, but being able to talk with dad, explore his thoughts and concerns, and send a message or question to the Gun was something I was able to do, that brought peace to Dad. I hope, anyway. Dad wouldn't really complain much. That may have been a good thing, or a terrible one. I will not know it in this world.

Nick is not really known as the Gun, in fact I think no one else even calls him Nick, but I just started calling him Nicky the Gun and he reacted with lawyer hilarity. He smiled and didn't say "okay" when I called him that. Like, "okay, that's enough…" I hate that energy. My people, they will tell you, this is not a conscious choice. More like a fucking liability. It makes me provocative. He didn't go that way. I was pleased. We both felt better. Dad liked Nicky the Gun, and all the while we were together, in Hell, we were always laughing, except the times when we had to stop and weep for a time. I think Dad was weeping away from me, because he saw me bleeding. I gave him his dignity, including mentioning that there did not seem to be any more reason to keep his whiskey under the stairs in the basement, and go up and downstairs to drink it, like he had for forty-four years in this house with Mom. I can count on one hand the times I saw him drunk in my life, and I was an adult for two of them, and one of those was in the future of Now. That conversation happened after I moved in, in the Fall.

The Code: Death/The Faye Brothers

The memory tsunami just grew, okay? It never slowed; it never shrank. It dulled when I had to think, drive, or smash. It accelerated and crescendo'ed the rest of the time.

***

I have been here before, to be sure.

This is where I saw my grandmother for the last time. This is where I saw a high school bully for the last time. His mother's screams and face that day haunt me still. I looked at him and was relieved he was one less problem. I looked up and over at her, and I hated myself for thinking that. He was a fiend, there is no question. He was also loved by many, and I wondered why someone so well-loved had hated me so much, or if it mattered to them, or if they knew, the face I knew. That was a long time ago. He hung himself with a belt in the police station in Wootown in 1986. I was sitting in the backseat of the car at my grandparent's house. Jackie's now, of course. My mother asked me if I knew this kid. I said, "Yeah, he sucks ass."

They both turned around slowly. I went instantly on guard. What's this, then?

"Not anymore," my mother said. She handed me a Camton Item. West Allenton youth hangs self in Wootown PD bathroom.

That was shocking. I watched the kids in my tiny high school walk around like zombies for a week. Nothing was ever the same again after that. We were a mixed group, but a small one, and the one suicide in my high school was a collective shared trauma, and a simultaneous comprehensive loss of innocence. It also changed boundaries between students and teachers forever. I had never thought so much about all this, but this too had served me, been part of my knowledge and experience, in my own walk as a healer and teacher. I took no pleasure in this kid's death. I was almost 50. He was always going to be 16.

I realized, standing here now… I may have hated this asshole in life, but he paid his debt.

Hate is a different kind of Acid. I learned not to waste time on it. I went to High School here. Now I look around and know how much I have changed. I never wasted a minute of my life feeling bad that High School was at best a mixed bag of experiences. All I knew was when I shared tales with Anghiel about the commonplace savagery I witnessed on a daily basis (not solely to me, mind you) she was shocked. Somehow, it always manifests, that everything in the Universe really does appear to be interconnected, into some crazy pattern. Like in The Wheel of Time.

***

Mr. Faye was a real pro, so it did not matter that we did different things for a living. It turns out, there are a lot of similarities between what he and his family does, and what samurai like me do. He's a mental health pro, by extension. Doubt it, do you?

Well, maybe you should contemplate doing your job,

which is to comfort people, while they shriek and tear out their hair, and curse God, when the dirt starts falling on the box their child is in forever. It's not easy. I saw him, and he me, and we recognized each other right away, and were brethren. Brethren in… some kind of Code. Healing, loosely, I guess.

He treated my father like a king. Dad planned the management of not only Mom's death, but his own. That was a fast 30 large. Thirty thousand dollars? Okay, that's for two. I would be half. Fuck, I need to be eaten by sharks, never recovered, or donated to fucking science.

"Not for some time yet, of course," Mr. Faye said, warmly clapping both of us on our shoulders. I wanted to turn around and hug him. Actually, that was all the time. He is a huggy looking guy.

"Gonna do some fishing, I hope. Need some canoe capability. You fish, Mr. Faye?"

"I haven't fished for many years, but my Dad and I used to."

"Well, maybe we'll take you out someday."

He laughed and nodded. I smelled it, the safe place. I went right in. None of that wall energy ("Okay, that's great. Let's sit down now, okaaaay?" sicky sweet pseudo courtesy passive aggressive shit that fires me up).

"No, I'm serious. Dad caught a striper on the marsh in Maine a few years back."

"Oh, really?" That was it…

As we walked out to the car, I had enough time for a few

stories, a drink recipe, and several pictures, of Ella, and being a Pirate.

"Dad's a pirate. All you have to do is come out with me in a canoe. I'm the King of all Pirates, sir!" I was laughing. This was fun, this… oh, yeah. Well, Dad and I concurred, as I smoked a bowl and he laughed and said, "Gotta get your EEns" and we were off to select a gravestone.

"That sounds fun!" He bade us good day.

They always said cremation, Mom and Dad. Dad had just purchased caskets, and we had gotten burial plots though Allenton Municipal Works Dept. It's one guy. It was the same prick who hung me up when I came back from Maine in U-Haul. I let Dad deal with him, and watched him with heavy lids and shades, encouraging respect toward my father. Town guy did not disappoint, to his benefit.

I asked Dad why the change. He didn't know. At some point, Mom changed her mind. It was news to me.

Hustle

I saw Dad and Mom every day. Sometimes she greeted me warmly like she had that last Christmas Eve. Sometimes, she didn't recognize me, or did, and told me to get the hell out of here. Sometimes, she was outside, and Dad was chasing her around. Sometimes, she was physically aggressive. Sometimes, without provocation or warning. I always wondered how, or if, this would come out. I never wanted it to be a bash on mom, or a whine from me. The truth is, when I was a kid, sometimes my mother could be physically aggressive with little or no provocation, or warning. And the face I saw on her now when she got pissed off was exactly the same face I remembered as a kid, and over long years that face had softened in my memory because she had softened with age, as a grandmother. I saw that face again now, and I remembered. It all came back in an instant, the years of my own healing path I had already walked, and how I was different now.

And it was OK. I saw my mom as she was, scared, confused, and defenseless. And I knew I made my peace with this abusive history, indeed I did, before that day I called her from South Twin on Acid and in grief. I spent my adult life unpacking this part of my upbringing, growing. Some of this unpacking was in view of my boys. They knew I had a rough time with Nana, and I said many times how she had changed, how she could be when I was a kid. I took all that, and took it back into the arena it lives, in the home, and I used my own experience to guide others. My own mom, I now saw back into the past with my grown-up eyes, was scared and confused just like she was now, and that was why she did what she did. She had never acknowledged it, but I made my peace with that too. The people I had treated, they were like her, and she, like them, and I found not only a new understanding, but a new perspective on things she said to me over the whole course of my life, able to hear them now and appreciate them, take the intent from them. As I walked with my mother under the Mastershade Locust tree, I had pure untainted love for her, forgiveness, if there needed to be, too, and profound appreciation for how much I was loved my whole life. In that moment, a doorway opened, because I was able to remember her words and sayings and lessons without the sting or bad taste that sometimes accompanied, and I heard many things from memory, yet for the first time. They had done their best, and I was who I was. Not everyone gets these things. I felt lucky. I brought them their pizza. Sometimes I cooked and put food for later, picked up supplies, stayed at Jackie's, visited Jon and Mary, and even got to help them do some of the insulation on their new house. They fed me, and we smoked together, and they treated me like a member of their tribe. Which I am. I wrapped myself in the Pieces of my new life and tried to be strong and brave, like samurai. It's funny that they always thank me for helping them. I just laugh and say, no. No, thank *you*.

The Dragon 88/Breana

I settled into my first routine. Mornings I had coffee with Jackie while she smoked butts and I smoked pot. She put me to work walking Lucifer, and helping her lift heavy shit, etc. I was trying to process the situation with my sons, and trying to be in the present for dad. Jackie also had a lot to share from her experience, which was a window from a different set of eyes on some things I had heretofore been oblivious to.

Like the fact that Marla had been taking money, a lot of money, from my parents over the years behind my back. And my mother had spoken to Jackie about Marla. More than once.

I started to open my eyes and wipe the blood away. I tried to think, and began to realize what was really going on.

I did not like being unemployed and trying to meet someone, but the truth of my situation I thought would be enough, for the right girl. I scrolled the dating sites, because I would be damned if I wasn't going to check my wide cast nets and just be pathetic, wiling hours playing games like Tetris and Candy Crush and Fruit Ninja on your phone. That was not unacceptable unless you're in the hospital or something if you're older than fourteen. I was hunting pelt, goddammit, I'm a red-blooded American single man. I took selfies and posted them. I composed titillating profiles and updated. I got scammed, almost, a couple times. I began to marvel at how stupid some people are. I'm an idiot, in many ways, but the idea of sending money and how prevalent that stuff was astounded me. It was like hearing about a giraffe your whole life, but never seeing one until now. I would really like to get a good successful date under my belt. For the Code, if nothing else. Sex not required, but you know…

I got a hit. The Fish Site. Tinder: I want to fuck, and I don't give a fuck. Bumble: I want to fuck, but let's try to have some class about it. Plenty O' Fish: well-named. It's a food chain, that's for sure. I'm laughing out loud in my car at nights between weed smokes and screaming harmonica if it weren't for both the drug experiences I've had, and all the crazy I've seen, I would be right out of my fucking mind. A flesh, separate and apart. Way of Samurai. Shock-Trauma/battle fatigue. Profound release and relief of being unmarried. All of it, all of it, swirling all the time around me, while I choked on blood and still managed to laugh my ass off every time I saw my peeps, like Jon and Mary, and especially Genna.

So, things were kind of OK, but it would be nice to meet a girl who wasn't, you know, awful. I got the nibble. All stop, quick quiet. Quiet in the Attack Center.

She said, "Your profile is like a breath of fresh air."

Okay, she was at least real and live. No typos with weird mathematical symbols, no off-putting syntax, like labels on Asian snack food: "The eating of this product should be making pleasure."

Ha! Okay, okay… live one on the line. Jackie smiled through squinty eyes that might have been bemusement, but she was trying to project maternal disapproval. She knew better than to horn-shame me.

Rocky Pond, Lambda Delta house, and working with all kinds of people for twenty-five years, you really have to know how to laugh at life, to survive in all those situations that were formative to the face I saw now in the mirror. I try not to horrify people, but sometimes, that gun, she just fires off, so, the fact that I did not want to creep this nice girl out aside, the voice that came to me now was perfect, except for the glaring inappropriateness of its source in the soundtrack of my ADHD mind. This voice is always the one I hear when it is time to get professional, get to work, go, team, whatever. It's always him, and sometimes, as now, it's just wrong, but there he is.

It's Anthony Hopkins, as Hannibal Lecter, when he says "Okey-dokey, here we go". He says it like three times in those movies, right before he does something awful to some poor motherfucker unlucky enough to have drawn his eye.

I have a lot of inside jokes with myself that I share with my circle when they can hear it with the proper set-up. They've read the books, seen the movie, whatever. I love this, it's like little pirate secret markers to funny, the funny that we use to navigate. Or to tell friend from foe, or at least those who know Code from those who don't. So, prerequisite credentials established, some people appreciate that I say this, sometimes out loud, when it's time to get to work, get to business… and no one has ever picked up on it, and said, "Wait, did you just quote Hannibal Lecter? Dude, we're about to teach a first aid class to girl scouts!" No one, except for a very select few, close friends, all now for many years, can really appreciate irony.

Tell me what you laugh at, and I will tell you who you are.

I like to know what people find funny, and those who squelch humor, well, we generally don't get along. Cristobal, Matty Mango… they would appreciate this. I spoke to both regularly in the early days; they were keeping an eye on me. People were still asking me if the boys had talked to me. It was still fresh.

I wasn't really feeling predatory. I mean, I mentioned that for a man, it had been a long time since, you know, but I'm a Man, not a fucking animal. Believe me, I have long contemplated the nature of want and need. There is no need that drives someone to overpower another in that way, physically or otherwise. Some things are so simple, yet they exist… sexual abuse… sexual assault… these are things beyond politic.

Is that not something everyone can universally get behind? Rape is bad?

I have standards for myself. I don't know about the rest of you, but I learned about making a fool of myself for pussy a long time ago, so, there's a point. There's a point I'll just say fuck it, and fuck a squash, or something. Coffee can full of raw liver? Dad? Weigh in on coffee can full of raw liver versus squash? No, I never had a moment of, "Eww, okay, that's enough." I mean, I could have found it, but his point would have been past mine too. There are lines, and they can be hard to see, but those are the lines that you want to have when you reach out blindly in the dark. When ya pucka tightens up, boyo…

I just wanted a drink and a laugh with a woman that didn't have my destruction and misery as her only mission in life. Okey-dokey, Hannibal, you slutty buttercup, here we go…

This girl was no newbie, and she didn't play games. Just grownups getting a drink. Only one place in the entire realm presented to me, for some reason, right smack in the middle of the Shire. We took to the phone. I asked her out. She knew the Dragon, and it was fucking *on*. Ha. All right. Jackie was bemused. Max told me to count my kidneys. I like that Max did not need a getting-comfortable-with-me phase before he spouted anything he felt like, or anything that came to mind. I didn't mind, because he was truly the high-water mark of reason, and seldom off base, although merciless in assessments, like now. The cliché phrase is "brutally honest". People say that instead of saying, "I don't give a fuck what you think, or feel, I like to tell everyone what is in my head, and if you don't like it, you're the asshole." Infantile, selfish, raw, unfiltered ego, in other words.

However, brutally honest is not inaccurate. So, rather than explain why I would not be following the advice of this 37-year-old (ex-drug addict with a half a habit still with Suboxone, who lived with his mother, and had no friends, hated his job, his life, and every relationship he's ever been in has ended like my marriage just did), I smiled and said, "You know, Max. I find your honesty refreshing." Maybe I'll help him get laid for once and he won't end up in court with no-contact orders. Jackie hopes I'll rub off on him, and says so behind his back. Nicky and Kevin, whose house this is, do not like having him here, and think he is a loser. Again, perspective. What he was, was my new fucking foster brother.

Max's sage and venerable guru-like cautions aside, I did NOT need Kidney-Shield 2000 by Ronco for Breana. She was fantastic. We had a great date, a drink, laughed. Absolutely no sexual vibe was present. Neither one of us cared. It never even came up.

We were both quite content to just talk with one another, like humans do. I realized something. I was devoid of this. I have many women among my friends, beautiful, powerful, but the option of anything else was always off limits, either professionally, or 'cause, you know, marriage, but it *was* an option here, the goal for both of us, even if it wasn't happening, and that was immediately apparent, and it did not matter. I was sex starved, yes, but I had been *this* starved even more profoundly. Breana was another angel along the way and she and I stayed in contact and friends from this early autumn night in 2019 until this very day, and always will. I can say I love the first woman I met out of marriage very much, it was immediate, and it was not a rebound. It turns out, contrary to my big slut talk, and wishes, I have actual standards. Nothing ever happened between us. But we continued to stay in touch. Would that have happened without the things that were coming? I think it would have, but most of the show was lined up, the Spiral was wheeling so fast and big it could not even be tracked or perceived now. The fact is, all sane people started to cling together. Breanna and I, we were kin from the start. She turned out to be important.

The early days of autumn brought crisp mornings in my car in Jackie's driveway with coffee and weed, frost on the windows, and dreams that I would find my way to the river again, with a dog. I missed her every day. And now, I missed my boys, too.

I didn't have much chance to talk to dad for long these days when I was at the house. I did float a test balloon about Mom going to a nursing home. He was not ready. I knew not to try to coerce him. This was going to have to run its course. I needed a job. My playing improved. I made the rounds on the phone. Lono was in touch regularly, and I gave the Treeherder updates in Maine. The Cid too. My friends were standing around me like I was in a hospital bed. They showered me with flowers of laughter and love. Hold fast lads…

"He who wishes to fight must first count the butcher's bill."

------Sun Tzu, High General

Armies of the Celestial Kingdom

"Wheels of justice grind slow but exceedingly fine."

------(also, Sun Tzu)

PART 3
NO TIME TO BLEED

Autumn, 2019.

Mile Hill Rd, Allenton, Mass.

All these familial relationships were new. Only the core—Genna, Jon, Noragee—felt… ordinary, like family. They were all kind to take me in, but I was careful not to present like I had any expectations on them. I sure wasn't going to hit them up for money or anything like that, but I had a mind that if I could model some kind of stability and general awesomeness, it could not hurt if the word went up North, although there seemed to be no real communication anymore, although I knew TC had kept in touch with Christopher and they talked cars and shit over Facebook. As far as leaning on each other, that had never been the way in our family. I had never not once as a child heard about someone borrowing money and not paying it back, for example. Maybe it happened, maybe it did not, but if one's own family is the template, I didn't see it, or hear about it. More like, heard about other people they knew who did stuff like that, and how they disapproved. Things like these get into your bones, the culture of your family, whatever there is. I had a large extended family. I had grown up surrounded by characters and yarns. I took it with me across the ocean, to Maine, raised a family, became a pirate, became a samurai… and now here I was. This me. With these they's. We were starting over. As a family dynamicist, I could see all this. All of it was overwhelming.

For my part, when I was at the house waiting for them to come back, I played harmonica as loud as I could, or went and sat in the woods in the backyard, hiding from the world, from the eyes of God, licking my wounds, and counting them, and finding new and deeper ones, and rednesses and inflammations, of little something extras that had been carried in and were now…

… suppurating.

I circled around to Jon and Mary's twice a week at least and helped them get their house finished by joining the Pierce-West insulating circus. They treated me like we did shit like this all the time, for years. Like I had never been gone, but it was an elephant in the room. Christopher's wedding was approaching. As the days grew cold enough to require jackets and heaters in the house they were finishing, I was not over there as much as I wanted to be. Sometimes, I saw Dad drive by with Mom.

The other thing, ever present, was TC and Keelin. I missed them mightily by this point and it was fucking awkward to avoid the subject. I tried to stay in the place I found myself in away from Marla, which was at its core, relief. I had been liberated from the camps, but I had pulled an ejection lever on my whole old life. This was what I had left. This was what I had returned to. I was here, and I had nothing really to show for my decades away but some sparse memories. It was getting hard to tell what was real and not, and everything felt surreal. The only thing I had going for me that was of any tangible use was my resume.

Paper does not float that well in this tempest… but it's better than nothing.

In the middle of September, I had to return to Maine. This time, it was to sign divorce papers. Marla sent me the wrong courtroom number. I fucking hate courtrooms. Some people hate hospitals. I don't like them, but it's nothing like this. I drove to Maine, and the plan was that I was going to go to the house, and switch out the cars, after signing the divorce papers. I walked into that courtroom high, wide, handsome, and happy, really happy. This was it. I was free. I shook her off, and now, anything she tried to say, wouldn't be a threat to me in my career or reputation. I thought all these things.

I retrieved my bare sword blade from the house in Scarborough. Shari-loo was there. I felt so bad for her and her lost son. I just smiled at her, not allowing myself to think too much about what she may think about me now. All I hope and pray for now is that Shari-loo, Rob, and their three surviving sons who all knew me well, will really think about what is said here. And know. Shari-loo, Rob… I'm sorry you were ever touched by any of Marla's filth, especially with what you had to go through. I loved all your boys. Know me. Know the truth, please. My sons are lost, and it is not right. I was wrong in many ways. The damage was done, and I still had no idea. I was glad to switch these cars, because there were leases involved and it was just what was agreed. Marla, in direct contravention to what I had begged my boys to shield me from, took this chance to fuck with me, and play power trip games, and gloat over her power over me, to make demands that I return within 30 days, and remove twenty years of my stuff, books and pictures, from the house that she had so efficiently run me out of, despite the fact that I had left her. It was petty, and small-minded, like her, but it still bothered me and I wished I could wipe that smile right off her face now that I was free of her. But I was taking the high road for the sake of the account I was trying to give of myself to my sons, and Marla got to play her little games. Her best friend was there, her only friend, really. We had all been close once, and I had taught all four of Rob and Shari's sons how to drive. Shari lost her third son the March before all this to a fast and sneaky cancer. She was here now, supporting Marla, and I didn't trouble her, but she had been in the courtroom too, and I had hugged her in greeting and whispered in her ear: "You know me, Shari. She's lying about me." Like I said, when I saw her later at the house, I did not say anything.

Two weeks later (she gave me thirty days, in her grace and class. So much for the boys not letting her play her petty control games. I was determined to do it sooner.), I rented a U-Haul and drove it up to Maine at five in the morning. Marla was there and all my stuff was supposedly packed and in the driveway for me. The theater around all this was grand indeed. Marla was really making it look like she had thrown me out, instead of me finally saying, "You know what? You don't work, you don't fuck, and all you do is bitch and whine, and it is time for me to fly." All of this petty indignity and the satisfaction she oozed throughout it fueled my wakening anger at the things I was starting to realize and learn from my conversations with Jackie about all the years, and all the things my mother said, and what my mother really thought of Marla, all along.

One thing I failed to grab was the Red Heart Stone, the one I found in Rangely the last autumn with Ella and the Treeherder, on the long ride to AnkleBreak. I really wish I had grabbed it. Looking back now, with all the truths that matter revealed at last, I really wish I had, because Marla never tried, never cared, and deliberately made me as unhappy as humanly possible, and she never gave a fuck about her marriage, or that rock. Or me. Or even her kids, for that matter. Not with what she did, she could not have cared about them.

But I had five hours in a vehicle alone on the highway to continue to see the layers fall away at what was really going on, and shock piled upon shock, rage upon rage, and pain upon more and more pain. Breana was horrified, later when she learned more about this, because when we met, what I shared then was nowhere near the reality that I had come to learn, and that she had seen me come to know. Athena has known me for years. She was not surprised, and she validated my rage I was trying to fight. Rage feels like clarity, and I had both going on. All these women…was there some way to raise their voice, raise voices, to give the lie, to call foul? To help me recover that which was stolen, and has hurt everyone around?

I did almost fall asleep at the wheel on 95 south. Tighten up ya pucka, boyo, whoooowheeeee. Yes, I did think for a moment, "That would almost be too easy."

There was construction on Mile Hill Rd., and the guy in charge was immediately and obviously identifiable as the Townie in charge. I explained to him I lived down that way, and he asked me if it was Dave Hamilton's place. Okay, cool. "Yes," I said. "Jackie's now, in fact. Do you know them? What's your name, sir, if you don't mind my asking?"

This guy looked me in the eye and declined to give me his name.

I mention this now for two reasons. Assholes like him are everywhere. Right here, right now, where I was, I encountered this from time to time, and just had to roll with it. I did not want to create any problems for myself, and give whatever Marla had hatched any nourishment. It's just that whenever I was getting tested, and boyo did this ever stay consistent, it was always outside of my ability or wherewithal to charge the dragon. I needed to focus on Not-Me. That was easy, to put Not-Me out front. Me was *hors de combat*. Not-Me tagged in.

I moved through one day at a time, touching base with Dad, hugging mom or dodging her (chasing, a little, through the neighborhood. She walked right out into the road a couple times, and I thought, "Well, here's where someone dies.") It was Jackie, coffee and just sorting these things I had. In the gaps, women swiped by and by and by. Some people have a package of what they like in a mate, and if you've known more than one of their partners, sometimes they all have a bit of a common look to them. I had the feeling of just spinning, trying to grab onto stuff, and tell what it was, if it was important, in the dark.

I tried to get my head above the chaos around and inside me, to balance it, and fit it all together and find a solid place to ground.

I was trying to shake the feelings and get right with this new paradigm. The leaves turned and the golden hallway on Mile Hill Rd blazed bright yellow for a week. All the trees are the same kind, and every fall, this little stretch of road looks just like that, a Golden Hall through the woods that were the specific woods that whenever I heard, "Over the river and through the woods, to Grandmother's house we go," had always been the only image for me of that journey. The horse still knew the way to carry the sleigh, after all these years and as I came to the intersection on Linden St, I found myself just sitting there, in my running vehicle, watching the thousand memories of my mother turning left to go to her job, or right to go up the street where everyone else lived, or straight, the tenth of a mile to my Grandmother's house, where I now lived, having lost everything that means anything from my old life, and trying to figure out how to move from that old to this new. It began to drizzle. Autumn, gray, and wet and cold is how I felt.

All I had to go on now was applying the words I had given others. If I could not use that now, I have always been full of shit. Part of Hell is not really knowing where Truth lies anymore, of self. I was clinging on for dear life.

I was just that, now, trying to rejoin this life, these people, that I had left behind so long ago. A part of, yet apart from. My Hell was mine; Dad's was Dad's, Mom's was Mom's and the one we were all in together was also all its own. It is the nature of Hell, to be at once disjointed, and hopelessly entangled.

Be Still, and know that I am. I am Samurai. Indeed, I have always been, and everything swirling around me now as

I sit next to the bonsai garden with my uncle's ghost, smiling at me though sad, but happy that this one has come home, was in testament of that, down to the stupid luck I kept testing, pouring nips of Irish cream and butterscotch shots into my coffee on the way home from Camton and a driving lesson for Little Jon. It is good to have reasons not to die. I have many, Thank God. After 32 years in Maine raising a family and walking a solitary path, I had become something, something that once was more common in the Old World. Something not seen as necessary now. For all of me, like in the movie, I cannot help but wonder…

What could be… more necessary?

I had to hang on tight to these things, because they weren't just for fun, or for talk, or to make life more colorful. It was all I had left of me, and I was in a terrible place in a way I had never known, and it wasn't getting any better.

Has anyone heard from my sons?

One of the things that started to flag for me as I spoke with Jackie about what I had just come from (I asked her, is five years without sex a good enough standalone reason to quit a marriage?) was that my mother trusted her as time went by, enough to include her in the circle of the family that we do talk about shit, a little. My mother never thought much of Marla's chronic complaining and ailments. According to Jackie, they seemed "convenient" at times. It pissed her off that Marla had refused to earn a paycheck, and that's when the first piece of the horrifying truth first knocked me upside the head.

If I had been working multiple jobs, and we had lived

paycheck to paycheck, what about all the money that Marla apparently asked my parents about regularly over years? Over *years*!

Jackie knew secrets. There were more, but I had to let that sit, for now. My mom had vented to her. What had Marla said to my boys to make them stop talking to me like this? It just didn't make sense, but I was seeing my own memories, through the eyes of my mother, and the things she talked to Jackie about. Over coffee, like we were now. This felt like something I should be paying attention to.

Nathan and Cody were about in these days, and I had time to just hang out with them. My conversations with Jackie were not allowed to just happen, because I would not air this in front of the boys, and when they were there, I wanted to give them attention and build that relationship. TC had sent me a cryptic message back during the first one week when I moved out of the house after trying to rescue Ella. It said something about "moving on to my next victims". A lot of things were in play, and I had been unbalanced for a long time, then, re-unbalanced. It's unsettling and unnerving and people get it and I had the benefit of Acid mind to just be able to tolerate how fucking insane and tangled up everything was.

This was the future. These are my "next victims." I felt like I had a chance to just demonstrate that Marla's lines of shit, that I was unstable? Crazy? Were just observably lies. She had tried to gaslight the shit out of me for years and everywhere I dug into her words I found more lies. Jackie knew that Marla's mother had stopped talking to us, and that she blamed me, but little was known about this. It had been shrouded in secrets at the time, and I had never seen these so-called letters, but I knew about them.

This is family, and I was here now; even though how I got here was not exactly in my life plan there were blessings abounding. It is just really hard to keep all these different things from clashing into one another. If things were as they should be, T.C. and Keelin would also be reconnecting with this whole side of the family again. It hadn't taken much, really, for there to be a strong foundation. And I had never needed to look at things the way I was trying to now, as in, what the fuck happened? But it was not, "what just happened".

I played through my harmonicas in the last warm evening rain in my car next to the Bonsai Garden.

(Hail Mary, full of Grace, I could use a little about now…)

When I first got home, we took mom to UMass and got her sized up. Her diabetes was my main concern at that point. It was odd to me that she apparently was not even diagnosed with cognitive decline, Alzheimer's, dementia. I met the doctor that had been charged with their care for the years since Dr. Hart retired. To say he was not on top of their health, either one of them, would have been an understatement, but he retired soon after all this anyway. None of her Pieces were falling off. Mentally, she was confused, angry, crying, and laughing and silly with dad and me; all over the place. Dad did not leave her for two days in the hospital, and I knew that moving forward I had to factor that into what we were doing. He would not leave her side, if he could. When they were letting mom out of the hospital Dad clipped a curb and popped the tire of his car. My phone had shut itself off without warning or explanation about two hours earlier…

***

It just quit. We were waiting to leave. My phone would not work. I started to panic. I breathed. I knew dad must be tired but all I could do was plan to tail him home and get them settled. It had been oppressively sticky hot all day and I was still not used to the foul air with no hint of ocean in it, only city fumes. Mom was okay, for the moment. She knew we were leaving, and it kept her quiet while we coordinated our departure. I saw him roll over the curb, and heard his tire pop. This was a real emergency. It was hot but the sun was going down. I told him to give me a minute and I would call AAA. I grabbed for the cylon as I remembered it was last reported tits up. It blipped on. Thank God. I felt like wanting to just weep when you're a kid, now I almost wept with relief. My luck, it seemed, was holding. I had been at that point where you just want to go home. I just wanted to go home, and I could never go home again. I looked down to the lake as I sat there waiting with them. I watched Mom and Dad sit, and chat, and pass the time, as they had their whole lives, and that was over for them now, as so many things were over for me now. All things end, this I know, and it is the process *of going through those endings that is the hard part. I learned to sail down on that water. Now, here I was again.*

For me, I look around at Earth, at the land, at buildings. I looked down across Lake Quinsigamond and remembered Al Fearne. I sat in the sail loft with him and he taught me to splice rope, and tie knots, and navigate the old way. I had learned to sail at Regatta Point, and later, as a Boy Scout, I got the idea that I could do a small boat sailing merit badge with Al, if he'd have it. Al was a teacher. As I would be. As I am now. The memory tsunami never really stopped, but it got more intense, especially sitting by a lake full of happy fun childhood memories, watching a sunset too beautiful not to just take notice of, reflecting on my sons and my own time as a father, and watching my father try to cling on to the last of what was left between he and his love. His pain was poignant, and my pain was too, and throughout all of any of this in the days to come I was ever struck by the way I have come to look at the world, after long years away living an illusion, and now looking at the world that had faded into the place where we remember fondly, and vaguely, and now it was in my face and up my nostrils and on my skin. It was an hour before AAA came and fixed the tire. Mom and Dad sat and chitchatted and I paced and walked over and told mom I was home from Maine for a while, and everything was okay, over and over. I got them home and before I made it back to the Bonsai Garden I stopped at Jon and Mary's. I just sat with them. They weren't saying much either, they were all busy, but I needed this place and these people around me tonight, even if I couldn't talk anymore. Dad and Mom were safe back at home and the sun was coming up tomorrow. I showered the hospital smells and the smells of city off me when I got back to Mile Hill Rd.

***

Dad and I had settled into connecting every day, taking care of the food and whatever needed to be taken care of, and I wandered between Jackie's, Rocky Pond, and Jon and Mary's house in Allenton, or the one they were finishing up in Camton. Whenever I was there, I felt okay, kind of, and they watched me with curiosity as I came out and they had fires lit, and everyone was hanging out and drinking beer, just like they always had. They had never stopped doing it. And I was among them, and we laughed. It got heavy at times when we discussed current family affairs, and Barts would always vanish. I knew the loss of their mother was hard on all of them, and it was Sherry's declining now that brought back their own mother's end of life. It also told me that they may need support from me in days to come, not the other way around.

I also scrolled the dating sites pretty regularly and Jackie and I had some good dialogue about what kind of girl I hoped to meet, and what kinds of ones I was going to first, especially if Max was around. He's never had a relationship that did not end in some kind of shitshow, restraining order, court, whatever. Yeah, Max. I'll take your advice on women. He seemed oblivious to the fact that Jackie was hoping I rubbed off on him, and said so over coffee talk, not the other way around.

One day, driving up the road on my way to pick up a steak sub and BLT for Mom and Dad, I just had enough. In my car, out loud, I beseeched God. Not on purpose. I think. Maybe. Yeah, I guess I knew what I was saying.

"Am I really destined to be alone and unfucked? Am I going to die without getting laid? Because if I do, wherever I end up, there will be trouble!"

Prayer. It comes from the heart. I did not hear this one get heard, as I would later. But it WAS heard. I thought I was just feeling sorry for myself. Is it funny or absurd that we think we can bargain with God?

Jackie took me on errands and kept me busy in her garden, kept moving water over me. We talked. I was in shock about my sons. It began with sharing memories she had of them, visiting when they were little. Visiting David and her, and something else. Something big, something that I had not thought about.

Before I left my home in Scarborough, I had been… scared. Scared for my future, because I sensed she had some nasty surprise, she was going to try and fuck with my livelihood, she was trying to accuse me of being an abuser. And she was leading me on with it, saying, "People *know.* They *know.*" And like everything else with her, she dangled implications and hints, and never said anything.

I had run away from that marriage screaming like a man who has been trapped in a mine and didn't know if he was ever getting out. I ran, I landed, and then… I had just completely changed my life, and decided to do what I can to help my folks. And something was looming, that I just hadn't put together. Until I settled down enough to think, eating Jackie's cooking ("I cook, you eat" she had told me when I moved in), and listening to some of the things she was saying.

My phone rang as I was talking with Jackie one morning on the back deck. Dad had been out for a drive with mom, one of the things he could still do to ease her that was left. I went over to meet them and he got out to get the garage door. As I pulled in behind Dad's car, Nana and Papa's car, it was running. My father had gotten out to the garage door, and my mother got out. His door was open. She must have told him to go in and check something, or something, because he disappeared stage left into the house.

I saw the look in her eye from twenty-five feet away, horror dawning on me. Twenty-five years of mental health, parenting, samurai, jedi… is it real? Is it imaginary? Fantastical, even?

Maybe it was my training, my experience, my good luck flowing free like spring water and defiantly tested occasionally. It may have just been Good Ole' God again. He seems to be not far away, these days. Maybe it was my acid trip, the heightened senses and perceptions. I don't know. I also have transcended caring. Has anyone spoken to my sons?

I knew as soon as I saw her eyes lock onto that spot on the car…

All thought ceased…

I made it to the keys with my sword hand, through the steering wheel, just as my mom plunked herself into the spot she had looked at, and her eyes had cleared. The driver's seat.

Mom said something weird as her eyes clouded back over. One face of her soul had passed by on the Alzheimer's carousel, and that face was replaced by one from the past; small, but older than the sibling I imagine she addressed in that moment. She had been thwarted and knew it when I snatched the keys and pocketed them, stepping out of range of her hands. She would have slapped me in the face. As I pulled back, I saw that look pass across her eyes. It was the older sister, babysitting and losing control of the situation and not wanting to acknowledge she has lost control, that showed up. I had known staffers, somewhere on this jumbled timeline, who had the same flaw. Teachers, babysitters… it's ubiquitous.

She said, "Arrr, now aren't you just a little firefighter?"

Another bullet dodged. Two, and the second would have been a mushroomed mess of an exit. Bone fragments, clipped artery. Third level fucked, because she absolutely would have put that car in reverse and backed it straight into the Superglue Forester I was still shackled to, a lease I had to transfer to dad, and simply give him money. She would have totaled both the cars. No question. Thank God. Thank God I was here. Thank God. If that isn't the be-still-and-know-that-I-am-God moment, I'll listen to rivals.

Dad came out of the cellar. As always, he greeted me like we weren't in Hell. Just genuinely and simply, pleasantly surprised to see me, and happy. Not relieved. Mercifully oblivious. I wasn't even going to tell him. Not today.

I burst into loud laughter. Mom joined me, and dad too, not even knowing what was funny. It was another snippet of something so natural, and familiar, but somehow also wildly out of place. Yet comforting. All three of us were laughing through tears, and it seemed normal.

Laughter, tears. What's the difference? Has anyone seen my boys? Has anyone talked to T.C. or Keelin?

Haw, haw, haw… Hahahaah… Ahhh… AAHHH! Waah! Waah! It was both. It was both. I remember now, because I can still hear it if I try.

The Wedding, Camton

(Petra, Jack, and Brooke).

After-party/Allenton.

Like I've mentioned, I was wrapped and swaddled in my family, not my lost family, my old-now-new family. I was the lost-now-returned. Just before Halloween, Jon's oldest son got married.

I saw all the West boys except Wonder Boy, and Chipper was there. So were Uncle Ritchie and Aunt Nora Gee, Ritchie's brother, my Uncle Paul and my Aunt Robin, Krissy's parents, more cousins. It would be the last time such a crew would be together, Ritchie's last wedding. Like so many times before, I remembered such assemblies. Weddings, including my own, funerals, Nonnie's eightieth birthday party when Mom got the three ladies who sang really high, like in "The Flower Duet". They had been a fixture at those events for years. Well, not the funerals. Standing in the middle of the wedding off to the side, taking it all in, I was hit with the thought of looking up the three singers for my mother's upcoming funeral, date TBD, and I guffawed so loud at the absurdity of it that I shook some water out of my mocktail and slapped myself on the forehead. Being hit by thoughts that just struck funny even in their morbidity was commonplace. When I opened my eyes there were eyes on me that I knew my whole life, and those of other guests to whom I was the wedding guest no one had ever seen before, and apparently even the guests on my supposed side of this wedding barely knew who I was except all the old people. I looked at them looking at me and laughed out loud again. My strategy for demonstrating loudly that I was not some kind of psycho was not off to a good start.

If we're going to use the image of an emotional rollercoaster for these days, I guess I would say that sometimes it was like that. Sometimes the coaster went at high velocity, shaking and clacking, and then, it would just stop, dead, with no jar of inertia. It would just be gone, like stepping into the cabin off a stormy frigid foredeck. And, like that. One second, rollercoaster, next second, stormy sea.

As I tried to regain my mind in the low din of a typical wedding, I looked in front of me, and there were all four of the main kids on this branch of the family. Petra, Jack, and Baby Brooke were Chris and his new bride's kids. Cyrus was Chipper's grandson. I was saved. They beat me to greetings and swarmed me. I had met them all at the tail of the summer, but this was a treat. I hadn't really thought about this, because it had been up in the air whether or not Dad would go, and I had been thinking more about seeing Chipper and all Mary's brothers. The younger ones and my cousin Nathan were good pals through high school, and I ran up on Petey and asked him if I could send a pic to Nathan. As always, part of my chorus in my head went off on a musical wonderment about how it used to be, when I would have said, "Smile!" and Petey would have, and I would then, subsequent weeks later, send said pic to my cousin in the mail and say, "Look who I ran into at Chris Pierces' wedding!"

But today, I just fired it off in a text message to Nathan in California. And right away I heard back from him… "Is that Pete West?!" And I confirmed it was, again, laughing by myself off to the side of the bar while people looked at me like I was on real drugs, not just a little baked like usual. I really wished Dad was here, for shelter. And credibility.

The kids were gathered near me and I eyeballed the centerpieces on the tables. Jack was looking at me and I nodded at the centerpieces. They were composed, primarily, it appeared, of Hershey's Kisses.

"Jackpot," I said, looking him in the eye.

He did not move away or ask for an adult, so I went on.

"Look," I said. "Hershey's Kisses." His eyes followed mine to the table I was looking at.

They widened. We smiled together. I laughed, inside this time. Don't scare the kids, it would be the trifecta and I'd just go home at that point.

His sister Petra came over to see what had drawn Jack's interest. She looked at me and smiled.

"Are you thinking what I'm thinking?" she asked me. This time I did laugh out loud.

"You beat me to it."

That was all they needed; it was a stamp of sanction from a "credible" adult.

They turned loose on the tables, laughing and gathering candy. At some point some other kids joined them, some of Mary's brother's kids. I'm so used to family horror I braced myself for a fight to start over the candy and for me to be blamed by the adults for starting it.

"Who told you you could take the candy off the tables? Cousin *Shiro?*" But that didn't happen, and again I found myself experiencing something I was going to enjoy sharing in years to come. The kids with me immediately pointed out where they had not yet raided and offered some of their own plunder to their cousins. Like good kids. I have to say, I really liked these kids from the start.

Absent from this wedding, sadly, was my dad. I floated the idea to him, and he had balked at the idea. There was no way. Not with mom, and he couldn't leave her at home.

Later that night found me at the house the Wests had all grown up in, that Jon and Mary were in while they built their house. Everyone was old school hammered. Genna and I were singing songs along with the radio, not goofing, but just sitting around a campfire drunk singing along with Neil Young. It was so normal. I could not stop seeing the place where my boys should have been standing in this group. They have a place here too, and they've never really experienced this side of their family, except for two golden weekends at Rocky Pond a lifetime ago.

In the morning, I came to pick up Genna. She was in the pop-up camper in the back. We smoked a fat J, and I took a selfie with her, and sent it to the pirates and samurai in Maine, that's friends, and people that were also workers like me. My lifeline now that my boys' absence was clearly not changing anytime soon. I sent a text with the picture.

"This… is my cousin, Genna. <3"

Laid over to a lee shore. Too windy for tea. Cold snacks and smoke. Wind slows and skies are clear at dusk…

Between the first visits and checkups, the sum total of that was that Dad had some Ativan that he could give Mom. It was a Godsend. I still couldn't talk to him with her home. We also briefly had a visiting nurse service. The nurses failed to show up when scheduled, or were late, and didn't have a whole lot to do. It was disruptive to Dad and I got calls from him whenever they were late. Or just failed to show up.

Mom was still combative without warning, and I knew that they were in real danger round the clock. I slept with one eye open a few hours at a time and continued to search for a job. I tried to breathe. I tried to stop bleeding. It got worse.

I explained that when the visiting nurse came next, we would ask her, the right way, to help us get this situation under control. My mom started to strip off her clothes one day but couldn't dress herself back up. Dad was out and it was just us. He came back just in time to help her get fixed back up, but we were clearly running out of time.

Dad and I wrapped up the last arrangements (he agonized over the perfect headstone and picked one so beautiful we just had us a moment, right there with the gravestone guy). When the nurse came next, we got it into motion, and mom went from a hospital ward to a huge imposing nursing home in Fitchburg twenty miles away.

I got hired for a job that was not exactly, or even remotely, really, what I had done in Maine, but it was mental health, it was with kids, and it was a job. And the company was located, of all places, you can't make it up…

… on <u>Sword</u> St.

I had a job, and a *date*.

Dickie-Kai, bitches.

Jackie and Max both approached me and tried to talk me into not moving out. I was touched, but that would defeat the whole purpose of why I had come back. I had a piece of the puzzle in place with a job, and I was going to pull off this date. I spoke to her on the phone in my car next to the bonsai garden. I was feeling pretty good when I went back inside.

I was scheduled for my first day on the job and my date in the same week, and it was time to move back home with my Dad.

"Ponder and deliberate before you make your move."

------Sun-Tzu

"Yesssss…"

------My Dad

PART 4
LIFE IN HELL

West Allenton, 2019.

Autumn.

My mom left her home for the last time in Autumn of 2019. She spent some time in Memorial Hospital and dad and I played the takeout game. It was the beginning of November when she landed at her first permanent nursing home. Phase 1, I guess, was complete.

Dad and I sat in the room I had slept in as a child, that they had sat in and watched Wheel of Fortune, the news, the Red Sox. The clock I used to hear chime through the phone in the background was now four feet from me, and the sense of being through the Looking Glass had not diminished since the Acid had worn off way the fuck back in Pootown on Midsummer's Night. Indeed, things were only getting weirder, and Dad not only jumped right into it, it was clear he liked this chaos better than the one we had just taken care of. He was beyond crushed, beyond heartbroken, and so was I, and it was what it was, but we laughed, and he surprised me more than once. We would now do the long wait and see her through. We talked of fishing. We even got out and did a little. He always caught stuff. I never did, and we laughed at that too. We got to take Nathan out too, and I took him to Rocky Pond.

All those years, I never once set foot over in the thick woods on the far side. In my old-worldview, that was beyond. Now, I took Nathan through that brush and muddy path over to the point, and set him up fishing, and just let wave after wave of all this energy, memory, I could not even tell anymore, wash through me like it had when I came and baptized myself. This young man lost his mother last year, and I did not know him. Now I do, and here we are. Now everything was fucked up. A lot of the things were great. It's just that all this great was taking place in Hell, and Dad and I laughed through our tears at that too. Nathan came over one night and the three of us just sat around the fire. The kid is an old soul, and tough as nails. He's a Pierce.

Hard to put value to things when you're in this place. Everything was gone, and there was this new stuff, being here, being part of life here. The life I had was not here. I had not been here. I was here now, but… I was not. Noragee was going to need help. Dad needed help. I know how fast ten years goes. In ten years, Nathan will be twenty, and Cody will be almost grown. Not quite 18, but close enough. Ten years. Okay. I could do this. With a dog.

I explained to Dad: we're just a bunch of assholes if we are without a dog.

We ticked off the days and bustled about the house. We went to Lowe's and got stuff to fix stuff. Whenever I said out loud I was looking for a toll or something, he would hop up and disappear, and come back with old and patinaed tools

I barely know the names of. He always had something to tinker with. We spoke of building a greenhouse and growing some weed. To my surprise, he latched right onto the idea. Mom would have been aghast, and we both would have been in deep kimchee. We laughed at that too. My sons would have joined us in all this enthusiastically. If they had been talking to me like normal. Blood. Still running.

Phone, as I had taken to saying to dad, went bing-bong throughout the days. Whenever my cylon went off, news, sports, the twenty odd apps that now spoke to me daily… bing-bong. Dad was also greatly tickled by the concept of EENs and took to referring to them while we were out and about conducting our myriad business, and I smoked weed constantly.

He adapted well to my antics and drama was a great listener as I brought him up to speed over coffee and birdwatching. There was a hole in the basement wall and the temp was going down. Not today's problem. We marveled at the state of the country and the political landscape, and what Mom would say ("Uh, Jeez, I don't even know…" was Dad's take. Exactly).

Often my phone would happen to deliver its daily Sun-Tzu quote as we were talking over coffee. It was either Mom, and what was going on with her (I shared clinical and medical knowledge, information about medication and facilitated his advocacy with Mom), or, what I was hoping to do for a living, eventually. They were not doing well with her there, and when he went and saw her, which he did every day without fail, she usually just said she wanted to go home. They were cold to her there, and it was perceptible. It made me sad, and for neither the first nor last time, I was grateful for her that she was not cognizant of the horrors developing everywhere around us. We also talked about the state of the house, and everything from imminent needed repairs to future plans for landscaping and fruit trees. I also spoke of my life when I was away, and what working had been like, and how much I wanted to get back to it. We spoke of the political state of the nation in 2019, and enough has and will be said about it that we don't even need to talk about that shitshow, and the best was absolutely yet to come on all that, as we now all know.

When Sun-Tzu arrived, I adopted a solemn air, and spoke in a guttural voice, like the narrator of Conan the Barbarian, the classic with Schwarzenegger. I read the quote, and Dad would nod, and say, "Yes…"

I pulled some classic clips of Conan. Cylon makes life easier. It really is an Easy button.

We laughed so much together, and had such a good time, it's hard to believe that we were in Hell, but it was hard to forget. If I could restart my career down here, and meet someone, things would be maybe a little bit okay. And that's when the Bumble bing-bonged.

A few weeks ago, when I beseeched God on my way to Steve's Pizza, I had been specific. I even had a glimpse of her. Not her face. My phone went bing-bong and I opened Bumble. Without thought, I bipped my screen enough to right swipe her before I even saw her picture. Now, I say this was completely unintentional. Later, when I looked at her pictures, and read her words, I knew I would have anyway. But I didn't mean to, and I think the angel in charge of my prayer just cheated a little and slapped my hand. I've cut corners like that myself for the greater good.

The New Kitchen

Wootown.

October, 2019.

I approached this with caution. Breana was one thing, like, a practice date. We still chatted. It wasn't romantic. This new woman had me from the get-go. Her name was Anghiel. She got right down to business, and we made arrangements to meet for an early lunch at a restaurant she knew in the Woo. I quipped something about being a medicine man while we were still on the Bumbly and I think I almost scared her off. Steady as she goes, laddies…

I had yet to hear her voice. I parked at the New Kitchen and waited. I tried not to look stalky. I was properly smoked and caffeinated. In theory I could be cuddled up to someone today, but I was realistic about my expectations. I just wanted to hear her speak. And laugh. At my jokes, hopefully.

All I remember is watching her get out of her mom-mobile and stand up. She was tall. She had nice hair. Something about her felt like I already knew who she was. I followed her into the restaurant without looking scary, or being seen by her. She turned around and saw me, and said my name inflected like a question. Her voice sounded like a clarinet. I was smitten. I was so fucking relieved to be able to tell her I was employed, and why I was living with my father. I had literally just moved from Jackie's the day before and started work three days this at Sword St.

No, I don't remember what we talked about over lunch but I talked her into a car ride and gave her a tour of the Shire. It took about an hour, and by the time I dropped her back at her car, I was hotter than a pistol and trying to play it cool. We parted with the prospect of meeting up again, and I was alive. Kind of. One thing I realized at this point, even though I might be about to get laid, it did not diminish any of my shock, pain, confusion or anger at where things were at, apparently, between my sons and me.

But I was guardedly fired up. I was at my office on Sword St, and I heard from her. "I have a thing with my daughter, but if you'd like to meet for coffee at Holy Ground we could do that."

All Stop/Quick Quiet.

Red Alert.

Breathe.

I'm in my new workplace. Take it easy. Find the Void.

I knew this was bad. I had reached the limit, on this one. Fuck it. I'm going to a professional. I knew it was important to be courteous. That's not a struggle. I am not inclined to just abuse someone, so I knew, that many guys might tell this woman to fuck off and insult her just to be a dick. It was a chance, no matter how small the sparrow that falls, to be different. Better, stronger, faster, all that shit, but also... Lean, Hard, Strong. Sharp, Bright, Quick.

Clinging to the Code will save your ass, boyo. It sure saved mine now. Class. Do this with class, and it ain't over till it's over.

"How nice to hear from you. I would love to meet for coffee. However, I sense that this is a termination meeting. If that's the case, two things, please. One, tell me now. I'm working and not of a mind to have this hovering about in the scuppers. Two, I hope we can be friends, because I think you're pretty great, and I was hoping to take you out again. Be clear, please, and thank you. Friends-only is a viable prospect I hope."

The die is cast. All quiet in the Attack Center. Fuck work, they saw me now, watching my phone, but no one seemed to really notice that I was perched on a precipice.

"I was thinking maybe we were not a fit, but I would love to pursue a friendship, of course."

FUCK… ME… RUNNIN.

The claxon was sounding in my mind. The lights and alarms rose to a crescendo and went silent. I was in a clearing in the forest in Pootown. Hagakure time. Do or die. I threw my last card, already resolved that this sexy bird was going to get away. I was undiscouraged. Plenty O' Fish in the sea. I laughed out loud and swept my eyes around the office. No one looked up. Lucky me. Nope, no crazy here.

"I would be honored to be your friend, thank you. In the new spirit of our friendship, could you explain to me why I am unfuckable, and what I might do to rectify it? Because I am on a mission now, as I'm sure you can appreciate."

And then… some long minutes later, maybe three…

"Oh, you are definitely fuckable. We can fuck, as friends, xxx %&^784, JGKhfh^%r": CRt OJHFdt%R."

Yeah, I have no idea what the rest of the message said. Everything got a thousand times brighter. It was like when the cold stinging rain finally stops after so long, and the sun comes out blazing all at once and starts drying everything right away, hot and sharp. Steam rose gently from the grass in the clearing in the forest of my soul. I had found a woman with nice hair, who was going to wrap her legs around my face. I had not been touched sexually by a woman in more than five years. And there were years of desert peppered with moments of hope. False moments. Oh, yeah. There was my tryst with Athena, but all I can say is, on paper is one thing, and it did not count. Not that it was bad, but… trust me, it didn't count. Foul ball. No goal. I needed… some real action.

I was saved.

Oh, glory. Glory, glory Hallelujah. And, considering my brief peek into the world of Tinder and Plenty O' Fish, thank God it wasn't a glory*hole*. How close a call was that? Maybe I will know, someday. But I couldn't give less of a fuck about that right now.

My luck was holding. Hell was not so bad. Beats being married to Marla, that's a fact.

So, I had built a firepit in the backyard before I even moved back in. I used the slate flagstones that had been under the deck when I was a kid. Mom and Dad had never used these, and they had never discovered I had cracked several into smaller slabs by climbing on them many years ago. I forgot about it, until I started moving them and saw the cracked one, just as I had left it, in 1982. Everything around me was like opening a Time Capsule. It was constant and overpowering. I built a slate compass rose around the fire ring and harvested rocks from the piles of gravel that bordered all our lots, the meadow this place had once been. They had just leveled it off and left it in piles on the backs of our properties. They were bleak and bare when I was young. Now they were covered with trees and blended into the forest. The whole yard had become a green enclave. It was beautiful and I had never seen it this way. The yard is bordered by two rows of trees, both planted by my dad. One is blue spruces and now they are taller than the house. I remember them. Two are fucked from me driving into them as a kid in the snow in my Cordoba being an idiot. They are more gnarled than the others now, they look older. The other trees went up not all that long ago, but different pine. Fast growing. They tower over the house and shelter the yard now from wind and sun. The firepit was my first mark being back. Then, I set up a proper campsite and invited my new girlfriend to hang out like kids at camp. Dad watched me intently, all the time. I became aware that he was following me around, and I made sure he did not think I was avoiding him. I certainly was not. He was institutionalized by my mother. I almost had been too. Nathan was out with Dad and I one night by the fire and I got some good pics of us all. These are the things you cling to.

We clung to each other. The first night, in my little river tent. Later, in the Big Tent, with the stove and air mattresses. She was shelter from the beginning. She perked Dad up, too.

Ever present are my sons, how we left, and what had happened up to now. It was such uncharted territory, and I was fucking up by taking shots at them asking what the fuck and trying to provoke a response.

Wales

A Tiny Distant Light on a Dark and Stormy Sea

(Hope).

Anghiel and I did not go out much, but we did run out together and get Eats or get takeout, but Dad was always trying to give me money. When I went to work, he asked me if I needed money. If I was going to get food, he would ask me if I needed money. He paid for takeout, and I didn't want to overdo it. I was mindful of my son's eyes on me and I did not want to give them any reason to think I was here taking the easy route, taking advantage or living the high life. This is the way it really was, but I had not come home to make my own life easier. I decided that I would not leave my dad to be out and about partying with my friends and shit. The possibility was there, but I wasn't into it. I could have been over at Jon and Mary's drinking, or down with Genna, or at Rocky Pond, but I didn't want to be. I wanted to be here with him. We had time together, and it was pretty great, even though we were, of course, in Hell.

Anghiel suggested going away for a weekend, and dad told me I was going, and gave me a hundred dollars, and told me to go somewhere nice. No saying no this time, so I took the money, and gave him a hug, and said, "Thanks, Dad," and when I came home on Sunday, I told him how we had found some awesome Chinese food late night. My weekend in Wales with Anghiel was a rebirth and I left those spooky woods with a *big* smile on my face. She was great. She was into me. She was smart and funny, and she had long legs and they were now not unknown to my face. I should have felt alive, and I told myself I was. But I wasn't. There was a new light in all this dark. It was like a candle left onshore. I used to do that, on big water at night. You can see that candle for a long, long way in the dark. I saw one now, off in the distance of my mind. Healing touch and stimulating intellect. The fun of cuddling. Lust. I was rejuvenated.

One thing Anghiel enlightened me further with was Reddit. "My crack," she quipped. I liked this girl a lot already.

"What's a Reddit?" I asked her. It was a joke that she was kind of amazed by how long I had held out resisting technology. I knew what Reddit was, but I had not heard the term Dead Bedroom, and, when she first shared it with me, I was enlightened. In the months to come I was amazed to hear these voices from all over saying the things that had echoed in the halls of my mind, halls that were vast and alone and uncertain. Part of the Hell of the marriage was the solitude and shame of it. Now, I learned that the vast halls are filled with voices with the same uncertainties and fears. My salvation began with this knowing, that I had never been alone, in fact, I had escaped a Hell that appears solitary, but from the outside, I looked back and saw that many thousands of people suffer in this same Hell, and not all of them could, or ever would, escape unscathed. I was amazed, and further horrified. It's called a Dead Bedroom marriage. There's a whole page, people just saying the things I said to myself, but hearing other voices.

"Get out."

"Not going to get better."

And there were conversations between sufferers, and people who would ask them, "What can you do better?"

Yeah. That started to piss me off. There is no getting better when you're with someone who just does not care. You're stuck to them, but they will not touch you, they will not be *emotionally* intimate. I would have lived without sex because of Marla's myriad ailments. It was the lack of any kind of warmth from her at all, ever. It's a cold, lonely road when you're with someone who does not love you back. I tried my best to make that marriage work. All my knowledge. All my skill. All my experience. If what I did worked everywhere else, why had it failed at home? Why was that the only fucked up thing in my life? I found some comfort, knowing I had never been alone, and that I was not the one who had some kind of problem. Being pressured to accept it as normal is gaslighting. I added my voice, and my comments, and I began to be seen in a world I had avoided like the plague. Funny, that, because there's no avoiding the plague now, is there? But we did not know that then. There's no stopping what's coming. My phone rang and bingbonged with messages from Maine, Cristobel, Matty Mango, and Kary, and of course, Lono, who was acutely tuned in to my loss of TC and Keelin.

Thanksgiving, 2019

Gardner Hospital and Nora Gee's

(Icy, windy, bleak, and gray).

As I worked with families that yelled at each other all the time, I began to see something. People who get frustrated will say and do stuff to parents of kids, especially kids with struggles or special needs, that are not okay. Working for years, I had seen it had been in a home when a teacher called and just made that parent feel like shit, and that was kind of why I was there, because what we knew was that they fought a lot about school. A little work and we uncovered this kid's needs were poorly understood by the professionals closest to him. It became a frequent story for all of us, and we collaborated actively on this in our teams and supervisions, and it happened enough that I began to realize it had happened to me all my life. My teachers loved to call my mother and tell her, "They just don't know what to do with him." That's code, you see. That's when teachers quietly encourage parents to lose their fucking minds; yell, scream, maybe hit. Punish. Shame. That's what school was like for me. And that's what school is like for a lot of kids. I am not a little boy anymore, scared and defenseless. Now I am a man, and I found the children still there, and still being mistreated by petty tyrants and closet psychopaths in the guise of educators. Nothing new, and we called it like we saw it. We field agents did not get invited to a lot of school picnics.

Now, after years of processing, that I felt like I had been thrown to the wolves by my mom as a kid, I found her defenseless and without voice, and even though unlike her I was really aware of how people can be, how cruel faces can hide in supposedly safe spaces, I was just as powerless to protect her as she was me. I knew, before she left that house, why that had been allowed to happen, and I knew it was not her fault. Before she left her home, my relationship with my mom was whole. They didn't want to deal with her at Thanksgiving at the nursing home, so they wait till someone yells or gets slappy, and they send them to a hospital for an eval, and that can take several days, so dad and I spent Thanksgiving in a hospital ward in Gardner for a couple hours with mom. Dad had to give the nursing home an extra thousand dollars so they would keep the empty bed for her. It's a huge scam. He had to do that again at Christmas, because they pulled the same shit. They didn't want my mom at their party, and I could not stick up for her. I wanted to just unleash on these people who so clearly did not give a fuck, and did not care that we knew it. They acted annoyed when we questioned them on anything. And I need to say, that teachers then and now, and all these people we met on Mom's journey, I will speak to the gaps and deficiencies, but there are shining stars of people everywhere, the sad thing is that they are so rare you remember everyone. They shouldn't stand out so much. We should all be so bright.

Mom was keeping them hopping at the nursing home, and they liked to call and tell us she was behaving badly. I thought of how my teachers used to do this, call home and work my mother up that I was a problem child, and she would lose her mind and scream at me for hours. This was a regular thing.

Dad and I went to Gardner hospital and sat with Mom at the end of an empty hallway. People gave us our room. It was neither the first nor last time I would see the places that are not happy, where the lonely and lost lie. I always thought of those "less fortunate". It was my mom in me, genetics or not. Nature vs. Nurture. I had studied this all my life. Mom was in and out and we sat and I played music on my phone and she would attend the music. So that's what we did: we used music and whatever else to connect with the little bits of her that were still hanging on so Dad could have the full measure, no matter how bad it was or would get. He accepted all this in stride and we talked of what the boys might be doing. I still had a lot of possibilities that I thought were viable.

Marla had lied to my sons. Made them hate me. I had not helped myself, but I was a little out of my mind. It was starting to look like I had been, in some way, but not what the boys seemed to think now. Even when Dad and I were together, we were in our own Hell. We spoke of this again through both laughter and tears and agreed that we were together and, Hell or no, we were kind of having a good time, if you thought of it as an adventure. Sun-Tzu came to mind, and Dad said, "Yes," and we laughed.

I brought Mom back down to near the nurse's desk so she wouldn't be left forgotten for the next several hours. It is the reality of things. She seemed occupied sitting there observing and telling people to get the hell away from her. It was as happy as she would get, and at least she wasn't crying and asking Dad to take her home. I wondered how many removals of his heart he had in him, because every single little detail about her lonely journey now ripped him to shreds, hot and sharp, and wet and raw and burning. He and I were both in Hell, and Hell is lonely, even if you are with good company. At least we were, and aware of that blessing.

Did the boys call Papa and wish him Happy Thanksgiving? They did not. We went to NoraGee's and the whole gang was there almost. I felt good because Allan hadn't seen anyone at the wedding of course. Dad was very happy and uplifted to spend time with his sister and it almost felt like old times, if we stretch "almost" like we do to apply to horseshoes and hand grenades. Dad and I made it home and settled in front of the TV, and we were together again as always. The comfort I was drawing from his proximity I hoped was matched by what poor measure of comfort I could be in now, but the fact is we enjoyed ourselves together as we always had, and despite our residence in Hell now, it wasn't so bad. At least I had a girlfriend. But the job was not meshing with my life in support of mom and dad, and hopefully, potentially to NoraGee with Ritchie, and for Nicky and his boys, a chance for us to stand in for what had been lost for others too. It would have been Mom's way, and Dad and I were sidekicks. I needed to order my life better every day.

TC. Keelin. Happy Thanksgiving. What the fuck? Boys… what the fuck? When am I going to talk to you again?

Vespers

And the Light shall pierce the dark… and show the way to safe harbor.

Anghiel was active in the Unitarian Universalist Church. It was an important part of her life, and her identity. She invited me to Vespers, and though I had no desire to rub elbows with people, I would not have refused. I'm so glad I went.

Christmas was approaching. Church at Christmas is something important to me, in the sense that if we went, it was either when I was a little kid, in the old church in the Shire that I drove by daily now, or when my own kids were young, we went to Mass with Marla's parents a few times.

Churches of any kind are always associated with memories. When people say, "Church is important to me, or important in my life." It's often code speak so you immediately know no dirty jokes around this one. It is the most fundamental, oldest, and most common mechanism of control, or imposing one's will on others. Don't do X, it makes me feel Y. That isn't what I'm saying. I'm saying that to be in a holy building or place of any kind shivers me timbers, and it has to do with power associated with a place. I think. Look, being a medicine man doesn't really come with an instruction booklet.

***

We had gone to the Catholic church in Old Orchard Beach, in the heart of the community I worked in, and I saw many people there from Saco that I knew from Sweet Shores. I was enjoying greeting my friends when Marla's mother did what she always did best: fuck with shit, just because. She glared at me, and told me to sit down. I was embarrassing her. Now, at this point, Marla's mother had been a bit of a scourge for years, especially at Christmas, and she brought such joy as this, negative energy. My patience with her had been dwindling slowly for years, and tonight I just had enough. I was going to teach her a lesson. I turned slowly away from the colleague who had greeted me with a wave and smile. When I had last seen him, we had been halfway up a tree dodging rocks; a runaway was whipping at us. Of course, we had nodded and laughed to one another. We served together. What the hell do you know about that? Someone was being an embarrassment alright, and it was time to set her straight.

I looked down at her pursed lip with a disdainful glare and said, clearly enough to be heard, "These are my friends from work, madam. It is you who are being an embarrassment."

Don't fucking scold me in public, bitch, especially in my town. I don't care who you are. Don't choke on it.

When people stood up to Marla's mother, she was unaccustomed to it. And she damn sure didn't like it. This was not the first or the last time I had to set boundaries, but it is one of my favorites. She also never forgot and held malicious grudges. I know now that Marla's mother told her for years to divorce me, hang me up with alimony, and take my kids away from me. She encouraged Marla to compromise me any way possible, including trying to provoke me to violence, which Marla had. I had never laid a hand on her, or stood to her, or done anything like that. Marla and her mother and sister all resented me, because I could not be bullied around like their men. And, they erroneously thought that that was how it was between Dad and Mom too. Many people did. It wasn't, though. My parents were a partnership. Yes, mom was CEO, but they did work together. They had, anyway. Before all this. Always.

***

Anghiel picked me up for Vespers and I was dressed in a way my mom would approve of. Dad and I laughed. She had been Death on any "Hoodish" clothing, and we had fought a lot about my dress when I was young. Dad and I always laughed when we talked like this. She made me stop and change my clothes more than once when I was young with friends waiting for me in the driveway. One time I had on a Metallica shirt that showed a zombie being executed in an electric chair on the front and a toilet with a dagger in a corpse hand coming up out of it and the words "Metal up your Ass!" on the back. In what, as I recall, she referred to as "druggie letters", was apparently her take on the production graphics and font. I almost made it out the door until she said, "No". And I knew I wasn't going to wear my cool Metallica shirt to Wootown Galleria that evening. Dad and I laughed like hell when we remembered shit like this, like now when I asked him if mom would think I looked nice. He just laughed and agreed, that she would.

"I'm glad you met someone," he said as I was leaving. "You need any money?"

By now, this was cracking me up when he did it, and I left him with us both laughing as I said, "I'm going to a church, Dad. Pretty sure I'm all set. But thanks."

When I came home, he was standing there waiting for me and smiling. I was grateful, not for my own contentment with this girl I met, but that he was happy to see me happy, and Mom would have been too. I hoped he hadn't just been standing there the whole time. Of course, he hadn't, but it sure felt like that. I think his pain helped me quiet mine out of the need.

The church was beautiful, and filled with her community, me an interloper in my solitude and pain. I bit through my lip to keep the tears in. I was overwhelmed with the Christmas spectacle, and I vowed that no matter how much it hurt I would never let this spirit die, even if only for the sake of the children. That's what Christmas time is supposed to be anyway. I got a great idea for gifts here this night, and the memory and emotional tsunami grew beyond my control and I surrendered and let it sweep me away. It was the music, you see. It's always screaming to me, but I love music, so I learned to do both, listen, scream silently, and cling to this world, this life. People need me, I have to care.

***

Ella, my sons, and my mother, all lost now in the road behind me. Death, Estrangement, Dementia. I prayed tonight that my sons were safe. I shared none of this with Anghiel, just put on my mask, and also genuinely took shelter in the safety and simplicity, and normalcy, that she brought to this raging hurricane in my soul.

***

Dad went to Fitchburg every day. I tried to make field work happen, although a mentor is not the same as a bachelor's level therapist, and I was limited in what I was able to do. On weekends, Dad and I saw Mom first, then figured out what to do. There was always something, somewhere to go, and I had Anghiel in the evenings to look forward to, either by phone or when she came over with those long legs I was growing quite fond of.

***

By 2018, we all knew that what we had known was over. Nana and Papa had not come up for Thanksgiving. T.C. had worked as a CNA in several facilities by now. Like everything else in his life, he approached it with shining teeth and bit hard. He excelled. His stories kept us all rapt. T.C. was the storyteller of the family, and every shift he came home from, whether it was the old folks, or when he was a firefighter, or driving a tow truck, he always had tales to make us laugh, cry, and everything in between.

We knew Nana had the dementia, and it was not a surprise. We made the decision to do something different for Christmas. We rolled down 95, like they had always rolled up, and I made lobster rolls. The silly card game with the little gifts, the little calendars and planners and little old-fashioned hand games, trinkets really, was only done in charade now. Nana could not keep up, and we were as she had been with all of us, save Dad and Marla. We had been the children growing and learning with her and now she was as a child, unknowing. Me and the boys got a bag from Cabela's, some cash, and a little stuffed dog. Dad had done all the shopping. Like nothing else, this signaled the death of the time of our lives when we were all a family. Nana would see another two Christmases come and go, but this was her last one, and our last one together. The ride home was quiet. There wasn't much to say. By the time the holidays rolled around again, I was with Nana and Papa on an empty hospital wing, just looking out the window and trying to keep us sheltered in the good memories of what had gone before, before everything started to burn. The absence of my sons in all this was deafening in my head. We focused on memory, and the day to day, as well as anything else. It worked as best it could.

***

Without her, he was lost.

The Holiday Sword St. Chinese Buffet Extravaganza

(Winter Solstice)

White City, The Shire.

14 degrees F and winy.

Through all this I was trying to do this job, but I knew I could not fit these two parts together. I loved this crew. I was joining with them, and we were getting to know one another, and I was up to my old tricks. We weren't even in fucking Maine anymore, so when I showed them pictures and spoke of pirating, it hit way above its weight class, because these folks were not accustomed to the visual embarrassment of riches that the natural beauty of the place gives. I missed it now, but they didn't know it. They ate up the pirate shit, and I started throwing around Hagakure talk. They ate that up too, and I was overjoyed. Some things survive and endure, I guess.

Making my way back from White City after the party, I struggled to feel okay. These things I was experiencing, new friendships, romance, none of it had any flavor. Everything tasted like cardboard. I forced new things into the wounds and tried to stop the bleeding. That's what this all was. I was clinging on to my sense of purpose without the boys in my life. I had to make new marks; I was not going to go quietly.

I knew I was leaving that job, but first, I wasn't going to miss a chance to make a memory, or at least to be seen here and now by these people. I was out of the sight of my sons, and I felt like I was disappearing. It helped. Good team. Laughs, Secret Santa. Needed it. I was picking up and finding new Pieces. When I was a little kid, I had a tooth pulled and the gas made me sick. Dad took me to the toy store that used to be where the Chinese restaurant was today where my work crew met. I got a metal plane, like a Hot Wheels. F4-U Corsair. Whispering Death, said the Japanese. When I got home to dad that day, I remembered this with him. He remembered too, and we talked about WW2 aviation for a while over a cold beer. It helped the memory tsunami, which had hit me like being swarmed by angry pecking birds as soon as I had stepped out of my car at White City. I was getting used to being able to see the real world and function, kind of, with blasts of sights and sounds every time my memories were triggered, which was pretty much everywhere I looked all the time. I had just started to get used to it. Like, if you're falling from an impossibly high peak, and you've been falling so long, you're not scared of the sudden stop anymore, you're just enjoying the view with resignation. Five stages of grief, gravity assist. The gravity was more than merely falling to Earth from the sky.

It was more like fighting against the pull of a blackhole in space.

Christmas, 2019

Ice and wind.

Jon and Mary's/Camton.

Like we had at Thanksgiving, we worked around Mom and seeing her. I found Dad one day in his chair with tears in his eyes, and a paper in his hand. He had always gotten her jewelry as gifts, and now, he was agonized that he couldn't give her something nice that she would appreciate. I comforted him, viciously stuffing my own desire to just break down and weep with him. Maybe I should have but I opted to anesthetize. It was the humane thing. Like he and Mom always had to me, I comforted him, and told him it was okay, and told him that the heart pendant from one of those Mint places was beautiful, and would be fine, and I'm sure she would love it. I got her some little plants that were in animal pots that she could water with staff or us. I wanted her to enjoy herself, play games and fiddle with magazines like she always had, and still could, kind of. Enough to give her some measure of comfort. But Mom pissed someone off; or maybe not; they just didn't like her at the nursing home in

Fitchburg and I got a call right after Christmas from Carlos the director, who told me that they just couldn't handle her, and she was being sent out. Again. Permanently this time. He was inconvenienced by having to make this phone call as a courtesy, so he withheld any courtesy, or sensitivity. I think he saw me as rude, because I did not apologize for my mother's behavior. Had he pulled this attitude directly when we were up there seeing Mom, I would have popped him. Something told me it was important not to create any problems that could be used against me in this situation with my sons. I still did not really know why we had this, at that point, six months after I moved out.

Christmas Eve saw us again in Gardner hospital with Mom, just the three of us sitting there. All I had in my mind was this growing sense of how wrong this was that their grandsons were not present for this in some capacity. We went back the next day and back to Jon and Mary's for coffee and pie. Dad and I laughed privately later together that we felt like we were standing there with holes blown through us, and no one could see or know, and everything was normal as far as anyone knew. It was surreal, but the moments we had with the other players were very real, and dispelling the surreal made it clear that it was surreal because real was alert, awake, and aware, like with anesthesia awareness. Mary had a C-section and felt everything. Dad had cataract surgery and felt everything. When I cleared my fog enough to actually enjoy mindfully these times with family, I became more aware of my own pain and loss, and now the loss of the boys was affecting dad too. It was a recipe for disaster with no defilade. But Dad and I went to Jon and Mary's for Christmas and got to see everyone and NoraGee again, and Dad and I were happy about that, and I helped him express the horror and absurdity of all this, and that we had moments of joy and fun.

Dad sent money to the boys and Marla for Christmas. I seethed a little at the Marla gift, but internally and did not interfere. I did not hear from them, and I think they called Dad to thank him, but as far as being there for him, and helping ease his profound pain, they were in the wind, and it was starting to piss me off. This had nothing to do with him. It was needless cruelty, and that didn't make sense. Until I took a longer, slower look, with Sun-Tzu at my side, and Dad, and began to see the full foul measure of what Marla had been up to, all those years when she wasn't acting like a wife, or mate, or even, apparently, a mother. Not a real one.

I quit the Sword St. job after the Christmas party. There was no way I was going to make this work with the other Pieces. I needed a full-time thing with a schedule.

Before New Year's Eve, we started to hear whispers of some virus circling way out in China. One more thing, as nightly Dad and I marveled at the Orange Clown, we speculated on how his story would end, and for all of us. The idea of a germ just seemed to be the growing action of the party we had arrived at before everyone else. We laughed at this in December. I wouldn't say we ever stopped laughing, but in the months to come, as we stood back-to-back holding each other tight while the world tore itself apart and Covid swept over the globe like fire through light and flashy grass, we had no real choice but to laugh. If we stopped having a good time here in Hell and failed for one instant to be grateful for the silver linings in all this godawful shitty mess, we would, without question, lose our minds and ourselves.

There were matters of import I had to sort out. One was ugly and unavoidable. Mom was at risk now, and around this time, we noticed the first set of suspicious bruises on her. I wrestled with what to do with this for a moment, because my father is a gentle man, but if someone was hurting my mother, I was going to have a rampaging Hun on my hands, and he was going to go to jail. The idea of my father running afoul of the law was so absurd, yet here it was in stark reality. I could not lie to him about the realities we faced with this. She had been in two different hospitals before she was in long-term care, and when we first got her in, she wore the staff out around the clock on all three shifts. I realized that Dad had been doing this work on his own for months. Mom also had not been medicated. Dad had gotten some Ativan for her early on, but he had to be taught how to use it, how to give her medicine when she started to escalate. Mom had gone from laughing to crying to trying to punch and choke us or go outside in the road when she had been home. I had only been able to check on them and help facilitate meals, any lingering presence messed things up. We had gotten her out of the house in the nick of time, that was just beyond question.

But now she had bruises on her hands and arms that told of being grabbed with excessive force. I talked about it with Dad frankly, and for one moment, for that one heartbeat again, I saw a look that said much. It said he was trusting me to take point on this, but there was a possibility Raging Hun would show up. I have never met Raging Hun, no one ever tried to hurt my mother, but I saw inside my father that day a creature that would be unleashed if anyone hurt his Babe. My father's heart was a deep well. After Mom left home, he spoke of buying guns, and getting a tattoo of a cobra. My jaw dropped at both. My mother would have been aghast at either one of these ideas. For all his unnecessarily surreptitious drinking in the basement, my father had an independent streak that was poking its head out. I found this, in all the horror of our reality, quite delightful. I showed dad various guns and tats on my phone. We continued to find things to laugh at and I found movies to share that he had never seen, but it was more clips of classics on my phone. One thing he would watch whenever it was on was any car chase movie. He was a nut for Fast and Furious. I told him about Paul Walker, and he responded with the obvious comparison to James Dean, which I think shows how keen and broad reaching his mind was, and though I knew my father was no dolt, this was something I never fully appreciated, until I watched him roll with his punches. How else could I respond, but to try to roll with mine?

***

These things are remembered now from the place that they reside in my soul. They did not always live together. They happened one at a time. Sometimes, a lot happened all at once. All I can say going into the new year, was that at some point, in that part of winter when it gets most cold, and the wind howls outside, we transitioned from one circle of Hell, into another. Perhaps it would be more accurate to say, we transitioned from one Circle of Hell into many at once.

***

I went to Pootown for the night in December. This was a complicated op, and I had built it up for a couple weeks with Dad. I explained to Dad that when we used to go camping and on river trips (particularly that; needing to get *to* somewhere, usually over water), I explained to him it was over water pretty much, because I like creature comforts and I can't hump a canoe's worth of gear up a mountain in a backpack. Water.

The objective was set up with the future in mind. Getting there after a shift at the Dep. That was one. No cooking. No showering. No puupen (I don't need to explain that, do I?). No dog. Just snacks in a cooler and Slim Jims and such, and the cold. And, the fabled Northwest Passage. This is the route to Maine that is not the highway. It is a whole different thing. I made it. I was not cold in Pootown. It was a good place to pick up where all that left off. I had Anghiel to think about.

Pootown

21 degrees F.

Cloudy.

It's empty. It looks the same, and the echoes of my otherworldly experience here a few months ago rumble all night long. But when I was here last, I felt Love for my sons, and their love for me is currently missing. The fire burns all night. No, it isn't fun in the winter without a dog.

***

Scooting up and back within 24 hours was also critical, because I was not about to leave Dad lying about the house while I went off and had a good time. And, as soon as it was feasible, I was going to work him into all of it. It took at least ten years to get our skills efficient on rivers. The trip to

Turkey Neck was exactly that, the kickoff of the season, and I always went with some new obstacle in mind to get better at cooking, cocktailing, adventuring. This is where the skills had come from. It was time to pick that back up, truck or no, to at least make what can be made ready to be so, for when the time comes.

I filled Dad in on this when I got back, and explained the merits of cast iron, and how the pans he had given me would be used in the bush.

Later that night we went outside together and cleared off the fresh fallen snow. Dr. Plow plowed the driveway.

Part 5
Plague 2020

West Allenton.

January 17th, 2020.

3:45 AM EST.

Howling Winter Wind.

2 degrees below zero, F.

I turned 50 today. I know they are not going to call.

Something was emerging as I tried to make sense of the hole in my life where my sons had been. Something foul.

These things, are facts:

Marla's mother liked to stir up trouble. It amused her to feel powerful.

She also developed an antagonistic stance toward me over the years.

Marla had surgery about ten years ago. At that time, there was some clear malpractice going on. I was trying to discreetly gather data from the nurses by playing dumb and paying close attention to what they were saying and were not.

Then Marla's mother showed up, and like she did in restaurants, immediately tried to bully her way around. You don't do that with nurses. The level of entitlement she exhibited in all things was hard to believe, and she did not like being confronted on her behavior. No narcissist does, clandestine of otherwise. The nurses circled the wagons and clammed up. I was furious, but I kept my cool. I had her thrown out, though.

Then, I went home and fired off a message.

I was never shown the response that came to that message. I was only told about it with no real reason to suspect the level of lie involved. Marla's mother tried to cut me out of my own family, to hold holidays at their place with my kids and Marla, separate from me. I said, "Over my fucking dead body." Marla backed me up, so I thought.

Sometime later, as Christmas was approaching that year, I wrote a second message. This one was to my sister-in-law, Vendela. In it, I open with the statement that my sons are sad, and crying, because their grandparents don't come around. I implore her to speak to her mother, to stop being selfish, and hurting people because she did not like that I was able to definitively corral her behavior for once. That was what she had needed, and I had waited for an opportunity to shut her down one day. I always thought it would be about the boys, and it's not to say there were no other transgressions against appropriate boundaries. In fact, that had been the point of my letter. That her behavior cried out for boundaries to be set, and from now on I would. What she had done at the hospital was not a game. It had consequences, and I had had enough.

I never saw Vendela's response either. This was always treated as an oversight and swept under the rug. It was a key part of an operation. A long one. One designed to do exactly what was happening now: to alienate me from my sons. That rotten trio of harpies had always wanted to take my sons from me. They had tried long before divorce was in my mind. Was there a chance I could reason with my sons about this? That they could see I was always up against this? That their mother was not trying to be married, she was trying to destroy everything that the marriage was? For years.

My sister-in-law, ever one to overplay her own importance, sent these letters, and another penned by her to my mother. I knew about this but had never seen it. Life was busy then. This was gaslit away from me by Marla, and by my mother, who was always one to try to avoid trouble. It's a damning flaw that was used against her by Marla. She counted on my mother never giving up those letters. It was the source of the last big argument my mother and I ever had because Marla had misled me to their content.

Those letters, and all the drama around them, and my mother's reaction to them, were all known to Jackie, and she helped me fill in some big gaps and realize that Marla and my mother had both deliberately kept these letters from me, but for different reasons. Jackie knew my mother's thoughts on many things, and I didn't have my mom's brain anymore; she had left a lot of information in Jackie's.

Those letters… could they be in the house, still? It had been about ten years, within that, that all this had gone down. Marla's surgery that started it all was in 2011.

I fucked up, then. I took any chance I got to scream "What the Fuck?" at my sons, directly, indirectly. I played right into Marla's hands, but I still had yet to put it all together. They still weren't talking to me, but I was able to make some noise from the fringes. That was the excuse they used to stop talking to their grandfather and make it my fault. My howling and lashing out in pain and rage and confusion piled on and on, old and new, and emerging deep and septicemic.

Dr. Plow kept our driveway clear, and I tried to stay ahead of Dad with snow removal, and despite his knees hurting him and being 78, I failed. Usually, the snowblower woke me, and I raced outside before he could start shoveling. Combat conditions. Heart a-what? I did not give a fuck.

In the Clutches of the Pestilence

The winter was long and cold. After the holidays, around the beginning of February, I got hired at a job I could work with. Dad still went and saw mom every single day. I usually did too. We had spent the few weeks after the holidays looking out the window in the kitchen at the birds in the backyard while we drank coffee, I smoked weed, and we talked and talked and talked. The conversation was ongoing, and covered all spaces, all memories and topics. I continuously related my work experience, and the things I had learned with experiences he and I had in common when I was a little kid. The more we did this, the more we remembered together. I remembered the python from my nursery school, and how I learned what a coleus plant is then and never forgot. I tasted avocado there for the first time, and found it disgusting, and now I eat them by the truck load. This was one thing I could do. Hang out with my dad. We could talk to each other and did about everything. I joked that I was glad I had met Anghiel because plan A had been a whore parade, and I joked that I may find the limit of his patience with my shenanigans yet. If my energy could sustain us through this, we may just make it into a future together. It was clear that Dad was aware and understood better than I would have expected for most people. Better than I was doing, because when you love someone, you have them in your heart all the time. Both of us were sundered from that which we had grown accustomed to. I missed my sons, and Dad missed Mom. We were alone, yet together. If I could ride the waves and rapids now constantly just with me, my normal self, we may make it up to Turkey-neck together someday. We also spoke at length about camping technology, homesteading, and off-grid things. There were little dots of light way across this dark water. Hope. Direction. Dad gave me cast iron pans for Christmas, and I continued to cook for him. Playing to his palette made a better cook of me than years in restaurants, wilderness camping where it became an obsession, and cooking for two growing boys. If it weren't for me, they would have grown up on chicken tenders and frozen French fries. See? They were ever present, so every minute or so, something just sent me bouncing off the walls of my solitude in my skull and I was climbing the walls, even in my sleep. The transitions and disruptions of moving and getting my driver's license and all that shit had all happened by now. These were the bricks of tasks and moments that made up our lives now, and I did my best to decorate with positive experiential and therapeutic energy. I am still a fucking professional, God damn it, and I can muster the nuts to do what I have to do now. Haga. Fucking. Kure.

This determination, while needed, was also dangerously close to the anger that comes from indignity and humiliation. Being fueled by it, you could say, as the hottest furnace of reserves burning. The nuclear pile, if you will.

We could do this. We could maintain. It was stability, for now, while Mom lived.

I floated the idea of building a greenhouse in the spring, and growing marijuana. Dad had no objection to this, and approached it with thoughtful practical questions and insights. We had a project, and I was eyeing a different tent, and toying with an idea that preceded the holocaust my life had evolved into. It was a remnant of what was and hope for what yet may be again.

We watched the many birds on the feeders in the yard on the Mastershade Locust tree. There were Cardinals, and Blue Jays, and all kinds of woodpeckers. Dad kept suet and seeds out there, and contended with squirrels, and something that untwisted the wire and made off with one of the suet feeders. I tracked it into the woods and found it. This was a fun and safe way to vent anger. Dad laughed. "We could have just gotten another one," he said.

I showed him my blowgun, the single best most effective tool ever for working with kids at risk or special needs, or whatever. Absolutely forbidden. I've used it many times, and left jobs, not over its use, but because of a culture that was incapable of *discussing* its use or benefits, even hypothetically. Limited thinking. Limiting thinking. Ever my foe. Dad understood all of this. All of it. I was impressed with him, his strength. I drew from it as I tried to supplement his.

Has anyone heard from TC or Keelin?

Depardieu, Part 1

Whatland, Mass.

The job would give me a predictable schedule so I could support Mom and Dad. It was flexible. And it was at least relevant. I actually got hired for two jobs and made an attempt to work both. I was thinking about the future, my future, my financial stability. The first job was in an inpatient hospital. I was not there long. In my short tenure there, my manager told me he was going to work me to death. The adolescent unit was completely out of control, and dangerous. The staff were widely varied in their competence, conduct, and demeanor. I met some incredible people, and was able to start establishing some relationships. All I ever have to do is work, and the respect and camaraderie follows. That I still have and can count on. And, ever emerge the petty tyrants, the control freaks, the whisperers in corners. There were plenty of those there too. I saw staff from orientation on meal breaks.

I encountered some shocking red flags, all too familiar. There was no way I was going to put energy into my work the way I always had. I was strung out under stresses, in shock. All I could hope to do was be a comfort, maybe help keep things safe, one shift at a time.

The orientation and training were a joke, and was dominated by a loudmouth biker slut who thought she knew everything because she had two years' experience with DCF. Now she was going to work in the finance department, and she had an opinion on everything. Some things never change, and I was grateful I wasn't going to have to deal with her on the floors.

Some of the people I met were really good, and many were clueless. Some were the combination of incompetent, characterologically flawed, and on a fucking power trip, not just at work, but everywhere they went, all the time.

This was unhealthy for me and I would have lost myself. I saved someone from choking at dinner one night, and later I got called to the adolescent unit to find a brawl worthy of a rural Maine redneck dive going on between the kids and the staff. All I could do was find a group of kids huddled together in a room terrified without supervision and tell them Pirate stories and show pictures of my old pirate dog.

I was smoking cigars on break and eating McDonald's on shift every day. Frequently, once a week, anyway, I stooped at the Shell station and chatted with Mark Gasss. He knew where Maine was and expressed interest. I had, mayhap, found a pirate down here. There were plans for that, too. Saco river. Turkey-Neck. With Dad. While Mom lived, we would see her through, and mark the time. I started to teach Dad chess, and we played a little cribbage, but not nearly enough. We were busy. I missed Ella and shared a lot about her when I told him of the wild beautiful spaces I had discovered, while they had been here living their lives. We got fishing licenses. I stayed in touch with Nathan and Cody and whipped up the excitement. Dad and I explored how we could help NoraGee who was doing this whole dementia circus too with Ritchie. It was around this time that Ritchie touched off a firearm in his house for the first time. We heard that exciting development via phone call from Genna. It worked out because I saw what real alarm looked like on Dad's face, so, you know, I could watch for it.

The hospital job was not going to happen, and we parted ways right after I finished the orientation at Depardieu. At the Hospital for Behavioral Medicine, they had whipped through things in one week, paper and lecture, medications, etc. Restraint training was four hours. And there was our bleach blonde tobacco know-it-all who thought she was co-teacher distracting with her loud constant clucking and annoying everyone. She had a tattoo of a coffin on her arm that said "Sleep Tight". I thought that was about the most cuntish sentiment I've ever seen expressed. That's knit-and-gossip while the guillotine does her work cold. She made me want to vomit. Most of us I think were nauseated by her. Except the Africans, we all come off the same to them. That's pretty funny too. People from Ghana, Nigeria, Central African Republic… I met many, and they all think we're nuckin futz. I don't blame them. Jamaica. El Salvador. Guatemala. Columbia. In front of my eyes was the change we were seeing in the world. My relocation brought the larger scale of our society, what we were doing, and going through, right in front of my face. Dad and I talked about events as much and as well as all the chats we used to have with friends in Scarborough, and even him, when they visited. We marveled at what we were seeing, and my job made it personal and real. If it weren't for the situation with TC and Keelin, things were going kind of OK. Less, perhaps, than *ideal,* but, also less than terrible, or at least, not as bad as it could be. World stopping pandemic aside, that is. And Mom, and her solitary journey of undignified useless suffering, of which we were powerless to control much, especially now, locked away from her. I provided stimulation, and distraction, for both of us, and mercifully all this compartmentalization may have helped in the management.

When Mom dies, the boys will come to the funeral, and I will need to play that properly, and not fuck up. I've fucked up now, because I'm really hurt and pissed off at how this has developed, but it can be salvaged, mayhap. When Sherry dies. Oh, Mom. You never stop giving. This would please you, and I wish I could share it with you.

At Depardieu, the orientation was *two* weeks. Restraint training was *two days* long. They brought in several senior staff to make sure everyone was seen doing everything, every particular skill, like hand placement, every time, correctly. I taught CPR, SafetyCare and Driver's Ed. Thirty-four years' experience, if you'll allow them to be counted separately. I know good teaching, and bad teaching. These guys ran the best orientation I have ever experienced in twenty-five years. Hands down. We were all exhausted by the end of it. We had all shadow shifted, toured campus, toured the school, ate the food. It was such a contrast to the Mickey Mouse operation at the hospital I was working so hard at and killing myself, it was a no-brainer to jump ship, and go to Depardieu as my primary job.

If I was on the fence, this did it for me. There were two people in this orientation who, like Klassy Kathy at the hospital, showed a blatant disrespect for the orientation, us and the instructors alike, by talking incessantly with each other like two kids in school without any hint of self-awareness. One, of course, was a teacher herself, and one was a prison screw who thought he was Vin Diesel. On the third day of orientation, they got pulled out by the guy who was our MC, Ryan, and chastised. We didn't see it, but it was deliberately obvious, that they had been dealt with.

But they hadn't. The next day they pulled the same old shit, and halfway through the afternoon, Ryan came in, called them out, and sent them both home. I haven't seen someone publicly slapped up like that for a long time, and never like this. It wasn't me. That was a plus. I felt like I was doing good. I bit my lip so hard stifling a laugh at some point during these shenanigans I told Dad, and showed him, for several days and he laughed.

I AM a fucking PROFESSIONAL!

They deserved it. The next day they both were late. She came in and had clearly been crying. Of course, she had. They always do. I've learned something. The ones who are the first to cry to get sympathy when they get caught, are the last ones to show any humanity or compassion when they have someone under their own petty tyrant thumb. He followed fifteen minutes later and tried to act like it wasn't unusual he was rolling in thirty minutes late. What, me worry? He also shot a look at the facilitator that told us all Ryan knew. Ryan even looked out at every one of us. The warning shots had been given. We did not need the first ones; we did not need any more. I pride myself on professionalism in these situations. By the end of the two weeks, these people knew I knew what I was about, and I had not needed to tell them my fucking resume. I had no mercy for these two and their embarrassment and struggled not to pile on. As it was, my

Ghanian friend Joseph didn't have a car and I gave him rides all through this, so we had a chance to shit on these idiots. By the time we were finished at the end of two weeks, these two clowns had shown their ass so much it had become funny to me, their fumbling through basic CPR after telling us how many times they've taken it. Patterns in shitheads always manifest. Some things just never, ever change.

It should not be a surprise, that although I never saw the female of this dynamic clown duo again, I would cross paths with the ex-prison screw frequently, and he really was unfit for this in every way. I took pleasure in watching the kids teach him what training and common sense had failed to.

There's a secret here in this. For the insiders, when you know you know? For you guys, the crew. For you out there among my readers, these little side trips up narrow waterways are for you, because I know you live it even now. Your managers are usually idiots, except when they're not. Your livelihood is the most important thing, and to do your job it all has to be on the line every day. You are part of a vast forest, that is not empty, but looks so. It looks like you are alone. Moving down here showed me we are Legion.

I shared all of this, with side dishes, to Dad, and we laughed, and laughed, and laughed. We saw Mom just about every day. We caught our breath, one night, watching the news.

From: Desiderata

Keep interested in your own career, however humble. It is a real possession in the changing fortunes of time.

Pause for Perspective

Dad asked me one night, "Hey, Son. I have a question."

My father was a good communicator. This was contrasted by his ability to get tripped up, and lose the tempo if the situation was chaotic, or many people were talking. He listened attentively to people, so when there was a lot going on or it was rapid, he could lose track, as can we all. This is a key component of working with kids and families, this managing of pace and tempo. When Dad led in like this, instead of just making a comment or observation, I knew he had thought about it, whatever it was, so I sat up from my texting, which was ongoing throughout every day keeping in touch with the Cid, and Lono and Kary and the rest, up in Maine. The TV was on, and the news was on, and as usual it was mostly bad, but now there was a disease moving quickly around the world, and it was becoming clear that even governments that were running somewhat properly, unlike ours, were struggling to deal with it. That was obvious from *"Ahh, 1918"*, and then we knew, that this was one of *those* situations. One that would be remembered in a thousand years, if we survived the next five as a species.

It was the earliest days, that the Corona-19 virus was out of control and there was no way at all of knowing how bad it was going to be. It was about three weeks before we all collectively realized it was bad, really bad, but his question was about an issue that had been building for some time across the country. The question Dad asked was about the other stuff, though.

"Don't *all* lives matter?"

The Four Horsemen

In 2020, I watched almost (almost, thank God) all of the nightmare scenarios that we ever talked about at my old kitchen table in my old life come to life. I mean society stuff. We were social workers, at our core, and the arena where we had all made our bones together was in the literal cracks they talk about kids falling through. The cracks are the system. Cristobal and Matty Mango were frequent guests, often in the wee hours that we live in, that I have always lived in. The places where there is no day or night, or season, sleep is caught as can be and all meals are eaten in motion on your feet. We talked about the viability of the rise of fascism in America, twenty-five years ago. Now, it was on the evening news, and I was here with Dad. We were back-to-back, and swords out.

I left that life in 2019 and watched my own catch fire. I came back here to find Dad fighting his own fire, and together we had…it's impossible to carry it further. Everything we both had known that mattered was ash. And then, the rest of the world caught up to us. It was no surprise, really, after the circus the Trump presidency made of American politics. And especially since this current climate in our country had terrifying parallels to history. It wasn't the political scene, of the insane inefficiency of the US Congress for thirty years prior. This was something else and it had both Dad and I concerned at least as much as the plague, until the effects of the plague made Dad's nightmare ten thousand times more agonizing for him.

Its's hard now to tell which thing was worse, because there was so much going on, that at all levels from our individual personal lives to apparently the entire fucking globe seemed to be sliding and picking up speed and momentum towards some unknowable horrible end.

"Yes, all lives matter. To you and me, and most people we think of as decent."

He was listening.

"However, at this time, one particular community, that of people who are… other than white, especially African Americans, appear to be getting killed by cops with numbers that do not make sense.

"We are conditioned to think 'Black Crime'. We see black men get killed in their cars, standing next to their own homes with their hands up. Shot dead during routine traffic stops. It doesn't make sense."

He was listening.

"So, you have group of people, in this case, let's say, Blacks. Ok? Blacks, in general."

"Ok."

"First of all, even the way we are presented with the facts is biased. Racially. Specifically, racially. *'The Blacks?'*… can you hear it?"

"I guess."

"Ok. We'll work with that. 'The Blacks' say that cops are little more than killers with badges, license to kill, like fucking James Bond. Or some western guy. Those old western shows we love… they do not depict a lot of due process."

He smiled.

"In black communities across America, people are getting gunned down. There are often suspicious circumstances. Body-cam footage should be readily available, every time there is such an incident, and they should be much less frequent.

"Black folk have been saying this for years. They get drowned out. They get shouted down about crime in their communities. And their brothers and their fathers and their sons and daughters just keep on dying.

"It might even still keep happening. Law enforcement denies there is a problem, despite the horrifying numbers of dirty cops, corrupt cops, gangster cops, and plain old fucking homicidal maniacs."

But I held up my phone. "Everybody has a camera now, and the ability to show anything at all to the whole world."

"So, when you have a cop, on camera, deliberately subduing someone excessively, someone whose supposed offense did not warrant such a response, and the person dies… what then?

"The cops shrug it off and say, 'he was resisting' or some other lame ass excuse. They don't have any camera footage, although they are supposed to. Funny how suspicious behavior of theirs is uncannily off camera. Like they know how to stay out of its eye."

"Cops are dirty. Not all of them, but if they all stand together, *and they do,* then they are all responsible for the worst of the lot. That's how it works. Cops are murdering black people in the streets with impunity, and the real story is that people are putting a lot of effort into minimizing that."

"All lives do matter, but to say so now, over the voice of black folks, is oppressive, and racist. Do you see that? These cops are often demonstrably dirty under close inspection. After someone gets killed. This pig had a history with this Floyd guy. It's always the rest of the story. I'll tell you one thing, Dad. Cops lie. Teachers lie. Everyone fucking lies. You know where the truth lives? In the streets. The streets always know the truth."

"But even with all that, the corruption, the racism of the system, the lies, the cover-ups, the incompetence, the poor training, all acknowledged and beyond dispute, you still have people with video cameras filming and spreading it, and without so much as a pause, voices shift gears, and dilute the message to apply to ALL lives. Its straight up oppression, racism, and gaslighting."

Dad took all this in. "Seems obvious," he said.

"It *is* obvious."

These were the conversations that kept it real. Sometimes I wonder, if there had only been one of our horrors to contend with, how much worse the one would have seemed, instead of just being part of some huge mess that was affecting the whole world not just us, which made it all seem strangely normal somehow. Reality. Hell. And all the Horsemen of the Apocalypse were riding the Earth. And here we were. I'm trying to breathe.

So, as a worker, my job was to figure out things. What someone is thinking. What they heard. What they think was said, what they meant to say, what they are trying to say. Also, of course, was there any peepee touchin' going on? That one is kind of standing orders to watch for. Anyhoo…

Now, with Dad, as I was and would more than I could know, I did this. I'm glad, because I think I changed his thinking about something important.

Dad was not a speller. In fact, me the future English major, etc., and Mom the teacher, used to ride him pretty hard when he wrote "shugar" instead of sugar on a grocery list. We laughed at him, with him. However, now, I realized, as I always tried to en fielde, as we say, (as I said to him exactly that sarcastic pseudo pretentious way, 'cause this was heavy and I wanted him to take it in, and I was in teach mode), he had lived his whole life thinking he was stupid. On some level. But of course, he was not. In fact, it really was simply a matter of explaining to him that taking words from his ears, and making letters out of it with his hands was the thing.

"You can speak, you can read."

"Right."

"You can Math, unlike me."

"Ok."

"When you hear words, you then have to recall them, and write stuff."

"Yeah."

"And spelling, in all that, making the one thing other, especially when you're also thinking about the whole thing, like, is it a question and you're writing the answer? There are several different things going on there."

"Right."

"For you, the you that there is only one of, that particular set of things gets tangled up, and you spell words, the way you hear them. Your spelling, when it's wrong, is wrong… phonetically."

"So?"

"So, it means that like kids in the 21ˢᵗ century now, in school, you did not have someone then, say these things, and then spend some extra time each week with a specialist figuring out how you yourself and no one else can learn to use you r own brain as it is, to do what you need to do."

"Ya…"

I'm losing him.

"Dad. It's 1955. You're in school. A little shy, and you know you struggle with this. In 2017, you may have an IEP, and a couple people who help you do the work around it. Kellin's a genius, you know this."

"Yes, he sure is. They both are."

---snick—a razor went across my heart at the mention of the boys, but this was important and I was hot for it. I pressed on.

"Dad, Keelin got reading help in school. You had 1955. Keelin also had a school that is making some progress around bullying. Not really, but for this, the most primitive and banal kind of bullying, they are on top of it. They don't let kids go 'um… um… um… b-b-b-' to the kid who stutters.

For example. Now. Sometimes. Kids still get bullied, it's a fact, and social media has made it beyond sci-fi futuristic nightmare. Back to you.

"You were shy, you were quiet. And like many, many people, you went through school and adapted as best one can, to a very, very, Dad… imperfect system."

"I wonder what Mom would say to that."

I laughed out loud. "I don't. I think I have an idea, because we went around about this on occasion, one professional to another, many times over the years."

I had to get to work. I filled my mug with caffEEN. I popped some nicotEEN. I had been good and high before my shower and this chat. I armed up.

"You're not dumb. You never have been. This is pretty much what I've done with kids all these years. Help them do what we just did."

"I love ya, son."

"I'll see you tonight. I love you too."

"And Mom loves you, too." I stopped and hugged him again.

"I know she does."

I rolled up to the Dep feeling good most of the way, until my sons joined me, and I wanted to be pissed off, but I wasn't. I missed them. I was pissed on behalf of Dad.

Dangerous.

My Parents

We went to Blaire Haus to see Mom. These days, she was often "zonked out" to use Dad's phrase, as in "I hope Mom isn't too zonked out today." It was hit or miss. We contended with the snow or rain, the traffic and the wind and the cold. I was aware that my dad's knees were shit, and he had delayed his second cataract surgery in the last year, because he could not do that with Mom in her rapidly declining state. It was after that last Christmas, I deduced, that she had really gotten bad, and so it hadn't been that bad. In fact, in larger perspective, the way things had shaken out had been somewhat fortuitous, especially when we considered the near misses we knew about. The deck would have collapsed, that was pretty clear. There was a hole in the basement wall as big as an open window. I stapled plastic in it, and we heard the furnace run and run and run. When we saw Mom, if she was awake, she would pretty much smile and chat, but not coherently, and in the three months I had been back that he had still been living with her at home, he had learned a lot about not trying to respond, answer or satisfy her questions, but rather to appease her. They call it the Long Goodbye. I always hated that term, but he needed the full measure. I knew there was no getting him to any kind of doctor until he felt ok about her. For now, he went and saw her every day, and I went with him, and I scrambled up to the Dep to my kids up there. Every day I had to leave him in the kitchen, with a hug, and telling him, no, Dad, I don't need any money, but thanks. Hopefully you talk to the boys tonight.

When we saw Mom, even if she was zonked out, if I played Oldies on the cylon her foot would tap, sometimes she would open her eyes and smile at us. Sometimes, she would open her eyes, and demand to know what the fuck was going on. Either way, it delighted Dad, and therefore me too.

Also, I now had a little money, and I bought a ten-foot canvas bell tent with a stove jack last fall, and I had my little camp tent, stove and snuggle den out there. Anghiel, in a refreshing change from what I was accustomed to, enthusiastically embraced the fun of snuggling in the snow on night so when she came to visit, carefully timed to be just before Dad went to bed, so I did not cut off time from him. She just was never a bitch. At all, and my friends struggled to understand this, and Anghiel found that dumbfounding, that men experience such things, in relationships. There was some measure of balance, and hope.

Boys call, Dad? No? Sorry.

Depardieu Diagnostic School

Whatland, Mass.

9 degrees F.

I started at the Dep in the dead of winter. After orientation I committed to three or four days a week. It did not take long to be recognized as an effective force, and I quietly did anything Kelsie threw my way. She was a soldier through and through, she ran her team and her group of kids with an iron hand tempered with flagrant love. She could kick ass when there was need, and was not one to be flowery with praise or compliments. If she walked through the unit and gave you a nod, it was a sign of respect and satisfaction.

Our unit was known as West Meadow 2. 1 was downstairs and had latency aged kids. Together, up and down were two sides of one team. We covered breaks for each other, and we slipped up or down the stairs when the calls for help went over the radio. We never had handheld radios at Sweet Shores, the last time I worked in residential. That was a game changer and I did my part to demonstrate good radio discipline. I did get carried away on occasion. Walkie talkies are fun, it is true. People will just pick up and adopt what they see that works, so our crew was good on the radio, clipped and efficient, and we often heard people around campus on the radio just babbling.

We also had pretty much the same core group of kids up and down. There were some changes, but most of the kids I met were there when I started working and still there when I worked my last day in early 2021. I've worked with innumerable groups of different kids. Some of them are… a great mix. These kids did not all get along, but they each brought something to the group, and I was grateful and blessed, that while every other part of my life was whipping and swirling and spinning wildly out of control, this felt like an oasis of normalcy, and familiarity. I was quickly recognized as the guy who could take three kids out of the unit, anytime and keep them entertained on the nature trail or the kickball field, or fishing at the pond a short walk off campus away, and divide the kids up is a good base strategy. I knew my job, and Kelsie liked that she did not have to explain shit to me, she could just put me on her chessboard and counted on me to do my job. She also started sending me everywhere else on campus, and I got in with the groups of kids and the staff at the different residences around the Hill, except for the all-girls unit, which was by far the most problematic and predictable for trouble. This is an example of the lines I had to draw for myself. I enjoy working with young women, too. That's exactly what they do need, safe men around them, and women, and to learn what that looks like and what to do with it. I explained to Dad that had I been back in the day, I would have been drawn there to help with the shitshow, but Lex and Jazz got their share of getting bounced around too. They did a lot of work with the girls. I could not, with my life now, make that level of commitment, because you need a few people at least, on the team, who will come in early, stay late, come in for four hours on their day off… Samurai. I saw many in action at Depardieu, and I enjoyed humbling myself, that I was not the wellspring and end-all of this, it was found everywhere, it was simply love, and honor, and professional ethics from those two things alone.

I was with a new group of samurai, and they loved the whole Hagakure philosophy. I had shelter from my own storms. I could do what I was born to do here, even if I felt like I was fading away and lost and alone. I could teach and heal, here, so I did.

Dad went and saw Mom every day, until the plague shut everything down. Then, I got to go to work three days a week, and focus on my little lambies. They had immediately been that, from my first shift. Thank God. I need an environment where you can at least know you're really planting seeds.

What is the brightest star in the sky?

No, smartass. Not the sun. That's just the closest. By now, someone has thought "The North Star".

The North Star.

However, it is not. It is not, but that is not the interesting thing. I've been asking this question of children for years. Adults, too, to (this gets complex) model for children that it's ok to submit to the learning process. If I tell my teammate on the unit, in the cottage, on the floor, in the fucking trenches, use your own parlance; if I teach something to them, they get to play it to the kids, and model prosocial behavior. Something like that. All I knew, was with a group of kids, I always tried to channel cool people and cool situations, to create experiences for others out of ones I myself had had, and therefore, knew about to share from memory and thus pass on. Legacy.

So, what is it?

Before the big reveal here, it's important to point out two things, the two things that make this something that has bugged the piss out of me for a long time.

The first is that people tend to think that it's the North Star. Why? I mean, they think they know it, and they say it. And yet, I cannot get my head around it, it is not. And all one has to do is look. It isn't on a wall in some cave in France. It's visible throughout the Northern fucking Hemisphere!

The brightest star visible to us is Sirius. The Dog Star. I have never been able to find a satisfying reason why people seem to think it is, even though it's right there in the sky. The only answer that fits the facts is so hard to believe I just can't, right now. The kids at the Dep were an engaged audience, and I quickly became the fishing guy. Got an App on the phone that made a reel sound every time someone caught a fish, and the kids got into it. I even connected (hooked up with?) with some guy, Kly05, who was near me, and caught monsters all the time, wherever he was almost daily. The kids became fans of the exploits of Kly05. When I shared this with him, he ended up mailing me a ton of lures for the kids to use, far better than the usual Walmart fare that made up most of what we had. I made sure there were enough poles and working lures for everyone to use one at my own expense, but Kly05 was another one of those random angels who just did something really cool.

Springtime in Gehenna

I watched the winter wane and we put together our plan for a greenhouse, to grow pot. He was a grower of things, the trees here now wrapping us in their arms were testament to that, and he loved the idea of growing cannabis, which was hilarious to me. I watched him do many things when I was a kid, saw, dig, measure shit. All that was and is beyond me. But, with me lugging the heavy beams for the frame, and trying to do the labor letting him do the actual carpentering, we put it up, over about four weeks, on my days off from the Dev. I could not keep him from working as hard as he always had. He would grab lumber. Swing hammer, and try to get in and lift stuff he shouldn't. I chastised him gently, but in the dark tone underpinning even our happiest and lightest moments, as these surely were, I tried to get him to take seriously the real problem of something happening o hi, or either one of us, really. We were in this together and as the sun grew in heat and length of stay day by day, I found a friend of Genna's who knew about everything there was to know about growing cannabis, and lacked only one thing. The very thing we had. A place to sow the seed. We built the greenhouse, and our mysterious friend came by and brought some seedlings. My dad was always a gardener and a planter. In his life with my mother, the idea of growing cannabis, legal or not (well, if it wasn't legal there would have been no way we would have been foolish enough to even discuss it with Mom) was a non-starter. If you actually know me, knew my mom, you're laughing right now, because "non-starter" to that idea speaking of my mom is like trying to vet a menu for a Hindu wedding that headlines a great big Flintstone's size hunk of rare roast beef. I believe Dad and I laughed in this vein many times. Mom's aversion to all things unclean or "low-class" was a cornerstone of the laughter and the conflicts that shaped our family.

So, I was surprised when my dad looked at me one day in the TV room, out of the blue, and said, "Hey, son… do you think we should get some guns?"

I was aghast, but that was funny. I burst out laughing. He looked at me with the smile I saw when he did something unusual. I saw it once when he got pissed off trying to pull out a stubborn unwelcome bush, and he just paused, growled at it, set himself, and tore it out by the roots. When he saw me standing there with my mouth open, he gave me that smile. One time, I saw him just pull like 500 dollars out of his pocket. I don't remember why, but I do remember I was like… 'What the FUCK… are you doing carrying that much cash around?' No answer. Just that knowing quiet smile. When I saw it now, I laughed harder, because without words, I and he were both laughing at this naughty streak he was manifesting now that he was cut loose from Mom, as awful as that was for him. There were parts of him that may well have been around in his youth, but he had married my mom, who was a nice girl, and never one for wildness. Indeed, she had tried to raise me with a pretty conservative mindset, one out of touch with the realities of the generation I grew up in. Not politically conservative, they were both socially liberal. Socially conservative. This was a profound lesson I would develop much of my professional skill and philosophies and practices from. One must have a realistic approach with children. If you live in a tough neighborhood, it's okay to teach your kid peace, but don't make him fear fighting to defend himself, or people will bully that kid. If your kid doesn't watch the show all his friends watch, it's a lot to put on an eighth grader. It can set them apart.

There is something here that came out in my talks with my dad, and he showed some startling understanding into the nuances of an art and science I had spent my whole life in quest of perfection of. There is a line between making choices for yourself and imposing your will upon others. In the political climate in America in 2020, there was a poignant relevancy here that we reflected on. It broadened the spectrum of our conversations. We continued to see Mom whenever we could, but there were weeks when we could not, and every time we did, it was clear she had slipped a little bit more. Most of the time, we did go and see her together and I tried to develop rapport with the staff so if I was around and she was awake I would go see her, but that, look so many things only happened once or twice and in the ever-changing dynamics of this many layered nightmares, it became irrelevant, because the Plague grew in intensity as the windbag's wind bagged, The Plague showed us what Plague is. Plague does not care. It does not respect or consider anything at all, and soon, we were all considering the Plague, and how to survive, all of us wondering I think, at least once, in our own heads during all of this, if this wasn't the Apocalypse, it would do just fine until the Apocalypse really showed up.

After the greenhouse frame was up, our partner started coming by and doing his farmer thing. Dad would go out and watch him intently, and ask questions, and I saw the two of them out there chatting away like old pals. Dad could talk with anyone. I was not unusual when I was a kid, if the weather was warm, to hear the lawnmower shut off, then long quiet. Mom would come out and I'd hear her whisper "Where the heck is your father?" And we would see him out there, chatting away with our neighbor Arthur. They could chat for hours, and did, as neighbors do. My dad was a great communicator. He could shoot the breeze with anyone. Arthur was deaf and mute. He did not speak, as such, but made loud vocalizations like: "Ahh! M-m-p-m-ffff. Aaargh!" And he and Dad would both double over and laugh. And slap each other on the back. More than once, I saw someone who would see them talking like this, and as we got closer, it was clear that they were having their own conversation in their own language. It took some by surprise, and never got tired for me. Dad never failed to know whatever Arthur was talking about. He could read lips though, and his two sons were both hearing children of deaf parents. The two sons would talk with their Dad, but only move their mouths, they did not actually speak. And Arthur would say "Ep. D-d-f. Gah." And they would nod, and say, "Ok, then." For me now, I just reflected on the communication skills I knew now, and how I had acquired them, and maybe where I had acquired some of them in a whole new way.

We got the plastic wrapped around the greenhouse and the plants went in and began to sprout. I did not bother trying to tell Dad he did not have to trouble himself to water them, because he did, every day. I said something about screening some loam and dirt out of the soil and gravel available to us on the property on day. When I came home, he had thrown together a wooden frame with metal screen in it. After that I was careful not to give him ideas like that. It was ok. He needed to keep busy. He went to bed when I got home from work, and got up around 7. I went to bed around two, and got up around 10. When I woke up in the mornings, I could hear him in the room that had been mine once, had been the room they sat and watched TV together in, planned Christmases in, spoke to all of us on the phone for hours and years in, now silent, but for the soft device sound effect of him clicking back and forth between the handful of pictures of mom that we had taken since she had gone away. When Ella died, I wrapped myself in pictures and memories of her, and I could see him doing the same thing. It doesn't make the pain any less, it just helps you feel the reality of how much you loved what was gone.

I never did wake up to hear him laughing on the phone talking to TC or Keelin, and that little disappointment started my day like coffee, and by the time I rode to the Dep for my shift, I had a pretty good rhythm going of feeling pissed off about how unfair this all was, especially if it was based on lies that Marla had told them. I still could not believe that's what she did. I asked Dad about the letters that had stirred up so much trouble long ago. He remembered all that, of course, but had no idea if they were even still in the house. I was hopeful that they were. I had never seen them and had always wanted to know. I was afraid there was some terrible hurt in there between me and Mom, that she had never told me about. Marla knew I feared this. She also knew that was unfounded, but she never stopped letting me fret about that. It helped her overall mission.

What I feared was that Vendela or Marla's mother had planted some terrible seed, and hurt my mother so badly with false or twisted words of mine, that she had left some final painful last word of a reply to me that said words to the effect of: "I guess I did not love you enough to satisfy/thank you for giving me Grandchildren though…" Some shit like that, that I could carry forever. Marla knew there was no such content, and she let me think there might be. Now that I was here, and my mother's impending death was here with us, this old fear rose in presence, and added to the nonstop combination of love and fury of confused betrayal, added my poor attempts at being Dad's sidekick in all this, not he to me and my fucking complex web of drama. What had seemed like an inconvenient circumstance, the fact that I had never actually seen this correspondence with my own eyes began to take on a new, deeper and far more sinister glow. It wasn't merely circumstantial. Marla had deliberately manipulated that situation. If she had done it as part of a larger picture to paint to my boys, to alienate me like this…. Then, she had been up to this for almost ten years. This situation with my sons now, it had not spring from the chaos Marla had made of what could have been a smooth transition. It had been her plan all along. And her mother and sister had been in on it.

I'm sitting here with my father, and I have things to do, and it was these little revelations that clang home in my mind with the undeniable ring of truth, that was hitting me like shots in a boxing ring. Marla. Did you really do this?

Do you know how sick that makes you, and that you

are a child abuser? Forget the financial abuse of me, and exploitation of my parents now becoming apparent. If you made my sons hate me with these filthy lies, you're a straight up child abuser.

It would be fair to say I was putting a lot of energy into containing my urge to find a foe to pick a fight with. Some people act out their anger with violence. I'm not like that, but holy Jesus if I had encountered someone abusing a puppy, I might have… indulged myself a little teeny bit, ok? The fury at these revelations coming on a time release dose is excruciating.

As the winter released its hold and the plague had us locked down tight, we began to address the other pressing things, like the sagging deck that had a hole in the wall downstairs with nothing in it when the temp had been five below except a stapled in white plastic trash bag. We needed that deck replaced, and the repair done to the house. I wondered for the first time what other unpleasant surprises were lurking for us to discover. I was thinking about the house. There were other surprises, and they were not just in the house.

My sons had not called me, and it looked like they were not going to. This ate at me like acid all the time and I worked through what I could and couldn't do. If Dad were capable, I still could not try to have him talk to the boys at all, it just was not in his ability to take that kind of delicate operation on. I had no one really, who I could even trust to do it right and not fuck it up, somehow help me be heard by them. Nicky, maybe, or Kevin, but that was a thin prospect, and the truth is, it was kind of like a dirty secret thing, people who knew I was agonizing over this were not able to really offer any kind of help, so they did not try. From Jon, I took it as his respect for my dignity in my pain, but from some it felt more like a lack of willingness to help me figure out what the fuck was going on and how to find my way back to them. These are the things that I ruminated on when I was alone, in my car, on the way to or from the Dep, so I had a little slow simmer going on as the tensions in the country and the world spoiled over everywhere. It wasn't remote shot on the news, we had idiots right here in our community harassing people about wearing or having to wear masks. I did get a lot of unasked for counsel that was not helpful, because they did not get the larger picture. When people told me to be patient, that time heals and all that, I didn't have the wherewithal to take on explaining, that no, it doesn't because there was a factor keeping these wounds fresh, and it was she who had inflicted them, and still was. My rage grew like a hurricane, and I used all my disciplines to keep it under control. Going to the kids helped, because even though their behaviors are often less than Southern-level manners, you're there to help them, and I knew how to shelve my own thoughts and focus on what I was there for, and we had a lot of laughs with those kids, but this place shocked me with how dangerously out of control it could get. I was never really worried about my own safety, but I did, especially for the littler kids and some of the huge violent criminals in training we were surrounded by. I didn't deal much with those older kids, but they never tested me either when I was called for shows of force, and I was grateful for that. This wasn't Sweet Shores where we were practically surrogate parents to those kids. You only expect the respect you earn, give them, and that they are even capable of. Any more is unfair to them, and you. I did my best to just do it good, and hope my new team, young most of them, were watching and learning. Some were, for sure, and Ryan really ran our shift. He was no newbie, he had a big heart, he was funny, and intelligent, and competent. Of course, he and I had become close comrades immediately, and so we remain even now. Just like Matty Mango, and Cristobel, and all the others in this long line of souls I've sailed with, it felt really good, to know that the line was still growing, My comrades. My brethren.

The weed plants were happily growing and the days were getting warmer. The Covid had everyone scared, especially before there was a vaccine. Anghiel and I stayed apart.

We have a lot of sayings in our culture that have lost their bite and fire. This is one, because it is never given in its entirety. People edit the message on their own. Absence does not make the heart grow fonder.

"Absence is to Love as wind is to fire. It extinguishes the small. It enkindles the great."

Anghiel and I were unable to enjoy the ice cream during the Rona, and we developed a deeper more intellectual and emotional connection enjoying the vegetables.

As the Corona-19 super virus escalated Dad and I watched. I escaped to the Dep to work, and found some measure of normalcy and peace. It occurred to me, that had I stayed in Maine, the effect of the Rona on my ability to earn would have been the ball game, and I would have been living in an apartment with a colleague… it was a what-if that was so much worse than the what-was. Like the deck that had not collapsed with them on it.

I kept Dad both entertained and occupied and we waited

for word that the facility was allowing visitors again. I had also been hired at the local driving school, but the math on the exposure was many times worse than one front line job. If Anghiel and I couldn't see each other to protect our parents, I wasn't going to make it higher risk for a few paltry scotch pounds. I finished this thought with Dad as the very words were spoken on the movie we were watching. Its title is Rob Roy, and if you've seen it, you know the scene Tim Roth speaks those words in. It was something I did when my kids were growing up, quote a movie while it's on without warning or explanation. Keelin had learned that if I just said something : "We're going to need a bigger boat," to watch whatever he was watching for it, and this tickled him, and it was like ten thousand inside jokes and chuckles I had with my sons before all this, the things that make up closeness and bond, and now, I tried to recapture these memories for myself, and share a laugh with dad, so when he said it on the film, I said, "There, see? He knows," and Dad got it and laughed, and we laughed again, some more, for a little while between all the internal screaming and the tears.

I stole moments on the phone with Genna and Dad and I made it over to NoraGee's for lunch. Seeing them together was nice, but I could never for a minute stop seeing what was not here that should be. I just struggled to maintain my positivity and advocacy around mom and support Dad, and try to build new and now from what had once been and diverged so long ago and was back together again. It is true that we did in those days make the literal comparison to Hell on Earth, and he agreed that it fit. We continued to laugh and quote Sun-Tzu, but Sun-Tzu was no longer coming daily, and I did not know why, but things were busier and that little detail did not flag as important until he started coming around again, and when.

Depardieu

Summer, 2020.

98 degrees F.

Sunny.

This workplace is an oasis. It says something that I have to come here and deal with trauma and violence and here I feel most like me, and normal. Being with Dad is great, but I have things I need to do, and I can't experience this for myself. I have to facilitate his, and ease what horrors of it I may. I come here, and the kids are screaming "Fuck you!" and running away, and throwing food, and fighting. Ah, Home.

No shift is ever the same. If they feel that way, you better check them all, right now, with your own eyes. We got shuffled around and moved and reassigned. We had to respond to problems that were not West Meadow's. We came to know who it was that was happy to see us show up to take our place in the line. In the old days it was Matty Mango, and Cristobel. Now, it was Perry, or Ryan. Or Jaz or Lex, who become much larger. Also, unlike my past experiences, here were people from all over the world with all kinds of stories and ideas. With the blatant reality that there was a rising tide of bigotry in our country going on in real time, it was hard not to talk about this with Dad, the obvious parallels, and the fact that Mom would be tickled that I was making friends from fucking Ghana. Perry, in fact, was Jamaican. So was Roshane. We had reggae music playing at bedtime one night and I nodded to them, that nod when good music is on, played by another, and you nod like, "Yeah" in recognition. I did that, and they both laughed right at me. I stopped halfway down the hall and looked back.

"White people think this is good vibes music" he said.

I looked, quizzically. Ok. I had just stepped in some White Man shit. This is also a new dimension. Fuck, it took ten years to get really comfortable with all the ways you can say the wrong shit to a female co-worker.

Perry was smiling at me. "It's all about poverty and shit, man."

I get it. "Guilty" I said. We laughed together. Is this the way to the future? Are we hammering it out? Here, and now, joined together by this noble purpose? Why not?

The kids at the Dep were great. By this, I mean, they were enthusiastic. They wanted to fish, and hike. OK. The backpack with the stove, and the briefcase full of tricks, rode again. Residential, again, after twelve long years. My tour with Matty Mango did not count. Elderly, intellectually disabled, and I was a manager and trainer, primarily. Not the same. They needed help, that was for sure, and it really came home to me that some things never do change. There will always be kids who fall through the cracks, who have nowhere else to go, and there will always be places like Sweet Shores, and Depardieu. There are many contrasts to be made between the two. The most important one is that Sweet Shores was the largest mental health agency in its state, and it gobbled up a piece of every pie with a flagrant disregard for whether they knew what they were doing or not. The side effect of this, however, had been that for years we often got to work with enough autonomy to be able to actually do some good. It is also true that Sweet Shores practiced blatant nepotism, and taking care of their own, and when it came down to brass tacks, they did not give a fuck about the quality of care they delivered. I dare them to come at me for this, please, God, let them come. Because everyone who worked there will back me up that it's true.

When I was fired from Sweet Shores, I had stepped on a lot of toes over the years. Sometimes it was funny, sometimes it was ill advised, but it never was for any other reason than what was best for us, now, kids and staff together, and it never wasn't dangerous to live that way. But it was worth it. Sweet Shores, because they were huge, and because I was poor, and because they could get away with it, stuck a little extra on me as I was leaving. For no cause, they told me I could not be on any of their property, and although I appealed to them to grow up and think about the ramifications of that for the people we both served, they blithely told me to fuck myself. I appealed one more time spelling out that since Sweet Shores was a large company, that prohibition was unreasonable, as it compromised my own ability to serve my people with that hanging around my neck like a scarlet albatross. They did not care about that. They threatened legal action. Oh, God… how I wish I could have charged that windmill. Alas…

For ten years I carried this disgusting affrontery of personal petty insult with me. Their dishonor is neither forgotten, or forgiven, and I speak of it here now. It will NOT be the last time. I think that when done wrong like this, this sneaky secret injustice, done simply because it can be done…that's evil, and though I lost that war in one regard, Sweet Shores is not regarded well by the community it serves. I am, though. I was, and am to this day. Sweet Shores…we are not through quite yet. But I have another war on my hands for now. You WILL hear me coming when I circle back to you. I will give you exactly as much quarter as you once gave me. And others, I have found out since. Watch for them, too. Truth will split all lies that cover it like the roots of the ivy shatter stone.

The kids at the Dep, like kids throughout my career, generally liked and responded well to me. Not everyone did, then, or now. In fact, less did than I was used to in the Old Days, and I worked on my percentage with that as best I could with some success, also as always. I wasn't getting told to fuck off as much as most of the staff. And, I was getting calls to work on my days off, and stay over, and fill in. Some things never really do change, and Kelsie's efforts were heroic keeping that unit fully staffed, no thanks to me. I could not prioritize it as once I had, when my own kids were young, and I scrambled for years to fill a coffer that never got any fuller…

But I know one thing. I wish I could tell you that Healing fell out of my ass in an embarrassment of riches, but despite what it may sound like here at times, the truth is if you're lucky, committed, disciplined, (*humble. Compassionate. Righteous. Honest.*) you <u>may</u>, repeat, <u>may</u> get it right enough to do more good than ill. However, though I wonder as I write these things if some kid may emerge to say "You know what, motherfucker? I think you were a mean asshole, and you didn't do shit for me but make my life harder! I hate you!"

Could that kid be out there? Absolutely. And if there is,

and God I pray there is not, but if there is, all I can say is this, and I say it on my life now and forever. Never, never once, did I ever try to hurt anyone, especially emotionally. I never treated anyone without dignity, even when we had to rough and tumble. I will say that to my Maker, so if it isn't true, all I can say is it is, as far as I know. I don't believe any kid I ever knew ever saw a cruel face on me. I sure hope not.

I do not have that worry about… creepy shit, though. I sure saw plenty of it. Close to a dozen people got caught at Sweet Shores over the years diddlin' kids, in one way or another. It's possible to diddle kids without touching them, too. No, I'm not going to explain, but if any kind of sexual energy leaks out of you around the kids, you're off the bases.

Ok, I will explain. I'm out with some kids.

I'm out with about some kids and one other staffer. We are at a seaside town in the summertime. There are beautiful people, everywhere, of all shapes and sizes. It is summer. Sexuality is in the air. People are lightly dressed. These are teenagers. Many have sexual trauma. Every fucking day, everywhere you look, there is always something. Ever believing you can sanitize an environment or a consciousness is erroneous. So, if some hot woman walks by around my age, I have the power to not be fake. I do not ignore, or look away, but I look at her like I look at everyone on the street. I do NOT check her out, and when I say this boyo, you better fucking believe it's a whole other level than checking out a woman and trying not to get busted by your wife for wander-eye. Trust me, you have to be able to not even THINK it. So, you don't. You truly don't. You leak zero sexual energy. Kids that have been abused have ESP. Just be pure and trust them to know truth.

Hopefully, the adults with the kids know how to work with what they get today. It's easy to get it wrong. You have to be…pure, about this. None of us are eunuchs, but kids don't need to be exposed to any more sex. That's a good rule to follow. There is a LOT of sex, everywhere. I know. I was in Dead Bedroom Marriage, and after a while it's like Chinese water torture. Is it just water torture now?

That is when beauty happens. Out of the mouths of the children.

Some will comment on people being scantily clad. It's a chance to teach them that the body is nothing more or less than a creation of Nature.

Some will speak about obesity. Some will test boundaries and make whistle or catcall noises. Some will snort when they spot a police car, or walking by a cop directing crown and traffic. They are children. Children say beautiful, and terrible things. Most of them, almost all of them, are true, usually. What you do with what they say is the foundation of literally everything, but getting these five kids through Old Orchard Beach in July without an incident report was my immediate order of the moment. But maybe… just maybe, they acquire something rare. Something so rare to them, for many they don't even know what is happening, or why, or even what to do with it.

So, you grab them all by their little shattered minds. And you give them a Day that was fun, and safe and not without adventure. We ran from cops once, with kids. We were not breaking law; we simply did not want any Imperial

Entanglements. We were doing Trust Falls in the woods at night, and we skedaddled. Oh, how those kids laughed. Later, at night, tucking everyone in, is when you tell them… Today was a good day.

So, they know. What a Good Day is.

Don't tell a kid not to snort or say he smells bacon when you spot cops. You use that to teach them that cops are who you do want, when things really do get bad. Don't retro correct kids. No, I did not write The Art and Science of Family Rehabilitation, but if I had, this is the kind of knowledge that would be in it.

Handling the little pervs requires a lot of patience. As a human being, I can tell you, what I'm trying to talk about is when some kid says some funny shit, you have to both acknowledge that it *is* funny, but make them submit to a lecture on why I am not laughing. If you can pull that off with sincerity, you're a samurai, or at least the right stuff for one. If you also recognize when to do shit like this, and how.

One time, on the fishing docks, I was with three kids. One of them was a little extra pervy, but they were all teenagers. We walked by a French-Canadian tourist. It is a fact of local culture here in Old Orchard Beach, that they are acceptable targets for ridicule, and we all grew up with our parents and grandparents cursing them for two main things; how they drive, and the ridiculous beachwear. The men tend to be blade slim or bulbously (*gross*) fat, but they all to a man-jack wear the bathing suit known by its brand name as a style itself (Speedo) but colloquially as "Banana hammocks" and "Grape smugglers". My background put Speedos in the swimwear of Olympic athletes, homo-seggsuals, and the

French tourists. I would not be caught dead in one, I'd rather wrap kelp around my wang and run for it.

One of my charges that long ago summer day in my old career, Pervy Kid looks at me, shuffle steps, looks back at me, and says, "Aww, come on."

One of our summer patrons is coming up the fishing pier towards us, and one of his balls is hanging out of his Grape smugglers. His Grape smugglers, they are not smuggling. They are, thank God, I think, steeling myself not to laugh, still hammocking the banana.

It took two seconds for the other two feral honey badgers to pick up on this alert. I swear, these kids are like an easily spooked herd of deer, all of them, ever, not just these three today. I was ready. "Nope. Nope. Nope." I said quietly. We have a good rapport. They trust me. I'm not worried. I know Pervy Kid is going to take it away. I could not, and do not attempt to flex at all on this. We all saw it. It was funny. We are fucking human beings. I will handle this like it was my kids, almost. My kids are not these kids, but we would have been roaring, and they did, many times because of course the story got retold.

"It's okay," Pervy Kid said. "He didn't want to rub the sunscreen off it with his Grape smugglers."

All four of us, in that moment, were not staff and kids. We all lost it, literally down on our hands and knees, in the parking lot, and we laughed about it all the way home. I admonished them that there would be one, and only one retelling of this, at dinner, and we could all take the heat. When they did retell it, they told it all together, like they rehearsed it. It brought the house down, and I got dirty looks.

"Two things," I pointed out later that night, after the kids were in bed. My crew was out fast, after fast uneventful showers. Good soldiers, when well led. They almost always are.

"Before you say anything, two things, and I'll take what comes. One, it was funny, and I'd rather have it out once, and get it under control, than circulate for weeks and turn into something that involves public jacking it, because you know damn well it *will* grow legs. We contained it."

This was a good crew, back then. They mostly got it, except a couple.

"The other thing… did you notice how they told the story, together, like, not fighting and stepping on each other?"

Two of four perked up, and saw where I was headed. They had been here this morning. They waited and let me bring it home.

"Do you remember this morning?"

The morning had begun with the very three that had shared this funny moment today, this *human* moment, this real moment, fighting over three separate things. One was debating which of the other two was uglier, one called the first one a nigger, and then we had an almost five-way melee in the milieu over the Nintendo. And tonight, they *all* bid each other goodnight.

"I'll take that for the price of a dirty joke. It happened. It was funny. It was all droopy and shit, guys, come on. That's what he said… he turned around and said, "Aww come on.""

My colleagues were laughing now, like we had a campfire burning low and the kids were in their tents, and we heard the resident autistic kid start a long low chuckle, and it got the entire cottage staff and kids, rolling with laughter again, after lights out, and they need that shit too.

"Heh, Heh, Heh. Heh, Heh, HEH. *Droopy"* I looked at my crew in mock horror. Whoops. Gonna have to ride this one out, guys. Steady… They had all been listening to me tell my version of Monsieur De La Nute Fuzz Wah.

Milieu was *melee* again, for a minute, but this is the other kind. The good kind of melee. The healing kind.

It was still funny. Dad's contribution was that maybe he was just cooling it off, and the Tale of Monsieur De La Nute Fuzzwah got some new chuckles, all these years later.

The summer days and evenings with the kids at the Dep finished with my arrival home, checking in with Dad, and tucking him in. On my days off, we did camp chores and I talked to him endlessly about the days at Depardieu, the nature of this work, and what it was I really did. He understood me well enough that I kept going deeper and deeper and he loved it. Life in Hell was not that bad, despite being Hell. We were in another level now.

The heat grew as the long summer days lengthened and began to shorten yet again. I did my three days a week. We were unable to see Mom. The ticks of the clock slowed deceptively, and our talk was about a future, and what we could go see, and do together. Hopefully, all of us. Dad, me, TC, and Keelin. In the stronghold, in Pootown. Camping, and having a good time. That's the path we should be on,

Dad.

Our partner in horticulture showed up regularly without warning to tend our crop. As we went out to greet him, Dad finished with this.

"You'll get there," he said hopefully, yet he had not talked to them. It was the Apocalypse, and they still were cutting me off. What the fuck could Marla have said to them? Did Dad know where the infamous Letters were? He did not. Someday, I hope to ask TC, and Keelin, if it was around this time, when I let myself get pissed off at this situation, pissed off at them, if that was the first big fuck up. Sorry boys. I was pissed, and you just cut me off. I didn't know what to do with that. It was Papa that did it for me, gave me a reason to be ok with being mad at you guys. You are innocent, yes, but Papa was hurt by this, and there is no undoing that. I made sure that we kept it on an even keel, and he never got mad at you guys. I never really did either. Not _really_, really. But I was hurt, and it wasn't going away. And there is no truth I say now in the eyes of God, and in front of the whole world as my witness, there is nothing even remotely true, to justify what we went through being cut off from you guys. You are innocent, but it was still a force multiplier of the effects of living in Hell.

Of course, it was not _actually_ the Apocalypse. Oh, no. But it did pretty well standing in until the real Apocalypse showed up.

I kept in touch with the Maine people with a vengeance. I filled them in on what I was discovering. They had stopped asking if my sons had called. Athena, The Cid. Matty Mango. Cristobel. The Pathways crew. People I didn't talk to all that often in Maine, but now that I was gone, I held them a little closer. I texted my old neighbor and good friend Tom Snow. This was a good man, and catching him from time to time to say hey for fifteen minutes or so was one of the small pleasures. He also had heard a good chunk of my story before I had left Maine, during that last week. The message bounced back. I should have been ready for it. I texted his daughter Erica. She told me he was gone. I was on shift at the Dep. I found out about Candace the White the same way. I called her while in the field and her man told me she was gone.

Speaking of Candace the White, I told Dad all about her, and explained why sometimes if he was watching, some hawks act a little funny, and I always nod and greet them. We saw a lot of hawks all the time. It is true, there are a lot around. Owls too. But I know her when I see her, and she was keeping her eye on me. Athena loves it when I tell her this, but she cries a little too.

Marks on the wall counting days toward the unknown…

I found snatches of summer. Anghiel and I snuck away to Cape Cod for a night. I did not go to Pootown. I went to Jon and Mary's place to swim and smoke, but I was always in some stage of getting back to Dad, not leaving him alone. This was good. We came home from the Cape and I told Dad we were going to have to drag him with us. Not now, because I knew he wouldn't leave Mom. But someday.

Fishbrain turned out to be quite a hit. I showed Dad the huge largemouth people were pulling within twenty miles of us. Kly05 was on there almost every day and I joked with him in his comments on the app that I had the wrong job. Of course, I'm driving a Fusion.

As the summer started to move at that fast pace it does just before you notice it is slipping away, when it still feels endless, I had to honor the Code. I brought the canoe that was here with me in Mass over to my cousin's place so he could use it, or Petra or Jack and Cyrus when they were there, if Jon ran out of shells to ride. My other canoe is in Maine. It sat at Lono's until the Treeherder learned it was there. He found the place on his own and asked me if he could retrieve the Discovery to the Stronghold, so there it sat through the spring of 2020. I could not transport two canoes on one vehicle, and my shells were 150 miles apart, one left behind in the old life, one I had hauled with me despite the fact that it had just been a whole lot more work not to just "stash it for now" at Lono's. I had been terrified of losing things that would be difficult expensive or impossible to repair or replace. I had fought against a feeling of going backwards in the marriage for years. It got harder and harder to go out with Ella or pals the last two years she was with me. Now I was starting to look back, at how things really had been and realize that had all been kind of by design, and deliberate, and now that which I never thought I could lose, that which was so dearer than the freedom a canoe brings, was ripped away from me.

One night in August I waited for Dad to go to bed, and told him I was going to take a run to Rocky Pond. I threw the kayak I bought off Jackie onto the Fusion and went there around 2 A.M. Dad knew I used to do this a lot, back in the First Age, with Ella, and friends. And sometimes, my sons. TC and I had been on that marsh late night a few times. These places are still there, waiting, for a future I pray is possible. Rocky Pond has never left, either, and though I told Dad I was scouting for fishing, I really just needed to be there now, and I made landfall at George and spent the night just there, in the quiet space trying to order the disaster that was going on inside me, and everywhere else. Dad and I were fishing a little, it was the one thing we could do with the plague, but his knees were bad. He was in pain, and I balanced trying to manage that without him thinking I was trying to manage *him*.

Rocky Pond was still there, and though I was not really there to do so, I did wet a line and the fish there are still just as big and hungry as they ever were. Bigger, in fact, and a little nuts, I told Dad when I came back that morning. Of course, Ella's spirit had been with me. Her distaste for the limitations of the kayak versus canoe found consensus in mine own.

Dad and I laughed. I had not been much, and yet… it sure felt good to know I could still do a little pirating. Also, I kept the kayak on the car for a few days so I could regale the Depardieu kids with sea tales. Make hay baby, while that sun shines.

Autumn 2020

Leaves of red and gold.

Late summer nights (as we clung on against brisker twilights) at Depardieu typically went like this (this will be familiar to workers everywhere):

1445: West Meadow 2/Depardieu Diagnostic School.

Supervisor and shift leader are in staff office. No kids are on unit. One is off grounds. Returning 5 pm.

1455: Unit.

Two of three scheduled staff arrive. Team equips with handheld radios and goes to pick up kids at school. Kids are spread in three classrooms. Staff coordinate who goes and gets who. One staff does not know two kids in the far classroom, but should not be left with primary larger group. This is a good team, and these operations are conducted quietly and efficiently. A quiet boat bespeaks good seamanship, and good command. We are West Meadow.

1501: School.

Team enters school. Fat staff from other units already wheezing, and we have a steep hill to climb. Easy to insert anecdote of arriving to full-fledged chaos, but that would be lazy and disrespectful to the reader. Blow the Death Star an hour in, roll credits. No brawl today.

1515: School.

Team and all but two kids are waiting to go. Kids are asking everything from what's for snack to can they call their aunt because they have to tell their mom that they need their

Pokémon cards for the weekend… Everyone… I hold up one hand, in a fist, and wait.

One by one, the kids quiet down, and wait. I've been doing this since my first day here, and it is not a dominance thing. That took a while, to work through their reactive responses. Sometimes, people try to whistle, or give the old "Hey settle down!" Military, cops in briefing, maybe Boy Scouts. Not these kids, not ever. Once they learned I was cool, the saw the dog and pirate pix, they dug the rocks, they saw the brightest star in the sky, all that shit… I had done my work by today. I put up my hand. The kids grew quiet. I asked them simply to be quiet, for a moment, while we gathered. Slowed the rising frantic energy building here waiting.

Most of the time, a little mellowness and respect goes a long way.

We are short one kid. This guy is a problem, I spotted him day one, and it has been clear, since day one, that he is advanced sufficiently in pathology, skills and commitment to be beyond any kind of truly manageable, and they have no idea. Kelsie does, but she and I both know we can't do shit. Oh, if this was the old days. Boyo, I'd help you, I surely would. But now, I have to keep these kids calm, while you throw a tantrum as a power play, because you did not get your turn in the game before the school day ended. Ok. Everyone waits for you, Little Baby. Pass the popcorn, it's a rerun. And, it may be better to you to be feared than loved, but these lambs don't really fear you, and you fear that. I know, because I point it out all the time, although it doesn't look like I really get the subtext to most of our group. But you and I… we both know you're a pussy, and I got your fuckin' number.

1516: School/Unit.

But we aren't playing, boyo. I catch eyes with Ryan, and we quickly split the group. I've got Perry and a newbie. Ryan will stay here and babysit the little baby. And he knows how to keep this from being too much of a win. Narcissists in training. If you catch them early, and you know how to kick their ass the way they need, and you got the stones and the ability, yeah, you can change the world. One little battle at a time. We get the kids back to the unit and run people in and out taking leaks, getting their games, and starting their chores. When Little Baby comes back, he is clearly expecting people to be like "Aww, I'm glad you came back to us." "Good job!"

The therapeutic antithesis looks different. "Perry… check this out." Perry's worth showing stuff too, he's very good on his own already.

"Glad you made it." I tell Little Baby. He is well aware I'm the one who took the drama out of his little play act. "I have your stuff ready when you rejoin the group." Your chore stuffs. He knows. I'm being supportive, and I truly am, not disingenuous.

Important, that. My intent is not to win, or feel strong, or feed my ego. This kid is a bully. He abuses kids right in front of staff, and dominates this unit like an abusive head of household. Some of the staff actually treat him like some kind of fucking trustee, blind to the fact that he is intimidating the other kids, and claiming the biggest piece of chicken for himself, always. He expects to be treated like the Godfather.

A few weeks ago, he pulled the same shit, in the gym. He started yelling at some kid twice his size, like he was going to kick ass. The North Wing kid was just laughing and telling staff to let him go, let him come at him. Of course, they would not do that.

Little Baby knows this well. He never talks shit or acts tough when he might actually get his ass kicked. We know it, and the kids all do too. Later that day, he was in my group outside. I had seen the group from North Wing go onto the trail on the other side of campus. Little Baby did not know they were outside. We strolled high wide and handsome onto the other end of the trail, and oh thank you Little Baby, you just kept talking shit about how everyone is lucky you didn't kick ass. You feel powerful right now, and you know you shouldn't even be talking about this, and you are waiting for me to say something so you can power play me, too.

Oh. God forgive me. Some days, I really enjoy my job.

Playing dumb always works on Little Baby, because he is a narcissist in training, so he thinks we are all dumb, and he isn't usually wrong. It works for him. The thug from North Wing rounds the bend into our sight. Little Baby goes silent, and ghost white.

"You were saying?" I asked. I took three steps playing dumb, like I did not expect him to stop, like I did not understand the situation. The two other kids stop dead in their tracks too. They were both in the gym, and they are weary of this kid and his bullshit. They truly are. This is not for me. It's for them, too. I am not worried about this punk from North Wing. I will protect Little Baby. I'm trying to rehabilitate. Ok, if I'm also trying to prevent one more asshole from just growing bigger and getting better at it, I'm ok with that. Little Baby shows everyone that day that he is just a little bitch, and he escalates and ups the ante for two weeks trying to gain face back, according to the world he has created here, but he never quite does again. At his humble request, we reverse direction before they get close enough to make contact. Close enough that we can hear that group laughing, though. I know it hurts boy, but you need this medicine. Even if it isn't enough, you need to taste this, and I'm your huckleberry. These are old stories, but by God, I guess I still got it.

1559: Unit.

He is pissed but regrouping. I'm taking three kids out fishing. See ya. I meant it when I told him I was glad he made it, and I would not have let him take the beating he deserved. Not from a kid from another unit. That isn't about him. No, Little Baby is going to fuck around and find out from one of our own lambies. I'll break that up, when it happens. In a minute, or two. Depends on which kid finally fucks him up. With all these kids, all the time, you have to keep it very real. Any subtext of smartass, or exasperated anger, and you're fucked, irrevocably, forever. As a practitioner, professional, therapeutic agent, I feel good about this, even though it won't do anything, for now, today, for the kids affected by this kid, and for him, I feel like I have done good in the world. I doubt Little Baby does. I do not doubt, that I could give a fuck about Little Baby's feelings. If I see him show any real ones, or say anything real, I'll be here, for real, to do what I can.

I do not waste time with committed sociopaths. Twenty-seven years now, and this is maybe the third or fourth real one I've met.

1600: West Meadow 2/Day Room.

Kids in Main Room have finished snacks and now check in. This group is special in a lot of ways, and I really like these kids. Even Little Baby has potential, if I had him in a different time and place. I can't save them all any more than I can adopt all the puppies I see on my phone that need a home. We split the group between the kids who are indoor cats in their previous lives, and want to play video games until dinner. Then we have four who want to go fishing, but only three can. If I catch you trying to manipulate who goes, like bribe some dimmer bulb with a fucking trinket like a Lego to trade for a spot on the fishing group, you are not coming with me. These kinds of rules and disciplines you can carve your own with your group. I cultivated my own respect and boundaries with these kids and enforced it.

1625-1800: Therapeutic off-grounds outing/No vehicles.

Fishing, Thayer Pond, Whatland, Mass. Three good size largemouth bass. Also, a snake, and some great birds. I hump my group, the hardcore outdoor cats who ALWAYS want to go outside around in the woods, over rocks, over concrete and water and true risk. I grant them the dignity of risk. We play out here, and laugh, and heal. I enforce kindness and respect. Here at the Dep, it took a lot of work to enforce one simple thing: wild creatures are not here for your amusement, and this is not a fucking free-for-all. You do NOT touch, harass molest or accost ANY living creature on your own, without checking with me, and being granted leave. Some kids respond to this new world order with a kind of defiant stupidity.

But rest assured. Test me and miss out on the fun next time. Kelsie backed me up on my own rules with my group. Besides fishing, we got to take vans out, and I explored my new office like the region I had as an in-home therapist… a *lifetime* ago?

I got one kid who is squeaky and unpredictable. He comes from a conservative background, and he is surrounded by kids who change their pronouns daily. He has been talking about being bisexual. I wonder how Jesus and his parents are going to feel about that. This kid is one that you need to watch, because you don't know what will set him off, and when set off he is like a shrew with rabies. Today was my day. He said something about Jesus, and (I really should have known better) I said: "Well, Jesus is not here with us. It's just us."

See, that's one of little moments I keep for myself. There is no justice?… However, my little banshee here decides to flip out 'cause I just said there is no Jesus. Everyone fucks up. What you do with it is not only who you are, but key to success. I need to contain this before we get on campus if I can. I'm the guy who never has problems in his group.

"Look, I didn't mean to say there is no Jesus! I'm just saying he wasn't coming down from Heaven and helping us hump it back before dark! Gimme a break, dude! No disrespect!"

"Yeah," pipes in Q. "This is why no one likes you."

Oh… from the mouths of babes, saith the Lord…

With a look to Q that said, "Okay, thank you, but I got this," I looked at my religious zealot on a tear. "I mean, he isn't wrong, guy. This kinda is why your peers… what's the word? Don't like you. Settle down. What, you want to punch me in the face?"

I stepped toward him, barely…barely. This is a precise thing. There is a real world out there, boyo, and you and your little tantrums are going to get you fucking curb stomped. We prevent it here for you like three times a week, it's kinda why you're here. You need a little dose of reality. Here I am. You have to teach them in the arena they operate in. I take my real joy doing this to assholes in our community who… Oh yeah… we have a word now. Karen.

I leaned in, and slipped a little Irish into my voice and dropped volume and tempo, just a leetle bit… steady now…

"You want to punch me after our fishing trip because you don't like what I said? Have you thought that one through? Before we get back?" Now I was between the group and campus, and we stopped.

"What? We good?"

See, you gotta play the role. And it doesn't matter if we were back on campus. When bullies try to flex, you stand your ground. I don't have anything to prove to these kids. But I walk it in the world exactly the same way. If you ever honked at my student while waiting for them to go right on red, you know this.

This is necessary. You cannot be of two ways in this. That… is no better than Vince the ex-prison screw, and it shows, not just to me. There is a guy here who gets this, and we get along great. If I weren't so busy, I'd draw him out. He was a martial arts instructor for twelve years. He and I ridicule (privately) the ineptness of the prison screw throughout my tenure at the Dep.

Squeaky has snapped out of it. Fuckin' *Je-sus*.

You just can't do it right and not be willing to take the risks.

I learned to stand my ground at the Old Blue Lambda Delta house. I enjoyed teaching it. This kid tried to have a hair across his ass because he thought he had an excuse. It's both his baseline dynamic from his family, but also the kid of shit we have to deal with, because when you have a Little Baby on the unit, no one ever really gets better. He tried to play fuck-fuck. We played fuck-fuck. He lost. He also just learned how to stand up to bullies better. The job never stops. This is as much for the other two, but they don't need it. I've been with them both all summer and we always have a good time. It's the third one, whoever it is, that is the test subject out here. I got Beansy and Q eating berries and leaves and shit. Had to tell Q not to just pick every plant when I saw him eating a dandelion flower and making a face. You really have to look at all the facets, with the neurodivergent, the maladjusted, the lost, neglected and complex traumatize mind. Of a child, no less. Adults are different, and not my bag.

There are going to be detractors here, who question the need to stand down all bullies whenever possible. If the world we live in as I type these recollections now does not back that up, I can't sway you. Sometimes, you have to get into the pit they are in, if they are ever going to get out of it. I got no regrets. I have a note from this kid on my mantle. It was one of my first accolades down here, the kind I really treasure.

1800-1830: Dinner/Games room, West Meadow 2.

Dinner arrives on unit and kids eat laid back dinner, transitioning to evening wind down so smoothly, it is not noticeable, until the vibe kinda just sets in. People feel safe, and are relaxed. Showers get done, no fights over whose turn. Some days we go up to the café, and every day is different, and you just never know what you're going to get when you drive up that hill onto campus. A lot depends on who is on duty with you, all over the hill, not just in your house. Today has not had any deaths, fights, restraints... *runaways... incident reports... med errors, fire drills, backup calls, assaults, rapes, inappropriate touching, sexual harassment, violations of recipient rights, boundary violations, ethical violations, plant failures, stopped up toilets, no feces smeared on the wall, no kids are sick, no hazardous materials exposure, no blood borne pathogens exposure, no trespassers, no allegations or contraband...* so far, it's been an okay day. We even caught some fish and had some laughs, and did a little teaching, loving and learning. Yeah. It's been a good day. They have not all been so. Last week I answered a backup call (no data, just a frantic call for backup… *outside*. Did not even know where to find them. The girl's unit, thank God my man-ness keeps me away from there most of the time, although, I do like working with borderline young women, because a true decent man is exactly something that is therapeutic for them. Takes commitment, that, like tattooing your corneas. Of course, that would not be something I would take on now, more like a special project with Matty Mango. There had been times. But with me in my life now, and the changes, and all that, it would not be right to let myself get any farther into these kid's hearts than I was able to back up. It was that way with all things, the Murphy's, and, should it ever present, it would be that way with Anghiel's kids too. I don't like letting people down.

That's really a thing, tattooing the whites of your eyes. I showed Dad. We both went "Eww." I wondered what TC and Keelin would have said. Boom. Right to the nuts.

1930: Day Room Hallway, West Meadow 2.

Nurse arrives with evening meds. Nurse is crabby, even for nurse. Beansy and Q are both excited to see her, because they like her, and they also like their drugs. Q is going to live in group homes and institutions all his life. He is 9. Beansy, if he survives and stays out of prison, could be a doctor, an astronaut, or anything. Literally, anything else at all. This is a high stakes game we all play. I'm a soldier. The battleground is the future. I love both of these two knuckleheads, and I enjoy a close relationship with them here, Dad knows all about them, and everyone pretty much loves them, and Beansy can be a fucking wild man. Some kids, they're kind of cool. Nerds, maybe, but that's ok. Some are just like you, but they live their lives in Hell now. Some of them are your little brothers and sisters right from day one. That was Beansy for me. He looked like Dennis the Menace; he was smart as a whip and fast as a mongoose. He took no shit from anyone, ever. I never gave him any, even when I had to help put hands on him a few times. When you have to do that, unless it is not indicated, you should be gentle and take care not to convey dominance, or inflict pain to get compliance, like cops. I'm not saying we never did that shit at Sweet Shores, because we were dealing with serious domestic violence dynamics, so if you're throwing food, breaking glass, or slapping titties, you're going the fuck down, boyo. I ain't tryna hurt you, but you started this, and I'm stopping it the only way you will allow. Your choice, never mine. Beansy, none of these kids, for all the crazy antics we had to deal with, and Beansy was above his weight class, none of them ever needed that. Just love, and safety. I was grateful to do what I do, and what I could do, for these lost ones too. I did not feel useless. I was… well… *samurai.*

1932: Showtime, almost…

Med nurse rudely tells both Q and Beansy to go wait to be called, crushing hours of hopes about what they thought would happen when the tell her about whatever it was… it was nothing, right? But she needs to be in control, and doesn't see their faces when she shuts them off cold. I did though, and Jaz and Lex were watching, because she did the same thing last week. I want to teach them how to ride the whitewater we just got handed, it's pretty much a usual thing, from someone. It only takes one. Today, it's Nurse Rachet's day.

She might have gotten away with it. I anticipated this, and set up Lab with my troops. I catch them as they sulk around and tell them not to worry about it, go take care of stuff, come back and tell her. Now, Ratchet heard this, and should have taken it for what it was, a cue. The kids like her. I do not, and this is why. Instead of just doing her job and leaving my kids to me, she barks at them to wash their hands before they come back. They are sticky with …kid detritus. Fruit, mango, I think. Fatal mistake. *Bitch.*

She knew it. She did it deliberate. It had been a good day, up till now. And, for no good reason, she just set off my little ticking time bomb, who did so well today. Fuck YOU!

Thank God, Lex and Jaz went from padawan to full Jedi in that moment. They each scooped one munchkin as they wheeled around like little gunslingers to become the teachers and we averted disaster, but not before Beansy whipped his juice box, at Nurse Ratchet and caught her right in the fucking maw. I was looking right at her. I had a quarter second to get it right.

Breathe.

The look on my face in that split second was clear. *"That…is what you GET. I am pleased."*

She took it. She did not try to make a thing. I barked at Beansy to get to his room. He did, and winked at me. Later,

I told him… that was so righteous… but it still was not okay. And that I still liked him, it doesn't work like that. I taught him a word. Unconditional. It was an okay shift. The next night I watched as the cops came to peel two girls of the huge transformer on campus between the school and the clinic. There were big bolts of lightning raining down and stinging high velocity torrents of late summer rain. That was a less than good day, but still, hey, no one died. Later. I told my mates about the time the Treeherder and I saw a lightning strike close aboard. Tighten up ya pucka, boyo, I said, much to the delight of the Jamaicans.

Africans should not be referred to by continent. Africa is many nations. I was still learning. I shared with Dad.

2100: West Meadow 2, Depardieu Diagnostic School.

The hallway is dark. We can see. I teach the crew how to close or cover one eye and keep your night vision. I explain the dangers of dazzling someone with bright light. Way of Samurai, new age. Fieldcraft. I make hot coffee with fresh cream out of my backpack while I speak with them. I pass around fresh fruit and warm sharp cheese with crusty bread. River lunch, I tell them. I'll show you all, someday.

Me and Jaz and Lex got the kids settled after our close call with Nurse Ratchet's contra-therapeutic style.

I have put so many children to bed for the night, tucked them in. It has been a long time.

One thing I like about this place, is that there are cameras.

They are not everywhere, but they are around enough that we do not have to watch staff we don't know. That's more about being new than creepy, but you should never be inside a room. Also, they roommate here, so we have to move around, and never let two kids be out of sight of us, at all, ever. Most of the time, they can't be out of sight at all. Beansy is asleep, having went one and one in chess, with me. Kid can play, and he knows when he beats me, I'm not letting him win. These things mean a lot to these kids. Always have. Some things do not change. I like having the cameras on me, even though I am furtively on my phone.

Beansy is downstairs on West Meadow 1. He was here most of the night because they were short *two* staff. Now, I get to do another part of the job, and this one has a twist.

2130: West Meadow 2, Upstairs. East hallway. Rm#09. Aiden.

It is not easy, after so many years, to pick the tales to tell as much of it as you may hope to know, without living it. Jaz, Ryan, Lex and Perry, Kelsie… like Kary and Matty Mango and Lono and all… all of them stretching back… and now, forward…

This one, is special, as are they all, yes. But, he had absolutely no business being there, except he had absolutely nowhere else to go. He was polite, and gentle. He endured multiple quarantines that would not have been out of place in an old Three Stooges routine, or a Looney Tunes bit. You imagine being quarantined with Daffy Duck and the Tasmanian Devil for four days?

Aiden came to us from foster care. Although he was very guarded with everyone, I worked on him, and paid attention, and I figured out a few things on my own. As I did, I would bring it to him, and he would confirm, "Yes, I was a little upset, earlier with Little Baby's antics." I did not target individuals, but this cat was 17, sharp, and decent. He did not have one single incident of being rude, oppositional, disrespectful, or really needing to be managed behaviorally in any way. Couple things are important here. This is a kid you DO treat like a trustee, within reason. You talk to him like an adult. You treat him like, I was about to say, like a man, but I was learning… that was kind of like saying, Hey, that's mighty white of you. People are not just men and women anymore, and it is not always obvious.

Oh, yeah. Aiden was also gay, but it looked like he had never said it out loud. At all. Even alone.

Aiden did not need to surrender his video game promptly at the stroke of lights out. No one does, but eventually we all go around and collect devices, and usually it's not a problem. Well, maybe 50 50. But this kid needed a chance to demonstrate a higher level, and I spoke with him about this, and he agreed to help me out.

"So," I began, "you don't need, like rules, or rather, enforcement, around these rules. I recognize this. Therefore, if you accept, I grant you the privilege of turning this in at lights out, like everyone else, but when you finish, save your game, all that crap. Ok?"

"Ok."

"Do you understand why this is a conversation?"

"Not really."

"Well, relax." I pulled out a pair of Slim Jims and tossed him one.

"You do not need me in your face telling you when to give it up. You turn it in, when you're done, without a problem, every night, without being asked."

"Uh-huh…"

"Last night, you turned it off and handed it to me, as always. However, I think you needed like 90 seconds more, to… wrap it up? Is that correct. Sir?"

"Yeah, but it's ok."

"It is not, and I will tell you why. Remain calm, it's my bad. Not yours. Allow me?"

This language and cadence and tempo, all that nuts and bolt shit? This is it, here, why you do it with precision. I'm talking to this kid like a good manager will someday, when he's done a good job. I must do what I can, to help him find his way there.

"Aiden, because of your impeccable conduct with respect to our expectations of West Meadow, you have earned the following courtesy. This needed to be created, for you, because…"

I raised my voice, just a hair, because I knew all my urchins were listening, waiting to get a hair across their little asses, especially at bedtime. Now I let them know I knew they were listening, that it was good they were listening. Jesus boy is the one who would come out with another hair across his ass that it wasn't fair, and he'd be right, so I'd grant him the same thing. If he woke up. He gets a LOT of meds at night. He stays asleep. I wake up my kids on heavy drugs so they can piss. Most of the time they appreciate it. If they don't get up and piss their bed, you help them, and be nice. If I hear you play that wrong, you got trouble. It's ok to say. "Hey, get up next time, ok?" It's not ok to say I told you so, and this little fucker in question will drink your fucking milkshake for that kind of transgression, even at 2 in the morning. This is the kind of shit Vince the prison screw pulls, and Screamy Judy. He doesn't wake up, anyway.

"You may, when you hear me collect games, take what time you must, to wrap up. If I find myself waiting for a minute, you sir, have earned that. For being you. All the time."

"Honor!" I bellowed, so all could hear. "It is earned and rewarded."

Back to him, "Don't mess up… Ha! I know you won't. That's for them."

Aiden's face lit up for a second. He felt good. The right good. Satisfaction good. Self-esteem good. Elite good. I bid him goodnight like a man to man. Person to person. Woman to non-binary dissociative identity system, it would not matter, and is not a fucking joke. We happened to be, as far as I know, old man and young man. If I did good here, now, that's what it is. I could give a fuck if he decided he was she six months from now, we were simply two human beings. I carried experiences like this home to Dad, and we watched the fascist homophobic racist scourge grow and get louder, and this became about more than ideas and saying shit to feel good. It became real, and personal, and… a battleground.

Oh, baby. It is, isn't it?

Don't joke about that shit. It's not LGBTABCDEFGEIEIEI fucking OH! Say it right, or say what you know, and be clear. Don't fucking play around with that shit. Ok?

As far as the video game thing, none of this was done with any kind of sanction, I just did it, and people followed, because it was right. I didn't have to sell it. We had a good supervisor and she watched all of us closely, and that was ok too. I did my best not to surprise her too much, and she gave me leeway. Less than I would have liked, but she also kept me out of trouble, and I had enough trouble. I came here for no trouble. The respect between us was so comfortable for me, I speculated to Dad about why it had been something rare enough to be sought and treasured.

Sometimes, you ask forgiveness instead of permission. She was ok with that, enough to make me happier more often than I chafed at it. The key here, is that whatever goes on, there is always brutal transparency and honesty. That's what she got with me, and she knew it. I had even gone to her with serious sensitive shit, and she did not disappoint in matters of leadership. I didn't need to. It was risky to me. But it was the right thing. My comrades were supportive, and we solved a major problem. For a little while.

I wish I could tell that tale, but, West Meadow business stays on West Meadow. That's why we were the best. Good Captain, good crew. Good kids too. Even Little Baby. The Code, Motherfuckers.

I did have to run interference for Aiden more than once, when people who were not always with us, or who could be a little too efficient or zealous, got out of hand. One staffer tried to push back and lecture me about rules. I shut her down without mercy. He gets to do it this way. That's it. Don't choke, it's just not your way. Sometimes, that's how it goes. This is one of those times. As I wrapped up my little sensei moment with her, Aiden handed me the device and smiled, oh so quickly. I think this kid's going to do just fine. Sorry, Nala. Did I *undermine* you? Let me just check… sorry, I don't even have a little teensy-weensy bit of a fuck to give you. Don't ever fuck with my kids on my watch again, though. You are not full time here. That goes for the little douchebags downstairs, too. We're done here. You got this bed check? Ok, great.

Good chat.

As the Holidays approached, our bonds with each other, and the kids grew in strength and intensity. The rest of the place ripped itself apart, but together with a little old salty guidance, we navigated all this, and I was blessed and grateful. I also grew lean and hard, running around in the woods every day chasing these guys.

2200: Hallway/West Meadow 2.

Everyone is asleep. Staff have been gathered in the central quad for 40 minutes. Ryan is finishing up paperwork. For all my relaxation of my own rules and boundaries around the Piece of marijuana, I have never been one to toke on duty. It is tempting, especially when I now have weed out there in my car or the ride home. It doesn't matter if it's legal, it sure ain't legal how I smoke it. But not here. I cannot, however, say that for everyone. I know stoners, and as the year had gone on, people definitely took little rides together throughout shift and came back with fresh coffees and the end of the shift in sight. I've done that many times myself on the job. In restaurants. I don't judge them They're young. They are good, high or not. I don't really give a fuck. I'll take my crew all day high before I'll take a shift with the likes of Nala. At least Nala is a hard worker. Some of the people downstairs, the old night hag who has the kids massage her bunions (ok, not really, but seriously, it would not have surprised me) are barely functioning bodies. They are good at pissing kids off by being cranky though, so there's that.

The kids are asleep. Ryan finishes paperwork and joins us. We check them. I never stop looking into rooms and listening for breathing. Little Baby's feet stink like a biblical plague. I do pray for all of them, even the real dickheads like this one. He is still a child.

We did hear a stream of backup calls with multiple kids screaming in the background from two other units tonight. We turned the walkies down before they woke anyone up. We could not help them, even if everyone was not pinned to doorways watching kids sleep.

And, for me, reading the Dead Bedroom thread on Reddit. Anghiel had mentioned this when we met, and she had been in one too. It isn't sex though. A Dead Bedroom is cold. Very, very cold. As I read the wailing suffering, the desperation, the not-knowing, that precedes the not wanting it to be true, that precedes the knowing, and then, the horrible decision making that takes place with lives in the balance, I was horrified, but also somehow comforted. It had not been just me… Reading these voices now, I heard them in my head, and they were not unknown. The lights came on in a big way. I relived the main bulk of everything went through, twice in fact, because I almost left her in 2009, and I hadn't been touched by her for going on four years at that point. So, I had been sick of tallying birthdays, Christmases, and summer days jerking off when I was fucking married. I almost left her, once, but she love-bombed me, and I thought we fixed it, and she did it all over again. And alienated my children. And robbed my parents' blind for …the whole marriage, it looks like now. While I worked overtime shifts and carved out Friday night Monopoly marathons with TC. Shifts here, in places just like this, long ago.

The irony of this was one thing. The irony that the lights had just come on, and that rage feels like clarity, and I really wanted to throw a fucking tantrum like these kids here did daily, but, of course, I did not really want to do that, and there was the rub, for me. Because I think I actually have an even temper, and if my life, and my conduct in my profession does not lend itself to believing that, what the fuck am I supposed to do with that? I was quiet, in the hall for the last bit of shift while the night crew settles in. At one point, I laughed out loud at nothing, but I just brushed it off, like a funny YouTube video I wasn't supposed to be watching, and in fact was not. I'm fine. How you doin'?

2220

It's been another day at the office. On the ride home, I pick up milk. And EEns. Dad is awake. He got to see mom today, without me. Blair Haus is open, for now, for visits, but they have to be scheduled. Until further notice, he schedules every chance he gets, and I go with him. Today she asked him to go home, and his lip quivers a little when he tells me. I have driven home feeling sorry for myself about my boys. This has become an unhealthy indulgence, but I have processed truths. Now, I feel real anger, at the hurt he endures, compounded by something foul, something unspeakable, and the wellspring, the backtrack, the fucking reverse fucking engineering… led straight back to Marla.

0207

Marla. TC. Keelin. The mysterious letters. Dead Bedroom. Parental Alienation. All the memories I now had that had a whole different look, when I considered the part of the puppet show I was not aware of. How could I have known, that my wife, my children's mother, would destroy her family, to hurt me? To win divorce? That is exactly what his was, but people were getting hurt.

Whatever else, I have to demonstrate that I am not… what they seem to think I am.

How to get that truth in front of them, cut off like this?

If I could do what I just did tonight, I must be a real healer. I must be clean, somehow. I have to be. I know I am not an imposter. I also have female friends of all ilk and a great girlfriend, not a fucking support group named after me. Do they not see these things? Do they want to?

Have you seen them? Are they OK?

For about a year, along with every other moving part and

crazy sideshow, this built up.

----night----

Sleep is never sleep anymore. Just nightmare awake or asleep, with the space between a rude transition every time.

0911

Click. Click. Click… click. I got up. Dad put his phone and the pictures of Mom down. The weed had come in. It was almost Halloween.

***

As 2020 was cooling off and winding down, Dad and I were in the yard, again, puttering about. I was speculating on all the raw resources lying about. There was compost, and gravel, and we could grow other stuff. Dad was knowledgeable and together with my back strength we had built the greenhouse and raised a crop of weed. It did not really save any money in the end, because it basically costs the same to grow it, but I did not have to trouble myself looking and there is always the weed store, brave new world we live in now.

There are tools here, and nuts and screws… every time I said out loud, I was going to pick up something like wire, or epoxy to fix my canoe, he would hop up and disappear, usually returning with something like whatever, or something better and more suited to my purpose than I had known existed.

We had taken Nathan out fishing a few times. I had taken him myself a couple more. Dad and I had gone out a few times too. There was never enough of this stuff, but it was because we had a lot of other stuff too, so it felt good, in a way, to be too busy to go fishing. I was trying to hit the balance point, the sweet spot, for my dad between self-care, and feeling guilty and missing Mom. I got it. I missed Ella, so much, all the time. If you think it's inappropriate to compare the love of a dog, or my loss, with his, well…you did not know her, and in case it is not clear, I was realizing that the love I had with Ella was the realest part of my old life as a father and family man. I did not regret trying to relocate her to Pootown and make a pirate treasure out of her shrine.

And that, the refusal to understand that the depth of my love for that soul was so intense that it was necessary to make some attempt at that, something worthy of legend, the refusal to be in their grandfather's lives, that 30-minute drive three days a week, and watching my mom die in the nursing home, while my Dad watched his own heart die were a lot to bear. My boys had treated me like I was some kind of rabid animal and had thrown me away like trash. I was angry, now. I was not unstable then. What the fuck had she said to them? Were the letters in the house? What did they say? Were there other secrets to be discovered? How can I get Jackie to talk to my sons? Why hasn't she?

It was a lot. I tried to maintain. I was in Hell; Dad was in Hell. We were in Hell. That's just the way it was as the pandemic whipped around the globe in waves, and we watched millions of people reveal that they had been out of their fucking minds, for years, and it was just now becoming clear. We had more than one pandemic. The Covid revealed the mental health pandemic. One thing good about the Covid…in 2020 the school shootings, and mass public shootings eased off. They had been picking up frequency so much, it was hard to even track them.

Dad, and Anghiel (who got the coded redacted versions) both were interested by life at a place like Depardieu. On behalf of the Melissa's from Portland Cottage at Sweet Shores fifteen years ago, to Vince the prison screw now, and all of them in between, for all of them now (and I do wish I could tell all your stories), I give you my favorite all time story, of someone who fucked around and found out. The old record was held by Donna Sinclair at Sweet Shores and had stood for almost twenty years. As much as I wish I could tell you about Donna Sinclair getting punched in the face, or a few other good ones who fucked around and found out, with great pleasure in the name of Karma, I bring you Screamy Judy.

Screamy Judy & Baby Huey

South Wing.

Depardieu Diagnostic Facility.

Autumn, 2020.

2115 EDT.

Screamy Judy started after I had been there a while, but my role here and now was not like my vocation once had been. I was compromised by the needs of my life and family now, and I knew this, and Kelsie knew this, and a lot of people have a lot of shitshow in their lives. I did not waste her time when she hired me, and she knew how to use all her instruments. I was the go-anywhere guy, the firefighter. I was not the only one, but she threw me around. I spent a lot of time on South Wing early, and had fishing trips with those kids too. I was happy to spread myself around, because you never know who the kid is that needs you, now, today, to melt their face, and change their life forever. You really can do it every day here.

The kids are bigger, older, stronger and more prone to acting out on South Wing, but only the half they struggle with. Half of them are gentle neurodivergents with the compound comorbid stuff, and they all are smart and knowledgeable in their own areas of interest. I do well with these kids, because I can hold my own on few topics and fake it properly. The sincerity is not fake.

Screamy Judy is not new, not to me. I try to like her, and connect with her, here in the line. She has red flags about her. She is where I once was. This is her full-time job, the insurance job. She is also a cop, on the side. This is a secret, and I respect it. I watch her, and feel a pang that I can't take her on like I would if I was a full timer with kids at home like her. I don't dislike her personally, but I notice she can be abrasive. I am too, I'm sure, so no judgement. I tell her about the owls in my yard, and she gets all spooky like I just pulled a Ouija board and a live chicken out of my ass and started spitting rum onto an open flame. It's an owl. I'm not being insensitive to your culture you are being insensitive to the native culture that I the white man have studied on my own, not appropriated… Yeah. I wasn't going to tweak her for dissing on the owls. She was an idiot. I've worked around them for years. I warned Jaz, Lex and Ryan about my concerns. This is one dragon someone else is going to have to slay, unless she pisses me off directly. She sensed me. I see you, too.

Baby Huey is an old person reference, but please, do the homework, it's worth it. It's there. I checked. This kid was huge, and gentle. I don't know much of his story except it was profoundly sad. He had poor hygiene. He accepted being treated poorly. The kids were pretty vicious to him. They all liked and respected me. I liked and respected Baby Huey, and my disapproval was ready, and the others knew it. They did test it, of course, but I countered by hanging out more with Baby Huey and less with mean fucks. One thing I loved about Depardieu, you could say it just like that. I told them I don't like mean people. I don't like bullies. The weak among us are not targets, and they are not weak. Test the gentle at your peril, I told them. I did like Baby Huey. I liked them all, even the odious redneck who wouldn't stop talking about pussy. Or Jews. Or Faggots, or Niggers. See? That feeling you get now? Well, when you're a professional, you have to figure out how to navigate that shit. With brown kids about who would tear this fat fuck to pieces, and only aren't for two reasons. They like and respect you, and they trust you to deal with it.

But the gentle ones, especially, you like more, because, they don't do that shit. And they are just full of surprises. Smart, and often funny, but hard to catch the funny, if you're just going through the motions. The kids always know. I never do, and that's why they always liked me, anywhere. It isn't supernatural. Baby Huey knew TV shows. We watched clips, and I showed him some stuff he did not know. What a game changer the cylon phone was. I still marveled. I kept Q quiet all summer at bedtime watching old Battlebots. I ran interference for Baby Huey when I was on South Wing.

I did not know what Baby Huey looked like when he

lost his shit. No one had ever seen it. But they thought they had. They thought it was him crying and slapping himself. I suspected, that there was yet another level, and it was… not going to be fun? We'll say that. I watched him, and the other kids, and tried to get a sense of the prior week before the day I happened to be there, sniff the simmering tensions. For safety, for Christ's sake.

I did two shifts in a row on South Wing as the fall started to chill. The first night, Screamy Judy was up Baby Huey's ass all night. He is the only kid here who will put up with that for more than five seconds. He will not put up with it forever. I have to wonder…does she think I'm throwing myself into the fray when he has enough? I've been here eight hours, and I've had enough. Jack and Joe, the two shift supervisors who were seldom apart, they had enough too. I really liked those guys. They did a good job. They knew who I was, too. Kris the other supervisor strolled through for five minutes. She had enough. They all told me they had enough.

I *tried* to tell you…Baby Huey is going to have enough, someday. I tried to be nice about it. You, madam, are a control freak. You are also flagrantly ambitious, and in your swift rise here in the trenches, you may have bitten off, just maybe, possibly, a wee bit too much of a mouthful, as large as your mouth clearly is. I tried, for the greater good, and because my fatal flaw appears to be giving everyone, absolutely everyone a fair shake… I had my doubts about you, and you failed. You shouted me out of your office, saying people knew well how you ran your unit, and if they did not like it, they could take her off her post. Ok, Screamy Judy. I find mixed feelings that I cannot pick up the gauntlet. Duty, the Shienarans say, is heavier than a mountain, and I must choose to let someone else teach you. Remember, you chose that.

About a week later, Baby Huey had enough of Screamy Judy. He became her teacher. He told her he did not like it in a way she finally heard. She got the lesson she needed. I did not see this, thank God. When I returned to rotation, Joe and Jack told me with absolute straight faces that Judy would not be back. That boy had thrown her about that unit like a teddy bear. A teddy bear in the mouth of a dog. They dared me, silently with eyes alone to react the way I really felt about that. These guys were friends, but they were testing my character. I was not happy someone got beat up. I was happy that Screamy Judy was not going to be screaming anymore, and that's a fact, and I'm not sorry. She asked for it. I split the difference with Jack and Josh. I looked them both dead in the eye, and said, "I'm stunned that happened. Hope she isn't too fucked. We tried to head it off…" They returned my looks. It's what it is. She fucked around. I tried to warn her. She found out. We three warriors… we accepted that. I was permitted this and other quiet moments of street justice. When it was just us.

West Meadow 2 is jealously, psychotically disciplined. I did not openly gloat about this. As far as between the crew here on the unit, they knew I tried to warn her, and they knew she should have listened. Only Ryan said it out loud, just he and I, before we went to get the kids a few days later.

"She should have listened."

"Thanks, Ryan."

That's respect. I worked on a lot of teams, knew a lot of warriors. For what it's worth this was a great crew, and well captained. I would miss them, and I regretted the what ifs of being able to lose myself in dedication to this the way I had as my kids had aged up and needed me less.

My only regret was that I did not get to see her off with a very cold I-told-you-so aspic with a flaming red hot Bitchcake for dessert. Breathe. Karma? Oh, God…please be real. I will take this for what it is. Joe and Jack, remained professional about it and I was alone in my satisfaction so I toned it down before someone got pissed off.

Also, of course, Karma.

Karma will have her due.

It was a fact, that life at the Dep was getting a little dicey and dangerous. I was less worried about personal safety, and more about catching a situation that would exterminate my tenuous dream that I might resume my career here, in home therapy, not, please God, not residential. Cort the karate guy is my age and has always done this. I cannot fathom it.

Sometime later, I took a deep cut to a finger from plexiglass and teeth marks on my head, no accident, in the same incident. It was the worst injury I had ever sustained, minor though it was, and it was also the only time I had been in any situation ever that was truly out of my control. The brawl at the hospital ("Cole's circus") before I came here didn't count. It did qualify, but this was worse. I laughed with Dad, but I dreaded one kid killing another, or themselves. We deal in the real, here. I did not burden Dad. I just added it to the whirlwinds I was trying to ride all, all, all of the fucking time, wishing they would just call, him, at least.

Holidays 2020

Thanksgiving and Christmas both passed by in quarantine and we were unable to see Noragee and the Jon and Mary gang, or anyone else, including Mom. We took comfort in her state of unknowing. I privately prayed that she was unknowing, especially if she had suffered any indignities. I mean, she had. We knew it. I privately prayed it was not *was suffering indignities*. We were powerless. TC and Keelin did not call. I did not have to work at the Dep, because Kelsie took good care of our kids, and by extension, us, and managed to get every single kid home for both days, and I was able to spend that Christmas just here with Dad in our sadness. We did not take any measures to keep it away, the holiday, like pretend it did not exist, and I told Dad that we would never let it get us down, because Mom would not want that. The kids, I said… it's always the kids, and if we run out of kids around us, like Petra and Jack, and Nathan and Cody, and mayhap even (dare I whisper it, my real Christmas wish? It won't be this year…) my own sons with us someday? Even now, I said with everything we had learned together, Marla could be with them, if that's what they wanted. That was what I had hoped for, before I left her. Things were what they were now, but we had this to give our attention to as best we could. Dad and I always had a good relationship. And we still did, Father and Son, clinging onto one another while Death walked the halls where his Baby now slept, in a nightmare that would only end with Death itself, and then, until Death yet again, he had the next one, the one of life in this world without her, would set in. We were in a nexus between worlds, and in that place, we had become best friends. I enjoyed this, here in Hell, and he did too. We both missed TC and Keelin, and while it is true I felt righteous anger at them for what Papa was going through now, I did still love them.

They did not call? Thought I heard the phone ring, while I was smoking. Your cell? No. Ok. Merry Christmas Dad. I love you. I love you too, son, and Mom loves you too. Even now.

I know.

There were plenty of things to watch on TV, and we ate well, as we always had, and as he and I would continue, in the Christmases to come, hopefully. We focused on the blessings, and the positives, and there were many, if you know how to glean out the silver linings. A lifetime ago, just as the flames really caught, at Pathways leadership training, we did an exercise called Silver Linings. I mean, some days, when I put shot like this together in my mind trying to make sense of it all, I felt like the universe had equipped me with my fucking spear and magic helmet, to ready me for the rising tempest, the fury of which I had only seen the dragonfly of and not the real dragon that it was.

It was in *this* place, that my Father and I stood together and talked as Men. I told him everything I could recall, ever, about everything. We spent the better part of the year under quarantine. Everyone, the whole world was in shock. I told Dad about shock. I told him about trauma. I told him about first aid, and CPR, and driver's ed. I told him of being a pirate, and a samurai, and explained the origins of both. I highlighted the difference between the two, what both meant. I strove for forensic accuracy. I will not brag or embellish. He's my father. I cannot. I must not.

I will not.

I never have, where it counts, and now it seems like I must not, absolutely in all things. To show them. My sons. I always identified with the Ranger, you know, must be Good in alignment, but can be neutral or chaotic good? Yeah, I'm chaotic good, I explained to Dad, on Christmas. Then, I explained to him how the Treeherder tends to view the world in three terms: military analogy, Dungeon's and Dragon's, and Chess. This, I explained, is Dungeon's and Dragons. Crickets. Blank stare.

"Remember the game Mom heard about, when she was a teacher, and it was called Dungeon's and Dragons, and she got it for me, and then there were like lead figures you could paint?"

"Vaguely."

"It came with like a book, and maps, and shit."

"Yeah, ok."

"Ok. Well…"

So, as we watched Fast and the Furious, I explained the intricacies of a game I never played, but I loved the books, and I did think the lead monsters were cool.

"But," I explained to Dad with a smile, "some guys discover pussy, or not necessarily pussy, but, you know, not that. Cars. Rock concerts."

Pause for ten seconds' video. It takes me six minutes to find on the cylon tube.

"Demented and sad, but social. The Breakfast Club. Put

it on the list, Dad, of movies and TV shows we need to get caught up on, you know. When we get a chance. We have to get you patched up. Justified, with Walton Goggins, from The Shield and Sons of Anarchy? Fuck, Dad. You have to LIVE," I said, laughing. "We need to get caught up."

Aah… *tomes.*

Dad did manage to have his cataract operated on in 2020. This had been shelved due, of course, to Mom's declining state over the last year she was home. He had convalesced and healed without incident. I dusted off some old nursing skills, as if the Dep had not pulled enough out of the attic.

So, me and my new best friend engaged in cultural, social, political discourse of every kind while I was home trying to at least comfort my family, protect them. It was cool, cause my new best friend and my father were the same guy. Christmas was kind of like all our days together these days, and while we remained locked down, we had the internet, tv, phone, computer, alcohol, EEns, canned goods and eleven Mason jars full of good old home-grown Mary Wanna. The apocalypse, if that's what this was, the plague? Hell was, it seemed, the place to be. There was a fair amount of drinking going on, on his part. I was not concerned that he was an alcoholic. The man was in his late 70s, and he has been coming down these stairs and taking a drink for forty-four odd years. What the fuck would I have said? Even if I was inclined to, and I was not, with Mom dying. I mean, on a long enough timeline, Dad was kind of dying too. He was in his late seventies. If he lived ten years, I would consider that pretty good. The women in his family live long. We will see. Breathe. See Mom through. Regroup. See what's next.

Between my limbo'ed career and my estranged sons, I was not looking for something to put Dad and I at odds. I was not worried about that, but the nightmare scenario was he'd get pissed at me and Marla and the boys would swoop in and run me out of here somehow. Ridiculous that may have been as a real possibility, the idea that she would have sought to do so is beyond debate. Especially now. I was smoking pot all the time, who was I to talk to him about drinking? I had two issues. I did bring them up. One was, why was he acting like he could not drink openly, and that I would care or did not know? That mattered less than this; he needed better booze. "You're 78," I told him. "And I'll be damned if you drink that shit under these circumstances. It's the Apocalypse for Christ's sake," I said.

"Ok," he said. "We should honor the club, or something. What you say."

I went right down to the floor and roared so hard I really did almost piss myself. Oh, baby that was better than pigeon McNuggets when I was a kid. Mom and I never forgot that one. Well… we had never forgot it until… yeah. I told my boys that one a bunch of times too, I wanted to call them and share the laugh, and there it was again. Trying to be happy and laugh, but I had to battlefield surgery my own memories and experiences or it was like grabbing a pan you do not know is hot until she's already burning your hand.

Could not tell mom. Could not call the boys. I did tell Anghiel, thank God that woman is entertained.

My God, thank God she's here at all. For both of us.

Fairview whiskey became Black Velvet. That's the best

cheap whiskey there is. I picked up some Irish. Maybe he likes cheap whiskey. Doesn't mean I can't provide alternatives.

It was a lucky break that we grew pot during the Covid. It did not really help with lockdown, but our farmer partner took care of that whenever he came by. With all the parts moving and sliding around all over the place the way they were, Dad and I reflected on the what ifs that would have been so much worse. We also discussed the truly minute by minute nature of not knowing how things were going to play out with mom. Would the Covid claim her? We almost expected that it would, and we both accepted that if that was how it went, her suffering would be at an end, and that's all there is with the Long Goodbye. You just don't want to see your person suffering. At the end of it all, that's all there is. There is nothing else to be done. They are not coming back or going to get better. You just don't want them in pain, or confusion, or fear, or despair, and they are. They are in all of these things, and no one can really do much about it anyway.

***

We were both acquainted with this part of the show. Dad's Aunt Astrid, the sweet lady who always gave me Jon and Genna clothes at Christmas had died of cancer in one when I was about 8, before my grandmother, Mom's mom, or Dad's dad when I was in high school. We drove by that nursing home every day, the one Astrid died in.

Sometime later, after everything was done, I was in the house alone and found papers from when I was in grade school. On one, I remember writing it, I remember that day, it said "I'll go home and to Knollwood." I was in third grade. But we did not go to Knollwood that very day, because at about 11 AM, when I was writing it in my 3rd grade class, Aunt Astrid died, and Mom and Dad told me when I came home.

***

We both knew the nursing home scene, and it's a terrible place to have to put someone you love to die. With Death itself walking the halls of facilities like these all over the world, we understood that most of the Butcher's bill was going to be extracted from the old, and feeble, and weak. But not Sherry. She caught fucking pneumonia, and survived that, but not the Rona. Mom went to the hospital and back several times during lockdowns, and we rolled our eyes that she was having adventures. That was a coping skill, it wasn't really funny, but like a lot of shit that isn't funny, like cancer, of Hell, or, like now, the horrors that walked the streets, the hallways, and our own fitful solitary nightmares, there was funny shit in there, if you just got numb enough, and beyond the end of your rope enough, to see it with the right kind of eyes.

Homecoming/Pathways

In January, I got word from Kary and the Pathways crew that there was an after-holiday Christmas party. It was going to be at Aiden and his missus's place, where I had lived for about three weeks with psycho Maggie when all this started. Maggie was long gone. I went up and spent some time with my old shipmates, and I had a couple drinks, but it was two hours' drive back down 95 to the Shire, so I took it easy. I did smoke a lot of weed with them, like we used to when Mom worked together. Not at work, Jesus. That was like oxygen again, and seeing them all from where I was now was like a

Zoom call from Antarctica.

There is no Jesus here. It's just us.

I did not get into my own business, now that I lived in Hell. It was Christmas. Twelfth Night, in fact. Just before TC's birthday.

And, there it is. Ow.

Long ride home.

Ow.

Event Horizon 2021

Things were winding up at the Dep. It had been a long year. I had watched the seasons run a cycle, and every time I reflected on it, I reflected too on Mom's life ending, and my own, in limbo while the sands tick down through the glass. Her suffering, such as it was, was an ordeal. However, she was not aware of the divorce, the alienation of TC and Keelin, Marla's treachery (Was she? Had she been?), the Plague, the Trump presidency, the rise of Fascists in America… She was already gone, as far as all that. That was Dad's and my time. You sure don't get any time lost back.

Dad, Anghiel, the Depardieu kids, my comrades, and pretty much anyone I could find an opening to do so, I told them about Ella, the original pirate dog. Dad was not warm to the idea of taking on a dog. This was the one thing I knew I was going to have to just override him. The pain of losing Ella had been with me for two years before all this, and that was a low place to leap from, considering the nightmare mess

Marla had made of our family. I was going to work a dog into all this, somehow. I had done my bit to soften up the ground on this. I had an app that showed me shelter dogs, and I saw about a thousand that I would happily have taken home. I was waiting for that spark.

I was used to being ready to be sent anywhere at work. This had been a bittersweet journey. For one thing, it isn't like the old days at Sweet Shores. I had a family to support then, and not only was overtime welcome, it gave people like me a chance to be mindful of where they spent their time. I spent a lot more time in Kennebunk than Arundel back in those days, because the relationships with the kids were more solid. It isn't a preferential thing, not at all. Some kids, you've seen for maybe six years or more now, in many different places. You just know them better, and they know you better, so they know they can trust you. When they really can, they know, and when they really do, it shows.

When they really can, they know, and when they really do, it shows.

Here at the Dep, it was kind of the same. I had been here one year. There were about two dozen kids I knew well, saw every day, and often had to deal with, but that also means there's a respect and trust there too. Out of those kids, of course you love all yer little lambies, but some of them you really join with. It's always the way. I try to give every kid something to show them they themselves are a person, and a part of this, whatever this happens to be.

Beansy was everyone's main favorite, because he wasn't

"good" all the time, sometimes he could be a Wildman. But he was capable of real relationships, so into those quiet spaces I tried to show people how to reach every kid. They did well with this guy, and most of the kids, most of the time, considering the different way things are now, and for the better, but not always the safer. I'm not trying to say I was like fucking Gandalf here. That was the old days. Here, I was pleased simply to serve as a rifleman in my beloved corps.

People like me, and the unit manager, and many of the staff, loved this kid, because he was smart, funny, and he didn't take any shit. He was also like TV show cute, which was a running joke when things got tough and he was about to go upside someone's head with a pipe. He'd look at us and be like, "Aw, come on guys," and we would literally say, "Bean, you know we love you, so think about why we aren't liking all this right now." Sneak Love in. This little dude's demons were real, they were large and nasty, and he did not give a fuck. He and I got along great the whole time I was at the Dep.

So earlier today, Bean had taken a flyer off the snowbank the kids sledded on and stove himself up. When they asked him if he wanted any particular staff, he asked for me, so they pulled me from upstairs and told me to get a van. It isn't totally professional, the smile I cracked when I drew this assignment, but I was not ashamed, nor was I alone, in being perfectly happy to do that instead of the shit night we had brewing, so common now it was routine, and I had been on South Wing for most of the past few weeks. Fuck, yeah, I'll take Bean to UMASS.

We watched surfing and whitewater canoeing videos in

the Emergency Room until Bean got hungry. I scored him some chow when the nurse came around. He asked me more than once to play video games on my phone. The second or third time I paused and looked him in the eye.

"Dude, there is no universe you ever touch my phone, unless we're on the rail trail, there's no one in sight, and I croak. Then, you may use my phone, to call The Dep."

He laughed. "You're just afraid I'll go on your dating profile and have more luck than you." My turn to laugh.

"Ha, jokes on you, I have a girlfriend!" I said this last loud and goofy and moved to like tickle him, but you never really touch them like that. It's ok just to convey the feeling, friendship, love, and it works. We laughed.

"Do you, really?" he asked.

"What? Have a girlfriend? Nunya."

He pouted at me and I could see it was important to him to keep it real here, so I let him in a little, of course. I was just kidding with him anyway. "Yeah, I do, and she's great, and that's all you need to know."

"I bet she's a princess…" He was teasing me the way a kid teases one of his own. It's a high compliment. Time to be a real pro.

"She is. She's descended from Russian Princesses, in fact. It never rains directly on her, and she never farts."

He dissolved into peals of laughter.

"Ok, she does fart, but they sound like windchimes and smell like silver and jewels. She's a princess, not a fucking mutant. Show some respect, God damn it."

He pulled up the blanket and giggled into it like Donald Duck choking. An Almost-a-Doctor walked by but ignored us. A warning shot. No fun allowed.

Obviously, this staffer has never dealt with Dep kids, or staff who never learned to keep it down, that's why I'm good, and both Beansy and I (without commiseration, that would have been unprofessional), saw it as a challenge.

That pissed me off, a little, so I went for the jugular on Beansy, to his delight.

"And I have to have her food specially flown in. It's fresh goose, from Narnia, and it is humanely killed with nitrogen while listening to classical music. Mozart, typically. Air on G string, my favorite all time piece of music ever."

"Stop! Ahhh! AH… AH… I'm gonna fuckin piss myself!"

Touchdown. The charge nurse looks directly in at us. I curl around Beansy like a wolverine and dare her with my eyes to fuck with this laughter that I have created. She stands down.

We giggled like kids at camp, in waves rising and slowing, for a while. Kids like this need moments like these, wherever you find them. Fuck Nurse Ratchet. Fuck her here. Fuck her back at the unit, Fuck them all, everywhere. You comfortable little buddy? All right, shut up before we get in trouble. I don't want to have to slap a security guard.

"Ha! I'll ankle bite that fucking rent-a-cop!"

"Don't swear Beansy." But I smile, 'cause he knows I could

give a fuck. One of the things he does really well is use the English language. It belies intelligence, so I helped him take his vulgarity up a weight class out on the rail trail with Q all summer.

I don't give a shit about me, or today. My battlefield is the future, and the prize is this kid's soul. Not for me. So, he can own his own.

I did laugh, then instantaneous straight staff face. "All right," I said, exactly that way, but ironically. He winks at me and smiles sipping his plastic round juice cup. We're in this together, little buddy.

This is a part that only the troops know, taking one of your kids you work without into the world for a doctor visit, or an emergency, like this, a regular kid emergency. Broken bones, etc. It changes everything. One, it shows you the worker how much you really care about these kids. When they live where your job is, nay, *are* your job, the bulk of the job is parenting them, but only around the one part of them that is so awry they can't even live at home like a normal kid. For that matter the word *normal…* That's one of those basic concepts that is nothing like what everyone thinks it is.

I think there will come a day when humanity, if we survive, will view the way we understood ourselves, and the inner workings and processes that drive us, and collectively as a society, a species, as being as primitive and limited as a time when the most advanced human science thought the Earth was flat, and the body contained four main fluids known as humous. We are in the Stone Age of human psychology and behavioral science.

A worker like me may spend years before you have to do an external op like this. It could happen your first six months. The Mango and I had to send two troops to fucking Bangor once so our guy could get dental work, because he was 6'4" and non-verbal, and when he got upset it was like when a Wookie loses a chess match, and he could pull people's arms out of their sockets. For things like dentistry with the disabled, you gotta sedate them.

These are just tales from the streets, the things you pick up like Christmas tree ornaments along the path of a career. Moments like these, when you get to stand in for all the other parts of parent that you do not get to do day to day, are good. They are powerful, and they should not be wasted or squandered. I've seen people just sit and ignore their charges. Make the most of every minute you get with them to enrich them any way you can. Teach curiosity. Inspire wonder, all that shit.

The nurse checked in again, and very politely moved us to the other room, out of the waiting area, and into a hospital room with a TV. We were quiet. He was tired. We watched some TV. We both needed that. He casually scrolls channels and leaves it on something that would never be allowed on the unit. I'm liberal, but he's nine and I see almost titties.

And then, my phone went Bing Bong. It wasn't Tinder, thank God, but of all things, Adopt a Pet. We found pets that match your search! Bean was in on all the Bing Bongs at the Dep. When Fishbrain made the sound of a reel snapping taut, he knew how to chant "Fishbrain! Fishbrain, fishbrain, fishbrain!" and stop and gather, because that's what Fishbrain does when someone also on Fishbrain catches a fish. Kly05 was our main thoroughbred.

This stuff, the fishbrain chant, utterly confounded other staff. The kids liked that too.

Some of the staff figured it out, and quietly joined the club, setting their phones up. When the sound came over one of their phones the first time, the kids looked around for me, and everyone laughed. The staff played it great. That's how you do it. Figure it out and get back ahead, don't try to chase it, ever. Way of the fucking Samurai, baby…

No, I knew I was not long for all this, no matter how much fun it was. But for now, let's see who's here. Bean perked up. He also knew I had lost Ella, and had seen many pics, and heard many tales.

"What do you think, Beansy?" I asked him. She was adorable. I knew immediately I had a winner. I was going to have to override Dad.

He approved, and that's why Beansy got to see me fill out and send off the application to adopt a puppy, at long, long last, sitting in the parking lot of McDonalds after leaving UMass. Neither one of us were interested in returning right at bedtime, so we agreed to get some chow and hang out before driving back to Whatland. I got us some food, and typed it up.

As I waited to hear back from the Arkansas shelter, I hit Dad with the dog thing. I just told him it needed to happen, and he gave in. It was the only thing I had asked of him, but the fact was that here and now, all the what-ifs that could have been, were all worse than anything we were dealing with. He gave in on the dog after a low-level campaign that began day one of being back. It had been four years since Ella and I had been parted. And, then everything else.

Beansy was excited and made me promise to keep him posted as I bid him goodnight. He loved the song, the Grateful Dead song (thank you cylon, again) and I played it for him and he sang it softly and fell asleep feeling safe and loved after a fun day despite the fact that a nasty knock on the head had been the theme. That's the job. Love them. Don't be a dick. Enforce kindness with determination. It was a good day. I waited until almost Valentine's Day before I heard about the puppy and by then, I had also heard back on a job, and miracles abound, it was back in what I really do. It was back on Sword St., too. That was just one more crazy thing about this whole journey that was just becoming commonplace. Coincidences, lucky breaks, and the wisdom of Chinese fortune cookies were the order of the day most days.

The truth is, it was getting scary around here. I knew I could not risk my future career with some shitshow waiting to happen, and I saw them all the time, every day. There were never enough staff. The bones that were working were like Nala, and working 80 hours a week or more. Everyone was burning out. Despite all the chaos and corners that got cut here and there, I watched these people perform through the plague, get kids home to visit, and make birthday parties for them when they could not. We all got familiar with Zoom for phone calls home, and life at the Dep had gone by so fast that my perspective on it was measured by the change of the seasons. Other revelations and rehabilitations that had happened was that I knew a full-time job in residential like this was in no way my future. I could not run with the big dogs, anymore. Physically I was past my prime, despite being in the best shape of the last ten years. That could have gone either way. Again, I found myself marveling in hindsight how much hinged on choices made along the way. Had I stayed at the hospital, my health would be going in the other direction. Dealing with diabetes like I have should be easy, but my life works against it. I never eat in the same place or at the same time, and sometimes I have to eat what I can get, not leaves and twigs and healthy shit. Aging is when you realize you could once do more than you can now, and it isn't coming back. I could stand with them but thank God I knew better than to try to run. I kept up with the twenty somethings. Middle aged folkie like me who can do that are appreciated. Most of us fossils by now occupy night shifts, where it's quiet, until it's not, and then experience is usually more valuable. That's where I saw most staffers my age, except for mutants like Cort and Arduous, both age peers of mine, and these two, unlike me, had done their whole careers in residential. That's the real hardcore.

Experience keeps people safe at night. I would have made an ass of myself trying to do more. I was glad to have this year of service under my belt. I had talked endlessly to Dad and the nature of the work past and present, and he had seen me in battle mode, with the subtle changes that come with changes in weather and season, or occasion. If I still had my old telescope, I certainly would have house it at the Dep and it would have been great, but I found compensations, thanks to the cylon, and we had the kids, especially Beans and Q, interested in the ISS when it went over, and I could still point out planets and stuff like that. Like how to use the Big Dipper to find the North Star.

And what the brightest star in the sky is… and is not.

Yeah, I am grateful, now. Looking back, if I had to choose between having that time with Dad doing my best to entertain him, for all the extra time we would have had, and him seeing me do what I always did, in one way or another…I'm glad he saw me, who I was, what I did, in action. The year flew by and the mass disruptions of the pandemic and the collective psychological trauma of the whole world just were part of the whole crazy show. We had seen Noragee a few times, Genna a few times, Jon and Mary a few times, Nicky and the boys a few times. We had been fishing a few times, and friends from the very old, old enough to have grown up here in this neighborhood with me, and very new, like Jaz, and Lex. And Mark Gasss. In fact, all three of them, and Lono were all here together one night. Anghiel came by. Dad had not stayed with us long that night, but often whenever someone came by, he was right there in it, and liked meeting people.

Lono and I were in regular touch by phone, and between text messages and phone calls missed and had, Dad had pretty much become a part of my life when I had come home and we had joined forces. He was my sidekick, or sometimes, I was his. The deck outside had been replaced in the summer. We were better off than things were a year ago, that was sure, even if Christmas had kind of been cancelled for everyone. Every day I was on the phone with someone and Dad took it all in. Whatever problems we faced, there were those that could be solved, and those for which we were blameless. If not for the Covid, and all the limitations it put on Dad's ability to love Mom while he saw her out, like not being able to touch her or hug her and those masks that she resisted wearing, because she did not really understand, it might not have been quite so bad for him, he could have held her hand and hung on, but all we could do was get there when we could, and watch. Getting Dad's health under control between the lockdowns and the fact that he revolved around Mom's iffy schedule was tricky. As far as I knew, he was in decent health. We go the cataract taken care of just before it became a serious medical problem for him. Another bullet dodged. He was up and down, up and down, up and down those stairs all the time, pouring drinks for himself down there and I just kept my mouth shut. If he wanted to drink up here, he could, but like me and my pot we kept our own counsels with our poisons of choice. The staff sometimes gave hints at why when we were not there watching over her, she often seemed a little roughed up. Though this killed us both, we also took comfort we could not do anything. Which is not to say when there were suspicious things like bruises or persistent skin issues that spoke of lackadaisical care, I reported them to the state.

I got the call about the puppy just before Valentine's Day. I drove to Connecticut to pick her up. Before I went to the shelter, I went to see Rig. Rig is another friend from college, and we are only an hour apart now. We have never lost touch, and this was the excuse to see him, so I did. Looking back, the last moments between dogs, and the pain I was in with the new stuff places this moment at a nexus of events. Before I went and picked her up, I saw my old friend for the first time face-to-face in a long time. He is also a swordsman, in fact. And it was he who put the first book of The Wheel of Time in my hands many years ago, with regret, he laughed. "There is no turning back," he said.

The Wheel of Time was always profoundly influential

to me in my practice as a healer. Warrior, healer, teacher… discipline is discipline. Duty is duty. Duty is heavier than a mountain, Death is lighter than a feather. I read those words long ago. I live them now. It boggles the fuckin mind, boyo! You feel me? I walk in a fantasy and dream world where nightmares live and Death stalks where my mother sleeps, and my sons are under an evil spell. Do you understand, if I hadn't lost my mind on acid at a Dead show years ago, how all of this would be a leetle overwhelming in its own right? Thank God for drugs… they gave me a fucking decoder ring for Hell.

Pause for Academia

The Wheel of Time by Robert Jordan is a great Tome.

I say this now, because I think it's important to state that I was guided my whole life by literature and cinema. Art in any way does not imitate life. Maybe it does, I'm not opening that debate. But what art does without question is *affect* life profoundly. People are inspired by it, and things learned in my grandmother's house among all the tomes (and not just the books, understand.) served me all my life.

Jordan's fantasy sci-fi adventure is superior to any other work in the genre, ever, save Narnia and Middle-Earth. Jordan was a veteran of Vietnam, and his works throb with a realism that is unsurpassed. The depth of his characters alone is worth study. I'm a fan.

Jordan's main hero is a swordsman, and Jordan's descriptions of swordsmanship are onomatopoeic and visual and brilliant.

At a point in all this insanity and that is what this is, the dual horror of being here with Dad trying to comfort him through terrible things, and realizing that my separation from my sons was done with malice and forethought to the very goal of putting me into this place I was in now, where it hurt to live without them.

I used the sword to calm and center myself as I always had. When I got my cylon phone, and with all the instant life changes that had come with it, it took a while what with all the other nightmares, but let's face it, also good times we were having, but one night it occurred to me to delve this a little more.

It turns out, some guys took Jordan's texts and interpreted the forms named in it, like Cat on Hot Sand, or Boar rushes Down the Mountain. The Wheel teems with action that comes alive with these descriptions and you see the steel flashing and whickering off the pages. I started reading the Wheel in 1995, when there were 5 or 6 books out. It was many years before all 14 of the books were even completed.

While he was writing this American Masterpiece of literature, he died.

He was eulogized by Brandon Sanderson. Brandon had read the Wheel of Time as a kid, like all of us with thirst in the years between, say, A Crown of Swords, and Path of Daggers. Mom gave me Path of Daggers for Christmas, years ago. My life and the life of my studies, both for pleasure and academics and vocation, all converged now to fit the needs of the fucking hallucination and despair that my reality was. Not having Ella was the first circle of Hell. Sorry, the second. Marriage to Marla was the first circle. Loss of Ella.

Estrangement from my sons. My mother's dying, my father's anguish. My powerlessness.

How many are there? Circles?

Sorry. Sanderson, like all of us students of Jordan, waited and watched while he succumbed to amyloidosis, a chronic kidney disease.

And the Wheel of Time was unfinished.

Sanderson eulogized Robert Jordan. His beloved widow Harriet, for whom he wrote that treasure, was so moved, she offered Sanderson the chance to finish it.

Can you just imagine that? He did. It's great. Read it. There are secrets there to sustain you when the world goes utterly mad, and when you're not sure you are or not.

I was watching the interview with the sword guys in Scotland sometime after this all happened. They really did an impressive job with it. I had the pleasure of sharing their surprise to learn that these beautiful descriptions of his (Hummingbird Kisses the Honeyrose, Moon Rises Over Water) were in fact likely originally sourced from real ancient texts, from Japan, that were his personal possessions that also contained illustrations, and such. If you read Robert Jordan, like me, you said in that moment, Ah-ha. Now, *that* makes sense. He took the real, and put it into Art, and someone took the Art, and made it real again, and new, though it was old. Old, and New, together.

And, sometime during all this, I went on the interweb and learned that the moves I had practiced, such as they were with a shirasaya, were real. Because on the intranet they have real guys, old guys, from Japan doing it for real. I had stumbled onto something, and I was not the only one. When I watched the old masters, guys in their eighties, in grainy black and white films from the 1950's, I saw something.

What I had been doing on my own was correct. I watched these swordsmen demonstrate, and it was familiar to me, like hearing music was now different to me. I always loved music, but when you play it, actually make it, you hear all music differently. Even me, weak on theory, and good with ear. This was the same thing. This was an interesting discovery, and these were the best parts of all. These. I could have not worked. I could have not focused on myself and truly gone to ground, and been Dad's *majordomo*, like Higgins on Magnum, P.I.

But I hadn't.

What I had done, was fold Dad's and my life back together, the way it had been when I was a kid, but we were roommates and partners in crime while the Apocalypse had literally come to both our lives and everything we had ever known and worked for, and then we watched the whole world go through those events that came with the Plague as all the hosts of Hell appeared to be unleashed upon the Earth. The surrealistic overarching vibe of it all, through the lens of shock horror and stress, fear of the unknown… never mind all the cool random shit we had seen, like the big ball of black snakes in the mucky marsh at Demond Pond in Whatland, last summer, all brought us together, Hell or no. We had seen a lot of cool nature stuff like the redtail hawk that had flown next to the car one day for a long time as we drove up Prospect St. on some mission, in the early days of this. It was that day, that particular event, that had prompted me to tell him about Candace the White, because he asked me why I said, "Hey," or "Hi," to hawks sometimes, but not always.

"Because it isn't always her." I had told him. That prompted further explanation, and I guess it was that day when something I hadn't thought we had room for with all the real world shit we were dealing with, made it into our conversation. In the end, I had not one secret from him, and he listened to my tales of walking next to the Gates of Heaven, right before I had returned to the Shire, and every other story, trade secret and tale from the trenches I ever thought of. He bore witness not just to who I was now, but to all I had done, everything I had ever achieved, barefoot rank or no, not in the Halls or Monuments of Man, but in the account, one gives to one's maker on that day we all will have.

I was of a mind to simply live a life that showed without question, that the monster my sons apparently think I am, simply never could have been. I had walked a tight line in many ways, although I was aware of some high-risk death wishy behavior, but that is also nothing really new. I guess I'm saying with a straight face that despite risky shit like Bailey's in my coffee rolling through Camton in those early chaotic days at Jackie's, I had been tested numerous times and had held myself together. That, job performance and stability, healthy relationship, good work with Dad…I was invested in these things somehow carrying weight.

And always, over and over, when we talked business, or took stock, I pointed out how lucky I was, how grateful I was, that I had made my way back here. Had things been different, like if Mom and Dad could have just grown old and died together, I realized now the Covid plague would have completely fatally done me, had I still been at Pathways, dependent on in home visits happening to get paid. I'd be absolutely fucked. I may have been a help to him, but he had actually saved my life, and now there was no other way to measure it. The very best I could hope to do was give back as much as I could to him. Thank God Mom was out of her suffering, and I could help my dad enjoy his life. And maybe, just maybe, we could help me find my lost boys. They call? No? OW. Anyhoo…

I think I need you to understand that these are the things I held on to tightly, desperately. Old values. Honor. It was talk for years. We fancied it was real. Now, I was in the crucible. This was all a crucible. The temperature had been increased by increments over a year and a half. New challenges and losses, anxiety about the future, uncertainty…

I just could not understand how I would have made it this far without the blend of experiences that are my own. There has to be a way for everyone to do that, some way to interpret the world and whatever is in theirs, and make it fit, and livable. It takes really high stakes to realize what really matters.

Before we go any further together, I want to lay it out. We need to.

My upbringing had traumas in it. Many people experience this.

I went back into the childhoods of others, to fight the

fight I could not fight as a child. As I learned how to be a healer and a teacher, I healed and taught myself. And I raised two fine sons. Many things I worked for, things I valued and felt safe in, like my relationship with my boys, were uncertain and fuzzy in my memory now.

I was a warrior. My path had been laid for me my whole life. I had the work, the bones, the feathers, whatever. I did these things. It has been an adventure. The adventure continues, here, now. My sons are lost to me, and the effect on me and my life cannot even be measured yet. All I have is what I am. If I doubted it, if I questioned it, I have proven my metal, here in the crucible. Not mettle. We deal in steel here.

I did from time to time hone my skills with my bamboo sword. Meditations come in many forms.

I need you to know that drugs, specifically LSD and mushrooms, and the spiritual experiences that had come with them, old, and new, are integral to my survival. Old, and new.

I was a professional mental health practitioner. What I did, and did with all of them through the years, and all of these soldiers now… it is real, because it affects the lives of others.

And, it is all I have to hold on to, because these are the effects of gaslighting abuse. I was coming out of at least fifteen years of gaslighting abuse, into the situation I had been blessed to be able to find myself in now. It was Hell, but Hell was not so bad. And then, there was Anghiel. She was normal and being with her… these are the things I clung to, and counted, and shook to make sure they were real. Dad was right here with me through it all, as I was trying to be for him.

It's important to pause and note that from the night I went to Pootown and took powerful drugs, I have not felt quite right, and things have just gotten bigger and crazier. I had a great job it took me a long time to find. Next thing I know, everything in my world had changed, much of what was lost, and then all of this was loss too. I never thought I'd be back in West Allenton, and yet here I am.

I just don't know, what the point of it all is for anyone when it gets like this, and I wonder what the breaking point of others is, because I feel like I've sailed past my own so many times it isn't really relevant to refer to it as that. It was like Aunt Stella's second man, Freddie, the one she insisted was just a pal for thirty-five years after Charlie died? Did Freddie Warren die of cancer? He had it since he was in his sixties, and he was 93 when he died. I don't think it would be right to say that the cancer got him. Breaking point for what?

My boys had cut me off. It was a soft cutoff, but that was what was going to happen.

Now I was realizing that the trials and hardships that had kept me up at night worrying were never real. TC and Keelin had no idea about this, about the full-time salary she drew off my parents under the radar.

She had set this up planfully. For how long?

Since I told her I wasn't fucking around, that I was going to leave her, if she did not make some serious changes? Ten years ago?

That's exactly what she did. She love-bombed me to stay, and spent ten years concocting this whole charade, and I had just gotten used. My kids did not know this shit. It would have to change their perspective, would it not? Waves of new knowledge as I had gained not only time and distance, but the long secret perspectives and thoughts of others. Three others, mainly. Dad, Jackie, and NoraGee.

All these things, the Tomes, the Code, the memories and tales of the spectacle of acts…These things I held tight against the storm. All of it just built. It wasn't like I could move on, because I was just starting to realize what had really been going on. The marriage hadn't failed. It was sabotaged. For at least fifteen years.

I wasn't married. I had trapped with a fucking sleeper agent. I had been host to some kind of demonic parasite. Oh, my God…

Dad sat with me as we picked this latest apart.

There's nothing. Even if he was, shall we say, suited to intrigue, or even sensitive topics to be carefully navigated, not only was it not his wheelhouse but the boys would have seen right through it. How am I supposed to build a new life and just what…leave them behind? That's probably exactly what she would tell them.

I should have been more… like Sun-Tzu. I should have just waited it out, but the travesty that my father was now paying the price for a lie that she told… and what about the fact that my sons had no father now?

Shock fueled the fire. I mean, it was a joke in the family that her mother and sister were some vicious petty characters.

Their behavior in restaurants, or to retail people when they weren't interested in actually doing business, just wasting staff's time and being controlling… Marla was the worst one of all. She was just… clandestine.

Fucking Reddit. Opening up Dead Bedroom was one thing; my lonely voice was suddenly a stadium filled with the soft cries of souls begging to find a solution. I actively told everyone I could on Reddit that if they didn't have kids to run, now, right now. Fuck Love, anyone who doesn't give a fuck about you on that level, trust me, cut them loose. I did, and brother the cost was dearer than I knew, but getting free was worth it. Run. Run. Run, now.

That had been going on for a while, since Anghiel shared this particular crack with me.

If I could save someone this pain, I would try, even a stranger.

But there are other threads there to enhance one's vocabulary, and thus perspective.

Like Narcissistic Parental Alienation.

Estrangement. Holiday's tough?

Ouch. No time to bleed, still. No time to bleed wasn't keeping my knee from folding every few months and taking me down for two weeks.

What… the FUCK am I supposed to do with all this?

I don't even have anyone really to ask, but Matty Mango, Cristobel, The Cid and all the rest, everyone, old and even new… they all surely knew that this was beyond belief, and some of these friends knew my kids most of their lives too. What the fuck was even real anymore?

Thank God the shelter called, because I could not take all this new shit, and still not have a dog, and I had found a good match.

It was unseasonably warm when I left the Dep, but by the time I got home to Dad it had started to cool off like February should feel. He gave in on the dog, and the next afternoon I was on my way to Connecticut to see Rig, and pick up… Holy Shit. It's finally happening. It's been four years.

Miss Fiona Honeybee

I did not change her name. It was perfect. On the ride home, I played the song that I played the morning Ella and I returned home after all night on the marsh. Keelin had picked us up. I just played Let the Good Times Roll and cried with joy in my basement that summer morning in 2016. I played it again, now, and cried with joy again as I rolled back north to Massachusetts and my father. When I went to work, Fiona could keep Dad company. There was a distraction, it was made of pure love, and it was jamming to the Dead next to me, as all the things that go to sleep when your beloved pet does as mine had, all the watchful instincts, all the good hearing and gut feelings, mine had all gone away before Easter of 2017. And since then, I had walked a Path that had beauty and agony abound. But now, I had her, and I was responsible for her, and we could love her, and puppies are also funny. A big part of me that had been in mourning shook it off and woke back up. I still miss Ella to this day, that never goes away, but now there is Fiona.

Fiona also arrived with a backpack, toys of her own, and contact info from her foster mom. We connected. I told her Fiona was definitely going to always be Fiona, and I told Miss Heather what Fiona could look forward to. Cause her new Daddy was the King of all Pirates.

By God, I was getting the Pieces together.

Anghiel was smitten with Fiona, and vice versa. Well, Fiona was smitten with everyone. And vice versa.

I took pictures of Fiona cuddling on Dad with my cylon. I sent them to NoraGee, and the crew. I kept this secret from the Boothbay boys. The trip to Turkey Neck was cancelled early in 2020. One of the Boothbay boys is a career respiratory therapist. He does not need to fuck around and find out, and it was called early, to everyone's disappointment. I was going to surprise them when I returned to SouTwin complete for the first time there in six years. And in light of everything that has happened, not only lately, but in the fifteen odd years that we have marked our lives here year by year, the trip upcoming is going to be a good one. Dad had always called Mom Babe. He called Fiona Baby. He also called her Fiora, and Farina, and I wished I could call my sons and make fun of Papa like things were normal. Fiona and Lucifer became fast pals. Nothing soothes this pain like a puppy. She was beautiful, too.

PART 6
APOCALYPSE

The Fog of War

As 2020 became 2021 we were locked down for the holidays, isolated from Mom, and I was wearing my soon-to-be 51-year-old ass out at Depardieu. I loved it, but I also did not have a full timer's obligations. I had spent a fair amount of time contemplating my path back to in-home therapy. I wanted my boys to see that I had a job, a stable relationship, new friends, and I was taking care of Nan and Papa. Nana was going to die, and her mental state made all of this far better, not worse. But Papa was aware, and he was confused, and hurting. I was too, but that clearly doesn't matter. I could go back to college and get a master's degree… yeah. I was a little bit concerned, but I kept my faith. I shot an application back to Sword St. I had been told maybe they could waive the degree requirement. I waited. I hoped. I passed the days with Dad and we waited and watched together. I kept putting in my time at the Dep, but the fact remains that I had been out for a week at a time over the past year with a knee that somedays just would not work, and hurt like a mad dog. Kelsie caught me limping once and sent me home, and caught me using a pool stick as a cane, and sent me home again. I had just returned from a week out and we had been able to see Mom around three days a week, on average.

Tick. Tock. Tick. Tock. Fiona kept things sane. Dad and her took care of each other when I was at work, but it was only a couple weeks and the call came.

I'm really stupid. Sometimes I surprise myself. I don't know if I could have done anything other than what I had done up to this point, but what I did was stupid, and backfired.

See, I thought I was innocent, so I got righteously pissed off, and I demanded they explain themselves. I had taken some shots at them after driving home from the Dep some nights, and letting my pain boil over, hoping they would take pity on me, and reach out. Then, there was the matter of how we left things, and the things I had left behind. Then there were the revelations since we had been cut off, that the marriage had not failed. It had been deliberately and systematically sabotaged by Marla. For years. While she exploited Nana and Papa financially. That my boys did not hate me because I was a monster. They hated me because Marla had told them I was, so she could murder my relationship with them, right in front of me, slow. She had apparently had this in mind for some time.

No. I should have sat on all that, and just let them know I loved them. But I didn't. At this point though, I still had a line open to them. I used it to tell them not to come looking for one of my kidneys, and the path back to me begins with a pick and shovel, and a funeral procession, long overdue, from Scarborough to the Stronghold. As far as I know, everything between us went wrong there, and none of what has transpired since is even close to right. Dig the hole, and let's start fixing things there, or tell me why we cannot. I wish I hadn't done that.

Peace

March 2nd, 2021.

We started the day like we had been. Coffee. Weed. Eens. Chit-chat. Random videos and movie scenes.

For the last six weeks, Mom has been on the decline. We have not seen much of her. Once a week, maybe twice. More than once, I called to check on the status of visits at Blaire Haus, and Steel Wool told me, Oh, gosh, golly. No one called you? We're so sorry, whoopsie.

Dad did not have many moments during all these things when he got visibly annoyed. There were even fewer when he got pissed off. Steel Wool brought it out of him, because she was an absolute incompetent idiot. She lacked professionalism, knowledge and respect for her own role and boundaries, and basic social skills. She was abrasive and sought chances to set rules and boundaries and be a petty tyrant. She bossed the nursing staff around completely out of the professional role she was in, and she and I had a history of me barking at her, usually when she was visibly wrong, out of order, or a hazard to Mom, which she was, because she tried to move her, and she should not, and she caused her pain several times. All of those times I had unloaded on her. To protect her, mostly. From Dad. Being careless or apathetic around my mom not only pissed him off, he did not miss a single thing. There were many incidents, and this clown was the main wellspring. She watched us like a hawk, during the Plague, like an adolescent hall monitor who has let it get to her head, like Dad was going to try to sneak a touch. She was a weak person who was queen of her dunghill. Her lack of true concern or empathy was viscerally repulsive, and obvious. One summer day during Covid, as my mother was dying, and my dad had dry but red eyes, she led us out to the back patio, complaining that the workmen on the roof were getting water where it was going get on her expensive shoes. She barked rudely at the workmen, inappropriately. You're the activities director, not my boss. Safety first. Shut the fuck up. Steel Wool needed far more Shut the Fuck up in her life. I'm so grateful I was able to give her some that day.

I tolerated this fool because she was between Mom and Dad. However, this pissed me off, because these guys were up there dealing with an emergency. I knew Dad caught it. He was a blue-collar guy. The guy trying to clear water off the roof was more gracious than I am. He tried to apologize. She cut him off, I'm not kidding, I swear, with "Blah, blah, blah." Literally those… words, and a wave of the hand. That to me felt like the most delicate cracking of a large and thick piece of glass deeply in the structure. Or ice. That was it. I had to. Suppressing this, this very thing here… well, I think it's fundamentally unhealthy.

We got through the gate and Mom was seated on the patio with her feet up. Her eyes were closed. I gathered my breath, and committed. I knew I was in a good place, because I saw and sensed Dad's futile anguish, at having to suffer this fool, and that Mom had to. Dad is not a man to speak up. In fact, if you provoke a man like my father to the point of action…well, you have both chosen, and earned what comes with that.

I am a speaker. As we settled in, I interrupted her nonstop babble. I waited until she took us through the forms. We were here yesterday, dumbass. No, we have not traveled out of the country. Saying so would cost us several minutes while she explained in her authorit-eye the rules. I did not like to give her any chances to play power. The only thing she does better than play power games, is explain why she never has any answer to any substantive question, like when visits will resume, and forgets to call us when they do, and why it is not her fault or responsibility. She was the activities director. She did not even do her own job well, but she had plenty to say about everyone else's. God. I despise souls such as these. I've earned this, forget everything else, anyway.

Sometimes, accounts like this, when you read them, they play like what you would have wanted to say. I promise you; I gave her the full Monty today, and what follows is pretty accurate. Think Christopher Walken meets R. Lee Ermey for the delivery.

"Charlene, before you go, I want to tell you…you know I'm a worker, right? I used to be a CNA/CRMA? Ok.

I find your conduct unprofessional, and offensive. I do not give a damn about your shoes, or how happy you are to be retiring this year. These are basic professional boundaries 101, Madam. Not only am I disgusted by your conduct, I lack the energy to deal with you, though I would like to. However, you continue to be a hazard around my mom. Hear me. Do better around her, or I will make it my holy grail to rain clusterfuck and wrath upon you and this place, and make sure, that they know why. Now, you are dismissed.

Thank You. Remember what I said, because I do not want to speak to you again about your conduct. Do better."

I can believe it, because I knew her, but I'm not kidding… she opened her mouth to reply. I literally roared "Do NOT!" and turned my back on her. She got the hint, and that's good, because there was no one else around, and I had a great big safe area. If she fucking opened her mouth again, so help me God, I was going to toss a couple chairs. She did not. Dad was watching me with a strange mix of expression, and I assured him with a look I was ok, but I was going to make a point, today.

I wanted to just keep my head down and take care of business, but doing what I had to do could have been disastrous. Getting brushed down here by Johnny Law was a nightmare scenario, which would have created some super nightmare fucking space vortex, or some shit.

That was over the summer.

If anyone doubts that I delivered this speech from the hip, just ask my friends and colleagues. Better yet, ask a Lambda Delta Brother. I got the Golden Jock four times. That's why. Good improv oratory. Or, at least have some good movie speeches memorized.

You know that part in Stripes when they all fight, and Bill Murray gives a Braveheart level motivational speech? I've done that, same speech, mostly, to many groups of kids, usually under similar conditions. In the business, we call that when *milieu* becomes *melee*. We're not Watusi. We're Americans! With a <u>capital</u> A, huh? Milieu good. Melee, *bad*.

We chatted that last morning for a while over coffee,

getting ready to ride out to Blaire Haus. Dad and I traded barbs about Steel Wool Charlene. I guess I have to say she did pay a small dividend in entertainment and humor value. Not enough to make up for her idiocy, but, whatev. The cylon went off. It was Blaire Haus.

My mother was at Peace, finally.

I looked at Dad.

"That was quick," he said.

When the call came that Nana died, I texted Keelin and TC both directly. Keelin and TC both called Papa separately. They were not coming to the funeral. They did not ask about me at all. I was starting to lose my shit, because I had invested a lot in being able to see them at the funeral and hoping for a miracle. Or, barring that, a good old fashioned white trash confrontation.

Nana's Funeral

I don't have a lot to say about my mother's funeral. I saw people who loved and worked with my mother, some I had not seen in decades. Family, too, that we really did not see that often these days, as things were for all of us. We were all making our way through and surviving and coping. Dad made it through. I didn't want Anghiel meeting everyone over Mom's casket, you know? Fiona stayed with us in the car at the funeral home, and she behaved herself graveside. There was no service graveside, really, and the whole affair was conducted in kind of a daze, because people were still locked down, unvaccinated, and afraid, or at least afraid of the fucking idiots who not only chose to challenge to Covid, but saw it as a principle of freedom that transcended public safety or the rights of others.

We had no idea what to do, as far as my mother's wishes. Later, we found her funeral plans neatly laid out for us. She had put it all together in 2006, when she had Thyroid cancer and had to have surgery. She was always deathly afraid of surgery, and she obviously survived to die slowly and obscenely with dementia, but it was clear when I read those to Dad later that summer that she was convinced she was going to die on the table, just like her cousin Jimmy had. But she didn't.

Jackie was aware that she was some kind of vessel that held my mother's thoughts and memories. I had the notion that she should try to take that to my sons. It was gnawing at me. I did not want to push it, but after Mom's funeral, when the boys had not come, I was horrified by the prospect that they simply may never know, and go on thinking I was a fiend, and fear me, and hate me. That was what Marla wanted.

People gushed over Mom's "beautifully written" obituary. I hope it played so well with the boys. I had this stupid dream that when they came to pay respects, that might be a thing to start building back that bridge. It cost a bit of money extra for the length. Dad was pleased. I helped him find ways to scream with cash. He bought some nice flowers. You've heard of war profiteering? There is death profiteering. The florist was a pro, not a crook. Shit's just expensive.

Nana's Obituary

Cheryl Olson [1944-2021]

Cheryl G. (Hamilton) Olson, 76.

West Boylston – Cheryl Gail (Sherry, Mom, Babe, Nana) Olson (Hamilton), 76.

Sherry Olson, beloved wife, mother, grandmother passed away peacefully at Blaire House of Worcester on March 3rd, in the morning, after a long illness.

Sherry was born in Clinton on June 6th, 1944. She was the first child and only daughter of Cecilia (Pierce) and Roy Hamilton. Her family, including brother David, would move to Boylston when they were young. She was untimely predeceased by her baby brother in 2015.

She graduated from West Boylston High School and subsequently earned her teaching degree at Worcester State College. She would serve her entire teaching career at Berlin Elementary, picking up two master's degrees at Anna Maria in the eighties and achieving the position of Principal at the school she loved so deeply and was so fiercely passionate about.

On July 30th, 1966, Sherry Hamilton married Allan Olson and they raised their son, Eric, in Boylston, and later West Boylston. Before they had Eric they traveled to the British Isles and Jamaica, and with Eric they took vacations every year to Maine, places of historical significance like Gettysburg, and fantastic big extended family trips to Disneyworld and Hawaii. Sherry and Allan, with their son and later their grandsons, spent their time creating and sharing grand experiences and adventures and that was the spirit Sherry exemplified in life. Everything was interesting and could and should be learned from.

Eric had two sons, Tyler and Elijah and Sherry retired from her beloved teaching to be a full-time Nana. Sherry loved her family with all her heart and for 24 straight years she and Allan came to Maine for the Christmas holiday. Sherry loved Christmas above all things and those holiday experiences they had with their son and grandsons were most of the year in the making and always involved gifts of an unusual or uncommon bent or theme which always led to many interesting conversations and knowledge.

Cheryl's life is marked and remembered for her love for her family and the generosity and giving that drove her in all things. She was an outside the box teacher and instilled in her loved ones a sense of community and humanity that would deeply influence the path of her only child, and many others. She appreciated history and delighted in discovering obscure facts and unexpected truths, the kind of thing you only hear on the tour at the actual place. She took joy in recreating old recipes from Grandma's cookbook, or exposing her child and grandchildren to a grand view, exotic location or new experience.

Sherry is survived by her beloved husband of 54 years, Allan, her son Eric, and her grandsons Tyler and Elijah. She had many cousins and missed those who went before, Jimmy, Donny, Kenny, and will be missed by Paul, Dickie and Candy. The nephews and nieces are numerous and so are their names, but they are all Pierces, ultimately and beloved cousins: Kevin and Tim, Todd and Kim, Kristi, Julie and

Joel, Donny and Jay, Rebecca, Amanda, and Meghan, Leeann and Greg, Scott and Heidi, and Susan and Steven. Her love for all of them endures, and she took great joy in watching her extended family grow down through the generations, including her many, many grandnieces and grandnephews.

Her many friends unfortunately cannot be named but her teaching colleagues that became lifelong friends were very special to her and her love for them equaled her love for her own family. Her best friend Ellen Power shares that she is remembered most universally for filling time with laughter and she was a very important person to a great many people. Sherry would be very pleased with this. Trudy, Cynthia, Jean and Janet, and all the rest, know that there was great joy in her life for sharing the times she shared with all of you.

Calling Hours are from 2 to 4 PM, Sunday, March 7th at Fay Brothers Funeral Home, 1 West Boylston St. A funeral service will occur on Monday at 11AM in the funeral home. Burial will follow in Pine Grove Cemetery, Boylston. In lieu of flowers the family asks that a donation be made in Cheryl's memory to: Berlin Teachers Association Scholarship c/o Berlin Memorial School 34 South ST. Berlin, MA, 01503.

Finally, because of the ongoing health crisis, the family wishes it to be known that the safety of our great family and community would be of utmost importance to Sherry and in that spirit, we request that people make their best decision for themselves and their families regarding attendance at this service. Your love for her is well known and she would not want anyone to be at risk for this, in all seriousness. Your thoughts and prayers are gratefully received and have been solace in this difficult time.

***

I really wanted to find those letters, but at the pace everything was starting to gather, the clouds of the biggest roughest storm yet to come, it really was hard to see anything in detail, or for long at all.

After all the hustle around a funeral, it gets quiet and the hours stretch out. People did not come, but Jackie called us over for dinner. Those are her love languages. Feeding you and yelling at you. It was fine.

Max poured Dad and I a shot of some excellent Scotch, single malt, at Jackie's after the funeral. He was so proud he was learning. Dad savored it, I watched him, and then looked aghast when Max dumped his, because single malt is an acquired taste. Dad and I laughed at Max, not cruelly, for hearing something is cool, and rushing out to join the trend.

"I didn't have the heart to tell him," Dad said.

"What's that?" I said as I wrangled Fiona out of the car.

"It's a sin to waste good booze like that."

For the rest of you, I learned something. When someone dies, and you want to say, "If there is anything I can do," just bring some sandwiches. You can't miss. We got sick of thanking people, well-meant though their sentiments were, but Dr. Plow brought a plate of sandwiches, walked in without knocking, hugged us tightly through tears of his own, and left without a word. It the scale of the whole scene, that stands out, because we ate nothing else for three days, until Dad got hankering for Sushi.

I took Fiona to the Dep. I sent pictures of her everywhere.

We went over and met Lucifer. The boys did not come to the funeral. I heard back from Sword St. Glory, glory, I found my way back. I was going back to in-home therapy. Marla was an evil sadist. My sons hated me. Dad was in shock. The boys did not come to the funeral. Dead Bedroom is abuse. She lied… she lied to them… she lied… they did not come… they hate me…

How many kids we got tonight? Holy fuck. I'm at work. Ok. That's it. I'm out. Right now.

But, before I quit, I said fuck it. My Not GivFuk boiled over. I called Keelin. Over and over again. Demanding he talk to me. He did not answer. He did not pick up. I sent text messages spelling out Marla's crimes and lies. What I knew of them up to that point, I did.

None of it mattered. I did it one night after work, and the next night, I started again. What the fuck, Keelin? How long? How long? Where's my shit? You know what? I'm coming.

I was on shift, hiding in the corner watching the hall. Jaz and Lex knew I was not ok, but they had me and we were ok. Then, my phone rang. It's funny. I thought it was Keelin, or maybe TC, for a second, and there was for one heartbeat a wisp of hope, joy that I had broken through. But it wasn't. It was the Scarborough Police.

Whoops. What the fuck, guys?

I knew I was risking it. I thought they would have mercy on me. They sure did not. Then again, they had Marla right there with them, didn't they?

One text message from Keelin, or any of them, telling me

to stop, and I would have ceased. I was not trying to test them like that. I did not think they would go straight to cops. They had, and the cop had called, and that was that. Ok. Dead end there. I seethed at this, now, after Mom's death, after the funeral. I guess I really expected them to show up. I wasn't in love with that scenario at all or the possibilities, but they had simply… not.

My dad came in in the morning. There was a cop at the door.

Good morning. Fuck. It was a restraining order. A civil restraining order.

That's a knockdown. 1… 2… 3… I can hear the crowd turning on me.

I staggered to my corner, upstairs, with Dad, and coffee. We just drank the coffee in silence. I had to muster out to my shift at the Dep, but God willing, Sword St. was where I was headed. I have never felt less psyched to make the drive in, but by the time I rolled up the hill, I was glad I had come here, and seen what I had seen here, and done what I had done, and found who I found. Shift was uneventful, and I thanked God, again, for small reliefs.

I was at the Dep long enough to ask Kelsie to find out if I had just ended my career. I had not. I knew one thing. There weren't going to be any guns. Not now. Glad I know how to use a sword, I guess, what with the zombies practically rising out of their graves and all. I was safe.

I took Fiona there one last time, and Beansy waved at us out his window over the snow-covered basketball court. I departed Depardieu. I had accomplished what I needed to there. Picked up some new friends. Reminded myself what I am and can do. Now, it was time to get me gone. I said goodbye to most of them, kids and crew. I never saw Beansy after that night. That was the last farewell there. Circles… well, you know.

Dance of the Damned

Portland, Maine.

April 8th, 2021.

I drove to Maine for the hearing on the restraining order a month later. I don't remember much of the time in between. Dad and I followed our pieces of regular routine, both of us now severely compromised. I had applied for a job at the old Sword St. company, but this time, it was for the work I used to do in Maine. It just seemed like things were starting to come together. We had replaced the deck, we had been planning the removal of the rugs, especially since we took a puppy home. They were coming up anyway, they were twenty years old. But Fiona made it the first big project we needed to do. Dad's knees were bad, and he was trying to keep that quiet, but we did not go out if we did not have to. He had been pretty isolated since the funeral. I was trying to keep that at bay, but now I had a whole other issue.

Portland was cold and windy, and the salt swept up from the Old Port as I tried to find a parking place. The memory cascade had brightened and quickened for twelve solid hours, and all the way up 95. I had called in some backup. Strategically, at this point, I was completely… out of Sun-Tzu. This had been layer upon layer, stress upon stress, and

I had invested a lot in the idea that when Mom died, the boys and I would at least be able to look at one another, and beyond that I had no idea.

But when they never showed up, I started to get a feeling, and it rose and it built, and I failed to manage myself, and I played right into Marla's hands, her manipulation using fears and hate and guilt and shame, and I had lashed out at the boys. Now, we do damage control.

I read something once about crisis, and danger, and opportunity. I was hoping that by putting myself in danger, I might find an opportunity. One thing was also clear now. Marla was not going to be happy until I had nothing left, no career, no sons, nothing.

Athena came to support me. So did the Treeherder. I stood outside the courthouse and Keelin came around the corner. He stopped dead, and I just stood there with a what the fuck posture, looking at him. I couldn't hold the pose. I was so happy to see him even like this I just wanted to run to him, to ask him how the hell we got here.

He would not allow himself to be anywhere near me in court. He was acting... like he was really afraid of me.

***

I need to pause, and reflect on my own state here, because I had no gauge on it, professional or not, and I knew I was in shock, and trauma stress, I had just lost my mom, I was worried about my dad...I was so far beyond what I had once thought of as the end of my rope, I could neither see the rope, or where I had even fallen from, anymore. I was already at the end when I had called Keelin. This reality check with the law had forced me to go cold to function, but again, you keep pulling reserves you did not know were even there, like the day I had tried to move Ella to the Poo. What happened next was when, after everything that had already passed, things really became surreal.

***

Athena and Pete eyed Keelin with some measure of bewilderment and disdain. I guess that's appropriate. These two friends were the ones who had allowed me to initially have and then process my anger at them for what to me was now a clear matter of manipulation and betrayal. I had lunch with Athena and we smoked a J in my car. I met Pete before I left Maine. He was focused on Keelin's affect in Court. He didn't believe he was really scared. I did.

They both expressed disgust at the way I was being treated by my sons, and further on behalf of my dad. The Treeherder also complained that I was not around much, and I told him, kindly, to fuck himself. I was with my dad and my life was ripped apart by …this evil witch. No one should get it more than him. I didn't have the energy to really get into it, but the Treeherder is resistant to my new line that I am no longer angry at my sons, they have clearly been manipulated since they were kids.

For me, that was a real turning point. I could not believe that he thought I would hurt him. I would not. I never would have. Even Marla, even now. She's still mother to them, from what they know. Some mother, to fuel these feelings in her son, to hurt me, with no regard for what it was doing to him, nay, glad it was hurting him, because he thinks I am the one doing the hurting. And she loves it.

I got home in the early afternoon. It was the only time I would ever leave Fiona with Dad for that amount of time. I was exhausted and after a brief report to dad on how it had gone, I slept for about three hours.

As soon as my body had recharged enough to even be awake, I was hauled from sleep rudely by cold hands around my heart and suffocating pressure on my chest. It was not physical. It was the loss of hope. I was dead to my sons. Keelin really believed that I would harm him if I could. I had no idea what TC even thought at all.

And, with that, I began my final descent, and transformation. For about 6 weeks, I could not sleep for more than about an hour at a time. I could not even lay down. I took to sleeping on the couch in the front room. It was the same feeling I had when Ella died, and I couldn't breathe, and I went to the marsh. Our marsh. That had lasted a few hours. I had my boys, and dogs don't live forever. This was different. It was away more intense and went for weeks non-stop.

One morning about 6 A.M. I snapped upright awake with that cold water doused feeling that now was part of waking up after about 45 minutes of stasis. I staggered into the TV room in a state of near panic. I looked at Dad.

"We really need to take care of you and your health. I can't deal with anything happening to you. I cannot."

"Nothing's going to happen to me, Son." He stood up before I could tell him not to, and hugged me. Thank God I am here with him. This really is Hell. It is the way I have come to look at it, and it is needed to just keep putting one foot in front of the other My sons hate me. They hate me, because of Marla's lies. I am losing my mind for real it feels like. Everyone is watching me and waiting for it, except Dad. This was bad. Really bad. And now that Mom was gone, he was in real freefall. The meals I cooked or we picked up went largely uneaten, and I watched this with one more thing to be alarmed about I threw on the stack. I had concrete Pieces of a future set up here, with Dad, and also for me. Some stability. I had this legal shit now, but hey, danger and opportunity. It was about this time, that inexplicably, I started getting daily notifications from Sun-Tzu again. and every single one of them basically clanged that I had really fucked up, strategically, tactically, ecumenically. As was now our normal, Dad and I laughed through the pain. However, his pain was now different, and cold. Very cold, with Mom no longer in the World. That had been the last scrap of comfort for him, was that she was still here, and not really suffering, fir all the suspicious things and poor care that I don't even have the energy to go into here, because people being slack, unprofessional and downright rude had been a measure of this from day one at UMass.

The accurate sequence, before we get to the all the way into Abyss that I traveled to during all this, is as follows:

In February, I decided it was time to leave the Dep, and I had reached out to Sword St.

Fiona came home on Valentine's Day, minus two days.

Mom died March 3rd.

I called Keelin and texted and let loose my last of three or four outbursts I had during the Plague. That was St. Paddy's

Day. No, I was not drunk, but I wonder if they think I was.

The last time I ever got drunk was either the day Mom died, or the day of her funeral. There were several people through that night, including Anghiel. I learned that night, forever, with my Dad, which is awesome, how much my absolute drinking limit is now, in my diabetic life. It had never been tested. I had drunk a little here and there, but that night, whichever it was, Dad and I drank a bunch of nips of Irish Whiskey and cracked a bottle of Crown Royal so old the bottle was different, and it had once resided in my grandparent's (*Jackie's*) house over in Allenton. It was at least 56 years old, and it did not taste like Crown Royal now.

When my old school buddy from two doors down was here that night I had him shoot a vid of me ripping some harmonica, one of the original twelve that I had with me that night, the last night of my old life, out ion Pootown on Acid, when Musician-me was born, and learned to scream with music. I did, tonight, and finished by bellowing "My momma got 'em for me!" as I finished, and you would be surprised to learn the sad backstory, if you just saw that quick vid of me and my dad getting a little drunk, and hooting it up.

When I woke up the next morning, Dad was sitting where he was last night when I ripped a little harp. I was not sure, and I did not ask him, how long he had been up, or if that was Crown Royal in his little favorite whiskey glass. It was.

I went to court on April 8th, thereabouts.

It was about two weeks later I heard form Sword St., and it was about two more weeks before I got up and running, training at home online, anyway. It was the only thing that stopped the freefall. I hit the bottom and bounced. For weeks, without sleep, I went through the ridiculously computer heavy training and orientation. This was all done on ZOOM. The plague had truly changed the world forever. If I had to get up, shower, dress, and go to an office where I could not smoke weed constantly, and sit in front of a computer for 8 hours… well, there was just no fucking way.

I remembered the early days when I had just moved in with Dad and started the first Sword St. job, how happy I was that I had not been out of the game long. We did not have their old computer running then, and Dad and I had since gotten a new one. I was able to recover from the effects of the court visit and haul myself back to the battlefield. The sound of the guns, I told Dad. I have a use. I am not dead. I can do what I do. There is war, and I am coming.

The phone calls texts and occasional visits from all my vast cast of characters was nonstop, and sustained me. This was truly my first ever round of being psychiatrically compromised. I wasn't. I tried to tell them, when Marla tried to tell me she was worried about me. She was not worried about me. Now I was. Quite mad, in fact ha-ha-ha-ha… Fucking trauma.

I asked Dad: "How the Hell did I ever say anything helpful, without understanding this the way I do now?"

Dad and I were having coffee, and I had been at it for at least two weeks, when I got my first phone call from a client. Dad listened while I was in the other room. I paced, and talked, and encouraged and charmed, the way I always had. This was something that had endured all of the changes intact. I had put it down to leave Maine. I had returned to my old roots and cleaned the foul years old taste of residential out of my mouth. I could operate in residential as well as I ever did. I drew strength from that, so by the time I returned to Sword St., I was lean and hot for battle, confident, and salty.

In the weeks to come, Dad and I watched the winter not go quietly, and the weather warmed gradually. The last snow of the season finally took out the circus tent for good. It had served well. Dad was glum but in good spirit, of rather, he was happy as he could be, but still profoundly sad. I still could not understand why the boys were not trying to talk with him more, especially now that I had a restraining order on contacting any of them. We talked much everyday about all things. He was Alfred. I was Batman. Fiona was a constant distraction, but in a good way, because we could not be long with anything, when she would want to play. It softened Dad's pain. His knee pain still concerned me. And he was definitely depressed, of course.

This is not the book I always wanted to write. That book did get written, while we were in Maine in the fucking wilderness, fighting stupid arguments over things that did not work for the treatment, and people didn't listen to us. When the smart people wrote that book, the one I always wanted to write, the one that became the standard, the nationwide, evidence-based standard, on these points, the ones we fought the hardest battles over, me, Candace, Athena, Mikhail, and some others. We were right on every last one.

If I could have written The Art and Science of Family Rehabilitation, it turns out, I actually did know what the fuck I was doing all those years. Go figure, guys. I told Dad all this with great joy and satisfaction. I felt maybe even a little Karma, and with that, some Hope.

Fuck you, Elizabeth. Fuck you, Lorry. Candace is a hawk now since she died. She says Fuck You, too. Fuck you, Jen and Becky, too. Fuck the whole fucking lot of you. You were all wrong. We were right, and the truth was here to be found, and I paid my dues at Depardieu, and I found it. Fuck… You. I spread this glory around ravenously among the old Pathways bunch. Told them, hold fast. The truth is coming. There were plenty of people who knew this tale, and they heard word that they were in the wilderness and getting it right with great joy.

Now, at this moment in 2021, I no longer had a book to write. Someone beat me to it, and I was glad. I could do it, the work, as it was meant to be. If it weren't for the shit between me and my sons, this would be huge, huge news. They knew well my crusades and trials fighting that particular war. I longed to tell them, but alas… I did not want to go to fucking jail. Jesus. I am coming, Shadow. I rise from ash with sword in hand. Mother fuckers. I felt good. It was, of course, still Hell. When I came back from Maine, Dad and I would get busy getting busy. He was enthusiastic. I did not think I would come home from Maine and find him dead of suicide. With some trepidation, I would have left him to that choice should he make it. I prayed.

The SouTwin trip was coming. I explained to Dad that we called it Turkey-neck because it's on Turkey Tail Road. I pulled it up and showed him on Earth, as always remembering how TC used to always come out and share vids and memes in the days when I did not have a device like this and had thought I would never need one.

But one other thing happened. It was not just a matter of a restraining order, because I went and got the mail just as a light drizzle started, and found a letter from Portland. From the DA. It was a criminal arraignment. I had gotten through my whole life without ever being arrested or being charged with a crime. Until now. My mother's ghost rumbled through the house.

"Yeah, I know," I said.

The rain slicked me as I walked back up the driveway. Fuck, again.

For what was becoming a pattern, at this point, I said to myself, "Shit just got real, now," and had no concept that that sentiment usually precedes the true arrival of the shit that gets real.

But…

There was something in there that changed everything.

I could not understand what happened with my sons. I could not make sense of it, a year and a half later. They had just cut me off, and they knew, they *knew* I was twisting and distraught over this. But why? It was not what we had discussed, what I had agreed to, when we had the last family meeting. It was a set up. Marla had told them something terrible. Something to make them okay with betraying me. Something to make them hate me. I had my suspicions what this could be. It was obvious, really, but here it was, in her own writing, on a police statement.

"He was physically abusive. Threatened to kill me and kids. I filed for divorce Aug. 2019."

-----*stop*-----

The house shook long and low, so low when it started, I did not perceive it. It rumbled. I tried to tell myself it was the train. I knew it was not. A surge of energy went through me, long slow and deliberate.

Dad came hobbling out, visible concerned, also visibly deteriorating now that he was not driven by his need to be with Mom. His knees.

"What's going on?" he asked.

"Train?" I was trying to hide the waves pulsing through me, as I had through all this, compartmentalize, somehow, what Marla had done so it would not hurt Papa. What a joke.

"Too early." He was looking at me the way he used to when he caught me smoking cigarettes. He would not tell Mom, because he would get it just as bad. Because he was a smoker once. He was looking me dead in the eye, and he knew I was lying right to his face. Or about to, to keep something from him. No. No, I would not. I surrendered; I don't want him thinking I'm lying, even in jest.

"Trauma flight to Lakeside?" I asked with an almost straight face...

"What just happened?" he asked me flat out. "Did you do that, like when Darth Vader--," pause as he reaches... Oh, Dad. I love you. This is funny... "--you know what I mean." He gestures, Sith-like, demonstrating Darth's outburst, when, newly Darth, he learned the awful lie about Padme. I laughed, again, here in Hell, at the wonderful terrible comedy of absurdity and horror my life was in this moment. With him.

"Yes, Dad, but no, I'm not really wielding the Force, like that. I think." I laughed again.

"Dad, you understand that I could not play harmonica the way you hear me play it, like, good, until that night in Maine I told you about? The acid, and the God?"

"Yeah."

"Well, I think I have a lot of energy and emotion and shit to deal with, and I am also a being of great healing power, as we've discussed, and because of what's going on, what has gone on, et cetera, uh, I don't really know. I was hoping it was the train. But I knew when you came out. It's like the time Candace came to us after she died, TC too." I showed him the various documents and data.

"I knew it was real."

-UGH- (not now, love-punch heart pain) at the memories of my sons, and the realization of the now.

When the cop called me that night and told me to stop calling Keelin, I asked if there was any safe person who could mediate. Between the cop and Keelin, that became "Could I send my friends to beat him up?" The Scarborough cop flat out lied. He scared my kid. Fuck you, liar cop.

Keelin… do you really believe I would ever have done anything to hurt you?

Who told you that?

From here on out, believe what I say, or not. It's all true. I never got to say it to them. I had chances. I fucked them up.

So, when I say that my Dad received this statement with aplomb, and accepted it for what it was, that was it. He just shrugged it off. Ok. You just shook the house with a wave of energy. You think we should get some sushi?

I wish I had always said yes to the sushi, and just went and got it. I was trying to exercise frugality.

-----heart/pulse-----

When I had looked into Keelin's eyes in court and saw fear of me in there, everything changed. It took a few hours, but for weeks I had been in a spiral, truly on a roller coaster I could not shake off. It is the very first time in my life I experienced actual symptoms like this. Thank God over and over again that there were three things that kept me here; Dad and being with him of course, but, for frame:

One was my experience in college at Blue House.

One was what had happened for me as a conscious being through psychedelic drug experiences, especially once my relationship with said drugs evolved to more than mere recreation.

And the third was a lifetime of genuinely trying to be the best I could be for the kids and families as a professional. And, also, my own, including Marla.

These things… were Truths.

So, the effect of Gaslighting abuse is difficulty perceiving reality, especially of memories.

But… and I knew as it came together for me, as soon as I saw her lie, and knew it was a lie, for real.

"He abused me physically."

I said earlier, I wish I could say there is no kid out there who would say: "You know what? I think you're actually a dick." I hope there is not. But I don't know. And by telling my tale, if that soul exists, may I get to see them again, and make it right if I can.

However, one thing I do know, is that no kid ever *saw* my dick. You see?

I know that. And I know what that knowing feels like. And that is the way I knew her lie when I saw it in her pen. And I was fucking saved.

I never, ever once, laid a hand on her, or made a move like I would. Knowing, really knowing that she had lied… it was the point at which I stopped being confused and angry and all that, and realized why this thing had happened between my sons and I.

Not only was it deliberate, she had always wanted to do this to me. Her, and her mother, and her sister Vendela.

It was bad, but it was what it was.

There it was.

It was May 2021. I have had since August of 2019, to try to make sense of the situation, and what I had learned down here. I had tried to tell the boys this as I had learned Pieces. Jackie knew, we talked about how she and my mother used to talk. Jackie holds the key, but I can't force her to action. She should want to, but… I got too many things going on to even think clearly. Legal trouble was nothing to trifle with. I needed a fucking lawyer.

"Hey Dad. Remember I said I was going to come to you if I ever needed money?"

Thanks to the Covid, and my out of state residence, this went onto the back burner, simmering. I had the data in my hands now. And, I was a criminal in the eyes of the law, and this shit, this domestic abuser shit that all Marla's lies hung on, well… People who really do this are pieces of shit. I have combated everything about this, abuse, violence, my whole life. I have nothing now. I am naked, and alone, in the fire. She lied. If I could not look down in my hands and see it, I would have struggled and I do not know what I would have clung onto. The only thing I had was the dead ass knowledge, that I never ever put my hands on that woman. It was black and white, and I needed that clear a thing to think straight myself. I had my footing.

I onboarded at the new job online with endless trainings while I chatted with Dad and talked to him about how the science of family treatment was growing in effectiveness as people got better at it. I explained I was excited to bring twenty-seven years of experience into this arena. We were excited. He was not eating that well. I chalked it up to depression. I watched his drinking, and it had up ticked a little. We began to look forward. I had just started this job, but I had a date with the Great North Woods. It was and would be the only thing that would take me away from Dad for more than 24-36 hours. I had to get back to Turkey Neck with Fee. It was the Code. Dad followed all of this intently as I made ready, planned menu and cocktails, and told him about how we did this, for years, and how we would do it now, with him. The fishing, I told him.

First, we need to get some shit squared away with the house, like pulling up the rugs. They needed to come up anyway. Fiona accelerated the priority on that. By urinating everywhere.

I prepared to return to the Great North Woods with Fiona. I felt like we had arrived into our new future, and I was going to go up there and kick it off. It felt right. I found my way back to my career. It was the sound of the guns, I told Dad that had pulled me up and made me arm up again. As far as TC and Keelin, now I had this charge to deal with. I was just hanging in the wind on that, without really knowing, exactly where I had been all along, no explanation, no closure. Anghiel watched me put gear and supplies together, and talk excitedly about the Doorway, although I had no plan to go with them. I showed her the little can that I carry the magic in. It held candy skulls, originally, and looks like a Day of the Dead Skull.

As the Spring of 2021 approached on the horizon, Dad and I took stock and prepared for our future together and Anghiel was part of these discussions too. And Fiona, of course. We were optimistic, and returning to Turkey Neck was symbolic. I planned the whole menu around the cast iron pans Dad gave me for Christmas 2019, that I cooked every meal with for us now. Things were looking up. The grueling pace of onboarding back at Sword St. had me tired, a year at Depardieu had me lean and hard, again. The sound of the guns had pulled me back. The situation with my sons was almost two years old, and it was a fucking soup-to-nuts catastrophe. One that now carried some real weight. I needed to clear that and it was going to be at least a year before I could.

What I did have going for me was a stable girlfriend who was credible, some new friends, and the kids in the family, who I was not getting to see much of, but it was the Covid. It just fucked everything way up.

The contrasts here were what was so crazy to deal with. I know we're more than halfway through now, but there is no horizon in sight yet, so we cling to each other and get by. Met Anghiel, have good thing going there. Marla sucked ass and I didn't have a normal life. Still assessing how bad that messes one up. I swear to God if being in a Dead Bedroom marriage broke my hog, I'll fucking buy one of those mini-Tesla coils I see on Wish shooting sparks out of dead shrimp and shove it up my peephole to get things going on. If I have ED when I have a girlfriend who is, well, you know, human, and not some kind of fucking sadistic mutant sex camel, I'm going on a fucking mass killing spree God, I fucking swear…

Oh, yeah. Probably shouldn't say shit like that, I said to Dad as we tucked into some calamari. Laughter: best medicine. LSD does a pretty good job, too. I told Dad that there would be no trip through the Doorway for this medicine man this spring at Turkey Neck. What I had just gone through scared the shit out of me, it was by far the most fucked up I had ever felt without a good reason, like being on fucking mushrooms, or delirious from fever. We weren't playing around with that; I'll just watch them and teach Fiona what it means to be a pirate dog. Things, for Hell, were looking promising.

Jazzy & Fee

Mossy Pond, Camton, Mass.

April, 2021.

Fiona's first trip on the water began where Jon and Mary ended up, the house they were still building in the hot frantic Indian summer of 2019. They found another pond, and as far as Petra, Jack, Brooke and the roughly hundred people that were in their orbit. Mary has 8 brothers, and their three sons are rich with friends, especially Padraig, the middle one.

Dad's birthday was last week. We got some good food and watched Fast and Furious, some new James Bond, and we discussed the various Bonds over the years.

Dad was delighted to learn more about Sean Connery, who was quite a model of noble strong man, in his life. Do the research. Daniel Craig was the best of all, I shared, and we watched some clips.

Fiona took to the canoe without any problems. At least she wasn't afraid.

It was really starting to feel like Dad and I could get about the business of moving forward. He had done what he needed to do, and I was grateful, because though we were not able to attend Mom in any way the way he would have unrestricted by plague and whatever, he was satisfied we had seen her through. The unspoken unmeasured tragedy that

TC and Keelin had been absent from the whole show was a large dark stain. But it was over. Dad and I were going fishing. Here, in fact, because the pond comes right up to the road where the canoes go in.

Jazzy loved it all. She was awestruck, and I was deeply amused, because here she was, looking at this little pond, like it was big. I remembered through a child's eyes. Jazzy, I told her…

"You have no idea."

***

"See her, now. My new girl." Jazz knew my teacher voice; we did eight months together at the Dep.

"Jazz… you know the Reservoir? That is an average sized body of water. It's a large lake, no doubt, but…imagine you could go on it. This, this outing today? Meal cooked on charcoal, lakeside. Frozen drinks. Put in at Old Stone Church. Take out, right over that hill. The North Dike. Right across the big open water. Maybe even rig sails."

She was just listening and her eyes were getting wider. I wish the third of our little ka-tet was here, Alexa.

"Jazz… by the end of the summer, you, me, Anghiel, and my dad and whatever pirates we can rally up could go up to the marsh, put in, picnic, party, swim… pirate. Ride the tide. Jazz there's so many birds and seals and shit it's like being on the Discovery channel. Four-foot sturgeon jump right out of the water, dude!"

***

Fee was listening too, we noticed, and we all three erupted laughing. She looks like she wants to swim. If she turns out to be a swimmer, that will be…something new. Ella could swim but would not unless she had a reason. Like following me. There were exceptions. One time, and one time only, she just leapt out of my canoe on the Saco and swam over, and rode with Treeherder Pete for a while. But she usually did not swim. Fee looks like she's a swimmer. I begin to wonder about the amount of Rhodesian Ridgeback and Arkansas Mountain Cur combo, and I realized something else.

Ella had to be part Rhody. No ridge, but…they don't need one. What I realized now, was her questionable other lineage was almost certainly another type of Cur dog. Black-mouth, for my money.

Fee and Ella were more breed similar then I realized, and four years later, Ella was still my teacher. Missing her had not lessened, but Fee was not Ella. And Fiona was a little Sweetie-bee, all on her own.

My two companions enjoyed their outing today. It was a first for both of them, the puppy and this young witchy woman that was my new sister. And, come to think of it… the first Pirate of the New Age! I told Dad later, with Fee fast asleep and pooped on my lap, there were many new things afoot, for me, for us, even ones with echoes of the spirit of the old, and he and I were poised to tackle it together.

Horizon-ho

Springtime in the Great North Woods.

South Twin Lake, Maine.

May, 2021.

There were no laughs or fires here last year. Here in my stone, I perceive great changes on the Earth. Their absence last year was an omen. The weekend that always heralds summer with laughter, and sometimes pirates, was silent, for the first time.

I am P'KtAAdn. I am the Stone that watches.

I am the Eye of the Earth, and the Scribe.

The pirate is with them. They arrive all at once. This has never happened.

The bark of a dog sounds across the lake in their company for the first time in six years.

There is a dog with the pirate again, and she looks almost, but not quite, like the Original.

Why… it's Ms. Fiona Honeybee.

Since that awful day in 2017 when he arrived here without her, they have made this trip about the Doorway. The pirate always brings the medicine. He has returned here with them every time, and they have all journeyed together, until last year, when for the first time, no one came at all, because of the dreadful plague.

They have taken this trip together every spring for fifteen years. The brothers lost their father a few years back, and they often speak of him now here, but only once or twice a trip, around the fire.

Their children have gone from Tonka Toys to college graduates. There have been many changes. Promotions. The dog and Pirate lived and died here. A lifetime of memories has been marked and measured here. The blowgun dart has been high in that tree for eight years through the bitterest, darkest, stormiest winter nights, when they are all far away in their lives the other three hundred and sixty-one days of the years they have spent here, and they come to marvel that it is still there every year, once they manage to spot it.

The puppy fits in to this ritual, this collection of rituals now, like she belongs. She does. The pirate and the dog. Without her, he has told them, they are just a bunch of assholes drinking in the woods.

He buried something here the last time he was here with Ella. Fiona and he look for it, as he has every year since she has been gone. They do not find it, again. They ponder the quality of pirate that loses his own treasure, and the drinks begin to flow. Then, they open the Doorway, again. This is now the central ritual, since that awful terrible day, when he arrived here alone and all the good memories were put on the shelf, complete. Never to be added to. Until now, a new set.

The pirate does NOT go through the Doorway with them. Another first.

Truly, all bonds are broken. All rituals new. What was is no more. What will be, will be. What once was may yet be again. Everything around the world is in flux, and everything has changed. The ripple effects are here now clear to me, P'KtAAdn. These men were like clocks, immortals, Archons in their energy here.

Until the First Age ended, just before Eas-- you know this… We have come full circle.

Circles open and close.

Everything has changed forever. Here. Out there. Everywhere. These men spoke of their sons and daughters for years. Now the pirate is silent, and waves come out of him that I can feel here, as they slowly pour into the Lake, vast reserves, of shock, and pain, and fear, and negativity that this one bears. He sailed the waters of it as vocation. Now he carries a weight few can even comprehend, and it is his own, alone, save she who birthed this obscene toxic dump of lies and hate that was their marriage… They are sealed together, and their Sons and the future are in the balance. The humans with him do not feel the gravity and weight of this. But I do. I have been here for thirty thousand years.

I am…

…P'KtAAdn… the Piece of the Big Rock.

The wave of pain he was in four years ago when she was lost is something else now.

Something far worse. This soul is lost and alone. Here among his brothers with whom he has been through so much you cannot see it, but he is keeping it down, so they can do what they do here, which is relax, and laugh, and have fun and recharge.

That is not what he does here, anymore.

This is Holy Water.

And as the boys spill out of the cabin in this new central ritual, the pirate smiles. And scoops little Fiona into her spot, to take her place, and join him on the most important ritual, honoring the Code. Honoring her. Her sister. He is holding her gently, pointing, and whispering to her, what all this is, and who she is now. And he is weeping, a little. A little with joy, maybe. She is not afraid.

The sun is coming around the trees. It is four years to the minute from the first time he did it, on impulse, shedding tears, and hot with fresh raw loss.

They slide out onto the lake. It is a mirror framed by green hills.

The secret ritual in Remembrance of Ella is now observed through her heir Fiona's eyes.

It is before sunset on the first day. They approach the island. The puppy is standing in the bow as they make their way nearer.

In the Lee of the island, the pirate produces three things. His knife from his belt. A name plate from an Old Town Canoe, and the shell. The shell is sounded before they round out of sight, as always.

In the quiet shelter from the wind across the big lake, the pirate looks at Fiona, and tells her, this is important, pay attention. Good girl.

The knife is struck to the nameplate. It clangs like a windchime in a Japanese garden.

"Only these two things in these two hands make this sound."
Clang. Again…

"Know me. And remember her.

"Great Spirits of the Lake, this… is Fiona."

-clang-

He rounds the lee of the island like he has since she has been gone. Not alone any longer. I still remember the howl he loosed upon us that terrible day.

Why is he now surrounded by shadows?

He has not changed, and yet…something is very wrong.

The shell horn sounds again over the water. Whatever else, there is one thing. There is one thing new again that was before once lost.

They are just a bunch of assholes without that dog.

They will never again return here together. This was an epilogue, pulled together for the sake of the Code, and memory. It is the last trip to Turkey Neck. I am the Eye of the Earth, and the Scribe.

Circles close, and open.

***

The ride home was swift and light. It would not have been complete without a dog, or breakfast at Our Fambily (yes, that's the real spelling) Restaurant in Dexter, Maine, with their awesome eggs benedict.

When I returned from the Great North Woods, I was rejuvenated. I threw myself into my work. My Alfred watched and we laughed. We talked of Mom, and fishing and how we were going to help Noragee, and how maybe Dad and TC and Keelin could hook up sometime, somehow, even without me. There had to be a way. I was crushed about them, and now we had some… regulation on it, which was good, except, it wasn't. I was up against this crazy alternate universe and I could not get to them. It was terrible, is your takeaway.

I could have handled this stuff, I think. What Marla did, the depth, the fact that it preceded even my awareness we were not happily married. My father's suffering. I need you all to really understand… that I was very, very lucky, to know what I had to do to survive, and I'm convinced the only reason for that cannot be about me. It must be about what I bring. It must be. From here on out, everything gets beyond fucking crazy and bizarre.

Wind

I was finally back on track with my career. I found my way back. I explained to Dad how I fought this silent crusade for years and how it turned out, the right way was the right way, and we were just the lucky primitives. This was going to be the big show. We had shit to do. Lono came with Mr. Nimbus and stayed for a couple days.

Almost all the Pieces were put together, and I had hopes that Dad and I could find some quiet spaces, and some peace, and continue with the good parts of all this awful. And maybe, just maybe, find some way to break through to my sons.

The greenhouse did not need to be built again, and the weed went in again. I talked to Dad about the house, and I had an idea. Shockingly, he thought it was good. I called

Lono and asked him, since he was van-living, having left Biddeford not long after I did (so much for the neighbor thing either way, and yet here we were again).

Lono could come stay with us and help us work on the house while he figured out his own shit.

Ok, then. I had high hopes to get some work out of this guy, help me keep an eye on Dad and Fiona, and just generally make life easier. Lono living here turned out to make life easier, primarily for Lono.

Yeah, when I came back from Maine, I was rejuvenated. We had Fiona to entertain and snuggle, Mom was at peace. It was time to go fishing. His knees were in obvious pain now, but he still would neither admit it, or give in to it. He needed new knees. Otherwise, as far as I knew, Dad was in pretty good health, for a man who just broke 79 years old and cared for a mate with dementia for around 9 months on his own when it was bad, and then had watched much of his world simply burn away, especially the parts of his world that were my world. They had called him on his birthday, briefly, while I was at work.

It was the Apocalypse now. We were surviving the real Apocalypse. It has not seemed necessary in this tale to reflect on the fact that all of this was framed by the circus of excrement that the Presidency had become, nay, the entire government, like a bad reality TV show that you could not turn off. As I was nonchalantly counting through blessings like rosary beads, I made the unforgivable mistake of wondering how it could get worse, for just… one… heartbeat.

***

The object of your desire comes closer.

You must risk the kingdom to achieve it.

The purity of heart guides a man home.

***

Weirdly timed and prescient Chinese Fortune Cookie Fortunes.

Also, Sun-Tzu for some reason returned to daily morning visits after I went to court, and every single quote from the Art of War was very explicitly about the things I had done wrong, in this war with my ex and my son's souls in the balance. I had not remembered my Sun-Tzu at all.

PART 7

INFERNO

Purgatory

June 30th, 2021.

Day 731, New Life/Day 1, purgatoria.

After the court debacle I had clawed my way out of that dark hole by riding out to the sound of the guns. I got established at what had been my old career. This was a major life goal for the future, and the possibilities that had been under consideration, like needing to get a fucking master's degree and social work license. There's a lot of talk of fortuitous and miraculous happenings. Finding my way back to my vocation in less than two years was one of the biggest ones. It would have been nice if I could just have that, and not be struggling every day with screaming in pain. Dad was too. We did not ever once try to sugar coat our realities, we simply learned to deal with them. There were a lot of things going on that were full of hope and promise. We had begun helping NoraGee with Ritchie such as we could. We had an edge over the Clinton clan. We had just navigated all this shit. Dad could be helpful to his sister and he was happy about that. So was I. We were working out fishing spots, with

Nathan and even maybe Cody. Hell, Even Nicky, if we could roust them out. I contacted Nicky the Gun and hooked him up with NoraGee.

Nicky the Gun is one of those players in all this that I thought would be mentioned more. Like my mother's closest couple friends, they were not as much of a presence as we would have liked.

Mom was gone, and the future was now. We had some loose ends. House needs work. Basement full of stuff. We had not wanted to do spring or fall cleaning while Mom was alive, getting rid of stuff or taking her possessions down would have seemed like we were hustling her through. She had been in God's hands, and ours, and of the three of us, the only one who did a good job had been Dad. Mom's final journey had been a fucking obscenity and the offensive conduct of Deb the social worker at Blair Haus, the lack of giving a shit exhibited by Steel Wool and the collective effect of trauma on the staff from Covid had all made her journey something I did not want to think too much on, because I had helped Dad do his best, and tried to do mine, compromised though I was.

Lono had arrived after three months living in his van between Maine and Alabama. I had called him after talking with Dad, and said if he wanted, he could come and live here rent free, and help me out with whatever presented. He was handy. He had sold the house in Biddoton after the Treeherder retrieved the Discovery and brought her to Pootown. He both this van, and now he was cleaning out my basement so I could get a hand around here.

Lono came up and poured himself a drink at my offering

and he and I and Dad sat together. The next night, he just poured himself one. The third night, I let him get his drink, and explained… hey… stock your own bar, brother. You're a farmhand, not a guest.

Lono left the stove on and fell asleep a week later. I went down and woke him up.

The second time he left the stove on, I pulled the fire alarm and ran downstairs shrieking "Fire!" for just one second, he wanted to get pissed off and give me shit about all the yelling and the false alarm, but when I saw that my blood went ice cold and I stopped dead. This was deadly fucking serious. You going to burn my fucking house down? No, not my house…

Lono did fall short of my hopes and expectations for a live in handyman, but barring a couple of things that stand out, it was good that he was here, and I was going to make some hay out of it. At some point I was going to tell him to get the fuck out of his Sky-Garden, and do some work for us, or start paying some rent, at least. I was not interested in his plans to take some fantasy electrical class. This IS your job. I need you. I did, and it was a good thing he was here, but he did irritate and tax me needlessly at times being a fucking millennial.

Lono had been with us about two weeks. I did not like the look of Dad. He had been depressed and was eating poorly. Fiona brought healing energy, but she was a puppy, and I was working a few hours a night. She seemed to be doing ok. I did worry as she grew stronger about safety. Lono had Nimbus downstairs and he could cover gaps if I was at work. In theory.

It did not get a chance to be tested, though.

I managed to find Dad a physician, Dr. Nur. Dr. Nur told me Dad was fine. Ok. At least we had a Doctor for him. It was time to plan for new knees, and Maine. He appeared to be in high spirits, yet, yes, also depressed.

Dr. Nur looked right at me that day and said, "No, he isn't dehydrated."

48 hours later, Dad was in the hospital getting fluids, because he was severely dehydrated. It's <u>Nur.</u> Nasifa Nur, in Wootown.

He was dehydrated, Dr. Nur. You are a bad doctor. Fuck you. Sue me.

I had a chance to tell Doctor Nur she was wrong that day, some weeks later when her office called me to schedule an appointment for Dad. How wrong, in fact, she had been. She responded with a letter that arrived in the mail flexing a threat that I would not be able to accompany Dad on visits if I spoke to her that way. I laughed loud at that one, although, it pissed me off too. Dad was not available then, in September, to share this with.

(Terror, neat. Make it a double).

It was the first week of July 2021. I had been back in Mass two years. Two years ago, I started running. The running had become something else, and something else again, and something else yet again. So many things had happened and changed I could not believe I once thought I ran.

I had a real job, my old job, and Lo and Behold, everything we ever fought for, fought about turned out to be right.

Someone had in fact written the book. I was feeling pretty good about this. Maybe I could add my story to the larger one. Hope. There was Hope around, although I was giving the Hope, I had about my sons CPR.

I was packing up my gear and consuming EEns. I went in to see Dad. He looked up at me, and that was the moment.

Blindsided. Nothing was ever going to be the same again. I didn't know that. I thought we had a crisis, not the opening act of what this turned out to be.

Dad looked up at me, completely unmasked. He had, it seemed, been keeping a brave face, stiff upper lip. Always his way. He had not been eating well, and I was concerned. Depression concerned.

Not difficulty swallowing concerned.

He looked up at me with fear in his eyes, and he was trembling, from obvious dehydration.

Did he know? I will never know. I can say, I can see how it snuck up on us, but I find it hard to believe he did not know that Death would be passing through on His way back around from taking Mom.

I could not help him to his feet. Ok, no plan survives contact with the enemy. I was going to take you to the ER. Now, we are calling an ambulance.

The Fire Department, in fact, came to help me get Dad out of the house and into my car.

As I had tried to with Mom when Steel Wool slung her around in her chair and whanghed her gout ridden toes off the underside of the table, I watched them transport Dad out. One young Firefighter banged Dad's knee into the wall turning the corner, and I said, "Watch his knees" and he told me not to tell him how to do his job. "Then watch his knees," I think I snarled a little bit.

I got Dad in the car. I got it on, and the AC adjusted. I had put Fiona out on her rope in the back yard before the fire department came. For safety. Now, I went in through the front door, and out through the back, and got Fee, and led her in on leash, and released her into the house.

And with a brand-new dawning horror, my eyes followed her as she brown-streaked her little ass right across the kitchen, right down the stairs, and right back outside, loose, and chasing West Allenton's fire engine up the street.

***

When these things happen, they happen fast, in slow motion. I had time to think, absurdly, of TC telling me that a fire engine pumps water from the hydrant, and a ladder truck is for getting to people to rescue.

***

I felt the old pucka tighten, Boyo, like a flash frozen ice cube, roughly the size of a softball, deep up my ass, climbing, expanding. Once again, I was in a full terror sprint before I even had time to think. I had an emergency on my hands with Dad, and Fiona had just broken the ice on Oh, fuck, puppy emergency. I thought as I cleared the driveway into traffic without so much as a glance to either side, that I was about to see our new puppy get cut in two by a speeding vehicle. There was traffic, and they were not too concerned about Fiona. This is Massachusetts. A loose dog in the road like that will prompt 50% of drivers to speed up, not to try to hit the dog, but because they feel they shouldn't have to deal with trying not to. People should mind their dogs. Justified callousness, and an opportunity to shame someone, or feel superior. Think about how hard some people work at it. Same people comment on loud kids in stores and airplane too.

God save us all from the actions of the righteous. What a committed zealot will do for the name of principle contains all the worst horrors of humanity. War, Inquisition, Enslavement and Genocide. May God protect us all from what people will do in his own very name.

I ran for several minutes and several hundred yards at a full sprint. I could feel my heart pounding. I saw Dad sitting in the car watching, powerless and scared too. This is it, I thought. I fucked up a puppy, I fucked up my dad… my sons are going to really think I'm a loser. See, even in the grip of immediate puppy life threatening terror, and the other terror that had shown up an hour ago when I realized Dad was not okay, they are always here with me.

I collapsed at the edge of our front yard. And it was Lono who managed to wrangle Fiona. So, Lono gets a pass on being a bit of a slacker and whiny bitch, because he saved Fiona that day, probably, and there would be other moments of greatness for him, even if it was only to bear witness.

When I got Dad to Camton hospital, deliberately avoiding the fucking New York City class shitshow that was UMASS ER, the nurse tried to haul him out of the car. She did this completely wrong. She bent her own body wrong, she bent him wrong, and I heard him grunt softly in pain. I told her to watch out and she told me not to tell her how to do her job, and I just physically interposed myself between her and Dad, peeling her off him. She tried to get affronted that I had touched her, but I just rolled over her. We got him in and the power trip nurse and I glared at each other. Push me. You were wrong, God Damn it. I was spoiling for her to say something, and it was going to be full formal grievance. What she did was on a camera out there, I had checked and there was one.

The Doctor came in and said to Dad that he had a large mass that showed up on XRAY.

They never say "Cancer" at first. They need to run some tests. But that Doctor knew, and she knew that I could tell, that he was a dead man, right there, right now.

-------b…----bre-----breathe……----------

Even though in that moment I knew, I forced myself to go by the book. When I made the calls, I said we did not know anything for sure yet. NoraGee and Jackie were the phone tree. They would send out the flares. From there the word would go to Camton, and Jon and Mary's crew, and south to where Nicky and his boys were. Mayday. Mayday. Mayday.

Immediately I wondered if anyone would think to send word to Maine, and what may come from that.

And I will tell the tale of my Father's and my parting, but know ye this. It has been some time, and although I recollect here and now, as of this moment, I was in a state of daze, shock, and just utter madness. From Camton I brought Dad to a hospital not far from where Mom's first nursing home had been. We had somehow…lapped ourselves. I left Dad there with a hug and headed home to a house that I was relieved was not empty. Lono was there to lean on. I needed to snap out of the shock of a very long but fast-moving day.

I looked up at the sun, standing on the new deck we were going to cook a lot of good meat on, in the timeline I now saw veering wildly off that way, as if we had just peeled on to an off ramp at high speed and watched the main highway head off into the infinity of what will never be more than a dream. The dream that we clung to like a life ring for two years had all been just that. A dream. I watched it go away forever along with the sunshine of that terrible day. I addressed God, directly.

"No."

The inferno had arrived. Ignition was explosive. When I woke up that morning, I had plans to talk garden and food shopping with Dad, and put Lono to some work that was not for Lono. It had been about six hours. Everything, everything inside, outside, above, and below me was now a solid wall of flames. I was blind and flailing. Anghiel came and held me with Fiona and we just sat and I tried to relearn how to breathe. How to breathe, while immersed in fire.

***

I have learned that when caught between such horrors, mounting, compounding, and not somehow progressing, as was the case with my boys, and things that are good (like the undeniable blessings that facing this, we were not also facing things like not having any money to deal with contingencies), one feels neutral and numb. It is hard to appreciate practical blessing that I had now in the face of loss and dying dreams. I think in pictures and this was a strength communicating with atypical children. The memory tsunami had never slowed, its volume increased and decreased depending on factors like where we were, or holidays. The Sacred Spiral had never slowed from the night I threw myself to its raging currents and whims. Now, I was at this pinnacle, balanced on the tip of a spear, moving at blinding speed, and spinning, spinning… spinning.

Ordeal

My father's suffering entered its final obscene stage with the official turning of his health. First of all, he had been walking on mushy knees. That he had pushed through the last two years, for that matter the last six, I would guess, was a testament to his stoicism and toughness.

He was in a hospital in Leominster for a few days. During that time, on a Friday at 1 PM, I conducted my last therapy session on the phone in the hospital room with Dad. These had all been by phone. I had no idea what the woman I spoke with those days looked like.

When the criminal arraignment had arrived in the mail, it was not as bad as when I had seen Keelin in court. Up to that day, I was angry. I had been wronged, betrayed by my sons, because they had swallowed Marla's story hook, line and sinker. I had had a show trial, that was what it was. They had never really heard my side, and I had not tried to spill to them the intricacies of the failed marriage between their mother and me. I would not do that.

But now I knew. Marla had. She had done it for at least ten years. And her mother and her sister had a hand in it.

Marla had deliberately used her children…*my* children, as pawns, to twist me up and make me hurt. It was beautiful, really. I mean, the commitment, the skill. It mattered to me, that she only could have done this if I had trusted her completely, because we were married. Also, if I had spoken at length, throughout my career, to her and in front of my sons, about the things I was learning, and doing.

And, discovering about my own self, history, and upbringing.

When I saw Keelin in court in April, and I realized for the first time they really hated me, and I knew most of why, I had entered a place I had never been before. That was the real Hell, that was the real Apocalypse. In fact, while we watch my father's last ordeal together, I guess that's the point. One of the points of all of this ridiculous yarn. Everything I had to do, coming back here, being useful, comforting, healing, and all the things on the table, helping NoraGee with Ritchie, supporting Nathan by being some type of cool Uncle, or whatever. There was a whole family here, around me now, and I had work to do, (with or without Dad) and nothing, no matter how intense, dire or anguish ridden all of this was, by any measure, the loss of the love of my sons was like comparing a mountain (KTAADN) to a fucking Mountain *Dew*.

My whole life has been a journey….and a gift. The privilege they talk about on the news these days? That defines my life. Thank God I have been something other than for myself up to now. A teacher, a healer… a father (OWWW, that one hurt).

When you brush the law like I had, (and whether or not I had in fact harassed Keelin was complicated. I had not meant to, of course, and meant no threat other than a father son sit down. I did not know that he truly feared me, and what I had done must have really scared him, and now I could not set it right.

Feeling suicidal does not make an appearance in this tale. For the record. However, I learned something scary. Suicide first appears in your mind, like a car, that drives by in the background on the road that runs through your inside mind. On the side, in letters…that's what it says. "Suicide." Well, it sounded more like "Suicide?" when I read the words as they faded up the road. Like… *"Hors-d'oeuvre?" "Italian?"* it simply rustled out there, in the dark. Suggesting that it was, should things devolve, an option. But I did not want to die, or kill myself, or anyone else. Ever. Not in these pages. Ever.

So, I had jumped through the hoops that one jumps through when you brush the law. Twenty-five years I pounded the streets combating domestic violence of all forms, and the short- and long-term effects. Just like that, I was through the Looking Glass. I was a bad guy. I wrapped myself in the credibility that I was not. The crew, old friends in Maine and new ones like Jazzy and Lex…I saw them as character witnesses, and that was how I saw my suggested therapy course. A chance to prove I was not unstable, dangerous. All the shit my kids thought I was. And now I was going to bear it on my own, because Dad had Death coming back.

So soon? Why, we just saw you.

So, I remember that I spoke to my therapist for the last time on Friday, and I had to cut it short because the doctors came in, but she told me in her assessment, after hearing my account, (and I had been both barrels unfiltered, it was sharks, pirates and LSD, I didn't hold anything back. She had been horrified by the truths I had told her. But not by me. I had been meticulous not to lie to her. Why would I?

They decided at the hospital that Dad had an upcoming appointment and he could come home with me until then. I got set up with supplies, and on the way home, Dad and I stopped for our last ever errand/adventure. I ran into the music store in Leominster and purchased a replacement harmonica. Hohner, Special 20. Key of D. The one I always break. The smell of cancer or death was on him now. He really had almost died last week when the inferno lit. He had almost just slipped away. I wondered if it would not have been better for him. He surely suffered mightily, and needlessly, before it was over, but we also had time together that now I don't know what I would have done if we had not.

It all comes down to what would have been, and what would not have been. Dad and Mom could have collapsed that deck in August of 2019. It had been a close thing; we both knew in our bones. There were things to be said, about the what ifs of them dying, together, quickly, before all this.

But what we had already had was something amazing, and from here on out, I would not trade anything, save one (two), for what we did attain together, both up until now, and from this point on.

Breana

We had stayed in contact throughout it all. The Plague, and our lives. She had a grandkid on the way, and was about to leave the area. I had caught her just in time. What we would have done without her is difficult to conceive, how much worse it would have been. We had become casual friends. She was nice, and I didn't have a jealous psycho for a girlfriend, so we had stayed friends. It did not hurt that I ran into her nephew Johnny at Depardieu. In fact, she may have slipped away during the chaos of the Covid, but I had reached out to her that night to tell her I met her nephew and we had resumed occasional chit chats, fortunately.

But now…

Breana worked for the best hospice agency around. She told me this when I told her what was going on with Dad. They had not given him his diagnosis, but I have two RNs in my orbit, Breana and the Treeherder. Their reaction to the news as it stood was all I needed to know my own gut on this was true, but we had to hold onto hope. You always at the last defend Hope, but this was the first time I had a period of weeks to reflect of the nature of Hope, and Futility, and how to avoid getting trapped in useless things. They both, when I told them it *looked* like Dad may have esophageal cancer, simply said "I'm sorry." They knew that it would be inappropriate, between professionals, to play the false hope game. Breana mentioned that Jewish Hospice was the best, and I kept it in mind as I spread these new Pieces out and tried to find my course.

Sun Under Lens

July, 2021.

Office of Dr. Sandramayan.

Dept. of Oncology

Leominster, Mass.

So, I had Dad home with me following about a week at Leominster Hospital. That week, here at home, I had taken a look at where he kept everything. I was careful to convey that I had the situation in hand, for when he was well enough to resume. I realize now, I did not have much an of an idea what he was really thinking. He seemed to be aware that he was suddenly very ill. There was not a lot we had already that looked good. It was almost certainly cancer. Of that there was kind of no doubt, but that's how you do it, as everyone knows who knows cancer. It was cancer. It must be bad. It was not a good kind of cancer. I wondered a lot what he had known, what he had thought as we were tending Mom. He would have ignored all pain. He would have just pressed on. I wondered further how long he would have lasted, had Mom not died when she did. He really had run himself all the way out.

It was not that different from what we expected to shake out when we went over this as a family, in Maine years ago, when Nana started to show signs that she was going to decline that way. We had time to wonder and speculate. The original theory was that Dad would press on until he could press on no more, and we would have to figure out how to take care of them. It would have been the natural progression. What had changed, in the big picture over the last two years was unimaginable, and poignant, both for what treasure had been uncovered in our time and experiences together, but also in the cutting pain of what had been spoiled forever by Marla, rendered to the dustheap of "If only".

If only Marla had cared about one single other thing besides hurting me, regardless of who else got hurt, my father's and my mother's walks to Death would have been substantially easier to bear, for them, and for me, and for the boys too.

The true scope of Marla's malice, and the cost of her actions and all that followed came crashing down with the finality of watching the Red Sox blow their last chance at bat on a sloppy foul ball, having come back from a four-run deficit, to the lead, briefly, only to see the heartbreak unfold that only Curse Era Red Sox fans can understand. Maybe the Cubbies, too, I don't know. Never been to Chicago. Either way, it was game over. Dad was in a lot of pain with his knees and I was doing what I could to get nutrition into him any way I could. It was juice and smoothies. Somewhere I had taken his card and some cash and bought a blender and some supplies so I could "take care of him." Whatever the fuck that meant. He was very, very weak. Know the smell of the cancer was thick, its cover blown. I played and replayed every moment I could, searching for something that would have tipped me off he was sick, when there may have been some time. As we ticked off the several days in hellish limbo, I tried to build his strength and spirits. Fiona knew something was wrong and was gentle and lovey with him.

I guess, I'm trying to describe one shock, one horror, one trauma piled one atop the other over a long, long time. All the dimensions were covered. We had loss already, impending death, and the fact that my sons were not part of all this, and their absence was a crime against God, for the love my parents showed my family, especially them. I had the stress of not having my sons, compounded by the stress of never having them, grandkids, or any kind of Christmas, really, ever again. I love my clan here, but holidays with them, fun, and awesome that we are together again, are impossible without the taint of what has been lost, and the rage at how that happened. Christmas had been my parent's, my sons, and their mother, mostly, and I was apart from every one in that Ka-tet forever. I did not see any more point in staying on Earth than I had in staying in Maine at Pathways two years ago. I did not want to kill myself, I just did not care about life anymore, and I entered the place of shock, constant action, unpredictability and numbness that had characterized my frantic leaving first my home that I worked and paid for and raised my sons, while my ex sat, and plotted, and robbed, and then leaving Maine, and then dealing with all of this, while trying to figure out why the only things that ever really mattered to me would not speak to me and were afraid.

It was in this high-speed, frenetic panic, so familiar, that we made it through the next few days with a little company of Lono and the Nimbus, who provided some distraction while Dad and I watched and rolled our eyes at Lono playing in his garden, as the grass grew higher in the yard. At least he was watering the pot plants, because I had forgotten all about them the day Fiona, and my Dad almost died.

The doctor's office in Leominster is on the same hill as my mother's first nursing home, the one where they treated her like the new kid at school no one liked. As I pulled in with my father, now visibly uncomfortable in any position, we both looked over there and remembered.

The closest they had come; I think I was there with them We were down the end of a Hallway in early December 2019. I watched them stand there looking out the window watching the sun move across the sky, and it's just a beautiful view, out the window of that building where Love says long goodbyes. It had not been that long ago. All this was jarring. It had to be to Dad.

That day, the cancer doc agreed with me that he was very weak, and she felt that he should be admitted. If I had known the circus of obscenities that was about to kick off, it would have been easier if I had just bundled him back up and took him home to die. I did not need to ask him. We were going to honor the Code. The doc decided to admit him, so we drove from Leominster to UMass Lakeside, (once more unto the breach) and my father spent the next eight hours in the emergency room surrounded by all manner of walking wounded. It was exactly where Beansy and I had been the day he knocked his head in the snow and I signed up to adopt Fiona.

I guess the next few steps are going to be told quickly, so I should pause here and try to give it the right frame.

We sat in the ER for eight hours. Dad grew weaker and less comfortable. I tried to get water into him, he could not eat. It looked like he had had difficulty eating for a while, and had said nothing and had taken steps to be low key about it. I'm sure this began in 2020 while Covid raged. I had to practically drag him to get his cataract surgery. Mom's and his family physician had retired around the time Mom left home. When I came back to Mass, she had no official diagnosis of dementia, and was on no medications. It was Ativan from the Tire -pop visit to the ER that had got him the medicine he needed to take care of her those last weeks. It had made a huge difference, to be sure. No, he had to know something was wrong, and, like I probably would have too, just tried to muscle through it, and now he was a goner.

He sat there in that wheelchair for eight hours while I slowly lost my fucking mind. In the end, the last hour before they finally took him in, I had called 911, and asked if they would come give him IV fluids in the ER as a rescue call because he was about to die right before my eyes. The lack of caring from the staff at all levels bespoke severe burnout, staffing problems, all that, and they were keeping a close eye on me. If I wasn't in trouble with the law, I may start making a scene, but there are people all around who are not here for scrapes. Many look almost as bad as he does, so, I don't mind taking a number, but this is ridiculous. I tried to call Dr. Sandramayan's office and they told me flat out I was on my own until they could take him in.

They finally did, and someday, I may know how close a call it was in the end, but I left him once I saw him hooked up to fluids and rode home with tears of rage, plus the usual loss ones. It was a double your pleasure moment.

Anghiel came over and Lono, Fiona and I ate and held council on what we were going to have to do, what realities were, until further notice. Lono tried to pause me down and I almost bit him. Dude, I told him, focus on what I'm saying, and let me worry about myself, ok? I'm more concerned you're going to burn my father's house down, so guru yourself, all right?

Anghiel, unlike any other woman I've been with, said little, hugged much, and just rode the wave. This one… when this is over, I'm going to elevate her to Keeper. It really is good, between us. We have four little road trips under our belt. Four times, we slipped away for the Cape, or Maine, (of course, Wales was the first) and I had left Dad alone, to what would have been his every day. He pushed me out when those opportunities came, trying to slip me some cash, and besides that I had two other overnight jumps up there, one of them had been for court. When those trips had happened, Dad and I were already talking about how he could get in on that. If nothing else, I said, for the fishing.

Over the next few days, they tried to get his strength up. I woke, tried to make sense of administration stuff for the house, spoke with Doctors, but not really. I had said I would like to be included in all conversations with my Dad, and they just went about their business. I couldn't be there at rounds at 6:16 A.M. and be any use for all the other things until 10, 11 PM.

I may have spoken to family members, but had little to tell them. Jackie came over with Nathan and Cody, to help me go over some bills. The first thing she did was bellow at the state the house was in, with my clothes still in the living room as my closet, and Fiona having the run of the house. I halted her right there that that was not why I asked her here, and if that was the help she brought, I was just going to hang out with Nathan and Cody and figure it out on my own. I had to bark at her again, a little, because as she was going over my mail and Cody was innocently running up and down with Fiona, she suddenly roared at him to knock it off, and it felt like Screamy Judy all over again.

I told her she was never to raise her voice to those boys here again, in front of them, and then I told Cody to relax and have some fun, this was my house, and my rules.

Whatever the mornings brought, I played with Fee outside for a bit, and made my way to Dad by 1 PM, usually. I would sit for an hour or so, then leave him to rest in the quiet afternoon on a ward like this, with people who are gravely ill. Sometimes wards are upbeat with healing, sometimes, they are resonant with dying. Like I had throughout this whole time, I tried to keep things comfortable, and light as appropriate. I moved between AC spaces, and blazing hot ones, reminding me that this right now was the high point of summer, about to turn, again, towards Fall and good sleeping weather. I blazed harmonica to and from the hospital every day, in traffic, at red lights, and told Dad I must be somewhat good, people were cheering on the road. He laughed. I played in my car when I went out for lunch for an hour, and I would come back in and hang with him through Wheel of Fortune. They were trying to get his strength up, and they came up with a Hail Mary of a plan.

It was either going to be a stent to expand his esophagus, or a G-tube in his stomach. I'm glad they went with the stent. At least he got a last meal. It was Crown Royal. That was later, at home. But he had sushi, and manicotti, and a couple other treats he really liked, but looking back I could have done a better job feeding him up, and I wish I had let him blow his money on sushi and Il Camino more.

Do TC and Keelin know Papa is dying?

Night Journey 1

Twenty seconds to midnight.

I left early the day they decided to go with the stent, but they were going to wait until something-something. I called Jackie. She called TC and Keelin. After making sure I was not going to be around or interfere, they drove down, and saw their grandfather for the last time. I don't know what they talked about. I hope they are at peace with whatever they said to each other.

Anghiel came to spend a little time. We were going to take shelter in each other's arms. As I was taking a shower at 11:21 PM, I was hit with a power surge, and this one came with a message.

No, it isn't like that. But I leapt from the shower and said to my woman:

"Change of plan. I'll explain on the way. Fiona, saddle up."

Did I say she is never a bitch? Did I say my buddies don't get it at first, I have to explain. Like this. She simply started getting dressed. No comment, no look, no pout. No bitch. She's definitely a keeper.

Even in the depths of Hell, love seems to have found me, because if this chick doesn't love me, what the fuck is she still doing here? It stopped being playhouse fun time a month ago.

***

I had stepped into the shower while Anghiel and Fiona

played. The surge hit me and I knew in that instant that I had to do something. How I knew what to do had never been something I worried about, when it hits, I have learned to just let it take me away.

What came now was the knowledge that I needed some kind of medicine. Dad was going under the knife tomorrow. He was at Death's doorway. If I did not act now, I was going to lose him? Was I? So, you don't take chances. I needed to get a little crazy.

***

Anghiel struggled to accept these things, but one thing she never ever did was complain that our plans were ruined. In fact, ruined had been one of Marla's favorite words, and I seldom heard Anghiel even think in those terms. Marla would have responded to this with a tantrum, and there would have been retribution. Not direct. Subtle, passive aggressive. Marla is a coffee-pot pisser. That's someone in the workplace who does that shit because they're antisocial, hate their job and that makes them feel powerful. Anghiel was in the car waiting when I came out of the house with Fiona. It was 11:41 P.M. It's seven miles to UMASS.

For the first part of the ride, I explained to Anghiel, again, what NotACunt was, and why she was that. And why I really appreciated that, above all things. That, and the sex. She laughed. She may never understand what it was like to live with someone who always found something to complain about, was never quite satisfied, someone who was a hair trigger for stuff to be "ruined".

And the weight of the fact that she had deliberately ruined her family to hurt me. There was no other reason that fit. It was pure spite, cruelty, sadism, and hatred. Very well concealed, over a very long time. My father was dying now, and I still could not stop thinking, bleeding, and screaming about my lost boys, my sons. It had not stopped, it had only gotten worse (and substantially more expensive now) every single solitary day and now all that had kept me afloat and made it bearable, and hopeful was wasting away, suffering, and alone, no matter what I was trying to do. God. Oh, God, Oh God.

God, thank you for stepping in at this point. You are truly omnipresent.

In my pocket are two crystals.

I'm not that guy. I'm not *ohm'ing* it, I do hug trees, but more for the Code and the spectacle of acts. I'm not a crystal whisperer. I like crystals like I like fossils. They are wicked cool. So are owl pellets. Understand. I'm a skeptic. This shit I'm talking about, that's the point. I never would have walked in the Spirit World or become a Samurai, but it turns out, I needed to be for my Destiny. And drugs. Drugs help; the right ones, in the right hands. They help you hang on when you have to make a breakneck run to deliver crystals and stave off Death. Otherwise, you just lose it and break down.

I was wearing the clothing I worked in on the streets, and now, here, on the streets and residential trenches. My work clothing at Depardieu had among it clothes I wore on the job for years. Robert Jordan's Aiel call it *cadin'sor*. Working clothes. Jordan's influence on my life and thinking shows itself here. His concepts have become mine own. They shaped me, the work I did, the life I have led, and who I have become. It is fast becoming the only thing I have left, and paper does not float well in the tempest of the sacred spiral. If it's better than nothing, I have yet to find that tide-line.

Something emerged that night. My past was gone, and I was ass deep in my future, and things were still out of control. The factor of the alienation of my sons took what would have been difficult life shit to a whole new level, and for all my snickers at the crystal whisperers, I did have an open mind. I mean, all the stuff I learned from Candace, that had started with the Crocodile. He was the one who first turned me on to shamanic medicine. He was the one who first showed me that book, the one I bought my own copy of in Boothbay when 25 dollars was a lot of money for disposable income, and I thought about how that had never changed. Even now. I lived my whole life up till now on a shoestring budget, real, necessary, or not, I had and I had learned things.

Below these latitudes, there is no more peace, not really. The way I felt physically was quickened. I was exhausted in layers over years. The reserves that were about to be tapped, I never knew I had, or maybe…

***

Maybe it was something else. In the days to come I would lay out my path for my father again, one last time. I was afraid and lonely when I was a kid, and the world looked bleak outside the windows of this house. Thirty years later, it was surrounded by trees my father had planted and lush and green behind. All I know is that while all this was happening, from Pootown until now, I had been picking up speed and spinning wider and wider circles. Through that had emerged a path forward, one that had room for everything we had to address, especially repairing the damage Marla did. That would be the work of the rest of our time together, but we can fish, too, I told him.

To have all of that hope evaporate now was bad enough. Losing someone unexpectedly like this, is bad enough. But I have been trying to convey why I felt it was needed to do some of the things I did, like trying to recover Ella to Pootown before I moved away from her.

***

Or why I was now doing seventy-five past the Wootown Country club and calling the hospital to get through security. In the last few days at UMass, when I measured time in weeks to days to sometimes minutes, security and the elevators were my two things that always brought that hourglass draining its sand right into my face. I had a little help on this one, because it occurred to me just in time to call, explain that I had a religiously significant thing to do before my father's surgery tomorrow, and it was imperative I made it into his room by the first tick of the clock of that day. Fiona did not make a peep, and neither did Anghiel as she watched me manipulate phone and wheel. I had slowed down. They passed the word, and for one and only one time, security waved me through and I rode an empty elevator that was waiting for me with open door as I panted and prayed and gripped onto myself as tight as I could.

At twenty seconds to midnight, I slipped into Dad's room. He opened his eyes. I kissed his forehead, and gently laid the two crystals on his sternum, where the cancer grew, and where they were going to cut into him in a few hours to insert a steel mesh so he could take in enough nourishment to make it home to die.

"You will need this." I said, and cried. A little, but laughed a little, too.

If we were playing a game of inches and seconds, I wasn't going to ignore feelings like the one that hit me tonight, spurring this ridiculousness. I made it.

On the wall in his hospital room are two large drawings I did while we were in here watching the sun go by in the huge window. They look different in the dark. On his table are two silly little sculptures I made sitting here, talking about working with kids, and how neither Mom nor I were artists with things like paint and clay, but we had picked up a little game as pros. I was also feeling a flowering of creativity in me that would have been bigger if it had room to grow while I dodged the storms. Underneath the poem on his wall, I had written and taped up with an old picture of Ella and the canoe in Maine, (for the nurses), I put the sacred crystals on his chest so he would survive hos procedure in the morning. When I tell you what happened after tonight, remember, he almost died twice already. I left the crystals there, knowing now what I had wondered a very long time ago, when I got home about eight hours earlier and wondered why I had bothered to take them in the first place, but I was trying to track all of his and my shit, and not lose anything, like, God forbid, my cylon, or his wallet, or the power of attorney letter I got form Nicky the Gun.

One ADHD brain fart, and I could really fuck myself. Still no time to bleed, no room for failure, and no real options but to wait and watch and play that harmonica baby…

And smoke lots of weed. If I were a drinker, wow… what a different picture this would be.

Night Journey 2

White Shirt.

Allan was up high on the lake side of the UMASS hospital. His window faced Lake Quinsigamond, and I could see the shore and the facility where I had learned to sail as a kid. Even after two years inland, I still experienced surprise at my perspectives on the size of water. This lake had been vast to me as a kid. We sailed around freely, and I had never been out of sight of Regatta Point. Now, when I looked at it, I smiled to myself, and shared with Dad how these bodies of water seemed so small to me know, after the waters I had come to know.

The sounds of Shrewsberry outside, here, in sight of White City, where my Daddy bought me a plane the day I had my tooth pulled, did not make it up this high, through the glass.

When I left him that night, I left him watching Wheel of Fortune. I screamed through the sticky heat all the way home, the music on full volume. I remember frying two harps during these few weeks, at least, screaming that damn second solo in One Way Out.

A week or so earlier, sitting with him in his hospital room, I had ordered what appeared to be a passable sword. It was less than 200 dollars, but this was Wish. I wasn't sure what I was going to get, but my father was dying next to me, and we were uncovering all the buried things and leaving nothing unturned. It seemed… appropriate, to get a proper sword. I felt a little underequipped without it. I guess I was scared about facing life without him, so it seemed, like I said, the right thing to do. We were playing cribbage for ten thousand dollars a hand at this point. I joked with dad that if I had a reckless gamble in me, he seemed like someone smart to rack up some debt to. We laughed, again, for a little longer, as the dark started to close in, and the sound of the wind in my head just would not stop, it got louder, and louder, and louder still, until I just got used to it.

It was a decent blade, when it came. The fittings were cheap, but functional, and for now, it was my first assembled katana. I practiced handling a shirasaya for almost twenty years, but I learned pretty quickly that while I had some comfort with a sword *out,* I had never practiced drawing it, or *Noto,* the way of returning it safely, and not looking stupid.

That is premature, my acquaintance with this weapon. For now, the point is that on day whatever of my father's ordeal, I returned to this house and found the sword, in its box, on my step. It was a most welcome distraction.

Later, about two hours later, after I had unboxed and cleaned the sword and inspected it closely and put it away, I was sitting at Command Central. My phone rang. It was Cristobel.

I was about to tell him about my father's cancer. I did not get a chance, because he told me that his dad had just died unexpectedly of a heart attack.

Cristobel and I have been friends for a long time, and we have both grown and been through many things together, including the births of all our collective children save TC. Both his father and brother worked with us at Sweet Shores, and I knew and liked both of them a lot. In those days, back in 98, I often wore a long-sleeved collared shirt as a smock, for when kids threw piss at you, or for cooking meals for twenty. Cadin'sor. Working clothes. So, say we all in Battlestar Galactica, too. There is a universality here I want to speak to, because though this tale is unusual, the trauma and all that is common. I was and am a healer. These things happened. I will use it, to teach, and heal. We all have our role models and influences. They certainly came forward now. I did not know then how big those books were for a lot of people.

The shirt was not always white, but I had more than one white one. Mike Sr. used to call me White Shirt. Cristobel would always bring that up, whenever he talked about his dad, like ten years ago, when he had called to tell me his dad needed heart surgery. He said it then, and all weekend long when Cristobal got married, and again, for the first time, maybe that it was more than just one of these things you laugh about.

He said, "My Dad always called you White Shirt."

I was not going to tell him tonight about my dad. I was just going to be with him about his, so all I could say was "Chris… I AM White Shirt."

"You are." he said. "You always have been."

"I guess you're right. Brother. I'm so sorry. I loved him too. Tell Mike too, that gun loving Trumper… I love him too."

We laughed through both our tears, and it was not the first time we had a moment like this, we had, I believe I have said, been tight for a long, long time.

I hung up.

"I am White Shirt". I said it out loud to the empty house.

Just like the last time, that feeling of something started to build. It always sounds like the rising wind that night so long ago back in Pootown.

Cristobel and I laughed sadly as we chatted about his family, his brother and kids. They were going to be ok. They always have been a solid bunch. I was so sad for him, but happy too, because he and his dad were close and had a great relationship. So had Allan and I, in a way Cristobel and most people never get to have. It was tragic, yes, but also beautiful. Chris's dad had not suffered, he had simply gone to sleep after a day of living his best life. He worked on his old Jeep, he had ice cream with his companion, he had dinner. The man had gone to sleep that night content and fulfilled in life in a way many do not get, and my dad had that too. I wanted to believe it. I said goodnight to my brother, and thanked him for his friendship, all these years (especially the last two, but that did not need to be said now).

The winds inside me rose to a roar, and I had clarity. I needed the power of ritual, and the power that comes with a true tale of acts. Especially pirate ones. Or knightly ones.

On the last night of my old life, I had set out on a journey that would open and close many circles. Some I knew about; some had been there without me knowing. In two years, I had changed from who I was that Midsummer night. I had experienced levels of feeling that I never knew existed. On this journey so many things had happened that I found myself moving from space to space, in my head and in the world, just trying to breathe, and think, and not bring disaster on myself or my family with stupidity, impulsivity, or rashness. I had learned, that when you find yourself alone, it can be hard to know what to do or what not to. I had been numb for so long, and when that changed, I entered truly uncharted space. This was yet another level that I had never believed could exist, in my life. It had been like waking from one nightmare into a worse nightmare, over and over again. It was like the funhouse ride back in the day, the one's in converted trailers, painted with bats and skulls and shit. They're like little indoor roller coasters… quick, terrifying, and over before the overwhelming stimuli and horror were even able to kick in. You see little kids stagger off these rides, and some are squealing with joy. Some are squealing with terror, and some are doing both at the same time, as the senses catch up in their little brains. This was my new normal, and now, by myself, I laughed, even though the crying inside was ever-present and cold. I could find moments of warmth, laughter, love, with Anghiel and all the others in my family. But inside, there was always the cold and numb.

To survive this, one must become a character in the story. Because one thing I knew and know now. There were things within my power. As the conversation with Cristobel faded into the walls and I gathered myself with these thoughts you read now, I knew what I had to do.

Uncle David came home from Israel once and gave me this bottle of holy water from the site, supposedly, of Christ's baptism by John. I had used it, years ago, to bless my weapons, my swords, shirasaya as I have said before. I liked the idea of whatever edge that brings, +2 hit damage on Shadowspawn, thank you Dungeons and Dragons. I'm not saying I *believe* in vampires, but I don't want to get slurped for lack of fighting back with the right tool. Or Instrument.

I didn't have Holy Water now. That bottle… who knows where it ended up as I left my old life. It was probably in the shit I left behind, the stuff I let get to me, that was a vehicle for my disastrous attempts to contact Keelin after Mom died, to demand an explanation, and redress. I was going to need all the help, all the magic, all the power I could muster, and if my beliefs and code were the only things that had enabled me to put my life into some manageable perspective, I was going to need to get outside the box.

There were no churches open in the Woo. It was 10:45 at night. The night was cooling off and fogging up after a long hot dry sticky day. As was so much a part of my sensory environment, weather always affected me, and I found myself thinking of Rocky Pond, long ago, when my parents used to tuck me in and you could smell mothballs a little, and outside through my window I watched the same moon over the water in the night, and had always thought that… that it is ever the same moon.

I thought of the Abbey.

The Abbey has real monks. They are the very same that make the Trappist jelly you see in the grocery store. Or not, consult the agoogly. It's a real place, in Spencer, Mass. I had gone there as a kid and found it fascinating. It looked and felt like a monastery in the hills of France in 1400. There was a sign: "No Women Beyond This Point" I can still see it in memory. I found that impactful. Monks. Real monks.

Of course, I had been a monk too, had I not? And though

Monk no more, what was I to be? If I was ever going to break the evil spell I now almost (almost) fully understood had happened to my family, and who was responsible, it was time to summon everything I could. And find my way, and back it up with acts.

I navigated the keypad to the infirmary. It was Brother Aldred. I opened laughing and thanked him for taking my call. I explained that he had never, likely, received a call such as this.

"How can I help you, Son?" he said.

"I have need of Holy Water. May I be graced with some?"

No inquiries. No questions. No pause. I felt like that was weird.

"Do you know the way here, Son?" He sounded bemused, I hoped. He was going to play along with the crazy person. Maybe it happens all the time, how the fuck would I even know?

"I do, sir."

"Come on down, then. Drive safe, it looks foggy. You know where the infirmary is?"

I laughed before I could stifle it. "I do not, Brother."

"Call me back when you get on the grounds." He sounded like he was smiling broadly, like he was old, but kind. A man of God, open to see what God was about to drop in his lap on what would have been just another night in that eternal sacred place. I wasn't even exactly sure. I was White Shirt. I needed to treat my Instrument.

I took a ritual bath (shower) and dressed in clothing I had worn on the job, in Maine, and at the Dev, here. Residential had altered my dress, and it was in the latest configuration that I rigged myself up as I would for the job. White shirt and all. I looked like I usually looked, like the selfies I took as I rolled out these last few months, overjoyed to see myself riding out to the guns, in new territory, ready to slay the dragon. The dragon, of course, had come knocking, but that did not matter anymore. I am White Shirt, and it was time to honor the Code. I loaded Fiona and my sword, and one more thing, and out we rolled into that foggy dark summer night.

It was 11:25 PM, EDT.

The night was crisp and electric, alive with summer.

Fiona and I rolled down Rt. 31. I think about the relativity of Time, because sometimes it takes forever to go a short way, and sometimes it goes by in the blink of an eye, and all the different levels and ins and outs were flowing at different rates. I needed a break, and time to reflect tonight, and also try to process another huge thing that had just happened for someone else, Chris losing his father, and bringing up the White Shirt thing. I thought about this as the black sea of trees next to me opened spectacularly over water and gloriously over open spaces, occasionally touched by starlight through the patchy clouds, where the blackness parted and I could breathe the air.

This kind of stuff, it's… impulsive? Childish?

Is it?

All my life, I have not had to look far for trouble. I

despise those who lament the unfairness of the system (NOT the system of racial oppression talked about in the Woke Movement). No, I mean "The System." The System got me, The System was stacked against me.

I was horrified to wake up to the real system, the one in our society that was absolutely the backdrop off all this small one-man drama played out to witnesses light years away, infinitely larger, and utterly uncaring. But that's not what I'm talking about. I'm talking about criminals who complain about the System when they get caught. When I taught driving, I was very clear with young drivers that if you are speeding, and you get stopped, the story is not about an asshole police officer. That just distracts from the fact that you were speeding.

I don't want to take away from the current climate in our society, the truths that cops are corrupt and flawed, and that the system, or systems, are certainly corrupt and power protects itself and its own. I definitely do not want what I say here now to be misunderstood as a lack of full hearted and full-throated support for all things woke. But I am not one inclined to lament like that. Sometimes, you just need to create something worth talking about.

The cylon led me to the Abbey and I remembered it from when I was a kid, a single visit in memory. The ride down had thankfully not produced the usual cascade of old memories because as a kid I could not have found Spencer with a compass and a guide. At night, when you can't see the little details, it's not so bad. In the daylight, when you see the sky over the reservoir exactly how it always looked, it tended to bring back high-speed floods of memory. Tonight, was not so bad, and I patted my new puppy and was grateful the pain of not having a dog was over, even though the pain of losing Ella will never go away. At least I know what pain is. When I lost her, I had to come to know it. I recognize it now, the pain for my boys, the pain now of losing Dad, and the pain of my powerlessness and the futility of it all.

I drove in the gate past the only spot visibly recognizable to me and up a long, long driveway to the proper Abbey grounds. I drove by a sign, white once, now white under scale of rust, and cocked over at the tilt of age, and also, I realized, surrounded by vegetation. The last time I had seen this sign, perched behind mom and dad, it had been bare at the end of a stone wall. I looked, in the dark. Sure enough. Since I had seen it last a whole copse of bushes and trees had grown around this little breadcrumb from the past. The stone wall was exactly where I had left it. No wonder it had not really looked that familiar. A whole forest has grown here.

"No Women Beyond this Point."

"Fiona," I said. "I'm going to call you Shrek while we're here. Shh! Good girl…"

If there be ghosts in places like this, they heard me laughing at my own absurdity all the rest of the way in, till the Abbey itself came in view and the woods fell away and the sky opened up behind it spectacularly. It looks like it should be in a Star Wars movie.

I called the infirmary back and waited, absurdly, under the starts and the fog next to a building that looks like a stone castle, and dialed the main number, and waited while I pushed the several buttons that took me to the infirmary.

Time slows way down, and all is quieter than it should be. Theis is a hilltop in south central mass, it is always a little windy, but now everything was very still. I breathed. Brother Aldred answered. He guided me to the door.

This hilltop is dark. The stone buildings ringing it look old, and medieval. There are lights through trees, and a light fog diffuses the light over the grass, down to the black tree line. I am on a promontory, domed over by wheeling stars. The moon is low and beautiful. It is silent here. Even the wind whispers. Fiona watches me make my way up the stone walkway.

If there is such a thing in this world today as a knight on a quest, surely, I am one.

I opened the two Poland Spring water bottles and took a drink out of each. I was actually quite thirsty, and there was an air of solemnity and respect I was trying to convey here, on my weird unusual quest. The water he put into my bottles came out of a heavily decorated thick glass bottle with pewter furniture and stones dangling and clinking. I secured the water in my Cadin'sor. I had taken one of the silver coins out of my candle lantern earlier, before I set out. It was a franklin half dollar. I carry a silver half dollar in my candle lantern. It's a Pirate thing. For moments just like this, although I had never ever taken a coin out and paid for something with it. I pressed it into his hand. He smiled. It may have been a smile that said, "Ok, crazy dude, now just be on your way, and don't kill me," or one that said, "I don't know what the fuck you got going on, but I'm glad I could help." I really don't know. I really do not care.

The fog was lifting. I drove back up Rt. 31 to home under

a blue-black jeweled night sky.

Later, after I settled Fiona in, I took the water, and like I had done with another blade many years ago, I washed it in the water. The weapon awoke in my hands. This is what it means to be the soul of the samurai. This was my first real sword, and it woke up and our spirits joined, just like in the ancient way. There were portals opening, and large forces moving about, as this last act unfolded. My father was dying. We were not going to KTAADN.

If I am going to have to live with the loss of my sons, I am going to tell true stories of swords, and holy water, and foggy nights in ancient places where silver quietly changes hands, payment for services not fully known. The gift of a tale, from which to mold a new reality, mayhap, mayhap only in a dream.

I am loose in the Sacred Spiral, wheeling wildly and trying to hang onto the things in my pockets, my Pieces, against what need may come. I no longer have any idea what is going to happen. Every plan I sustained us with is gone.

After this night run, during this stay in the hospital, I joked with Dad that as hard as I had tried not to take any money from him, I had, for a lawyer.

So, I told him as we passed the time in the hospital room, you should let me try to win some back. I dealt some cribbage hands, and poker hands, and we joked that we were playing for a thousand dollars a hand, and I could maybe try to clear this debt, since I wasn't going to pay him back, just in case.

That was bad idea. When he left the hospital, I owed him three point one million dollars.

Sequence Forensics

Dad got sick the first week of July. He spent about a week in the hospital. We bought a harmonica together on the way home, our last run for an errand.

We had an appointment for oncology in a couple of weeks, so we marked those two weeks. Looking ahead with time running out sucks, you want to slow it down, but, you also don't. He was in a limbo of suffering.

When he went to the cancer doc, she decided the best thing for this 78-year-old with advanced cancer and sore knees was to sit in an ER for eight hours just to run his clock almost all the way out. He was a week in the hospital at Lakeside. That was when the boys had come, with Jackie's help to facilitate. He missed the scan for the cancer because he was in the hospital.

My day was divided between trying to take over all the house bills and make sense of the finances. I am uniquely unsuited for this. I never dealt with money in my marriage. I trusted my wife to handle that, because she could not work, because she was sick.

And of course, I now knew she drew a full-time salary off my parents behind my back the whole time we were married. I laughed out loud out of my thoughts.

I gave Fiona some time and attention and cleaned the house. Getting Lono to even pick up after himself was like pulling teeth. He was acting like a whiny teenager, and I needed a soldier. No time for that.

The first time Dad was in the hospital at Lakeside, and

missed his scan, I knew that was bad. This cancer was moving toward a terminal line. If it was in his stomach, there would be nothing they could do, and they could not even do the test now. Then they had to just keep him alive long enough to come home, so he could get the test.

Somewhere during these hospitalizations, I took two hard fast visions, and had to do some odd shit. The crystals before the surgery were the first. The sword trip for holy water was the second. I ran through the blazing hot summer sun through traffic pounding coffee, sucking Eens, smoking pot and screaming, thinking of my mom, my lost dog, my lost boys. My new puppy took all this in stride, and I was grateful that I had taken care of that Piece before all this.

Dad was able to leave from the house and drive with me to get the scan test for his cancer. There was one more trip to take. A few days later, we drove back to Dr. Sandramayan's office, and she put the scan up, and his death sentence was final. He looked up at me.

"Well, that's that."

He seemed a little surprised, and I will never know. I think, like me, he just decided he had no time for it and he was in the hands of God, and now he truly was.

After I went to court and saw my youngest son look at me like a monster, I had been a little disconnected from that. I had to put it down to return to work. That was the only thing that had pulled me out. Dad watched me and knew. He knew what I had done all those years.

When I got him home, he entered his home of almost fifty years for the last time, never to exit again, I carried him in. At the top of the stairs, I almost teetered backwards with him in my arms. I made it back, and just as I did Lono's hand was also there. It was a close thing. The other close thing was for the first time in my life I think, I almost threw my back out. One more thing to check, if they give you your stats in Heaven. I got him to his chair, got him something to eat and drink, and lay down on the floor with hot iron in my back. If I was really hurt, I was fucked.

I almost died once because I took a powerful time release opiate without prescription. Mikhail gave them to me, because in 2012 I fucked my neck, or my shoulder up at Turkey Neck, and I asked him for some drugs to get a good night's sleep. And I almost became a statistic. Never mind scaring the fuck out of everyone around me. Stupid. I still don't get how I was that stupid, I truly don't. I thought I was happy, in 2012. Is it possible I was flirting with going out like that, on top? I still do not know, but the only reason I mention it now is that started with a casual attitude towards some dangerous drugs. I never had a taste for the drugs that now ravaged the country dropping people like machine guns at The Somme. I had liked having them handy for painful emergencies. And that little bit of carelessness almost killed me. I did have a near death experience, and it was the only time I ever confronted my mother, or my father directly on some of the shit that happened in our family. It was a quick exchange, in the hospital that day and nothing had really come of it, but there was nothing unsaid between us, that is a fact, and Dad and I had spent a moment recalling those events in the two years we were here together. The point is that when that happened, I promised TC I would never fuck around again and take something not prescribed like that, and I never had. Until now. I had to, and I thought to myself, the ramifications of this simple fact would surely damn me with my sons, but I took my mother's Ativan so I could take care of my father, and then I stopped taking it after about a day and a half, and I was better and the rest of the Ativan still sits it the cupboard next to the dishes, untouched. And then I thought, What the fuck does it matter? They are not here.

Now at the end of it the whirling, whirling winds of my life came to their pinnacle. I was untethered, almost totally.

My back got better and we waited for the hospice nurse to arrive. There are a lot of stories that did not make it in here, because I've probably run you through a lot of mazes up to now, but like Screamy Judy, Baby Huey and Steel Wool, some moments stand out for their exemplary teaching and historical cultural documentary value. These are two.

Nurse 1

Unknown agency.

Nurse 1 showed up, and made one point. Several times, in fact. "I can do nothing for you."

Nurse 1 did not stay long.

I called Breana. She took over.

I called her and told her about the debacle of the morning. Twenty-four hours later, she walked into the house, clapped her hands twice, and the doors opened and people came walking in, and went walking out, and Dad had a new hospital bed to die in, and all the supplies like creams and soaps and lotions and diapers, then Carter has little liver pills, my parents used to say, if we needed them. The frantic, wild, intense raging shitshow of the inferno was quenched. It was Deathwatch. Hospice care. She left me with enough drugs to kill thirty people, but we weren't going to hustle that. Just keep him comfortable, she said, and hugged me.

She left and I went back in with Dad. Fee came in too. What a good girl she was being.

Later when Dad was sleeping, I thought about all of it. I walked outside, by myself, loosely following the path I walked with Mom that day so long ago. I watched the moon pass over through white smoky clouds, backlit and beautiful. My whole life up until now, I had ever and always been safe in their hands. This was the ending. Had I done my duty? I don't know, but on any alternate timeline, all I saw was disaster, what with the plague, and my legal troubles. It was no small advantage that states separated us, God knows how it could have played out that night in March if I had merely been a few miles away. Showing up there demanding audience would probably have been in play, and I would be in a whole lot more hot water. This…it wasn't nothing but it was bullshit, and I didn't GivFuk, at this point, I still thought they should be here somehow.

For the next couple days, it was blazing hot outside, but Lono and I had put in the air conditioners at the end of June, just in time. The back half of the house was cool and quiet. I moved between the front, hot part, and the back cool part bringing Dad drinks, or just sitting with him. Throughout all of this, we continued to talk about this and that, and sealing wax, as we always had.

Japanese Shrine Music

After Breanna had got us set up, everything was different. It was over. This was Deathwatch. I wanted to rage at it, but I did not want Dad to have that. I needed to do this as best I could. I knew it was not going to be enough. As always, I could only feel this so much, because I needed to stay operational, (like I was on any level at this point is a joke) and I just missed my sons. They still weren't here. Even this had not broken through. I was so far past stunned, so far past shocked, so far past numb.

Some people take little sharp things, and clip and nick away at themselves, trying to feel any sensation at all. I never got that personally, but I understand it completely.

I don't know what numb is, what pain is, what anything really is anymore. Everything that ever made sense to me about my own family had been an illusion. I had no gauge at all. Everything in the universe was at once clear, and yet mysterious and it was in that very duality that I found a quiet space to exist in, sheltered from the Fire, sheltered from the plague, from destitution, I was at peace, and grateful, as always for the good fortune Dad and I had seemed to enjoy despite this, this... reckoning.

I spoke to Dad again, about how Candace died, and how I still encountered her, and he had seen when I believed I did as we walked with Mom through plague to Death.

I told him I believed there was a bridge between worlds, and that that could be bridged somehow too. I told him I would get some tattoos.

The night was clear and warm, and fresh breezes gave a

dynamic to the night wrapped around us. The air conditioner had kept things cool and comfortable. Dad was resting but awake. I had Japanese music playing in the front room and it was faint and distorted when it reached us, eerie, but appropriate to this culmination of otherworldliness that had been our last time together. Deep blue-black burst with white flowers of clouds and moonlight as the moon came up behind the trees in the back yard. We could feel ourselves, here, now, at the end of it all.

"I love you, Eric," Dad said.

"I love you too."

He always said that. I always said it too.

"You helped me a lot."

"I'm so glad I could, Dad."

He lay back and looked up at the ceiling, as if reiterating it to himself. "You really did," he said.

Trying to keep the horror and sadness, the awful powerlessness to virtually nothing to alleviate his suffering, and yet there was so much here that I was truly grateful for.

Dad closed his eyes. I squared his pillows and told him I was going out to the front room. Fiona had been silent, and was bearing all if this, as she had from the very beginning, in good stride. I brought her in to say hi to papa and left him to rest for a time.

I went on the deck with Heiwa no Dogu. I drew, and replaced it, and felt my stance and steel collect the power and energy of the night into myself. I moved through Deflecting

Wind into Stingray Strikes. The cool night air parted for my instrument. I channeled my energy into its vessels. It is what it is.

Later, after a few moments of practice, I went back inside. The air was thick with sweet summer flowers and heavy with particulates. Inside the air was cool and still. Dad woke up as I went down, and I bought him some orange juice. He said he was comfortable.

"I could use a little drinky-poo," he said.

Crown Royal. Neat.

All the bustle had stopped, all the talk of the future, the one that had guided us through Mom's journey, was over. But we still spoke of fishing, and the Great North Woods and Mt. Kineo that he would never see now. I showed him pictures. This phone had really been a character in this story, and now we sat, and I should him some of the places, and told him some of the tales that had happened in them. The house was quiet and still, and we felt it heat throughout the day, and slowly cool itself down as the night enveloped outside and the yard. The last days of our time together were ticking inexorably away. For my part, I was holding on so tight I was numb despite respite in Anghiel's arms. The wind swept over the house and through my soul and I stared at the empty chamber I was in. I tried to remember to breathe and be still and hang onto my mind, and comfort Dad.

In the evenings when Dad slept, my friends ever steadfast called to check in, and I called them. Garry Sloane did not know about Dad. It had been him I had spoken to so long ago, sitting in my car next to David's bonsai garden. It had been he, in those very first days that had said the words aloud that I already knew but had not heard in my heart yet. Mom's time at home was done, and I needed to protect Dad from the hurt that comes with the disease. Their love was pure and perfect as Love ever gets, and after the night I had spoken to Garry, in the weeks I remained at Jackie's and made Death preparations for both Mom and Dad, with Dad, I knew that the immediate priority was to minimize the hurt my Mom was inflicting with her words on Dad. He had no shield on it at all, and it cut him when she did it. The truth is that I had grown up with both of these people, the loving mom and the one who could say hurtful things, and I had long ago learned to live with it and overcome it, and even make all peace with it with Mom, with myself, and with Dad. There were no topics off limits during our last two years together and the only thing that remained unspoken was how terrible those last days with Mom had been for him. He had put it away. It had no place, it was an anomaly, like an injury, and it had healed such as it could, as all the other wounds came slicing in, removing forever pieces of our lives. I for my part felt like a man without limbs, but it was part of my soul that had been excised. There was no need or place for that awful episode to be spoken of, so we did not.

Breanna came by and I was again struck by the change in our relationship. We had remained friends and had clung to each other these last two years. I had Anghiel for a girlfriend, but there's nothing wrong with friends. Breanna both warmed considerably, and was huggy and comforting, but this was also what she did, and she operated with an impressive air of professionalism, despite the personal warmth and support she was giving me. She was an angel, and I told her. All the angels were making their appearances.

One showed up, quite unexpectedly.

Cassiopeia (The Code: Duty & Love)

Right before I left Maine, I had seen Cassiopeia face to face, which was rare over the twenty years we had been friends. She and I had been in contact over about two weeks, as I was hustling around the Biddo thinking my biggest problem was transitioning into a new life. That was pretty funny since that new life had lasted a total of 26 days before I had pulled up anchor for real. Cassiopeia and I spoke on the phone about three times a year, and I always called her, and it always took a couple days of messages before we connected. She had been a lifeboat to me, a death row reprieve. Seeing her in Maine, when I did, had been a critical dose of love, and friendship, and support. The thing is, she and I had never gotten together, but the fact that that chemistry and attraction was there quite transparent. I didn't creep at her in these phone calls, but as the years went on it definitely came up, from time to time, that we would have been good together if things had been different. Of course, by the time I left Marla, Cassiopeia had been married fifteen years. But we had a close and intimate friendship. That bubbled with lust on occasion, and she had been my companion in a way for many years, in a Dead Bedroom marriage, and she knew it, and it was kinda hot, and still safe. If I was a gentleman about it, which I was. She let me get away with being flirty and sustained that part of me for years. Her and most other women.

Dad was sleeping in the other room as comfortable as I could make him. I was out front with Fee. My phone went off, ringing. I was shocked. It was Cassiopeia.

I was so happy to hear from her the fact she had called me escaped me at first. This was highly unusual. We spoke on the phone for almost 90 minutes and had the most unbelievable conversation of my life. Top ten, easy.

So, I told her what was going on. She shared the health and status of her family, including her brother who was an old worker form the trenches of Sweet Shores who I knew and liked well.

Then, we talked at length about us, the two of us, and what our relationship has been.

I told her, again, how important she was to me. She's a smoker, and I always encourage her to take better care of herself.

But...

The discussion we had on the nature of Love was and remains profound. She was married, and I was with someone I cared about very much, so there is no question on either side what we are and are not talking about here. It's probably better to just outline out agreement with each other that came out of this phone call.

We agree that we both love each other a whole lot. We also agree that it has a romantic and sexy side, this friendship. We have kissed, once, long ago, before I remembered I was married. We spent a moment indulging the sweetness of this chemistry we have.

But it also came out that I love her so much, that if she is happy with her life, I would, in theory, give a kidney to her man should he need one. Do you get that? She did. Its fundamental.

The talk I had with my old friend and wife in an alternate reality did so much for me that I had to just give myself a shake. I could lament the awful, or I could appreciate things like this, that I had such friends as both Breanna and Cassiopeia, that carried a little extra spice, but not too much. And a girlfriend who I could be honest with about such things. In all this pain as the wind picked up outside and a light summer rain began to fall, I could not help but to just give myself a moment to appreciate and be grateful. The wind blew outside as my father lay dying in the other room. I had peeked in on him in the hour I was talking to Cassiopeia and he was sleeping. I went in to check on him. I hugged him gently and got him into a more comfortable position. Fiona nosed into the room quietly. I made him as comfortable as I could. I brought him some Crown Royal. I could hear Lono in the basement with Nimbus.

Secrets

While Dad was dying, I played the Japanese music for a while, I paced, I went in and out of his room as I saw him get tired, it was minute by minute. People called. Jon came and said goodbye, stoic. Jackie came. I made the mistake of leaving her alone with Dad. But I had no reason not to trust Jackie.

I was on the floor with Fee. I let her in to say hi to Dad and it cheered him up. I was scrambling to just make him… at ease. I looked around the room. I started to poke around, watching Dad for signs of distress at this. He was merely curios, and engaged, and ready to be helpful, like he had been, every minute for the last two years. For me. For a lifetime, with Mom.

I found some letters. My heart jumped and seized. If these were the infamous letters, the timing of their discovery was most inappropriate, and I would have to decide, to keep them to myself for the sake of his peace? I did not have to make that call. It wasn't them; it was something beautiful.

When my mother had thyroid cancer some years ago, she panicked about having surgery. She, of course, had written letters to her people in case she died. Uncle Jimmy's death scared the fuck out of her for the rest of her life. Facing surgery back then, she was terrified. Thank God, despite the suffering she had endured, thank almighty God, I thought now, that we had seen our course all the way through.

She wrote letters to me, my father, and each of the boys. We read them, now, together, laughing, nodding knowingly to one another, weeping and absorbing this amazing thing I uncovered and was able to share with my Dad. He had never seen them, of course. Nana was a little dramatic. She loved spectacle, as do… well, you know by now, or I have failed.

There is a picture of my mother in my room during these two years. I have come to realize; it is the prettiest picture of her there is. She hated being photographed, and hated being fat. She is smiling, here. She does not look fat, she looks sweet, and nervous, and cute. Knowing her as I do, the picture is rich, for me. I do not remember it in the Old Shire, but I love it, and I put it on Dad's hospital table next to his hospice bed. I knocked it off. The frame broke, but I picked it up, and it wasn't well and truly fucked, just… apart. That picture had a fold in it.

On the back of the picture was a message written from Mom to Dad in 1963. It was early in their walk. She calls him a name I have never heard. No one has. It has never ever been known. I read it now, and Dad's eyes get a little wide for a second.

"I haven't heard that name in a very long time." He smiled at me, then at the picture, and drifted off to sleep. I put everything back together. The picture frame, not the disintegrated mess that was all we had worked and hoped for.

I told him he said that like Obi-Wan Kenobi, and he said, "Yes," and we laughed a little bit more.

In the coming days, the last we would ever have, I spoke to him about how I was going to move forward in the world without him. Sometimes I stopped to weep, but we talked of the world and what we watched in it together. I kept coming back to the idea that I had been a warrior, and I would continue to be a warrior. If that was all I had, then that was where I belonged. I told him, that I could hear the sound of the guns, yonder, and that there were those out there that needed protection. Dad had seen me doing what I did all those years in Maine, saw me doing it like I always had, with my whole heart. He was proud of me and what I did, and I knew my mom was too.

Dragonflies

I woke up at about six in the morning after about two

hours of sleep. Fiona was lying next to me and there was no sound from the other room. I paused, for just a moment. If Dad had died during the night, his suffering was over, and that was that. I readied myself for what was around the corner and stepped into his room.

He was awake and looked as surprised and happy as me. We began another day of this ordeal. I fixed him up with some orange juice, and gave him a dose of Haldol, and one of Morphine. I helped him get to the commode chair. He was getting to experience some measure of what Sherry had gone through. It's better, at the end of things, I think, to have as much of the real as there really was, as much understanding, as much experience and empathy. My fear is that I will get to the end of my time, and realize I had been doing something wrong, and had missed out on something important. So much of how I felt was indistinguishable from that anyway, like the idea that I had wasted a LOT of time chasing my career and employment, when now that had not mattered a whit.

Except it had. It was the difference we had now in what was never to be. If he had not *seen* it, it would not be as real, as powerful, and I would not be as proud as I am, in his understanding, and appreciation, of what I truly mean about the Way of the Samurai. He had seen it, and now, he could tell mom. All of it, as awful as it all was, seemed right in its way.

This may have been a week before he died. I don't know, because at the time, it's simultaneously happening fast and slow, like a train wreck or an unopened parachute. After, though, in memory, everything went by in the blink of an eye.

We carried on minute by minute. I tried to feed him, or bring him juice or any other nourishment I could. I spent time trying to contemplate and predict such things as him expiring from dehydration, perhaps, before he suffered greatly from the pain of cancer. All I could do was watch and try to hang on.

Then, one afternoon he was getting back into bed, and I saw him put his right foot down, and he made a sound of pain. It was a simple thing, but in that moment, I was back there, with Ella, and the choice was the only one that Love can make.

When Dr. Michelle told me it was cancer I knew. The shock I felt then w existed in my life so I could deal with the shock of this now. It was identical, except with Ella it had played out over days and hours, and with dad it had been two months of fucking circus and ridiculous. In the abstract it was one thing, but the simple fact for both of them was that every minute they remained, the chances of their suffering grew. With Ella, there had been no choice to make it the one of Love, and it was the choice we faced now.

***

Dr. Michelle had left the house in Scarborough and left me in my shock and grief. I had to go to work. It was that night, the one I spoke of back there, that I came home, and found myself unable to breathe, and walked down to the marsh, and on the bridge under the stars as the hot tears coated my cheeks the whole marsh had gone silent out of respect.

***

I spoke to Dad later that day, as he lay in his uncomfortable bed. The sun was rounding the side of the house and speck of dust floated their way across their cosmos.

I asked him what he wanted to do. He figured it may as well be time.

He asked for a little drinky-poo with a smile. I burst out laughing through tears.

The freshly opened half gallon of Crown Royal stood on the kitchen counter, next to the morphine and Haldol. I pulled fresh syringes and loaded them up with Death and juice. Release, and juice. I knew this was an act of Love, so I refused to let it feel like preparations for an execution. But that's what it felt like, like the old movies about the French Revolution. Everyone feels terrible about it as they all do their part to escort you. To the Guillotine. I shook it out. I would not let such foulness creep into this. It was his cry of pain that did it, that gave me the steel to nudge him through. At this point, I'm pretty sure now, he was just sticking around for me. I felt selfish enough. It didn't matter that I had come home to help him out. Thank God I knew that. But the reality was if I had never come home, I would have crashed and burned, probably before the plague even showed up. They had always given me everything. Now I knew that they had given far more than I ever knew, and they had just given me everything all over again. I had mixed feelings. It was hard to feel good about any of it. I had to do something with it, and we had.

The house was still.

We sat for a while in the room. There was nothing left to

say, but that wasn't a bad thing. I kept thinking of my friends who did not have this, what he and I had had. By now he was struggling to speak, and his words came in a breathy whisper.

"I love you."

"I love you too, dad," I had said it more than once, in the days before. When we knew our story had reached its final chapter. I knew what I had to do. We went over it one last time.

"You guys gave me everything, my whole life," I said.

"I can only do one thing now. I must take what I have been given over and over again, and give it back, every way I can." The ideas that would lead me down my path were just forming, but turning Death into rebirth was what I had, what we had, to finish. The idea had formed enough that I knew this house was going to become something more. A sanctuary, where all are welcome, and we tried to bring light into the darkness. Somehow, I would make that reality. A knight I have apparently always been. The Hell we walked through together made it very real to me. I could not live in this world alone and I had only survived so far by thinking like a warrior. Dad *understood* all of this, before the end. It was only one of the myriad blessings that abounded in the hot dry fleeting summer of 2021.

That moment and conversation is marked as the birth of the Sanctuary of the Mastershade Locust Tree. It's to be a modern, American, Order of Chivalry, retooled for today's world. Not guns. Steel. And Skill, and Honor to back it up.

"I will do everything I can, give all I have, to fix what happened between me and TC and Keelin. I'm sorry you don't get to see it through with me."

"It'll be okay, someday. Sooner than (he paused and took a breath) later. Hopeful…" he exhaled and let it trail off. It was okay. We had thrown everything that was not nailed in, everything that we could lay hands on, overboard in completion of the tasks we had.

"I fucked that all up. I should have just kept my mouth shut and went looking for the evidence. I did not follow Sun-Tzu." Like with everything else, that was bad, but he smiled and said, "Yes," like he had when we used to do Sun-Tzu over coffee in the mornings.

"You and Mom saved my ass Dad," I said. "Just like you always have."

"I love you. Mom loved you too."

"I know."

We had our last drinky-poo together. Crown Royal, from his big half gallon bottle. A few minutes earlier, Lono had emerged from downstairs, and I poured him one too. Join us, I said through grit teeth, for my Dad's last drink. I did not mean come to the room. He got this. He raised his glass and we nodded. The Code.

He sat back and let me squirt the two syringes full of a lethal amount of Haldol and Morphine into his mouth. I held his hand, and hugged him, and cried a little, but I tried to be brave. Brave and strong, like my father had been, all my life. All my life, in every way.

The sun was shining in on him.

I sat with him. I checked on Fee. She was ok for the moment, and puppy though she was, just like Ella, she demonstrated in this moment what a dog is capable of. The thought of all of this without her could not have even entered my mind then. Even now, it still holds, I can barely think it enough to share it here.

After dad died and I tended him for the undertakers, the feeling came over me and I followed the impulse to take Fiona outside for a while. Dad was in his bed, and it seemed inappropriate to hustle him away. He put everything into this house. I had helped him arrest the decay that had outpaced him. He had had to make choices, as Mom's illness and needs had almost outpaced him. The house was sound. And they had never sold it and moved to Maine. It was mine now.

So, I would say that when traumatic events are in progress, it's hard to think straight. I knew that I could not digest all the ramifications of what reality was now.

I went outside with Fiona. The air was tropical but comfortable. There was a fresh soft breeze.

I turned around, and stopped dead, so suddenly my next step's momentum almost took me off balance. Fiona stopped and looked up at me inquisitively. Then, she followed my slack jawed gaze up, up over the roof of my parent's house, now my house, now the Sanctuary of the Master shade Locust Tree.

Over the house, in a large impossible swirling mass, were thousands, *thousands* of dragonflies.

Lono

I have thought a lot about Lono since these things happened. I have things to say I have not said to him, and he knows that he will hear it here for the first time.

I want to explain that Lono was here at The Sanctuary when it was founded, before Allan died. He loved the idea. It was Lono who thought bringing Ella to the Stronghold was beautiful, alone among all I shared my intent with. It was he who had first told me that I was not crazy, or an asshole, to have come to where I was, and he validated that the nature of it is solitary, and therein its sinister strength. Lono, who had consistently called while I came to understand first that I literally was in, and learning how to navigate Hell. Although Lono had been alone virtually in much of the support and validation I had gotten before the fire really caught, he had not said anything that had not shown to be solid counsel.

Lono was the second to last Pirate of the Old First Age/ *interregnum* and Mr. Nimbus had been the first dog aboard with us since Ella. That day on the marsh I remember the current had been strong, and so had the wind. When it's extreme conditions the best you can hope for is to lay over in some defilade, usually little indented irregularities offer shelter behind grass that is not in a straight line. If you can position your little clamshell of a canoe with the long grasses between you and the wind, you can regroup.

At high tide, you're fucked. There's not enough depth for cover. Lono told me that day that I was neither crazy nor an asshole to not want to be married anymore. And what had happened between then and now was beyond imagining, and yet, here he was now.

Lono was here when Allan died. He saw the dragonflies. He heard the first words spoken in The Sanctuary, besides my father. The ghosts were there too.

Breana told me when the time came, she would come herself and pronounce him. She did. My sister now. She mixed the drugs with dish soap and told me I had done well.

One Week

The Faye Brothers came and took my father's body away. They were almost totally silent. They had handled Dad and I with great care and now they were more than pros the way I had been more than a pro. They paid me the highest respect of being human with me. Being on the other side of this gave me great joy in all this sadness and uncertainty and fear. On that score, that was the right thing to do. When people are hurting, give them dignity and special treatment, the right way.

Fiona and I and Lono and Nimbus were all here. I spent the next couple days catching up with people. The phone rang.

Lono came upstairs as I was sitting with a pile of paperwork, the same paperwork that had been in my face when I should have just been sitting with him. Now he was gone, and it was on me to make sense of it. Someone was mowing the lawn. That's it, I thought. The neighbors have finally had it. It was Dr. Plow. He was mowing my lawn and tears were flowing down his face.

We spoke for a moment, and he expressed his sorrow.

They had been friends and neighbors for forty plus years. I gave him one of Dad's Franklin Half dollars.

It was a blur. I set about pretending I had things in order. I knew I had to breathe long enough to get to Maine. I wrote page long emails to everyone, anyone that had been involved from the bank people to the people in Berlin where my mother was a teacher, to I don't even know. I did trade a few emails with the Faye brothers. I think it's safe to say I left them laughing, if a little bewildered. Every staff member at my Father's funeral got a silver coin. Mr. Bill Faye got a Peace Dollar. Pirates tip silver. I had put Dad in a gorgeous black Ralph Lauren suit, and my Mom's ghost had popped in to quip that we should have bought it for her funeral, so he looked nice. He did look very slick and handsome, for my Mother, when he did finally go to see her. I asked him, when he saw her, to make sure he told her what he saw me do, for just a little while. I was their son. I would live every day of my life with that in mind always. And tell her, I said, I'm sorry I messed up so bad with TC and Keelin, but I was going to try my whole life to make that right too.

"That isn't your fault" was one of the last things he said to me. That and "You helped me a lot." And, "I Love you", of course. Oh, and… "I'm happy for you, son," which had dropped me weeping to the floor.

And I had told him that the boys loved him, and it wasn't their fault and he had nodded. He and my mother loved them so much.

Another Funeral

All the same characters were there. When Sherry died and we saw everyone it had been one thing. Everyone said how beautiful the obituary was. I had worked hard on Dad's too. It was even longer. Mr. Faye said it wasn't quite a record, but it was up there. A lot of people opined on the content in a way they had not about Sherry's because I said in it, pointblank, that Allan's beloved grandchildren were estranged from him the last two years of his life because of an unspeakable act by his daughter in law. Out of a Fury which hath no like in Hell. Dad knew I was going to do it, and he was ok with it. I couldn't care that people were offended, or aghast. I could not have really cared less, in fact, and I restrained myself from grabbing people by their jacket lapels and screaming into their faces, what they might do, in my shoes. That said, I gave people a chance to speak on this by asking them directly, so I wasn't going to vent on them for being honest. It just helped me gauge that no one at all knew what it was like to be here. Maybe someday I will find those who can commiserate with me on this feeling, but there were no faces I saw those days that had any idea, and the fact that they thought it was ok to tell me showed me that I was pretty alone, as I had been. I longed for the last breath of summer on the river, to put it all in order and reflect. I wanted to feel like I had done a good thing, but it was hard.

I know I helped them, especially Dad. Coming home sooner had not been an option, I think many people face these dilemmas, especially when separated by distance and with their own children at home. My good fortune on the timing of how it had all played out was damn near ideal. And I felt awful about it.

During the funeral, Jackie informed me that TC had sent her a message the day before Allan died, and she had shared it with him, but not with me, and she was waiting to share it with me.

-----heart-pulse-----

"What?" I asked. That can't be right, what I just heard.

She repeated this. She said it again. I wanted to think I heard her wrong.

"You put a secret between my father and I before he died? Why?"

I must have set off Jackie's defenses, because she started to get worked up. "I don't know, I thought it was best." My fury at this insertion, this invasion of her into these affairs, when what I needed was my mother's voice that she had remained silent on… and now this. I was fucking furious. This was out of line. Oh, my God, Jackie… how?

And where the fuck do you get off playing pick and choose games with your play here? You're supposed to be on my side. What the cinnamon toast FUCK?

I did not say that. I did not even say she had five seconds to produce that message or I was going to fucking choke her out in front of God, my father's body, and all these people who were already salty about Dad's obituary, and fuck their mood on that, by the way. I didn't say that either. I don't know what I said, but Jackie stopped fucking around and showed me TC's message. In it, he states explicitly, that it was because of me that his other Nana did not see them the last years of her life. He also talks about what a monster he believes me to be. But the first thing, that is the nut. My mother knew, that it was Darlene who wanted to split from the holidays. That rotten demonic bitch had lied to my sons on her deathbed, when the three of them went up to see her and say goodbye. And Jackie knew this was bullshit, and she had watched a golden opportunity to speak go sailing by. Why?

My father had died sending love out, indeed I was sheltered in it in every way now, and Marla's mother had lied on her deathbed out of hate and spite.

Jon is great. We don't get to see each other much, that's a fact, despite me being here. He had nothing to say about what I wrote in Dad's obituary. That's the kind of 'stfu' respect that I appreciate. That's why I hide treasure at his house. Turns out, hiding treasure is another way to be in the pirate club, but I also grew up with Jon in canoes so, he kind of has been as long as me anyway.

Allan's Obituary

Moon Metal.

The day before the funeral it occurred to me to look in the steel bank box in the armoire. I knew it contained my father's coin collection. I knew it was there. Dad and I had discussed coins, and Keelin's love for them during our last run, but we had never gone nosing around in the collection. It was one of those things we were waiting, to deal with when we had some time. It had sat in his armoire that I had dove into while he was dying, trying to figure out how to take over the ranch.

The box contained a bag of silver quarters, and dozens of other coins. Most were silver, but there were old things in there, too, and 2-dollar bills and stuff. The memory tsunami crashed over me, and I remembered sitting on the floor in my grandmother's house while my grandfather had shown me this very bill in my hand now, almost half a century ago. In fact, the box was full of things I had seen at one time or another, in one house, or another, all my life. I saw some things that were not Dad's when I met them, they belonged to my grandfather. I had never seen them since they had made their way here. It was one of the least known things to me in this time capsule that was now the Sanctuary of the Mastershade Locust Tree.

I know Lono is no thief, but there's no need to be ignorant about things. I did take that box over to Jon and Mary's and let Jon check it out. The glee he showed diving into that box and forgetting the rest of us were there for a few minutes… well, I wished I could tell Dad about it.

My parent's last giving to me had begun, and it started with a treasure chest. I felt like a real pirate and I laughed and cried again at the same time, for a couple minutes, then I shook it off and stowed the treasure back in the armoire, until I took it to Jon's.

Two hours between the funeral and my bugout, my phone rang. It was Max. He had almost died crashing his car. It was totaled. When I returned to the Shire this man was full of rage and pain and hate. He absolutely represents everything I try to stand against. To be a friend to him was not a choice, and I brought my whole heart into trying. I told him when I came back in a few days, I would scoop him and Anghiel up and go back up to Maine.

The man in my kitchen today is different, and I will see what we can do with that. It may be, I have the first… candidate?

PART 8
THE QUIET SPACES BETWEEN THE WHIRLWINDS

Pootown, Maine.

Pirate Stronghold.

August 29, 2021.

79 degrees F.

This story begins and ends in the same place, in the same manner, and among mostly the same company.

It is two years since I have opened the Doorway at all. Since then…

Since the first night in 2019, the last night of my old life, I have crossed some hard terrain.

Circles close, and open.

After Max left, I stood in my kitchen with Fiona for a while making my plan to bug out. I had no idea what was coming. I just knew I had to get to that place. I piled my tent, stove, cooler and packs, bundled the dog, made sure I had all my necessary *accoutrements*. The ride to Maine went by in a blur as the sun went down over my left shoulder. It was just growing dark when I opened the gate at the Stronghold and ate my medicine for the last time. I had more than one home now. I had started this journey here, and here it would finally end. The Treeherder was there. He knew I was coming, and he knew I was coming in hot. He had set the stage well, despite the abuse I rained on him all night for that damn foul candle. There was magic in it after all, it turned out. He had found this large Hindu funerary candle at Pick a Pound and was melting it into his copper firepit. Before long he had a bubbling cauldron of flaming smoking acrid oily wax.

The Echo in the Halls of Heaven

The Doorway was opened. I made preps. I found a good place for Fiona, where she could lie down, run around, and watch us. She barked a lot. This place must have been wildly stimulating for her. I took her around on tour while I waited for the feeling to start. I was numb and in shock. The legal trouble with Keelin had been present with me throughout Dad's deathwatch we had spoken much about what I was going to do next, now that I had a whole new world of options. Dad was in the ground now, and I was in the safest place I know, and I needed to see about what to do next. I was in shock, and pain. It was time. My numbness started to give way to adrenaline jitters and I knew I was in the Spiral. It had been a little more than two years since I had started this journey, in this place. And in the company I was in. Ella's spirit before, now… Fiona… watching me, tongue out, curious but not scared. I minded on her and tended her, but she settled down and watched the fire. As I stood there with

Pete, just in silence, looking at each other. He knows where I am, and he has watched me do this before. The forest woke up and shook like an old hound dog. The trees began to hum softly. A dirge, for my father, for all that has been lost. The tears of grief and love and joy and wonder and gratitude and loss and pain all came flowing freely together. I was here again at long last and this was the closing. Even with the act of retrieving the Medicine for my journey here, the one clear thing in all the pantheon that my father's passing had been, I had not really had a plan, or known what to expect. Even after last time. It makes sense now, because it was now that I realized that the book I always wanted to write was a dream, and it was ok, because it did not need to be written. The book I was going to write was this one. I knew it, in this moment, and all the years I wanted to be a writer I told myself I had something to say, but I really did not. now I really did. The stars started to take their seats in the gallery. I felt like I was on a cosmic stage, being watched. Hail, yon Pirate King… From whence come ye, briny, bloody, burn'd, and torn? The forest greeted me with familiarity as I saw the Scared Spiral, and realized I had never stepped out of it from Midsummer's Night when I decided it was time to leave Marla for real, and I thought of the things I had come to know since.

The smoke rose out of that pit and circled around the flat area where we park and hang at the fire. It's framed by Pete's camper, a large hollow leading to the river, High Hill, the road that would gain a new name tonight, but not yet, and the frog pond and a little grove complete the circle. Next to the road at the front of the grove is the big stump, also to be named tonight. Right now, in fact.

"The Altar!"

Pete looked up. "Mm?"

"This," I said. "It's an Altar."

"I guess."

I had put the latest offering on it. The Altar has accumulated a little minibar these last two years. Every time I've been here, I've left a nip or the rest of whatever came with me. Tonight, I placed the jug of Crown Royal on the Altar, where it sits to this very day.

After I took a good, long, pull.

I turned around to face the Treeherder. I was starting to feel it all, catching up. All the feelings I had kept mostly down while I took care of business with Dad. The business was done. I had done it. I knew I would spend the rest of my life thinking of ways I could have done more, or done better, but I had come home to the Shire, and helped Dad finish it. My sons were the great joy of my parents' lives. The experiences they shared were so vast and formative and my mother was much more happy, much more satisfied, as a grandma, Nana, than she had been as Mom, but I knew now that she loved me. I had never doubted it, but it was Dad, who always finished with "She loved you" who drove it home, over those short frantic beautiful two years we had had together. He had seen me perform at the work I had always done; he had walked with me on that journey back to that same place I had left almost two years earlier. I don't know why that was so important now. It seems like more of a waste of time I could have been playing cribbage with Dad, but to have lost what happened would not be worth it. He had *seen* me, and before he died, I had told him, that when he saw my mom, tell her I love her and miss her, and to tell her what he saw me do. I would not have traded that, or the secrets we had uncovered together in those last days of the last summer. He suffered so much before the end, but what would have been lost after so much that has been lost was inconceivable. I had been showered with blessings. My Dad had told me how proud he really was of me, and that I was a good man. He had laughed with me at the utter absurdity of life as a mental health worker, especially a roving gypsy maverick like I seemed to be, no matter what I tried to do.

I was in full swing now, standing there in commune with the forest. The contrast of the loss and pain, not just of my parent's but with my sons, was offset by the feeling of being blessed. There is no conversation that Dad and I did not enjoy the luck of leprechauns throughout all phases of our journey together. I was overcome with the duality of it, and how to fit and carry both within my soul and survive. The red and orange of the fire was so thick with smoke it looked like the night was a tiger, with its black and orange striping. Above me, the green of the trees lifted the eye to the heavens, and the deep blue black bejeweled Maine summer sky.

The Doorway was open again, and this was the last act. Whatever happened tomorrow, this, whatever this had all been, and yet would be (I still had a pending harassment charge to contend with), tonight, it was over. I felt my energy rise, and just like two years ago when Pete asked me if T.C. was gay, as soon as I thought of Keelin and TC, I got clobbered with a wave of Love that drowned out all though. All but one. I made my way to the grove, and stood for what seemed like a long, long time, weeping with grief and rage but also gratitude. People lose people to Death, but my sons were alive.

"God… please. Please. Please God, please… Please, God. Please… Please, God, watch over my boys. Please. Please watch over my sons God. Please. I cannot. God, please."

The tears fell and washed my face of road and funeral. Baptism, again. Baptism of Atonement. My hurt pride and ego, honor, justice…there was nothing at all left, only that.

"Please, please, please, God, please watch out for my sons. Please. Please God."

I knew, from what had happened with Anghiel, that one does not simply pray. It comes from the heart. My words were all that was in my heart, all I have or ever will have. I love them. I'm so sorry. I love them. Please. Please, God…

I released the tree and realized the bark was imprinted into my hands and face from my embrace of it. I caught a full lungful of cool clean night air, and had one heartbeat of perfect silence, just me, and my love for TC and Keelin, as it is at its core, untainted, and as ever present as the North Star.

I let that breath out with one last whisper: "Please. God."

And I watched that prayer, the deepest prayer of my Heart, the thing to me most dear in all the universe float as a wispy mist, up, slowly, over the gravel path, up above the trees, and up into the sky, directly toward the spot across the river where I had seen Heaven a little more than two years ago. My Prayer. The deepest prayer of my Heart. All the power of my love. I watched it go, and I heard it, I HEARD it, echo in the Halls of Heaven. I heard my prayer heard in Heaven. I did.

-----heart pulse-----

Paladin/The Bargain

I staggered out of the Grove, wet, hot, sticky outside but clean. I felt Love flowing through me, pulsing like a vibrant new star. I felt my own power. It has never left me. I am… this. The morning I left here on the first morning of my new life, I had felt so much pure unspoiled love for them, and from that day on, I had seen their love for me murdered in front of my eyes. I had driven them away. I had played right into Marla's theater of damnation. I didn't care, anymore, about my stuff, or that they lied, or anything. Whatever they did, they did because of what she told them, or made them believe. I am a fool, but an innocent one. I love them, and they have no need of forgiveness, they are innocent too.

It was hot and so dry. Fee was just watching the woods; this is a first for her. She is happy. I am happy to see a dog with me, again.

"Love Heals, Pete," I said through my deep hungry breaths.

"It does."

"My sons are alive!"

The Treeherder nodded.

"Thank God they aren't soldiers."

I felt a fresh wave of relief at that. I also thought about today, and tomorrow.

"Pete…" I said. I could feel the words rising and I knew my voice was still being heard. "If anything happens to my sons…"

We were silent with that for a moment. I felt another wave of energy hit me. This was all different. When I came here before I had opened the Doorway to set off on a journey. Now I had just completed one. There were other things. I had a companion who was caring and loving, and at this point, surprisingly, still around. I had Fiona. I had been safe as the plague had raged outside. I was grateful. But, I realized, only one thing mattered, and prayer was not going to be enough. I was befuddled for a moment with this conundrum, and I paused to contemplate the future. If anything happened to my sons… what?

Pete spoke, "You know, I've been thinking about something."

I was standing with Fiona. She took all of this in calmly and she seemed content to watch Daddy lose his shit. She was safe. She knew it. I'm sure she was just glad to be somewhere besides the house.

"You've talked about this Samurai thing for many years."

"Okay." I was intrigued where this was going.

"I get that, the Bushido, the service. But it isn't quite right."

After the last two years, if he was about to suggest something silly like a "Bard" I would have been pissed. I have never felt more like a warrior. It is certainly something, not the only thing but something I could not have survived this, indeed would not survive this, without. I braced myself for whatever wisdom the Treeherder was about to share.

"You're a Paladin. A real one. If there is such a thing possible in the world we live in, you are definitely it."

There was quiet as I absorbed that. He was right. This is what I am. It is what my entire life has prepared me to be. A Paladin. A warrior with healing powers, who serves Lawful Good. Yeah. That is me. He's right. A rare bit of wisdom, from the Treeherder. They're rare cause when they come, they're big. This was. Life defining in fact. If I had any hope that God would watch over my sons for me, I was going to have to earn it. And watch over everyone else. Okay.

The trees and the night continued their color and light show, and it was quiet.

It came to me. I drew my sword out of the back of the car. I felt the steel in my hands, and I felt power surge through me. There is only my sons, and I will do what I must to find them again in the dark.

But...

Without thought, I moved to low guard, and I stalked up that path all the way to the end, where it opens out into a vast cathedral of trees. Behind that, is the river. The Hall of Trees swayed in unison, and I felt great power in the moment, and in the spot. Starlight played through the trees, and I followed it down, down to the ground, sliding over my unmasked blade like oil.

I breathed slow and deliberately.

"If this is the Bargain you offer, I accept."

"But, if anything happens to my sons, I am going to come looking for answers. And before I do, I will unleash the other spirit within me upon the World. And then," I realized I was roaring like thunder, like a Titan the way I had that day so long ago, up in the Great North woods. "And then I will storm the very Halls of Heaven itself. Watch out for my boys, and I will watch out for the whole world. As I have always been."

I realized that my voice was like thunder, and echoed through the night, along the river. The power flowing through me was nothing new, but I have ridden this ride too many to many times and I would not be standing here now, without the power of this sacred medicine.

There was one heartbeat of still. Be Still. And Know That I am God. God heard White Shirt's Vow. My end of The Bargain.

I do not doubt the things I have said here. I believe them all, and if they are not real, I am not real, and nothing I have ever done has been real. That is what Marla would want. In that instant her foul presence manifested, the power in the moment, far beyond acid trippin' instantly diminished....I had truly been in the company of God. Directly this time, not just across the thin place between worlds that we now know as the Cathedral, what opens up into a vast beautiful green space in the forest with only the river behind it, and waves and whispers with the voices of the Universe itself and all that lie within it. Witnesses. Good. I knew it then, and I still believe it.

I had just struck a bargain with God.

The path would be long and hard, and I could not even begin to see it, only the promise of what may be over the horizon, if I could be worthy.

If I could but truly be… a Paladin.

The Gates of Hell

I returned to the central area with the fire. Pete was still there. He had of course heard me raging at the Heavens, making demands and threats to God himself in the name of the Love of my sons. I was transformed, forever, here and now.

"I am Paladin." I said simply.

"You are." Pete said.

Fiona barked, and I went over and played with her for a minute or twenty. Time is different here…

10,000 degrees (kelvin).

The huge funerary candle had been melted for a while and the whole mass of liquid was bubbling at a full rolling boil. I remember when TC was with the Fire Dept, he talked a lot about fire science, and I knew that that flaming cauldron of oil could actually flare up. I've seen turkey videos of people burning their house down. Same process, scientifically.

I kept feeling an anger, but not the cold desperate rage I had learned to live with, the one that got worse and renewed every little layer of Marla's evil that I had uncovered. No, this was the anger when someone farts in your car. Friend anger, like "Dude? What the ever-loving FUCK?" The cauldron was bubbling and boiling and giving off putrid smoke that smelled like diesel and Death. And Brimstone. I moved closer to the fire, but before I did, I looked over at Pete, and it really hit me. If I was going to be Paladin, I was going to have to contend with this demon.

"Pete… how could she have done that to my boys?"

He was watching me and said nothing.

"She's their MOTHER!" Two years of shock and discovery erupted out of my heart like pus, the way light exploded out of me at the mention of TC's name here that night so long ago.

I wanted to give Pete shit about this foul smoke. I kept trying to haze him, ask him why, why Pete, did it seem like a good idea to fill the night air with funerary smoke that smells like Brimstone? But then, I kept bursting out into laughter, spitting and tearing hysterically, because it was so fucking funny, not that he had done it, but that I wanted to bust his chops for it and couldn't, because it was so fucking funny. I took a good hard pull from the Crown Royal.

"I know one thing, by God" I said, and he was watching me.

"We are still from that old blue house and there will be no dishonor here."

"Pete," I said to his silence. "Where in the name of God would any of us be without that old blue house on School St?"

We will never know. But this is better.

I was not done. There was another place to visit tonight, and I had not really expected this. The realization that I had just spoken aloud came at me hard, and I realized, standing there, in that thick black smoke, I'm sure it reminded Pete of the Iraq war, the first one, when the entire sky from horizon to horizon was this, this thick oily disgusting choking deathsmoke.

It was exactly what we needed to finish this. Heaven, and now Hell.

Throughout our journey together, my father and I had spoken of the joy we had together, in spite of the circumstances. In time we had come to accept that we were in fact both in Hell, and Hell was not so bad, for Hell.

Now, the thick smoke obscured Pete from my vision. I had seen Fiona sleeping in the car, and now, I was utterly alone.

The smoke ringed me, and the flames climbed high up into an arc. I looked into the bubbling flaming oil. The heat was singeing me. I stood in it. I knew where I was.

I did not know why at first, but I had an impulse to launch myself directly into that flaming oil. Face first. I pondered this impulse. There is nothing, NOTHING, in all of God's creation, in all the vastness of the universe, as pure, as strong, and as enduring as the love I have for my two boys, and if I had any way to know for sure it would work, to save them, I would throw myself into that fire, even if it meant Hell for me. To save my sons, I would sacrifice myself, all I have, in an instant, without hesitation. Even my Soul.

And THAT... is Hagakure. I really found it. In front of

the Gates of Hell.

I would die in a second for my sons. Marla put them in danger. She put them in danger of Hell. For her own selfish reasons. It wasn't the first time, but I felt sick with that, and this was it, this was the paydirt, the final ultimate breakdown of all this. Whatever else was to be said, Marla could not, and did not care about those boys first. I did, and I still do. Knowing that, I withdrew from the edge of the fire, now an 18 feet high arc of flames over the copper pit. The Gates of Hell itself, real and in the flesh, drugs or not. Daring me to just step in through and take the short and easy road to giving all I have to give to my boys. It would have been so easy.

No.

The arch receded back into an earthly fire. The thick smoke cleared as I felt myself swelling. When the smoke thinned enough for us to see each other, I was standing with my sword, shirt off, shoes of on that sharp gravel slicked in sweat. He was eyeing me warily.

"Relax, brother," I said.

"What the fuck just happened?"

I looked at him.

"You, the fire… it all just disappeared."

"Your fucking smoke got thick dude." It was funny, but I did not laugh this time.

"No, dude… for a minute or two, you, the fire, the smoke… just was not there."

A lot of weird things have happened at that Pirate Stronghold in the woods.

I moved off to a safe distance and just… let go. I just surrendered. The steel in my hand leapt awake, and together we moved all the way from the Common to The Landing. I could feel and hear the blade move in my hands, and I did not wonder why, but just casually noted, that I had no idea what I was doing, but I was doing it right. The gravel did not cut my feet, even though we cannot walk up there comfortably without shoes on it. Tonight, I never even felt it. I knew that some of what I was feeling was like those people that walk on fire or broken glass. No thanks, but I have no doubt I could have done either.

I came back down and did a nice clean Noto. I returned my instrument to the car. Fiona was awake, and I let her out to hang out by the fire. In that moment I looked at her, and she at me, and we had our "It's you" moment, like Ella and I had so long ago. The thought we had simultaneously was "Home".

"Yes, honey," I said. "We are home for each other."

"You're pretty good with that," he said, nodding at my instrument.

"How the hell would you know?" I asked him back. Fiona barked. Yeah, Pete. How would you know?

It was different than the last time. The last time, Midsummer's Eve, 2019, when all this began, it had taken all night, hours. Of course, between then and now I had been burning the candle at both ends a bit, and maybe it was me that was different now. It sure felt that way. I had never come back through the Doorway I opened here that night, I just kept passing through more and more. This transcended chemistry now. I no longer required the assistance of chemicals to access this world. I had relocated, chosen my residence in Hell, when I escaped the marriage. I would never have sacrificed my sons for anything. Their mother made them into sacrifices.

Tonight's journey had ended however, the same way it had begun. In the same place, in the same manner, and among the same company. I spent the rest of the night sitting by the fire, feeding it, and watching the meteors shoot across the sky. I knew my destiny, after all these years. I was Paladin, and I was going to do everything I could to right the evil that has been done to my children. The Long Evil. The Many Evils.

Between the Path of God and the Cathedral, and the Gate of Hell, the drugs I had taken were barely noticeable. They had come hot hard and fast and had blazed out in incredible intensity.

It had been two years to the day since I had returned home to Massachusetts after a lifetime in Maine. I sat as the sky began to gray, like it had when all this began. I reflected. I tried to really reflect, that when I was here at the start of the journey, I had no idea what was coming. I only knew I could no longer even live in that marriage. It wasn't about the day by day at that point. I was desperate to have some kind of normal life, now that the normal-est part of us had been raised to men.

On the score of the kids, even with all that had happened, even with all that had been happening for years that was unknown to me then, I had no regrets. Not about what kind of Father I had been. It had taken a lot to pick my way through this thorny path. Now, this morning, I had some kind of map in my head about the high points.

I addressed the Treeherder.

"I'm going to the first hill."

"Okay."

***

I thought I was alone; I went on as Pete settled in, walking with me through this deconstruction, the first time I was connecting all the dots, all of them. I almost had it when Dad was here, but fucking Jackie and her meddling had kept that last clue until after he was in the ground. Its ok. We were almost all the way there, and that didn't matter anymore, either. For two years I had railed and screamed at the injustice of my sons going no contact with me. I did not understand why. There was no truth they cold know that would justify what had happened, and it turned out, it was no truth that they knew.

I had missed some truths, too. I had been so obsessed with Marla's bad behaviors that I failed to realize that the slow turn of the screw she worked on me, that long game… that had affected me, and what the boys saw was the strung-out man, not the guy being quietly tortured by their mother. And, I knew from TC's message to Jackie, Marla had constructed her own web of lies and manipulation around them, and her fucking rotten sister and mother had been a part of that.

When Marla's mother died, she had been away from the family for some time. We had seen them at events with Marla's

448

extended family, cousins, and shit, but they never came over. I had never seen the letters. Marla and the boys went to Lewiston, where her mother was dying. Even though this was not done secretly, it was *conducted with the old-fashioned air of keeping me away from all of it that her mother had excelled at. I was silent on this, trying to be supportive of their loss. As far as I was concerned, the matter could have been resolved a long time ago. They went. They came back home. TC and Keelin both shot looks at me when they came home that night that escaped me at the time. Now, I knew, that their grandmother had used the last time she saw them to tell them she was sorry she turned away from them, by that it was all my fault.*

I wonder what my boys would say, if they had heard my father recall that Marla's mother, with her filthy talents, managed to almost make my mother feel bad about something that brough her great joy. One Christmas, my father recalled (I remember this, I remember her saying it) that as TC and Keelin were opening their gifts from my parents, Marla's mother rolled her eyes and said, "We can't compete with this." That pretty much sums up the whole score. She was jealous of the way my parents spoiled my kids with gifts. That may have been true, but we didn't raise spoiled kids. My mother loved Christmas, so Marla's mother had tried to take a shit in it for her. It was ever, and always, her MO.

Standing here now, the idea that I had been married to my worst enemy, who deliberately and systemically tried to undermine my relationship with my sons for years, and then successfully murdered it… I felt myself begin to swell. Waves of rage flowed through me. Rage, and Hate. Shock. How could someone do such a thing? Pete says now that he saw me… transform. I had almost forgotten I was in the Spiral again, and that I had just put my father in the ground, and that TC and Keelin were not a part of any of the last grand act of my Parent's lives. Now, it seemed like both dementia, which shielded my mother from the horror of this reality sprung from Marla's hate and diabolical mind, and the Covid plague, which would have kept the boys away, at least physically making some of their absence irrelevant, were their own kind of blessings. What was lost had been the opportunities to Zoom, and talk to him on the phone, and love him, and thank him, and remember the laughs and the love and the good times. He deserved that, and earned it many times over, infinitely many, and it had been denied him out of a most cruel web of lies, years in the making. They should have been with him any way they could have, and they had not, except that one whirlwind operation that had brought them down to see him, all tubed up in the hospital and wasted away to gaunt, that one last time. If they ever came to understand what they had done…they needed to know that it was not their fault. They are victims, of child abuse. What has been done to them, this manipulation, this carefully constructed story about how Nana V. left the family and it was all Dad's fault cause he's an asshole… that was a demonstrable lie. TC's message to Jackie, the one she fucking meddled with instead of just passing it on, stated that specifically. That he blamed me for that. He did not seem to know that I had tried to put it right, through my parents, to encourage Marla's mother to try to be a little less selfish and petty and rejoin the Holidays. TC and Keelin did not appear to know that. But Aunt Jackie does. Directly from my mother. If I could find the letters, maybe. That and the forensic bank documents they kept, the Christmas lists… the records of all the money they gave to Marla, and one note I found early, one titillating clue where my mother backhandedly states that Marla takes them for granted and Mom had to tell her no this year. I had that one clue to start the treasure map. I wasn't thinking about this now, I was climbing back to the Poo from the Pit.

My rage at Marla's evil gave way to Love, again, for TC and Keelin, and I remembered the Bargain. If the creature in me that had just stirred was ever unleashed there would truly be no going back. I will hold my end. I must protect them. They are innocent.

But…

What I did not know two years ago was that nothing was ever going to get better with Marla, because Marla was determined to make me as miserable as possible, every day. Taking my kids and leaving me for dead or on the hook as her fucking pension fund had been in her plan for years, that was apparent now, and even though I had yet to find those cursed letters, I knew, I finally knew, just how evil and selfish my ex-wife had been, to hurt everyone around her and destroy her family, out of spite. Because when we were in college, I had cheated on her, and she never got over it. She milked thousands and thousands of dollars out of my parents the whole time we were married, knowing Sherry would never say anything to me.

If I had not lost my mind (when Sherry died) and caught that charge, I would not have one thing I did have. Marla's written statement in her own hand calling me physically abusive. That, I knew, was not true. I never laid a hand on her, or acted like I was about to. That would have brought an immediate total victory to her years ago if I had, now that I knew I was little more than a hated pet in a cage to be tortured at will. The last two years had been more harrowing than almost anything I could have ever imagined. But the truth, the red-hot toxic truth, was out there. There was a way back, there was a way to break this spell of lies. There must be. I will live every minute of my life trying to find the way. I will hold my end of the Bargain. My sons live, and they are not soldiers. I will protect the innocent and help the needy, in the spirit and memory of my parent's lives, their love, and the undeniable absolute practical truth that they have always, in every way, given and given and given to me and mine selflessly. they were together again, and I was still here, and everything they ever loved or took joy from was partly a lie, and now lay in shit covered ashes and debris across the beautiful story that our family had been, in the most important ways. Marla.

The night was cool but not chill and the air carried the good sleepin' weather vibe of the last hurrah of summer. The coming day was going to be hot, and I was sticky, gouged and covered with leaves bark and pine pitch. Fiona and I had torn into the woods after all this died down, and she went nuts terrorizing the little forest critters. There's a dog on the scene again, bitches. You can't hide! We crashed into the thick evergreens, me roaring laughter and Fiona barking maniacally.

***

After the rapid and intense first couple hours, I spent the rest of the night with Fiona while the Tree herder tended the fire. It was not like last time. By morning, I was just awash in love, and cared nothing for anything, except my boys, safe in the arms of God, if I could hold my end, and be Light, always. So, they may yet see.

We go up the road to Azz-waschay Beach, to wash up. Or, waschay. It is the Baptism that closes the circle, and opens the new one. There have been undeniable endings, and there will be beginnings now, and in between all those whirlwinds

I had to learn to find…

You know.

Contrast

Pootown.

Morning.

Hot dry/insects buzzing.

I called my lawyer in the morning as the medicine wore off. The past twenty-four hours had gone by in a blur. I had about six hours sleep since… well, July.

My lawyer's name was Dick Burn. That about sums up my experience with him. I'm probably fucked. Fuck it, throw me in the Klink and I will minister to the lowest of the low. Will that convince anyone?

Not long ago, yet… a long, long time ago, in May, I had called this man and agreed to pay him. He told me, this is how it works. This is clearly all bullshit. You have been through a lot, it sounds like. Let's do this and let me make it go away. Dad was right there, I wanted to say, "Let's ask him, ooh."

Then, he got my check.

The next time we spoke, I asked him some questions, or tried to. He was surly and unprofessional from the moment he had my money, and he had my balls in his care.

That all went on pause when my dad got the cancer. For

a while, I had not worried about this legal trouble. It was bullshit, I knew that. But it was a nuclear pile of it, and I was under the pile. Now, Dad was gone. My time had run out on this, it was coming down. I was looking at a plea, or fighting it out. Taking all of this into a courtroom, forcing Marla to put her hand on that Bible and lie in court… if I could do that, at least, I would. After last night I had made my peace with many things, as I watched the blazing light of my love for my boys make everything else not matter. I didn't care about anything except them, and that had extinguished the petty grievances I had over how they had done me. They were innocent, and they were victims.

I've said a lot of things about Marla here. Today, sitting in my hot car, smoking weed, and cuddling Fiona, coming down of the acid, I made peace even with Marla's crimes. Having recently toured the foyer of Hell, I prayed for Marla's soul, I did. The depth and malice of her crimes against my parents, me, and our sons was so profound, that in hours after I heard my voice in Heaven, I prayed for her not to be damned to the fires of Hell. I did. I truly did. For all the destruction she wrought in all our lives, this foul abuser, I had that measure of forgiveness. If it fell to me, I could not Damn her. Or, I surprised myself, her mother, or Vendela. That was this morning. There were still secrets. And I may find them, and change my policy, but today, no. Even after all you have done, I would not Damn any of you if I were given the judgement over you. Maybe there are secrets yet that will change that, but, I could not, in the eyes of my sons, even allow myself to hate you. You ain't getting my kidney, like Cassiopeia's husband if you need it though, go fuck yourself. Unless you tell the truth.

I will trade anything for the full truth if I could draw it out of your diseased sadistic mind, but I cannot hate you because you gave them birth. Your crimes against them are unforgivable, in this world, or the next, and I have to let that part go. To get to the truth I will cut my own heart out on National TV. Would that convince you then, sons? I love you so much it burns me to the bone, and I will not loosen my grip on that ever though I turn to ash and stone. I feel like ash and stone anyway, without you.

Well, then. I am going to have to take this onto a bigger stage. Starting with telling the truth for the world to inspect, and judge.

Walkabout

I went walkabout for four days after the Circles closed in Pootown. I took Fiona around the old haunts, Seavey's Landing, the strip in Old Orchard, and just enjoyed the attention she got from people, and the idea that at the end of this there was a new era ahead and I had all the necessary Pieces. Dog, Truck, Canoes. Girlfriend. Money. Friends. The memory cascades will never stop, I know that now, and I drive the roads I drove all these years in another lifetime now in this one. Fiona riding next to me, out of the corner of my eye, I could almost… but of course, we will not. Ella is no longer in this World. She remains in the Universe and stops by from time to time. Fiona is here now. There is a whole new set of stories to be written. Now, the stakes are all our souls. I have to be who I really am, not the monster the boys think I am now. I must raise the voices of all the cosmos. I will stop at nothing… nothing.

***

"Duty is heavier than a mountain. Death is lighter than a feather."

That's a saying in the Borderlands, Shienar, in the World of Robert Jordan's Wheel of Time.

***

I drove past the road that turns to the beach after I pulled out of Suds and Such, after screaming some music for about an hour. Fiona had loved the beach, and all the sense of starting so many things over again, from scratch, did not seem all that bed.

At this point, I was awash with love for the world and a desire to carry the legacy of the profound love of my parents into the world in a way that would make my parents proud. And maybe, just maybe, TC and Keelin.

Right now, I am as content as one could be with what I have, except, you know. The play is pretty good, said Mrs. Lincoln. In fact, I am pretty unbelievably lucky. The way things went down with Mom and Dad…I was so grateful, in the shadow of what had been ripped away so wrongly, for what I had been able to do, and also what had come out of it. There was no way not to be, it was their last giving to me, and they would be at peace with the peace I found in that, that I was, if naught else, glad they were together, and out of suffering. I did always love them, maybe not as well as I could have or should have, but I would carry forward what they would want me to. And I will never, ever surrender my sons to the Shadow.

The idea of making knights, justiciars, I liked, and I thought about it. It was Max who came to the Sanctuary in pain when Allan died, because he crashed his car. I was kind of the closest thing to a friend Max had. I invited Max to come camp out for a night, and me and Anghiel and Chief Soda—Pop, an old pirate and samurai himself, my friend of twenty years and likewise friends with Matty Mango and Cristobel, came up and went through the Doorway by himself. Me, Max, and Anghiel heard him howling down by the river far into the night. This was a week after my solo walkabout.

Later, he just appeared out of the woods. We were sitting at the fire. Just a little weed and Crown Royal, Dad's Crown Royal, tonight. No acid. Just a little drinky-poo.

"That's good acid," he said and ran up the path of God toward the Cathedral, screaming and laughing.

I looked at Max and Anghiel, both uninitiated, and far from being ready for this kind of healing. "It is." I told them, as they followed his antics up the path with amusement, and a little uncertainty. "It is *really* good acid. A direct phone call to God, in fact," and I fell off my chair laughing as hard as Chief.

Jimmy Buffet, the Grand Bard of the Brethren, knows.

If we couldn't laugh, baby… we'd really be fucked.

The next morning Max dove in the river and had a transformative experience. A baptism. No drugs, no shenanigans. Just the Spirit of the river. Two hawks circled us overhead. Anghiel smiled when she heard me greet them. Candace? No, not today. Just friends. None of us commented, we just let him flounder around for a while, and fished him out. Fiona, it turns out, unlike her sister, is a swimmer. Just friends swimming in the river, a woman who loves me. Oh, God. What now?

Treasure Hunt 1

Two years ago, when I was getting an oil change on the car I was still driving, I spotted a brand-new Ford Ranger in the showroom of the dealership. I took a picture of it with the cylon. It's weird to think how new this sidekick was then, considering the things that have happened through it (and sometimes, because of it). The truck was beautiful, and that day, I looked at it lovingly and dreamed. Dreamed that I could put my life together, and be in a proper vehicle for the life I was trying to make. It was the truck.

That poor Fusion. It was a great car. It carried me through all of this, and never complained. It had served well. It was also a lease, and the lease was coming up. I had enough money now that I could seriously consider what I needed to do, and I was hoping to be able to buy a ten-year-old Tacoma. It would do. I had forgotten all about the picture, of buying something so nice, and new, and full of promise for the future. The Fusion was the vessel that carried us, all the way through all of the fires and shells and gas and horror, in which we had laughed and cried, and in which I had brought Fiona home. It deserves a medal.

I was in my parent's room, thinking about this. The hospice bed guy had come and removed the bed, and the room now looked like someone had died. The house was in a new phase. I looked at the floor, under the little desk table thing with the marble top. It had old meds and other shit on it, and the last two years had gone by with this little corner being quite undisturbed. There were some cases and an old doctor bag on the floor under it. I looked at one of the things on the ground. I had seen it. I knew it was there. I just hadn't really had time to register it, or ask Dad. This was one of those little details that started to pop up after Dad was gone. When Lono moved in, I had asked him, flat out…Is there anything in the house that is valuable. He said no.

My Dad never lied. But that was not accurate.

I brought the safe into my room. It was locked, and I could hear that it something in it. Papers. I went to the armoire, where my dad kept a dish full of every kind of key you could imagine. There were several examples, including those little round fuckers they use for electrical box locks and stuff. I grabbed what looked like a safe key, I guess, and wondered about the hammer and crowbar option, and how bad I wanted to see what was in here.

The key slid in and the box popped open, and I looked at all the little envelopes in there, neatly packed, and labeled. 200. 500. 300.

When I was done opening the envelopes, I had fifteen thousand dollars in cash on my air mattress bed. When I regained my senses, slightly, I scared Fiona howling laughter like a madman at the ceiling. It was… Truck-in-a-Box.

Sunnyside

The dealership that sold and serviced both what would be TC's first car, and the one my father had just passed on to me, was down the street from Anghiel's house, oddly enough. When I first came back to Mass., I inserted myself into certain elements of infrastructure that were in place. Auto insurance and my own auto needs, I had adopted both of Dad's teams. They treated me well, too. Sunnyside had serviced this vehicle since I came back. Now, they were going to help me dump this lease and buy a truck.

The guy told me that he had a new vehicle that was not much more than the used one I asked about, of course. But it was such a big leap for not much more money, I channeled TC's attitude, and decided to go big, or go home. I never had the financial situation I currently had. I was not going to live high wide and handsome, but my days of being ok with being poor were over for a little while. This was a necessity, not a luxury treat.

The new vehicle he just happened to have on the lot was two years newer, and a crew not a king cab, but it was identical to the Ranger I drooled over two years ago, when it was a faraway dream. With an ocean to cross. And here I was. Fiona felt my moment with this coming home to me, and started to bark, snapping me out of it.

"I don't need to test drive her. She's all mine. I'm taking that beauty home. Today, if possible."

Bill the car sales guy reacted, barely perceptibly. He was a cool cat. They all are here, and they all have a sense of what I am going through, at least their own instincts are capable of reading my state. Or seeing the haunted look of me, how it's grown over the last two years.

Sold is sold. He did not fuck around. When you walk in with ten thousand dollars in cash, they don't care that you are wearing jeans and a hoodie, and have a crazy puppy in tow. They do not fuck around *at all;* they are fucking professionals.

Everyone got tipped a silver dollar. Pirates tip silver. These aren't my Dad's coins. I bought a bunch to use for tips. It's the same amount of money. When the guy came to jump start Dad's car, I tipped him a silver quarter, but he did not notice at first, and kind of gave me the "Oh, thanks! I'm eating lobster tonight, high roller!" vibe, so I said, "Hey… take a closer look, amigo. I'm a pirate, not a chump. That's a silver quarter."

He looked down again, and immediately snapped to, grateful. I explained, "It isn't worth a whole lot, but it's more fun than a ten-dollar bill, ya?"

He agreed. It's fun being a pirate, even a sad one. Dad always tipped people. Marla's mother and sister liked to fuck with food servers, Karen-style. We just called them cunts, people like that, not Karens, when I was a cook back in the day.

But that pretty much says it. Dad was a tipper. Darlene and Vendela were opportunistically cruel. There lie the high and low tide lines of human behavior, at least on this scale.

Karma

The medicine for both journeys into the Spiral came from the same source. It was a friend of Lono's. I had casually asked Lono about this so long ago, and he gave me a phone number, and without that simple thing, I have no idea what story you would have read, but… it would not have been this one, or by me, I reckon.

Marla liked to cite Karma. She also had three favorite quotes she loved to cackle out to contribute to whatever was going on.

"It's not what you know, it's what you can prove."

"Keep your friends close, and your enemies closer."

"Never put anything in writing."

The irony of these had not been lost on me as these events unfolded and my nightmare grew every day since I left her. I had been led like a lamb to a slaughter, I just jumped on my own at the last minute. If she really thought I was dangerous, why did she throw TC at me every chance she got for years? Now I got it. She was a toxic cunt.

She also loved to spout "Karma!"

Please, God…

Anyway, I was in the front room with Fiona, and I was contemplating the radical change in my life, and how for the first time I had money, and my sons were gone, and what the fuck had it all been for anyway? How did I deserve such good fortune? Because if it was a tradeoff, I am not happy.

The source of the Acid that fuels this ride came from

Lono's friend. He was now dead, and his face hung below me somewhere on a tapestry in my basement.

And then, my floor slipped away, and my walls faded away, and it was just me, looking down impossibly into my basement, through where my floor was supposed to be, and the face on the tapestry looked up at me and winked, like it was okay. It's all as it should be. That was weird, by itself, but Lono's dead friend's name was Karma.

Later when Lono returned to the Sanctuary, I told him what happened, but first I just mimicked the exact little nod I had seen, and asked him if it meant anything to him. Yeah, he said. You looked like Karma for a second.

"Sit down, please, Lono." I told him about my disappearing floor.

Treasure Hunt 2

After that little surprise with the truck in a box, I started to wonder what else might be in the house. I found a locked metal safe under the stairs, and I placed it back there, and forgot about it. I forgot about it, because I was going to return to it, but when I stood up, I tapped my memories of this basement, and I sniffed the air, and I sought.

And I opened my eyes, and I was looking at a box that had been sitting right there, in the open. While I was in Maine for four days, for two years while a dozen people had been in and out, like out Farmer Pal. These people were friends, but…

The box was labeled "Coins" in sharpie. I knew this box.

I had seen it long ago, and never again, but there it was, right there in the open all through this, and I was just registering it. I knew there was something in it, and I slid it off the shelf. It was heavy. I knew there was something in it…

I got the box to the top of the stairs and sat down and dug into it. Fee was curious and I told her to spread out, honey, good girl…

In terms of raw junk silver alone, at the prices in Sept. of 2021, I had about thirty thousand dollars in my hands.

In terms of what there may be for numismatic value, my brain clicked, and shut off a little… Keelin is a coin collector. The last eyes in this box appeared to be his and Dad's because both their handwriting is clearly visible on plastic containers.

And, this collection, about half what I see, was previously my *Grandfather's*.

There are at least eighty little brown med envelopes that contain anywhere from two to several coins. They are all marked in ancient pencil in a hand instantly recognizable as my mother's father. This is his coin collection, the rest of it. The part I have never seen before, just because of chance. I have heard my mother, grandmother, grandfather and father all speak of what may be in here. Every envelope has numismatic notes, specifying the coins inside. Mintmarks, wheats… errors.

This could be worth literally hundreds of thousands of dollars.

It belongs to TC and Keelin.

The Pirate King has a real Pirate treasure. And it's going

right where I said I would put a thousand ounces of silver, someday. Where Ella should be. Right on the banks of the Ossipee, where I saw the City in the Sky.

The Last Secret

It was at least three weeks after I returned from Walkabout. I remember sitting in the early autumn night, trying to find that quiet space. I was still in shock about the treasure hunts, so much so that I had yet to really take a close look at the old coins.

But there was one thing that had eluded me, and the truth was, it was here. It HAD to be here. I was seeing Christmas lists, and random notes jotted down. It was the breadcrumb trail my mother left as the lights went down. She had known much, and maintained some measure of control over things, long enough for what had happened to happen. I had been lucky. Escaping Marla, even at the terrible cost… well, never once have I doubted or regretted leaving her. The hard part has been never even once letting myself regret I married her. There is nothing in the universe that would make me change one thing about my sons, and that was the important thing., They had not acted wrong, and I was a fucking idiot to have ever let myself get mad at them, or have expected them to have any capacity to deal with what had been done.

I got up slow in the still of the house. Fiona followed me down curious and anxious to participate as always. It was cool and fresh outside. The plants, abandoned when Dad became sick despite Lon's presence here, swayed outside in the backyard of the Old Ponderosa. I sniffed the air. They had to be here.

And then, as I for the first time really slowed down until the whirlwinds stopped, right where they should have been, I found them. I found the letters that spill the lie. And they had a name now, because my mother clearly knew from day one the value of them. She had them neatly packed and filed, and marked in her own hand, **The Poison Pen letters from Vendela**.

The Poison Pen Letters

The message that Jackie had shown my father, but not me, was from TC. Jackie decided on her own, to show that to Dad and keep it secret. She had told me about it at the funeral, that she had received a message from TC. She said she was not going to show me, ostensibly to "protect me" I guess.

In that message, TC explicitly states that his other grandmother's estrangement from our family had been my fault, that he put it squarely on me.

I thought of that message now, in memory. What, exactly had it said?

"Because of my father we did not see my other grandmother the last few years of her life."

THAT… was BULLSHIT.

Jackie knew all about that situation. My mother's memories of it live in her. My mother trusted it to her, it seems, because she knew…she KNEW there may be need someday.

Marla's mother had sent me a letter in response to an email I sent her informing her flat out that in the days to come, I was going to take a more proactive stance dealing with her rude and provocative, and after the events of that day which prompted said original email, dangerous behavior.

Marla's mother had sent me a letter in response. In it, she states and uses the word "Divorce" i.e. "We are divorcing ourselves from you, but not our family".

I was never shown that letter. I had inquired, and as the years had gone by, I knew that there were secrets in that whole situation. In fact, the contents of the messages to follow... wait, man overboard...

I was never shown that letter, but around that time, that was exactly what Darlene and Papa V. had done. They had attempted to alienate me and tried to conduct separate holidays. Marla was strangely silent in all this but seemed to agree that it was not ok to go to Lewiston for Easter and me be deliberately not invited. They were welcome here whenever they wanted. I had simply set some boundaries, because her behavior had demanded them.

I wrote to Vendela shortly before Christmas one year, because Marla had stated to me and the boys that Nana and Papa were not coming for Christmas. Now, as I look back on moments like that, I remember what I failed to see for years going on under my nose. When Marla dropped that bomb that day, I was in the kitchen. She and Keelin were looking right at each other, and I now knew that many times right in front of my face, Marla communicated one thing in the open, then another on subspace channels with subtle looks and gestures to imply, generally, that I sucked, and shit was usually my fault, to my boys. She reinforced this with talks that took place when I was not in the home, or simply in another room. For years, she had made a show of suffering because of me, and let them think that, and experience stress because of it.

And it was all a fucking fabrication.

The very last message TC ever wrote that his grandfather saw contained this lie. It was the core of Jackie's fucking playing games and making herself the center and shit, when she should have played it straight and still wasn't. This very lie was still floating around. It was almost like even if things hadn't happened on my spark, she was prepared to take my sons form me with this lie someday.

And here it was, in front of me, in their own hands.

I wrote to Vendela because Darlene and Rene' were not coming, and Keelin was crying, and that was not okay.

Vendela responded to me, but I never saw that either. Why, you ask, did I not simply demand to see these letters and emails? I did. I did. I hit a brick wall every time. Do you see? Shock, again, familiar and comforting, because now with these in my hand I felt the other spirit in me stirring and I could not, could not give in to my reaction right now, seeing it, reading it for the first time, and knowing that when the boys went to see Darlene on her Deathbed, she had used her last moments with them to solidify this ruse, that their father was a dirtbag. She went to death lying to her grandsons so her daughter could cut me out the way she had. They had actually conspired. *I held onto shock desperately kicking at the monster trying to wake up and take over. Breathe. Be Still.*

What Vendela had done, was to send all of this to my mother, with a nasty little letter saying I was an abusive violent unstable, yeah… all that.

But… there was one other nugget to plop out of this disgusting web of lies…

Marla had always let me worry, that Vendela had told my mother that I hated her. These letters and their content had been the wellspring of the last real fight Mom and I ever had. I called from the field and brought them up, that I should see them, and my mother as always stonewalled me, and I got pissed off. I didn't want her to think I hated her. I never truly had, but I had had to do a lot of work to be able to really love her. My whole life, my vocation, my own healing path…all of this had revolved around who I was and what I chose to be. Part of that was understanding my childhood, and it had neither been a brief or easy path. That's just the way it is. their relationship with the boys had been amazing, and that was why what had happened… what had happened to all of us, because of this, these filthy little packet of lies, poured into my children's ears, spawned of hate… everything that was now written in the books of time because of Marla's abuse, and thievery, was done. This was the smoking gun I had prayed was in this… sanctuary.

The letters were in an envelope scrawled on in my mother's hand. I realized that I could tell from her penmanship when she had written stuff. In fact, the reams of written notes by her, and dad too, were a forensic roadmap of the progression of her disease.

My mother must have always known wat manner of odious creature my sister-in-law was.

The envelope said… oh, I just realized… I don't have to write all that, Mom can speak for herself.

Because here, in their entirety, unredacted except for names, are the complete Poison Pen letters.

It was my mother who named them that. It's right on the envelope I found them in, and that's what she calls them. Vendela's Poison pen letters. Here, see for yourself.

Sons…

Read them.

If I am to be judged, READ THEM. Overlay them on what your mother has said. Also, ask the entire world. Because I will never, ever stop screaming, or fighting, or burning to rescue you from where you are now. You think it's me, but it isn't. Just fucking look, please… I'm not innocent, but this is beyond, and the hurt done now is hard to just get my head around the bloodthirsty never satisfied monster that had them close tucked in.

As you will well see, it's Nana's writing, the Nana who never did anything but love you, the one who never lied to you, the one who did not try for most of your lives to split your parents up. That Nana. Do you remember?

I had found the last treasure in my parent's home. My only hope now is to preserve these, to make my case, and keep it. For them. It isn't about what was done to me now, it's about what she's done to them. They must know that they are innocent and I was wrong to get angry at them. She has them under an evil spell. It was sealed with a Deathbed lie. There can never be any doubt now that Marla deliberately and systematically destroyed her own marriage, and her own family when I could not take it anymore. Only a Paladin can break it. And Paladin is what I am now. What I must be. What, according to the Treeherder, I have always been. But now, it's going to be for all the marbles. My destiny is clear. I will stop at nothing for them. There is still the matter of this criminal charge I'm facing. Alone, now, and truly naked before the Storm.

I'm not the abuser boys. Your Mother is. She deliberately and systematically dismantled the marriage and our family. She was doing it from the time you guys were young. Darlene and Vendela helped and supported this. Your cousin Debbie too. They are all complicit in this abuse of you, of my parents. This thievery. She took a full-time salary from my parents behind my back for twenty years. She defrauded the State with false financials, and she built a nest egg while she slowly tortured me, every possible way she could think of, and showcased my pain to you guys as me being unstable and abusive. And it isn't just me. A whole lot of motherfuckers get done just like this it seems. Wife's always miserable, can't seem to please her, you're never right. Undermines you to your kids, your family, your friends, your community. To think I was aware of some shit in the world, so I thought, and she had been able to pull this off anyway, the extent of the manipulation, the hate. Indeed, Marla really never did anything else, but this. Work toward my ultimate destruction.

And she failed. And this isn't over by a long shot. I may be dead, but I seem to still be standing and my grip is good.

Bees

That fall I floated and drifted and screamed with my music and tried to take care of the ranch. I practiced the sword every day just to find the peace of it. Every day when I go outside, a single dragonfly lands, and looks me over. I know it's Dad. The dragonfly showed up for the last time of the season long after you would expect to see one. It may have been like around Thanksgiving. The carpenter bees returned to the shed. I had sprayed them that one summer we had here together but not when we got Fiona. Now, I thought about this. I don't like to kill, but maybe I could use the bees to train the steel?

Well, that's not what happened. The bees seemed to know what I was doing, and they got right into it. They moved with a strange sentience, and they taught me the real use of the sword. You don't believe me? Come see. They really did that. Anghiel saw, a little, of this strange happening. And in the spirit of my Dad and the plans we had together, I got my first tattoo, at 51 years old. Midlife crisis much?

Ella, with pawprints. Over my heart.

Epilogue

Tick Tock

So, that was that. I found myself here, in my house now. Safe. All of it, had come and gone. And it had been worth it. If the road you're on leads you to this…

I only made it here because I was strong going in. I only was strong going in because I have always been strong. Everyone can be strong. Strength and courage are the same thing.

I am dead in the water. It might have been Jaz who saved me, but it might have been Kary or Jesselee too. I can't remember now. But all three of them are on TikTok. So, when they sent me videos, I picked up the app. It was just the anesthesia I needed. I am still in shock. I am doing my job, but something is very wrong. The only thing that seems to be as it should be is that I still seem to have what it takes, but I do not feel the way I used to. I made it to February before I decided why am I working sitting on this pile of money? I'm still screaming, nothing has stopped or changed.

I got drawn into TikTok because it wasn't immersed in the sewer of sandbox shitheads that Reddit had been. Maybe it's because I'm not really a rookie anymore. I saw my friends, and I saw a lot of other people, and a lot of funny and thought-

provoking stuff.

And I withdrew from the battlefield before I could crash and burn, because that's what it felt like was happening. For the last time, I walked away.

I was lost. The winter wind is whipping up again and there's still the same old drafty doors and windows. I'm going to hear the furnace kicking on, and it's going to be a cold expensive winter. I had no Knights to train, and I was watching the needle, waiting. Listening to the wind and water of the universe, Paladin now, still lost wounded and alone. I was going to have to earn it.

I popped in a live accidentally. Immediately, the host greeted me by name. Eric White Shirt. I felt it course through me. I said hello, and then I was out, but later, when I saw him again on one of his vids on my For You page, he said something that immediately became the Creed of the Sanctuary, forever. It was perfect. It was an Oath anyone could swear and follow, no matter who they were before. It was a Code.

The Code of the Sanctuary, by Bobby Opp the Navigator

If you wear a hijab, I will sit with you on the train.

If you are trans, I will help you find a safe bathroom.

If you are a person of color, I will stand with you when police stop you.

If you are a woman, I will help you get home safely.

If you are a child, I will watch over you.

If you are an alcoholic, I'll help you feel comfortable in your feelings.

If you are an immigrant, I will help you find resources.

If you're tired, I'm tired too.

If you need a hug, I have an infinite supply.

This. This is what is needed here, in America now. Knights. What a coincidence. I have been trying to make some.

I shall. And I will cut anything down between me and my sons.

If you come here and learn swordsmanship from me, you may **never** *carry one, unless you carry it in the Name and Cause of the Sanctuary.*

***

The legal issue, between Keelin and I, remains open. I coasted my way out of all this trying to figure out my way back to both of them. I love them like the North Star. Not the brightest star in the sky, but the truest. So be it. Right now, this is what I got. If I can do something spectacular for the world, let them see they are all that has ever given me strength and courage, but with power like this, I am not allowed to just lay down and die. I must do something with it. I shall.

The End of this Tale

All of it is true. If I can't make myself heard by them, I will tell the world. I look at the things that endure, to measure authenticity. One thing friend and foe alike will agree on, I tell it like it is, I say what people are thinking and are afraid to say, and I truly do not GivFuk.

I did GivFuk, once. I GavFuk when I was young. When I was told that if you played by the rules, you could be happy. That turned out to be a lie. Maybe I had different rules. I don't think it was a lie on purpose. I think parents try to tell their kids what the world should be, by they tell them like it is that, and kids meet the real world, and they feel like they've been ripped off. I was lucky. I found or forged my own way. If you can be proud of your friends, and enemies, you're doing something right. I know this, because when everything else burned, the Code, the Way, whatever the fuck it is for you, that's what will get you through. Honor is a gift you give to yourself. No one can take it away. Same goes for knowledge.

I had to make everything fit. That's how you keep your sanity. I also had to embrace a little prescribed insanity (chemical, spiritual) just to survive. If someone here finds peace, or truth, or healing, or even simple laughter, I know just maybe it is not all just full of sound and fury, signifying nothing. It is definitely a tale told by an idiot, this. But it is mine, and it is true.

And, they are still out there, the pirates. The samurai. The places have been there for thirty thousand years across the realms of Maine, and barring lack of ocean, Massachusetts is pretty nice too. I have found blue and green spaces, and some peace for what I now must prepare for. It does suck that I can't bring Fiona anywhere around the Reservoir. I spent more time around the res in the last two years than I ever had before, unlike Genna and Jon whose high school is just down the road, making those grounds hooky woods for Allenton kids for years. Not me, though, and I will not see some of those places again, while Fiona and I sail together. It is a place I will associate with my work with children here, that brief beautiful wild apocalyptic year, and fishing, in the swift running rapid of time I had with my Father, before he went away, and before Fiona joined the team. But the Treeherder, and Chief Soda-Pop, Matty Mango, Cristobel, The Cid, The Druid Priestess, The Blacksmith and all the merry gallows fruit at Pathways, Depardieu, Sweet Shores and Sword St., all true samurai everywhere… they are all real, and they are all still out there, waiting, and working their asses off. The places aren't going anywhere, either.

My sons are still out there. This tale doesn't resolve the loss of them, they still hate me, and I cling to Hope against hope. These things are just facts. The best I could come up with, was to be something that the voice of the whole world, nay, *ALL worlds* will say, "That man was never the monster you believe he is. Open your eyes. Be proud of your father."

There's Nicky, and Nathan, and Cody. There's Petra, Jack and Brooke. There are kids and families down here who need me, I know I have already seen… I will unleash my Light on the world and pierce this darkness, no matter how much I must burn or blind myself. There is Anghiel, and NoraGee and people who need me to be here. I have to show them all. I will raise the voice of the entire world in my defense against this obscenity. I have acquired some new tools, and skills.

I love you, TC. I love you, Keelin. I know the truth doesn't bring you back to me, but I hope it sets you free.

I love you, and I will make sure I give you everything, the way my parents did. I have a little treasure chest going here, every Christmas and birthday I put some silver in there for each of you, to mark. This year, because of the bounty, I did five thousand dollars in gold, but that is not there. An old friend from *Sweet Shores* went down the Saco like a good pirate and lost his fucking leg, so I reached out in the spirit of your grandparents' generosity, and gave him five grand interest free. He will pay me back in Gold, when he can. That's for you too. I love you boys, and I am still and always your father, just a man who tried to raise his family and have a good time, and was done a little dirty by some people. That isn't your problem. I'm sorry. I love you always.

Marla… shame on you. All of you. Vendela… you eat spit and pubes in restaurants. Your mother did too, I have no doubt. I saw the looks you got from food servers back in the day. You've eaten pubes, and that's a little Karma right there. *Bon appétit*, I'm sure you're still a cunt in restaurants, and you still get a little special sauce from time to time. This pleases White Shirt.

For the rest of you, you *can* find your way. I hope this helps. I am on a quest now to save my sons, and myself. I will be out there, somewhere, waiting for you with hot coffee and maybe a J… and some tales to share and perchance, to spend a little time… a few beats of the fragile Heart…

… in the quiet spaces between the whirlwinds…

Appendix

Allan Olson [1942-2021]

Allan V. Olson.

West Boylston – Allan Victor Olson arrived in this world in the usual way in Clinton, Mass., on April 17th, 1942, during one of the darkest and most uncertain times the world has ever seen.

Jeanne and Helmer Olson welcomed Allan's sister Norma to complete their family.

When Allan was a young man growing up, he rode his bike all over to go fish or just explore new places. He had a lifelong love of fishing and the outdoors, and an appreciation for nature and the environment which was an extension of his appreciation for the rich fullness of life in all things. As a kid he and Norma went with their parents to many places. Allan described for his son in later years how Helmer and Jeanne, in those thin times, always found places to go and were able to enjoy themselves in a way that is beautiful in its purity of what was important. The stories told to his son and recalled now were of packages of saltwater crackers and cheese so sharp it would take the skin off the roof of your mouth, "kept warm," he said, under a tall glass jar in a little country store near Bonny Eagle Pond. He spoke of how Helmer would bring fishing gear, and it was fresh hornpout for breakfast up in Maine. "Sometimes," he said with a smile that summer night two years ago, "it was for lunch and dinner too."

Both Jeanne and Helmer were Old World Anglers, and that skill was deep and strong in Allan, as it is in Norma, though it does not run as strong in his son, which was a source of many laughs and jibes over the years, especially last summer when Allan and his son were able to do a little, on reflection far too little, fishing, and he found a little peace while dealing with the hardest thing he had ever yet dealt with.

Allan was a hard worker his whole life, and recalled how he worked at Van Brode's in Clinton as a young man, mixing up what to his son sounded like proto-granola bars, "Lard, Oats, Salt, Barley," but also tending the overall complex taking care of whatever needed it. It is not hard to imagine him doing this, in that big ancient mill complex that still stands today in his old hometown, shops and karate dojos now where machines used to turn out everything from strangely yummy sounding granola bars to little plastic toys like Cracker-Jack toys, small white people figures cast in that 1950's plastic that doesn't bend and shatters like glass.

The only soul that has ever been documented to be affronted by this gentle kind man was a little girl he called a name when they were young. The story goes, another kid got in trouble for it when the girl went home and told. Technically, that unknown person is the affronted one, because the little girl ended up being the love of his life, Sherry, and they told that story many times to their son from the time he was old enough to tease the girls in his own class. "Watch out" Sherry used to say, "You might end up marrying her!" But, as far as anyone can tell, this man spent his entire time on Earth treating everyone and everything with kindness, compassion and generosity. There are no statues of him or buildings that bear his name, but his impact on this Earth because of his simple decency is still felt today, and the good that he put out into the world continues to flower and spread.

Sherry was a schoolteacher, and Allan worked hard in his own vocations, Bigelow's Nursery, and then Jamesbury. These are the jobs his son remembers, his knowledge of plants and landscaping picked up from the one, and the perpetual odor and presence of oil and metal, and the little magnets, from the other, but there were other jobs too, mixed in, and Eric remembers waking up at night and riding out with Sherry to pick him up at a moonlight job he was working extra. Maybe some of that was why their son enjoyed so many opportunities growing up, to go places with them, and also to go to different camps and experience a childhood steeped in curiosity and wonder, and widely varied experience. Allan worked for years after Eric left home in a widely varied jobs that all had the same things in common. He worked hard at them all, he did them all well, and the people he worked with treated him with the respect a man who works hard and doesn't make any trouble gets. Genuine, universal respect, and he did not command that treatment of himself, he inspired it.

They raised that son and sent him off to Maine to college, and then, in 1996, they became grandparents. In 1999, they welcomed their second grandchild. For a decade they had enjoyed their "Empty Nest", quiet summer mornings at Rocky Pond, coffee on the old metal table watching the sun scatter diamonds on the water, but then they jumped into their role as grandparents with a zeal that shone hot and bright for many years, and they were actively involved in their grandsons' life, and their son's family life, until the boys reached their majority. Allan's grandsons were estranged from him in an unspeakable act committed by their mother out of the fury which hath no like in Hell, but by then they were grown men, and he was focused on his duty. Sherry started to experience cognitive decline and for over a year, Allan kept her at home, and safe, with him. Then, when she couldn't be at home any longer, he went to see her every single day until the plague came, and then he went to see her every opportunity that was presented, without fail.

Allan and his son were back-to-back against all challenges over the last two years, taking care of his love, and supporting and reconnecting with family members. He was saddened by her loss after 54 years of true bliss but was actively planning and preparing for a final chapter, a sunset act, of living out his days, for once, without having to take care of or worry about anyone or anything. He was setting up a full knee replacement and listing places in Maine he has not seen that his son has, and they were going to work through as much of that list as possible.

This remarkable soul has been a source of strength to his wife and child as constant as the North Star, and an example of generosity that is seldom matched, and never as discreetly anonymous as his greatest acts were with Sherry, like buying Christmas presents for entire families of strangers, or sending Easter baskets to Eric at college the size of, in fact actually were, laundry baskets to share. It is fitting to end that thread on this note: Allan and Sherry gave everything of themselves to their son and his family, over and over again, and on his own, without his beloved Sherry to guide him, he was there for his son as he always had been, all the way to the end.

Allan will be remembered and missed deeply by his beloved grandsons Tyler and Elijah. He spoke of them often with love throughout this time and he died knowing they love him. His most beloved sister Norma, and her family, nephew Todd and niece Kimmy, Todd's three sons and his own three grandchildren, and all the many cousins and their families that make up this blessed clan. There were many people who called him friend, and many thousands of people he didn't know at all, except that he had seen them often enough that he knew them "by sight" and always greeted and was warmly greeted by these not quite strangers. Sherry had many friends through her career, and Allan was universally liked by all of them, too. In fact, Allan and Sherry used to joke that people used to seek him out to talk with at these things, other spouses bored with all this, as he never was when helping Sherry, and never was talking about the weather or anything else with anyone. Allan was a universally good communicator, and in years gone by he could be seen often on the North property line, having an active conversation with our neighbor. In total silence, because the neighbor was deaf, but to see Allan talk with him one could not tell.

Allan missed Sherry profoundly when she passed away in March of this year, and when it was discovered he was dying, just in mid-July, it did not take him long to find the silver lining that he and Sherry were not going to be apart for long.

Allan Victor Olson left this world on August 24th, 2021, at home with his son, peacefully, to find his love Sherry, during one of the darkest and most uncertain times the world has ever seen. It is safe to say, it is a little less dark and uncertain for the time he spent while here.

For an hour after he was gone, in the sky over the home where he and Sherry lived their lives, were thousands of Dragonflies.

A Funeral Service will be held Monday, August 30 at 11 AM in Fay Brothers Life Celebration Home, 1 West Boylston St. Burial will follow in Pine Grove Cemetery, Boylston. Visiting Hours are Sunday, August 29 from 2 to 4 PM in the Funeral Home.

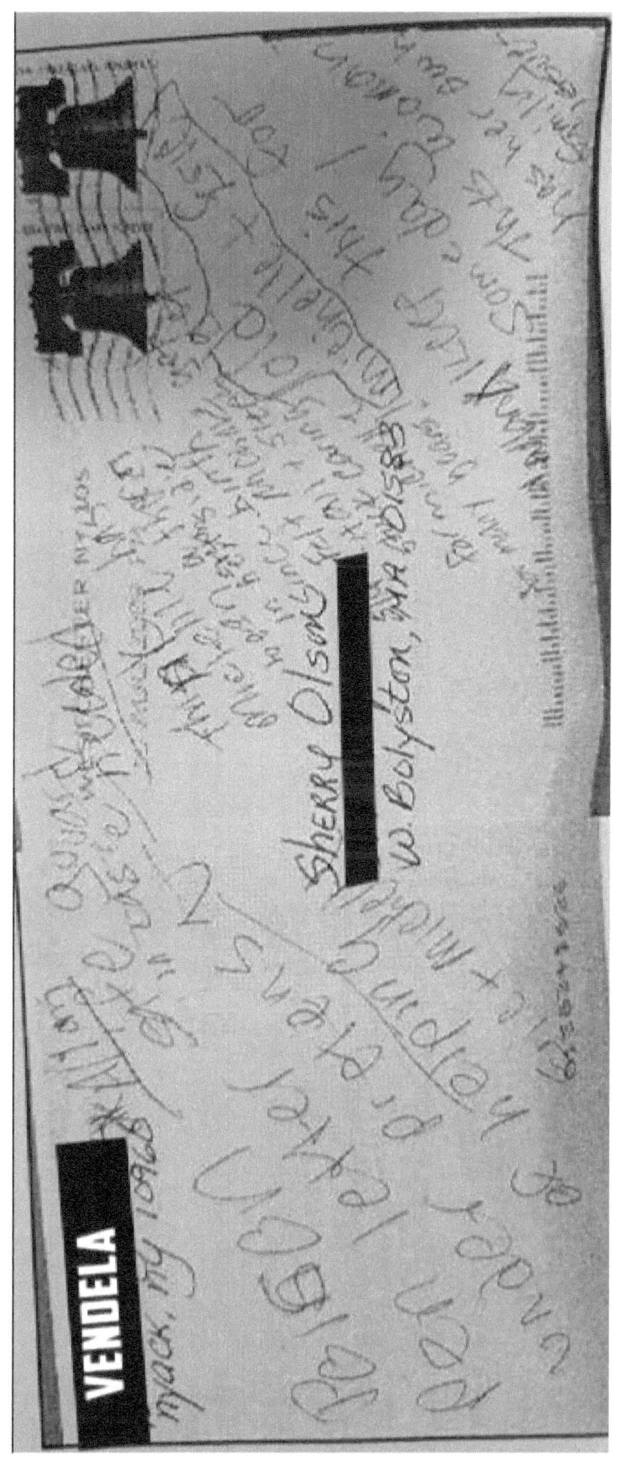
VENDELA
Sherry Olson
10 Bolyston, MA 01583

From: " MARLA and Eric" [redacted]
Date: April 5, 2009 9:27:21 PM EDT
To: "Mom V" [redacted]
Subject: time to get it straight

marginalize. devalue. invalidate. look them up. this is what you do to me. there will be no talk about it. just cut out the sick dysfunctional sh
it ruins everything. not just for me, cause I don't believe you give a shit, but for the whole family. when your mother died you made your girls
promise to tell you if you ever got like that. I never met the woman, but i'm here to tell you, for me, you suck to deal with. I usually ignore i
because I don't want to be part of the problem, but your daughter was in a hospital bed and you are still trying to push me aside and control
everything. By no measure is your behaviour even close to appropriate, never mind healthy. And don't give me some shit about being worried and
stressed, it's the same shit you do ALL THE TIME. You weren't even able to knock it off in a real by God crisis.
I'm not interested in any discussion about this. You've crossed a line with me. knock it off, now, forever, and we'll move on. Keep it up, and you
are going to step onto a whole new playing field. I just don't have the time or patience to indulge you any more. I will not conduct a dialogue by
e-mail, so don't bother replying, and I won't shame you by sharing this with any one else, but you should be ashamed. get your shit under control
and maybe you'll salvage the memories we'll have as a family. If you don't, from here on out, you've got a whole different me to deal with. Believe
it, up until now I've been nice. If I didn't think you'd eat most of them for lunch, I'd suggest therapy, but I really don't care what you do. Just
stop being the unhealthy influence you are on my family. And that means no more veiled suggestions that you suspect me of being some kind of abuser
too. Just do your job. Be Mom and Nana. Take this like an adult and take responsibility for your behaviour, and maybe you can repair the damage.
even with me.
eric

From: "MARLA and ERIC"

Date: April 5, 2009 9:27:21 PM EDT

To: "Mom V"

Subject: time to get it straight

Marginalize. Devalue. Invalidate.

Look them up. This is what you do to me. There will be no talk about it. Just cut out the sick dysfunctional shit. It ruins everything. Not just for me, cause I don't believe you give a shit, but for the whole family. When your mother died you made your girls promise to tell you if you ever got like that. I never met the woman, but I'm here to tell you, for me, you suck to deal with. I usually ignore it because I don't want to be part of the problem, but your daughter was in a hospital bed and you are still trying to push me aside and control everything. By no measure is your behaviour even close to appropriate, never mind healthy. And don't give me some shit about being worried and stressed, it's the same shit you do ALL THE TIME. You weren't even able to knock it off in a real by God crisis.

I'm not interested in any discussion about this. You've crossed a line with me. Knock it off, now, forever, and we'll move on. Keep it up, and you are going to step onto a whole new playing field. I just don't have the time or patience to indulge you any more. I will not conduct a dialogue by e-mail, so don't bother replying, and I won't shame you by sharing this with any one else, but you should be ashamed. Get your shit under control and maybe you'll salvage the memories we'll have as a family. If you don't, from here on out, you've got a whole different me to deal with. Believe it, up until now I've been nice. If I didn't think you'd eat most of them for lunch, I'd suggest therapy, but I really don't care what you do. Just stop being the unhealthy influence you are on my family. And that means no more veiled suggestions that you suspect me of being some kind of abuser too. Just do your job. Be Mom and Nana. Take this like an adult and take responsibility for your behaviour, and maybe you can repair the damage. Even with me.

Eric

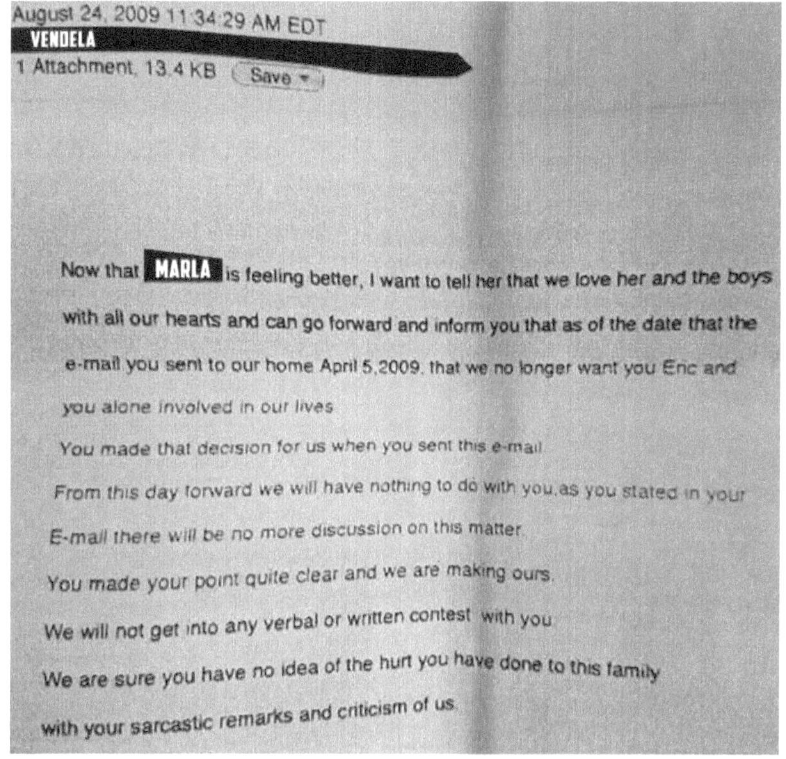

August 24, 2009 11:34:29 AM EDT

VENDELA

Now that MARLA is feeling better, I want to tell her that we love her and the boys with all our hearts and can go forward and inform you that as of the date that the e-mail you sent to our home April 5, 2009, that we no longer want you Eric and you alone involved in our lives.

You made that decision for us when you sent the email. From this day forward we will have nothing to do with you. As you stated in your e-mail there will be no more discussion on this matter. You made your point quite clear and we are making ours. We will not get into any verbal or written contest with you. We are sure you have no idea of the hurt you have done to this family with your sarcastic remarks and criticism of us.

From: **MARLA** and Eric
Subject: desparate times/desparate measures
Date: August 24, 2009 2:50:50 AM EDT
To: **VENDELA**

Hey **VENDELA** Eric here

My son is crying because your mother informed him that they will not be here for **KEELIN'S** birthday, Thanksgiving or Christmas. This was her capper on the way home after the kids went and spent the weekend there. She offered some transparent reasons, like how they haven't seen you for a few Xmases etc. but **TC** knows the score. Actually, it appears that your mother does not realize what you have made pretty clear to **MARLA** and I, which is you stay in Nueva Yorka because you don't dig the hassle up here at the holidays. I hope things go well for you down there this holiday, seriously. I mean, if her hate for me is so strong its driving her down there, the groundwork isn't really too solid for a pleasant holiday, not my problem. Actually, if I wanted to be selfish, I'd allow myself to be thrilled I don't have her behaviour sucking the shine off my favorite time of year like it usually does, but I try not to be selfish.

My problem is what I laid out to you the night this all came to a head, the night we spoke on the phone when **MARLA** was in the hospital. I need not reiterate the long and well established pattern of poor, tacky and tasteless pathological behaviour I have put up with over the years. Rather, since I sent a pretty direct message in which I stated some clear limits and policy shifts, your mother has chosen to "divorce" herself from me (her term). If you haven't seen the e-mail, read it. I stand on every word, its a little undiplomatic to be sure, but it needed to be said every last word and I'd say it all again. Your mother is pretty good at twisting things around, read it, its all there, I'll send it to you if you can't get it from her. **MARLA** and her have not really talked and they have been pretty much out of the picture. This is all very unnessecary and sad, and at the expense of the kids, and **MARLA**.

I don't know, really what I can do by way of intervention, but the situation is not getting any better. What I will not do is negotiate with a terrorist or come to some mutual reconciliation table. If I could I'd tell your mother that for me I say Good Riddance, but she is hurting her family a lot all because someone finally said no to her and backed it up. If she really loves control more than her relationship with her family, I for one am glad she is not around to poison shit with her toxin. However, her grandkids miss the relationship and I'm sure it's killing conrad. Anyway, she's acting like a spoiled child who is going to make people pay that she didn't get the big cookie, and we are all sick of it. And make no mistake, the kids are told the truth about this. I will not enable her by keeping ugly things secret. I was willing to put up with a lot, and did, for years (the insults, the tacky behaviour like bringing her own food to Christmas so she didn't have to eat mine, the trying to get me and my mother to fight, all that shit) but no more. The line is crossed. This ends with her changing her behaviour and taking some ownership, or as far as I'm concerned, she can invite herself to New Jork every damn holiday.

I don't expect any thing from you, nor is it your responsibility to do anything. I just figured since you are hearing it from one side you may as well get the other. Je Assume. Maybe you are not hearing it, but I notice you and **MARLA** haven't been talking as much, and that concerns me. If you have any questions, feel free to ask. There is nothing going on here but simple folk trying to make their way in the universe. I am not sorry they somehow feel that I am not good enough for **MARLA**. Sometimes I feel that way too. But right now, I am not hurting her and her kids unlike some people in this equation. I love my wife and my kids and I am a good husband and father and I don't need or want or give a flying fuck about her approval. I suspect it is my inability to be emotionally levered that pisses her off about me, since it has always worked so well for her with everyone else. Actually, I could give two shits what it is. I just wish she'd stop hurting my family. narcissists never have any insight into their own behaviour. Anyway, thanks for listening. If I thought she wasn't in the hands-over-ears la-la-la stage I'd ask you to forward it to your mother, but one thing I know is not to put any high (scratch that) any expectations on her behaviour, just predictions.

e

From: MARLA and ERIC

Subject: desperate times/desperate measures

Date: August 24, 2009 2:50:50 AM EDT

To: VENDELA

Hey VENDELA, ERIC here,

My son is crying because your mother informed him that they will not be here for KEELIN's birthday, Thanksgiving or Christmas. This was her capper on the way home after the kids went and spent the weekend there. She offered some transparent reasons, like how they haven't seen you for a few Xmases, etc. but TC knows the score. Actually, it appears that your mother does not realize what you have made pretty clear to MARLA and I, which is you stay in Nueva Yorka because you don't dig the hassle up here at the holidays. I hope things go well for you down there this holiday, seriously. I mean, if her hate for me is so strong its driving her down there, the groundwork isn't really too solid for a pleasant holiday. Not my problem. Actually, if I wanted to be selfish, I'd allow myself to be thrilled I don't have her behaviour sucking the shine off my favorite time of year like it usually does, but I try not to be selfish.

My problem is what I laid out to you the night this all came to a head, the night we spoke on the phone when MARLA was in the hospital. I need not reiterate the long and well established pattern of poor, tacky and tasteless pathological behaviour I have put up with over the years. Rather, since I sent a pretty direct message in which I stated some clear limits and policy shifts, your mother has chosen to "divorce" herself from me (her term). If you haven't seen the e-mail, read it. I stand on every word. It's a little undiplomatic to be sure, but it needed to be said, every last word and I'dsay it all again. Your mother is pretty good at twisting things around. Read it, it's all there. I'll send it to you if you can't get it from her. MARLA and her have not really talked and they have been pretty much out of the picture. This is all very unnecessary and sad, and at the expense of the kids, and MARLA.

I don't know, really, what I can do by way of intervention, but the situation is not getting any better. What I will not do is negotiate with a terrorist or come to some mutual reconciliation table. If I could I'd tell your mother that for me I say Good Riddance, but she is hurting her family a lot all because someone finally said no to her and backed it up. If she really loves control more than her relationship with her family, I for one am glad she is not around to poison shit with her toxin. However, her grandkids miss the relationship and I'm sure it's killing CONRAD. Anyway, she's acting like a spoiled child who is going to make people pay that she didn't get the big cookie, and we are all sick of it. And make no mistake, the kids are told the truth about this. I will not enable her by keeping ugly things secret. I was willing to put up with a lot, and did, for years (insults, the tacky behaviour like bringing her own food to Christmas so she didn't have to eat mine, the trying to get me and my mother to fight, all that shit) but no more. The line is crossed. This ends with her changing her behaviour and taking some ownership, or as far as I'm concerned, she can invite herself to New Jork every damn holiday.

I don't expect any thing from you, nor is it your responsibility to do anything. I just figured since you are hearing it from one side you may as well get the other. Je Assume. Maybe you are not hearing it, but I notice you and MARLA haven't been talking as much, and that concerns me. If you have any question, feel free to ask. There is nothing going on here but simple folk trying to make their way in the universe. I am not sorry they somehow feel that I am not good enough for MARLA. Sometimes I feel that way too. But right now, I am not hurting her and her kids unlike some people in this equation. I love my wife and my kids and I am a good husband and father and I don't need or want or give a

flying fuck about her approval. I suspect
it is my inability to be emotionally
levered that pisses her off about me,
since it has always worked so well
for her with everyone else. Actually,
I could give two shits what it is. I
just wish she'd stop hurting my family.
Narcissists never have any insight into
their own behaviour. Anyway, thanks for
listening. If I thought she wasn't in
the hands-over-ears-la-la-la stage I'd
ask you to forward it to your mother,
but one thing I know is not to put any
high (scratch that) any expectations on
her behaviour. Just predictions.

    E

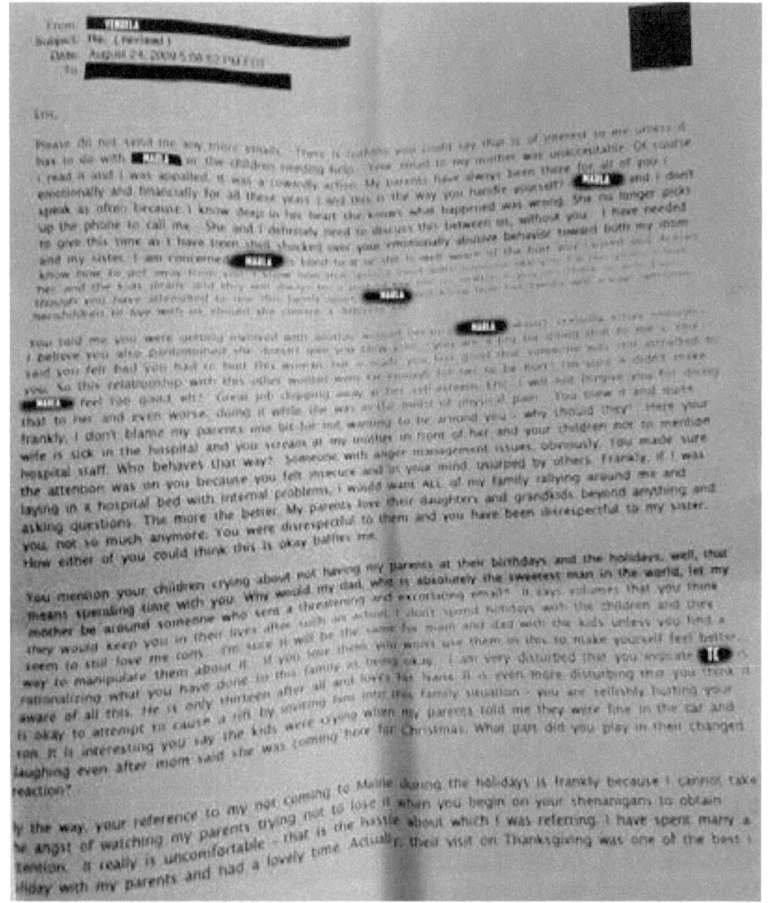

From: VENDELA

Subject: Re: (revised)

Date: August 24, 2009 5:00:52 PM EDT

Eric,

   Please do not send me any more emails. There is nothing you could say that is of interest to me unless it has to do with MARLA or the children needing help. Your email to my mother was unacceptable. Of course I read it and I was appalled. It was a cowardly action. My parents have always been there for all of you (emotionally and financially for all these years) and this is the way you handle yourself? MARLA and I don't speak as often because I know deep in her heart she knows what happened was wrong. She no longer picks up the phone to call me. She and I definitely need to discuss this between us, without you. I have needed to give this time as I have been shell shocked over your emotionally abusive behavior toward both my mom and my sister. I am concerned MARLA is blind to it or she is well aware of the hurt you caused and doesn't know how to get away from you. I know how that goes. I lived with someone like you for ten years. I love her and the kids dearly and they will always be a part of my life no matter if you are there or not. Even though you have attempted to tear this family apart, MARLA will know that her family will always welcome her/children to live with us should she choose a different life.

You told me you were getting involved with another woman because MARLA wasn't sexually active enough (I believe you also pantomimed she doesn't give you blow jobs - you are a pig for doing that to me). You said you felt bad you had to hurt this woman, but it made you feel good that someone was still attracted to you. So this relationship with this other woman went far enough for her to be hurt? I'm sure it didn't make MARLA feel too good, eh? Great job chipping away at her self-esteem, Eric. I will not forgive you for doing that to her and even worse, doing it while she was in the midst of physical pain. You blew it and quite frankly, I don't blame my parents one bit for not wanting to be around you - why should they? Here your wife is sick in the hospital and you scream at my mother in front of her and your children not to mention hospital staff. Who behaves that way? Someone with anger management issues, obviously. You made sure the attention was on you because you felt insecure and in your mind, usurped by others. Frankly, if I was laying in a hospital bed with internal problems, I would want ALL of my family rallying around me and asking questions. The more the better. My parents love their daughters and grandkids beyond anything and you, not so much anymore. You were disrespectful to them and you have been disrespectful to my sister. How either of you could think this is okay baffles me.

You mention your children crying about not having my parents at their birthdays and the holidays; well, that means spending time with you. Why would my dad, who is absolutely the sweetest man in the world, let me mother be around someone who sent a threatening and excoriating email? It says volumes that you think they would keep you in their lives after such an action. I don't spend holidays with the children and they seem to still love me tons. I'm sure it will be the same for mom and dad with the kids unless you find a way to manipulate them about it. If you love them, you won't use them in this to make yourself feel better, rationalizing what you have done to this family as being okay. I am very disturbing that you indicate TC is aware of all this. He is only thirteen after all and loves his Nana. It is even more disturbing that you think it is okay to attempt to cause a rift by inviting him into this family situation - you are selfishly hurting your son. It is interesting you say the kids were crying when my parents told me they were fine in the car and laughing even after mom said she was coming here for Christmas. What part did you play in their changed reaction?

By the way, your reference to my not coming to Maine during the holidays is frankly because I cannot take the angst of watching my parents trying not to lose it when you begin on your shenanigans to obtain attention. It really is uncomfortable – that is the hassle about which I was referring. I have spent many a holiday with my parents and had a lovely time. Actually, their visit on Thanksgiving was one of the best I have had in years. It would have been lovely to have had MARLA and the kids with us. I am looking forward to my folks Christmas visit and it will be nice to finally have family in my home after all these years. Yes, how awful that my parents and your parents are kind enough to bring food to your home because they know you are financially challenged. Again, you take it as an affront. It seems my parents are only the good guys when they write you two a check, paint your ceiling, give you a car, buy the kids clothes, buy eyeglasses, help pay a bill, send a food gift certificate when you were fired, etc., etc., etc. Yup, mom is just a horrible person.

Eric, you detonated a bomb and you now have to live amongst the ruins of your own doing all because of your insecurities. You targeted my mom and in doing so, have hurt all of us; it is irreparable. Shame on you. You have accused your own mother of being "abusive," as you recently told me on my last trip up to Maine, and you have confided in my mother on many occasions your feelings about how you were raised. Did it bother you that DARLENE stuck up for your mom – you know the mother who always financially bails you out of your money troubles that are never ending? Interestingly enough, it is my father who decided to not have you be a part of their lives, not my mother. He is beyond angry with you. All your vituperative accusations regarding my mom seem, in my opinion, to indicate a projection on your part – you are doing exactly that of which you accuse her. My parents are in their golden years and do not need to be abused by you. I will not have it ERIC. I will suggest they get a restraining order on you if you attempt to contact them.

In my opinion, you have serious issues that need to be addressed. You are approaching forty and it is time to act like a man and get your emotional life in order. Additionally, no more cellar trips with a leather belt and TC in tow; seek anger management help instead. Perhaps you should look inward for awhile and see where you stand in all that has happened. You are proficient in blaming others for everything even your wife; it is time to be less insular and seek therapy.

Let me reiterate, do not email me again (or call) unless it has to do with an emergency or if the kids/MARLA need something. I will always be there for her and her amazing children. If you attempt to make any additional threatening comments, emails, or any correspondence to my parents, I will call the authorities and put in a complaint. I have shown your emails to the police and they said (verbatim) you are most likely just an insecure bully, but should be monitored. Your emails sound like a person who is losing it and I have concern for the safety of my family. You will not get away with this abusive behavior. In every email you send, your words indicate your insecurities and issues with abandonment. I do hope you love your family enough to seek professional help so you and your loved ones can be happy in life.

This will be our final correspondence.

VENDELA